MIDNIGHT ON LIME STREET

MIDNIGHT ON LIME STREET

by

Ruth Hamilton

Magna Large Print Books
Long Preston, North Yorkshire,
BD23 4ND, England.

British Library Cataloguing in Publication Data.

Hamilton, Ruth
    Midnight on Lime Street.

    A catalogue record of this book is
    available from the British Library

    ISBN   978-0-7505-4332-3

First published in Great Britain in 2015 by Macmillan
an imprint of Pan Macmillan

Copyright © 2015 Ruth Hamilton

Cover illustration © Margie Hurwich by arrangement with
Arcangel Images Ltd.

Published in Large Print 2016 by arrangement with
Pan Macmillan Publishers Ltd.

Magna Large Print is an imprint of Library Magna Books Ltd.

Printed and bound in Great Britain by
T.J. (International) Ltd., Cornwall, PL28 8RW

FOREWORD

The Invisible

No city sleeps.
New York, Bengal, London, Paris, Moscow,
  the shadows are there.
Not rodents, not insects, not ghosts of times past.
  People.
The forgotten, the criminal, the unloved, the
  embarrassing, the surplus.
Ralph McTell said it all about London.
I'm looking at Liverpool, my beloved home of
  choice.
And I'm searching for the invisible.

RUTH HAMILTON

Dedicated to Gill Currie, who has looked after me and my household for two decades.

In memory of Red Rum, the greatest ever steeplechaser. I salute the owners, trainers, keepers and riders of this most wonderful horse – I met him on Southport sands.

ACKNOWLEDGEMENTS

Thanks to Gail Stanton Friars
(new researcher) and Avril Cain
(my forever researcher).

I send heartfelt gratitude to my readership.

AUTHOR'S NOTE

Although the books are fiction, I try hard to adhere to the (f)actualities of the era in which they are set. In this one I wander off a bit, for which misdeed I beg tolerance.

Mad Murdoch is a pale imitation of the aforementioned horse, and his owners are ... unusual.

I allow women to ride in the National rather earlier than they did in reality.

The phasing out of hospital matrons had already begun at the time.

We were relatively unaware of the long-term effects of LSD and similar drugs until later.

For these and all other mistakes, I ask pardon.

Ruthie

One

There were shoes everywhere: strappy sandals, peep-toes, flats for wearing with jeans, stiletto-heeled pairs, silver ones, gold ones, patent leather slingbacks, wellies for God alone knew when, scarlet skyscrapers, boots in suede and leather, plus one man-sized brogue in brown (no lace). The room resembled a colourful maze, or an obstacle course for small animals. Or was it more like a jumble sale after closing time?

Eve Mellor stood in the open doorway, a fat hand wrapped round the handle. Somewhere out there in the city of Liverpool walked a man with half a pair of shoes. Perhaps he had only one foot, though she couldn't recall admitting a disabled man ... no, that wasn't true. Tom Duffield had just the one hand, since he'd lost the other while operating heavy machinery, but that was different and didn't involve a brogue without a lace. Eve sighed heavily; this was going to be quite a fight. Her thoughts wandered unbidden back to Tom Duffield; he was clearly falling in love with Belle, another of Eve's girls. Life was a continuous bag of complications.

Baby Schofield (real name Barbara or Babs) was out for the count and snoring like a drunken sailor. She specialized in acting the little girl, frilly knickers, a skirt so abbreviated that she needed to keep her neck clean, white blouse undone to her impressive cleavage, a carelessly knotted school tie, straw hat with a band round it, a prefect badge on her blazer. Dressed and ready, she looked cute, though fast asleep and with her mouth wide open she was somewhat less than attractive.

'Baby?' Eve called in a rough, growling voice born of too many cigarettes. 'Babs, wake up. Where the hell did you get this lot?' she asked, though she was beginning to suspect that she already knew the answer. It looked as if Donald Crawford had definitely lost the plot. He was aged, probably senile, and rather unpredictable these days. And he was creator of the gathering storm.

The woman in the bed moaned, swore, and turned over, holding her pillow close to her chest. 'Bugger off,' she repeated.

'Wake up before I send for the ambulance.' The owner of the farmhouse picked her way across hazardous terrain and pulled back heavy velvet curtains. 'Opening a shoe shop, are you? Changing your name to Freeman Hardy and Willis, eh?' She struggled to contain laughter; for some inexplicable reason, she was fond of the nuisance under the covers.

'Aw, shurrup, Eve. I'm not in the mood. Donald's retired and shut his shop up Lord Street, so he's give me all the size fives what were left. Oh, and right as well as left – they're all in pairs.' With her eyes crinkled against the onslaught of daylight, she finally managed to sit up. 'What do you want, anyway? I'm supposed to be resting.'

Eve snorted with suppressed humour. 'So that's what he had in the massive suitcase when I

18

picked him up. And one man's shoe?'

Baby yawned loudly. Last night's makeup had not been removed and, in this state, she looked a great deal older than her thirty-one years. She wanted to scream, though she worried about not being able to stop screaming if she started. There was no life round here, no shops, no houses, little traffic. And she was sick unto death of playing the child for dirty old perverts – there had to be more to life than this.

'If you don't start cleansing with cold cream every night, you'll end up with skin like a rhinoceros. What's the matter with you?' Eve's tone was becoming caustic.

Barbara Schofield shrugged. 'I can't be Baby any more. Shouldn't Sally do it? I'm fed up with being given lollipops and chalks and colouring books.'

'You get paid,' Eve snapped, 'and the johns are used to you – they like you, especially the old ones.'

'And you take nearly half of me money. Go away, I'm tired. I had to stand on a chair reciting me three times tables last night while Donald slapped me arse with one hand and helped himself with the other.'

Eve drew herself to full and not inconsiderable height. There were occasions when Babs had to be chastised, and this was one of them. 'I've a mortgage to pay and a house to keep nice' She folded her arms. 'Look at it this way – if he's hitting your arse while you say your tables, he's leaving some real kiddy alone. You're providing a service that protects the community.'

Babs was almost awake and alert by this time. 'I was tired. I needed my sleep. What the hell do you want? Is it dinner time? I never heard no bell.'

Eve bridled. She was a well-organized woman of substance who took no prisoners. Few people dared to get on the wrong side of her, mostly because she was built like a Sherman tank. And she was thorough. Everything was timed to a split second, and all coins and notes were accounted for at least twice at the end of each session. Like Scrooge, she left nothing to chance in the counting house that was her office.

Baby sighed; she knew what was coming. The Lecture.

'Listen to me, Barbara Schofield. I look after my girls very well. There's no pimp to beat you up, no chance of being caught out here in the back of beyond and, on twelve to fifteen quid a week with tips on top, you earn more than most bosses in big offices get paid. I do three pick-ups a night, I pay for petrol and take the men back to town when they're all finished with business. You're safe, fed and clothed. If you're not suited, get your arse down Parliament Street and wake up a bit dead the next day.'

But Baby Babs was not for giving in easily. 'Have you woke the other girls up as well?'

'No.'

'Then why me? Why rattle the bars of my playpen? What the hell have I done this time, eh?'

Eve relaxed her shoulders deliberately; she needed to present a less formidable front, as this was going to be a delicate business. 'You want to get away from here for a while, yes? Live where

20

there's shops and cinemas and pubs, a bit of life.'
She sat down. 'It's Donald,' she said, her tone
softer. 'He's retired because he's not up to the job.'

'He's not up to much,' Baby replied smartly.
'He's bloody useless.'

'Useless and rich, madam.' The light dawned
fully at last. 'Did he bring this brogue last night
when he gave you all the women's size fives?'

The younger woman nodded.

'He's mixed up because he's going senile, Babs;
he's rolled half his marbles down the drain, poor
fellow. Don's health's in a hell of a state, and he's
got nobody to look after him. Months to go at
best, that's all he's got. It's his heart. He wants
you to move in and live with him, look after him,
feed him and play Baby and Daddy with him.'

Babs blew a loud, damp raspberry. 'In his
dreams,' she hissed.

'Think about it.' Eve's tone had reclaimed its
acidic edge.

Baby rubbed her eyes, spreading black mascara
all over her face. 'In Southport? Isn't that where
everybody goes to die? There's nursing homes all
over the place full of old folk. And loads of kids
come in summer, too.'

'He won't see 1969, Babs. What's six months at
your age, eh? You'll be in his will, babe. He might
even leave you his house and everything. Think
about all the clothes and jewellery he'll let you
buy. Think lap of luxury and all you could want–'

'Oh, stop it. Lap of luxury? It's his lap what I'll
be sat on while he ... how shall I put it without
bringing the tone of Meadowbank down? While
he tries to rise to the challenge. I'll get bored. I

21

get bored easy, me.'

Eve rolled her eyes up to the heavens. It would take more than a verbal stumble from this little minx to bring the tone down. Meadowbank Farm was classy and discreet. 'He's got a horse,' she said quietly.

It was Baby's turn to fold her arms. 'Has he? Just what I've always wanted, a bloody horse. Ooh, I'm that excited I could dance till Thursday without the seven veils.'

'Well, it's a special horse and he owns half of it.'

'Which half?'

'Does it matter?'

Babs grinned. 'Better the eating end than the shitting end.'

Eve wagged a finger. 'Thoroughbred hunter, sired by a wild Arab, no fear in him and tipped by some to win the National once he's sorted. Think about it.' She left the room, banging the door in her wake. She would miss Babs, but oh, she was a pain.

Babs rolled out of bed and sat in a wicker chair. It was painted pink, because this was Baby Girl's room. The wallpaper was pink, as were eiderdown, curtains, carpet, lampshades and some items of furniture. 'Thank God none of these shoes are pink. Pink is the sort of colour that could drive a girl to the edge of madness. I hate pink. I bloody hate bloody pink. I want purple. I'd like a purple dance frock with sequins. I wonder if he'll buy me that emerald green suit in me catalogue? And to be fair, I suppose they do have some nice shops on Lord Street.'

She looked in the mirror. 'I'm a rancid mess,'

she told her reflection.

Southport was rather sedate for Babs. It was Victorian, all canopied pavements along the main road, and little arcades running off it. Quaint was the word, she supposed. Liverpool was where she wanted to be, but perhaps she would have to travel the long way to Liverpool: turn right into Birkdale and follow the road home after Donald had given up the ghost. 'Six months,' she whispered. 'Can I put up with him for six months?'

She sat for a few minutes and thought about Donald. He'd never married, because women were too old to suit his requirements. Teachers and mothers had stopped him hanging around in parks and playgrounds, so he now visited her, his pretend child, at Meadowbank Farm in the middle of nowhere, nearest shops in Knowsley, quite a stretch away. Don's footwear outlet had possibly been closed down because he couldn't be trusted to deal with the feet of little girls, and to top it all, it looked as if he'd a few slates missing off the roof. Who wanted to live with a crackpot?

Barbara Schofield sighed heavily. She had been picked up almost five years ago during one of Eve Mellor's recruitment drives. Babs had been looking for business at the bottom of Lime Street when the van had pulled up. 'Get in,' had been Eve's greeting, and she'd got in, because Eve was roughly the size of King Kong, and the weather had been bad, freezing rain turning to sleet and threatening to deliver snow.

So she'd been driven out to this godforsaken farm where she'd been given hot soup and bread, a bath, a bedroom and the promise of a safer, warmer life. Eve had examined her while she'd been naked, had forbidden her to diet in case her bosom sagged, had named her Baby, and here she was, going on five years later, still stinking of Johnson's baby powder and with freckles painted on her nose. A doctor had poked and prodded at her nether regions before declaring her clean, and she'd been stuck ever since in a pink room while Eve Mellor paid the mortgage and the bills out of 'her' girls' earnings.

What about the other men who wanted Baby Babs? Hadn't Eve just said that they were used to her, that she couldn't grow up and be a normal, common or garden working girl without freckles? 'She's bloody sold me,' she hissed between gritted teeth. 'She's sold me to a limp old kipper with bad breath, false teeth and combed-over hair. Southport? Who wants to live there with Droopy Don and half a horse?'

She ran downstairs and into the enormous kitchen. This was where Eve's girls lived when they weren't on the job, but all the others were still where they belonged, upstairs in their beds. There were two large, custom-made sofas, two padded armchairs, a massive Welsh dresser, a huge table and, in the corner, a television set. Cooking and washing up went on at the other end of this thirty-odd foot room, and such activities were in the hands of Miss O'Gorman, who was now too old to be on the game.

Kate O'Gorman turned when the door slammed. 'Hiya, Babs,' she said. 'You look like you fell off a midnight flitting; you've black streaks all over your face. Have you been with a coalman?'

Babs offered no reply.

'Did you lose a shilling and find a penny, love?'

Babs continued to ignore her; Kate was from somewhere near Manchester, so she talked funny. There was no sign of Eve, and Eve was too big to hide behind anything less than a double-decker bus or the Mersey ferry.

Babs crept down the hall to the office and pinned her ear to the door.

'Don, she'll do it, I promise you. What? No, no, don't cry; we can't leave you ill on your own, and we won't. Look, slip me another five hundred and I'll pass it to her. I promise. I'm happy with the grand you gave me, but she needs an incentive, too, doesn't she?'

Babs bit her lower lip; she mustn't scream. The old bitch had sold her like some poor sod off a slave ship, or a sack of spuds. 'No bugger owns me,' she whispered. 'I'm not for effing sale, Miss Eve Mellor.'

'I'll ring you back later, love. Eh? No, you won't kill yourself, and of course I know she's the love of your life. Yes, yes, I'm sure she knows that, too. Get yourself a double Scotch and put the pills away. I mean it, lad. Any more of that talk and I'll send an ambulance up to your house. Yes, I mean that, too.'

Babs heard the ping when the receiver hit the cradle. She dashed back upstairs, reclaimed her breath and sat at the pink dressing table. When Eve returned, Baby's face was smothered in Pond's cream, which was just as well, since she was alight with temper and her cheeks were glowing.

Eve closed the bedroom door. 'He'll give you five hundred to show goodwill,' she announced. 'Five hundred in cash, girl. Now, what do you say to that? No, you're not interested?'

Babs shrugged – at least the boss was being honest for a change. 'Tell him I want the five hundred and half of his half of the horse.' She turned and faced the boss. 'How much did you sell me for? A grand? Two?'

'That's my business.' Eve's voice was dangerously soft.

'It's mine, too. Listen to me for a change. I don't want to live in bloody Southport with Don unless he gives me a chance to win big on the National. Even then, I'll probably die of boredom. Have you seen what he does to me, eh? Shall I show you my bum after he's hit it with his flaming long-handled shoe horn? My top half's covered in love bites because he gets mad when his personal equipment lets him down, which is nearly every blessed time. I have to use makeup on me body so the other guys won't notice till it rubs off. If he does get anywhere, he nearly drops dead with the shock of it. There's not much fun in this job, but just one dirty old man? At least there's a bit of variety round here. And me mates, too.'

'You'll miss the girls, I know, but it won't be forever.'

'Then there's his foot thing, sucking at me toes like a piglet stuck to its mother. That's why he had a shoe shop, because he loves feet. He's weird.'

Eve closed her eyes for a moment or two. 'I bet you he'll be gone by Christmas, poor old Donald.'

'How much?'

'What?'

'How much will you bet? Stick your money where your mouth is. I'll put my five hundred in the kitty if you'll match it. With a thousand, I could buy meself a nice little semi or me own flat, and not in stinking Southport, in Liverpool where there's a bit of life.' Babs stared hard at Eve. 'Cat got your tongue, has it? Good, because it'll make a nice big meal for the cat and it will shut you up.'

The boss of the establishment took a step towards this damned cheeky young madam. 'I don't gamble,' she hissed.

Babs delivered a hollow laugh. 'This place proves you do, Eve. I can have the farm raided quicker than you can say knife, so don't threaten me, you fat bitch.' She was surprising herself, because no one ever stood up to Eve. It was almost funny, since all three chins had fallen like collapsed layers in a badly baked sponge cake. 'And shut your gob, there's a Kirkby bus coming,' was her final suggestion.

Eve faltered. She wasn't a falterer, and she was beginning to realize that Babs had grabbed the upper hand. But yes, there was an answer. 'So you want Belle, Cynthia, Angela, Mo and Judy in jail, do you? And young Sally, too? What about poor old Kate? Because she'd go down with the rest of the crew.'

Babs shrugged.

'Are you evil enough to send the old woman you scarred to jail?'

'Don't forget yourself, Eve; you're the queen of the rats, so you can help them all to jump ship, eh? Read my lips. I'll lay five hundred quid that I

27

can keep him alive till Christmas.'

Eve blinked stupidly. 'Look, you'll be minted when he goes, girl. A grand's going to look like small change. He owns property as well as half of Mad Murdoch. That's the horse.'

'Is it mad?'

'He was. Wouldn't let any bugger near him, wouldn't take a blanket, let alone a saddle, kicked everyone and upset all the other animals. Gordy Hourigan has him just about halfway tamed. He's famous in racing circles is Gordy Hourigan.' She stared hard at Babs. She was a short girl with an hourglass figure and a pretty face, a face that was currently concealed behind half a pot of cold cream. 'All right, then. Kate can hold the money.'

'Pull out and I'll shop you,' Babs advised. 'And I'll give the girls enough warning so they can scarper before the cops arrive. Oh, and you can drive me to Southport a few times while I get used to all this. If I can't stand him and his messing about, I'll walk out and all bets will be off. OK?'

'OK.'

'And I can come back here?'

'Yes.'

'Will you train Sally for all the daddy-men?'

Eve nodded.

'Does she know?'

'Not yet.'

'So the poor little cow will get this pink room? Well, good luck to her, because she's going to need it. I'd best get this muck off me face before I turn into an oil leak.' Babs swivelled and faced the mirror once more.

Carrying the strong suspicion that she had just

been dismissed, Eve crept out of the room. She'd never liked short women; what they lacked in height they made up for in the cheek department, stretching their personalities as a form of compensation. Good things came in small packages? Yes, and so did poison. Barbara Schofield was possibly dangerous ... yet she was lovable. 'The daughter I never had,' Eve mouthed.

Downstairs in the office, she phoned Donald Crawford yet again. 'She'll do it. She wants the five hundred and a quarter share in Mad Murdoch.'

'Bloody hell, Eve. She doesn't care about me, does she?' he asked in a tone that managed to convey both grief and resignation. 'I'd give her the world, but she'd never love me, and why should she? Have you told her she can have other men as long as I can watch?'

Eve took a deep breath. 'No, I haven't. She may look young in her outfits except for her bust, but she's an adult, Don. I'll bring her to you, only you're the one who has to persuade her to stay. Any negotiating is down to you and her.' She ended the call, stood up and walked to the window. While Don Crawford presented as a harmless old man, there was something in him, an element that rang alarm bells in Eve's experienced mind. She decided it was dementia, which rendered unpredictable all who suffered from it. Anyway, Babs was capable of looking after herself, wasn't she?

She stared out onto the flat, green nothingness of the Mersey plain. Kate O'Gorman, cook and housekeeper at the farm, often commented about the boring dump, as she termed it. 'It's bloody pancake land,' she sometimes moaned. 'No ups, no downs, just boring. In Bolton, we were surrounded by hills and fields. It were great.' The girls would often sing, 'We'll send you home again, Kathleen, to visit all the Woollybacks,' in a poorly adapted version of an old Irish song. Anyone without a Scouse accent was dismissed as a country bumpkin.

Eve nodded; Kate was right, because Meadowbank Farm sat on flat earth behind strategically placed conifers and thick bushes. It was safe, it was hidden and yes, it was dull. But a move nearer to Liverpool was out of the question. The purchase of this house had been a deliberate act arising from the need for concealment. Leaving Kate in charge, Eve drove to and fro, there and back, the van sometimes empty, often packed with men. She went to Liverpool and picked up clients at pre-arranged and constantly changing locations. She took them back as well – at least half a dozen trips hither and yon most nights. This was the only way to run a secret brothel.

She sat in a chair by the window. 'I'm getting a bit old for this,' she mumbled, comforting herself with the knowledge that Don Crawford's thousand quid would go a long way towards paying off the mortgage. 'Except if Miss Frilly Pants wins her bet,' she added in a whisper. The job would have to continue unless she sold up, since a house of this age required maintenance, and she was probably stuck with it. Anyway, who else would want to live in a farmhouse without land beyond its own admittedly large gardens? Perhaps it could be made into a smallholding where vegetables might grow and a few hens could be kept – perhaps pigs and a goat, too. But it wasn't everybody's cup of tea.

Miss Frilly Pants. Ah yes, there was something in her, too, something with a red-hot temper, sharp reactions and a venomous tongue. Twice, she'd lost her rag here; twice, she'd been removed and stuck in solitude up in one of the attics. On the first occasion, Baby Babs had smashed pots and had thrown a pan at poor Kate; then last year she'd kicked a bloke where it hurt because he'd wanted stuff Babs didn't allow – to this day, she refused to perform any act she considered radically unusual. 'She'll keep him alive till Christmas,' she whispered, 'but God help him when it comes to Boxing Day, because she'll have him breathing his last. God, I'll miss her.'

An uneasiness crept through Eve's large body; she should have thought things through. Donald Crawford and Barbara Schofield were each unstable and unpredictable. He was senile, and she was without patience. It was down to the question of which one would crack first. If he made his baby girl into a cabaret act with himself as audience, he'd better hide all sharp knives first. 'I'm in danger. If he kills or hurts her and gets arrested, he'll tell the cops where he bought her, and if she's caught for attacking him, she'll blow me up without a second thought. She'll plead ... oh, what is it? Mitigating circumstances? Undue provocation? Having been sold like an animal? Shit. What have I done?'

Kate knocked before entering the office. 'Dinner's ready,' she announced, referring to the

31

midday meal, a kind of breakfast-cum-lunch. 'I'm going to ring the big bell.'

'Shut the door and sit down for a minute, Kate. I think I've been a fool.'

'Never in this world,' was the answer, delivered in the flattened, slower speech birthed in cotton towns. Although mills were gradually being silenced, messages were still mee-mawed, as if fighting to be lip-read across the hot, sticky din of hell itself.

'I've sold Baby to Don Crawford,' Eve said.

Kate pursed her lips.

'Did you hear me?'

Kate answered eventually. 'I thought she were in a bit of a mood half an hour since. She threw no plates and pans, but she looked like a cornered cat ready to get its claws out for sharpening.' She paused for thought. 'Can I talk straight, Evie?'

'Course you can.'

The older woman sighed. 'Look, lass, you're my best mate in th' 'ole world, and I love you like a daughter, only you don't own nobody. Even if you were me daughter, I wouldn't own you. Think back. We were on the game for years, love, we never had no pimp, just our own little 'ouse in Dingle, and you saved like buggery to get this place. I were never no good at saving, and you minded me when I retired. But even though we liked being together and looked after one another, we didn't own each other, did we? It's wrong to sell the girl on. And if you were selling some working girl, she's not the right one. In fact, she's a wrong 'un from top to toe, and well you know it.'

Eve dropped her large head into plump hands.

'I still 'ave the scar to prove it.' Kate rubbed her forehead.

'I know, Kate. But what I don't know is how I undo it.' She opened up about the bet, the horse and Baby's attitude to the proposed move, her dislike for Southport, the old man's idea of watching her with other men. 'She would object to that; I said the two of them have to negotiate terms. But do you remember the identical twins?'

Kate nodded.

'One finished with her and went to the bathroom, and the other one took his place for round two. She nearly blasted the roof off with her yelling that night, frightened other clients halfway to death screaming that she wanted paying twice. The second twin had a slight cast in one eye, and Missy spotted it right away. I'm not sure she'll agree to perform with Donald watching. She's that sharp, she should be kept in a locked drawer or a toolbox.'

'You're going to need to put a stop to it, Evie.'

The big woman raised her head and shook it. 'I can't.'

'Shall I talk to her, then?'

'No. You never know which way she'll jump, and she's stronger than you. I've seen more flesh on a string bean, sweetheart, and you know she's feisty at her best and ruddy lethal at her worst. I must be losing my grip, Kate. Maybe it's time for me to give up and turn myself into a bed and breakfast – we're near enough to the main road between Liverpool and Manchester.'

Kate shrugged. 'You'd not clear ninety to a hundred and twenty a week at that lark. This is what you know, Evie; this is what we understand. Men need women, and they can't always get them. In fact, the government should be behind us, because I reckon we save a fair few girls from getting raped.'

Eve nodded. 'An essential service. Try telling that to the bastards in charge. Yes, it's time the world grew up, but that isn't going to happen until I'm pushing up daisies. Ring the bell, queen. And keep your ears open while they're all eating, because I need to know what's going on.'

'I always keep tabs. You know that, Evie.'

Kate left the room, and a loud bell sounded three times. One long ring meant fire or cops, two shorts in succession meant an unexpected daytime client who had made his own way here, while three shorts summoned the girls to table.

Eve tried to count her blessings, though she didn't find many on this occasion, since her mind was fully occupied by speculation relating to Baby and Don. There had to be some way of making herself and this place safe. Aside from throttling Don, Baby or both, there was no ready solution. Never mind. Kate would bring her meal soon, and Eve loved her food.

The escape committee met behind a redundant air raid shelter on the top field. Grass on the top field was left untended, so the Brothers Pastoral seldom ventured up there, as wild and damp herbage tended to wet their long, air force blue habits.

But the boys got together not to discuss clothing; they were gathered to condemn their supposed saviours for bad behaviour. The orphaned, the abandoned and the unmanageable had been delivered here to be fed, clothed and educated by men of the cloth in this new order set up to care for unwanted and difficult young males. The six boys who had come together today were going to travel beyond difficult and all the way to impossible; it was about revenge, personal dignity and freedom, and the greatest of these was freedom.

'Did any of you tell your welfare people?' Ian asked.

'No,' chorused the other five.

Ian had to admit that he, too, had failed to jump that particular fence. 'Who's going to listen to us?' he asked, knowing that his question was rhetorical. 'I've been done for a load of shoplifting, Pete stuck a craft knife in some bastard teacher's arm, and the rest of you are down as bloody trainee criminals as well. So, let's see what we've got.'

Each laid down prizes. They had wire-cutters, a Swiss army knife, a crowbar pinched from the wood and metalwork room, a hammer, an axe and an assortment of food stolen from the kitchen. There was a bag of mixed clothing, a torch, some matches and a packet of Woodbines.

Ian eyed the knife. 'I know what I'd like to do with that,' he said, his tone grim. 'I'd like to cut Brother Healey's bits off and shove them down his throat.' He spoke to John, who had a terrible stammer. 'Just nod or shake your head, lad. Have we got some money? Good. Are you sure you know the way to that old scout hut? Great. Are you sure nobody uses it no more? Brilliant. Tonight then, lads.' He sighed. 'I wish we could take some of the little ones, but they're too noisy.'

'Now, we need paper and pens or pencils, some envelopes and some stamps, because we're going to tell people what's been done to us. It'll be easier in writing. I'll get that stuff while I'm cleaning Brother Bennet's office. Remember, we all need to be shut in the basement tonight. This is the first time we've wanted to be locked up, and the last time they'll shove us in clink, I hope.'

The school bell sounded, and they dispersed, each boy changing into indoor shoes as soon as he reached the cloakroom. For what they hoped to be the final day, they dispersed and went to sit with their fellows in two separate classrooms. The Brothers Pastoral were back from their session in chapel, where, no doubt, they had prayed for their own souls, because some of them were monsters, while almost all believed that corporal punishment was good for the recipient. Why couldn't they be more like Brother Williams, who was firm, but fair and always prepared to listen?

Ian Foster shook his head almost imperceptibly; these men of God were allied to the devil himself, especially Brother Healey, who taught Divinity. Divinity? What did this terrible man know about that? How could he possibly be close to God?

The boy lowered his posterior onto a hard chair, all movements slow and careful, as he had been left bleeding last night. At the age of fourteen, he was now judged old enough to show his love for God in the fuller sense, and the wicked so-called brother at the teacher's desk had raped him. Ian needed to lead the other lads into trouble as soon as possible so that Healey would send them to the dungeon.

He closed his right fist and imagined the crowbar gripped tightly in his fingers. Behind lowered eyelids, he watched himself bringing the metal down on Healey's head until it burst open like a ripe melon; even then, he didn't stop raining blows, because the creature at his mercy was lower than an amoeba and must be rendered unrecognizable as human.

'Ian?' Healey called. 'The seven gifts of the Holy Ghost are?'

Ian rose slowly to his feet. 'Wisdom, understanding, counsel, fortitude, knowledge, piety, fear of the Lord, Brother.'

'Ah, you remembered them at last.'

'Yes, thank you, Brother. I got no sleep last night, so I learned them.'

For a fleeting moment, a glimmer of fear showed in Healey's eyes. 'Sit down, Ian.'

The boy remained standing.

'I said sit down'

'It hurts, Brother. Something happened to me, and I've been bleeding.'

Another boy rose to his feet, as did a third, a fourth, a fifth, a sixth. They weren't all on the escape committee, but each had been a victim. Usually too scared for words or actions, they followed Ian's lead, because Ian was a natural born genius and top of all classes in all subjects.

'Go.' Ian's voice was soft.

Seven desk lids were lifted and slammed shut, lifted and slammed, lifted and–

'Silence!' Healey roared.

And slammed.

'Stop!' Ian's voice rose above the clamour. To the

37

tune of a well-known Christmas carol, he sang into the sudden and deathly silence, 'We will get you, get you, ge-et you, we will kill you, kill you, ki-ill you, we will hurt you all we-e can, evi-il, stinky-y, dirty-y man.'

White with shock, the man had remained immobile during the delivery of the song. 'Out here now,' he commanded loudly, his face turning purple with rage.

Almost casually, Ian approached the lectern behind which Healey sat. The teacher climbed down from his perch and grabbed a cane. Ian Foster held out his hand, never flinching throughout six heavy strokes. Determinedly, he stared into the eyes of his tormentor. When the caning stopped, he managed to smile. 'Thank you, Brother.' All boys were trained to thank their betters after punishment.

Healey was sweating and breathing hard; it was clear that the caning had excited him.

Ian continued to stand his ground. 'Are you all right, Brother Healey?' he asked, his tone saccharine sweet.

Four of the escape committee were in this class today. The other three members stood and walked to the front in response to Ian's nod. They stood behind their leader, arms folded, mouths tightly shut.

Healey panicked. He raised his weapon once more and lashed it across Ian's face. Stammering John grabbed the cane while the others jumped on the man. They were fourteen years of age; they were strong; they were healthy and, beyond all that, they were furious. John used the cane, slashing once at Healey's face before lifting up the hem of his robe and beating his shins. He then dragged the monk's legs wide apart while the other three kicked their torturer repeatedly in the abdomen and testicles.

Ian placed his hands round the creature's throat and began to squeeze. 'Always remember, Brother, that there are more of us than there are of your scabby lot. Always remember that we'll grow up unless you kill us, and that we will talk. Oh, and we do pray. We pray to St Jude, patron of hopeless cases, because you and a couple of your mates need to die so that we'll be free of you dirty, mad, rotten bastards. You're in Liverpool now, and Scousers take nothing lying down. Right, lads, that'll do for now.' The four of them returned to their desks.

Brother Williams burst in. 'I'll get an ambulance,' he cried when he saw the state of his colleague.

'And fetch a doctor for me,' Ian hissed. 'Because that filthy swine shoved something of his up my back passage last night and I've been bleeding.'

Williams, a true Christian, simply stood as if riveted to the floor. 'What?' he managed finally. 'And why is your face marked?'

Ian stood. 'He caned me across the face, so we did the same to him. There's Healey, Ellis and Moorhead. They interfere with us, Brother Williams.' Inside, he was shaking, as the hormone that had sustained him thus far was dispersing fast. He glanced at his three friends; they, too, were trembling. They needed to be put downstairs in clink, because the prison cells provided the easiest escape. He hoped that the other two prospective escapees had misbehaved in their Latin class, so that they, too, would be placed down below.

'Shall I get the police, Brother Healey?' Williams asked.

'No,' groaned the felled man. 'Remember? Father, forgive them, for they know not what they do.'

John jumped up. 'J-J-Jesus said th-th-that on the c-cross. You w-w-w-will nev-v-ver be for-forgiven. E-evil f-f-fucker.'

Brother Williams, a calm and gentle man, led the class out into the corridor. 'Be still and quiet,' he advised. 'This will be dealt with.' He returned to the classroom and closed the door carefully. Ian crossed the fingers of his left hand – the right was too sore. 'Release us, God,' he prayed inwardly.

To keep his mind further occupied, he listed the names and addresses he intended to use. The Queen and the Duke of Edinburgh, Buckingham Palace, London. The Archbishop of Liverpool, Archbishop's House, Liverpool. The boss of Liverpool Corporation, the Welfare Department, Liverpool. Dr Masefield, Heathfield Close, Hunt's Cross. Ian's own mam, who lived in a refuge somewhere in West Derby, and– Oh, God. He probably wouldn't be cleaning the office today, so paper, envelopes and stamps might be unattainable.

He sent the whisper down the line. 'If you clean the office, get stamps, paper, pens and envelopes. Leave them behind a milk crate on the steps.' He hadn't thought things through properly, had he? If he was the brains of the outfit, God help them all.

The whole class stood for what felt like at least an hour. Although they listened, they heard not a word from the classroom.

'P-please, God,' John prayed. 'Get these bastards for us.'

'Amen,' breathed the rest of them.

'I've been on this bloody beat for eighteen months now, and I demand a recount.' Constable Eddie Barnes was not in the best of moods. Quick Mick was snoring in a stall in the gents' toilets. 'I wouldn't care, but he smells worse than the urinals. I wonder when he last had a wash or a bath?'

Dave Earnshaw shrugged. 'About 1947 when he left the orphanage. It's your turn, anyway. You'll have to climb over and get the bugger out.'

'Shit.'

'Yes, he might be doing that, too.'

'They should give us protective clothing for jobs like this,' Eddie moaned. 'He could have fleas, scabies, dry rot, rising bloody damp – hey, if he bites me again, I want a tetanus jab.'

Dave couldn't help himself; he burst out laughing. 'Listen, you go in there, lad, and I'll get you swilled down by the fire brigade after we've done here. Anyway, I've got to shift Smelly Nellie, so you're not the only one with a problem.'

'She's not shut in the lavs, is she? You don't have to throw your leg over a door and split your difference if you slip.'

Dave shrugged. 'Like I said, it's your turn – simple as that.' He walked towards a slight, stooped old woman at the other end of Lime

41

Street Station's public area. Constable Earnshaw had a soft spot for poor old Nellie. She wasn't the most fragrant companion, but there was a strange dignity about her. Well spoken and gentle, Nellie was something of a mystery. Her whole life was contained in a coach-built Silver Cross pram whose undercarriage had been replaced many times by her associates, one of whose number was currently comatose in the gents' lavatory.

'Hello, Nellie. How are you doing, girl?'

'I'm well, thank you, which is more than can be said for Mick. Has Constable Barnes found him?'

He nodded. 'He's locked himself in one of the lavs, and he's snoring, so we know there's life in him. I think we'll have to take him in before he does himself a mischief. How does he manage to get hold of the booze, Nellie?'

'I have no idea.'

They were a clan, and he knew it. Solid as a brick wall, they stood together, one for all and all for one, secrets buried deep inside, locked away in minds that refused to open to authorities. How many welfare workers had the 'family' chewed up and spat out? Yet Dave tried once more. 'Where do they go during the day?' he asked. 'We see you and a couple of others out and about, but what about Quick Mick and the rest of them?'

'They sleep here and there,' Nellie said.

'And they burgle at night?'

The old woman cocked her head to one side. 'You know I can't answer these questions, constable. We live how we live because life let us down, or we let ourselves down. And we serve a purpose, as you very well know.'

He had to agree, though he did it silently. The Lime Street Gang, labelled such by the police, had rescued many a runaway who had landed at train or coach station. The latest had been returned to her home only to disappear again within hours, probably to London. London was the Other Place, and few returned from there. But he didn't tell Nellie, because she took these things very seriously. 'Have the ladies been out tonight, Nellie?'

'They have.'

'How many?'

'I didn't count them. Look, Constable Dave, they do what they do, and don't judge them. Some have children to feed, clothe and shelter, and for others, it's the only way of life they've known. They are a necessity.'

He pondered for a few moments. 'Where did you get all that wisdom?'

She smiled at him.

'Where did you go to school, Nellie?'

'If I told you, you wouldn't believe me. Look, there's Eddie with Mick. Look after him. He's no longer Quick Mick since the fall, so be gentle.' She took the handle of her pram and began to steer it through the station. When she reached her prostrate friend, she lifted something from one of her many pockets before placing a hand on his head.

Dave watched as she turned into Lime Street. How old was she? Where had she been born and raised – where had any of them come from? And he felt almost certain that Nellie had just put holy water on Mick's head. She was a mystery, as were many of the other rootless souls who haunted the station.

Ah well, poor Eddie would get some relief, since Mick was literally legless. Eddie could radio through for a jam butty, as police cars were named in this city. And God help the poor lads in the vehicle, because they might well be gassed. Quick Mick was now slow since his accident. He was pickled in booze, almost ready to shuffle off into the afterlife, and he stank like an open sewer. It would take an age to get him into the police car, and another age to get him out.

Dave joined his colleague. 'You stink,' he said, 'and I think an ambulance might be better. He's very yellow, isn't he?'

'There's blood in his vomit,' Eddie said. 'I think he's finally blown his liver to kingdom come. And I have sent for an ambulance.'

Two young men in uniform stood in the station's entrance. Behind them lay a dying man who was probably under forty years of age. 'Why do they do it, Eddie?' Dave asked.

'No sodding idea, but I wish they'd die on somebody else's watch.' He turned and wiped a tear from his face. Sometimes, he hated this job.

'You all right?' Dave asked.

'Something in me eye. Mucky places, these stations.'

'You're right there, lad. Enough to break your heart sometimes.'

See, I'm the only one who knows that Jesus forgave Judas. Yes, I realize I'm talking to myself, but who can I tell? Not Laura, not Joseph at work. Nobody.

They came to me that night a couple of weeks back. My kids, Lucy and Matt, were asleep in their beds, as was Laura, my kind and gentle wife. I went downstairs after kissing all three, and I grabbed a beer: it had been a long shift sorting mail at the post office; it's a boring job.

I was sitting there thinking about Joseph Turton, who is probably my only true friend. He still lives with his mother, and she needs looking after. He and I enjoy a pint or two with the rest of the two-till-ten shift, though we usually chat just to each other. He's a good man, paying folk to see to his mam while he's at work, sitting with her when he can, seeing to her medicines and her bedsores and all the rest of it.

And there they stood in front of the fireplace. Jesus was in a long, white robe, and Judas was dressed in something similar, but he had a necklace made of silver coins all linked together. Yes, he wears the thirty pieces, and his sins are carried round his neck. He reminded me of Jacob Marley, the first ghost to visit Scrooge; Marley dragged his sins behind him in heavy chains.

The good Lord raised a hand and blessed first Judas, then me. And He spoke. To me. Jesus spoke to *me!* He told me about Mary Magdalene and her repentance; then He spoke about those who stain the streets with their bad behaviour. 'They sell their bodies,' He said, 'and the streets must be cleansed.'

So I'm special.

I don't know who drank the beer; the bottle was empty when they disappeared, but now that I think about it, there was a glint in Judas's eye. I hope he enjoyed it. I had to smile, because he's still up to his tricks, right?

Chosen by Our Lord, I will come to no harm. I am above and beyond the reach of men's laws, as I am directed by the Son of God to do His work. No one will catch me. Like Judas, I will link my deeds together, every one connected to the rest, because I am guided by divine hands.

This is my job, my task. Of course, I'll carry on at the post office – I have a family to support. If I'm on a day or an afternoon-till-evening shift, Laura will think I'm out bowling or having a drink with the lads after work. We're happy. We love each other and go to church every Sunday and teach our kids good manners.

I will bury no bodies. I'll leave them in plain view so that others can see them displayed as vessels of sin. Each link will hark back to a previous removal. Judas's chain of coins gave me the idea. It was the necklace that helped me know who he was. So I'm here with my first. She made no noise while I used the garrotte. Her head's at a funny angle, and her skirt's too short for modesty.

She's got bright red lips and cheap plastic earrings. I've taken the cross and chain she wore round her neck – that's link one. The next one will wear it. Laura's making shepherd's pie for tea. She'll have saved some and I'll have it for my supper.

Nobody here on the coastal road. Not that it matters; I won't get caught. I'm special, see?

Two

Babs was reading an article in a magazine. It was a piece quoted from *Women Objectified*, a book by some London doctor called Alexandra Sefton-Hope. 'More like Sefton-bleeding-Hopeless round here,' the reader muttered. She turned the page and read on. This author insisted that females ought to stand up and be counted in the workplace – equal pay, no sexual harassment, and the same opportunities for advancement as men. 'She should look at this workplace,' Babs whispered, 'because we don't stand up to be counted; we lie down most of the time and have to let men think they're in charge.'

But were men truly in charge here? 'No, they're not. They're as much in charge as a nail under the hammer.' She placed the magazine on her windowsill. No, men definitely didn't run Meadowbank; they came here because no other women out there wanted them, so they had to pay. This was one place where females held the power. Each girl had an alarm button and permission to refuse to serve an abusive client, while Eve was definitely female and absolutely in charge. She did the counting, but she sat down to do it.

Eve Mellor had invested real money in the farmhouse. Three large attic rooms were now made over to Belle and her massage, Judy with her reflexology (I'll get you going, lad, because I know which part of your foot to stimulate) and Angela Whiplash's chamber of horrors. Oh yes, it was all very well thought out and beautifully appointed. Eve went so far as to bring in part-timers whenever one of the girls had her monthly 'problem.' 'She's efficient, I'll give her that,' Babs muttered. 'And while she's being efficient, my lifespan is getting shorter and I'm bored. Can a person die of boredom?'

The whole place apart from the kitchen was red, black, white and gold, all subdued lighting and erotic prints on the walls. Men arrived here looking tense, probably afraid of their wives, their neighbours, their colleagues and their own shadows. They parted with good money, and left in a happier state. Cynthia, Mo, Babs and Sally serviced clients in their bedrooms, and that wasn't fair, but neither was life. 'Yes, I have to get away, because there's chances out there. This is a rut, and I want to get miles from it. Bloody pink – I've had enough.' If Don had anything pink in his house, she would give the article a decent funeral.

Right, it was time to go downstairs; she was tired of the smell of sex and stale sweat, bored by constant bed-making and sheet-changing, fed up to the back teeth of a life over which she had little control. Eating in the place where she entertained customers was not pleasant, so she must return to the kitchen and face the music. No. To hell with facing it; she would write the score and the bloody lyrics.

She picked up a hairbrush and raked through her tangles. Several plots were hatching under her mop of long brown hair; she could do better than this, a bloody sight better. It was time to face the congregation, and Babs intended to conduct the orchestra and manage the auditorium too. This was her way of standing up to be counted, she supposed.

She dressed slowly, donning jeans, a blouse and flat shoes before capturing her abundant tresses in a pony tail. Let the rest of the girls settle round the table before she put in an appearance. Satisfied eventually with the way she looked, Babs descended the stairs.

Several differing points of view hovered in the air above the gathering as Eve's girls sat to eat dinner/ brunch two days after the transaction between Eve and Donald. They had talked, of course, but Baby Girl was expected to join them today, so their conversation was confined to matters mundane until they worked out the lie of the land.

Babs stood in the hall and listened; nothing of interest reached her ears. She had eaten in her hated room for two days, delivering a close imitation of life only for clients, as she'd had a great deal of thinking to do. But at last, having given Eve time to spread the news, she joined the other girls.

An uncomfortable and sudden silence accompanied her entry into the arena, but she was ready. Babs made no effort to communicate as she walked in and took her place at the enormous table; it was up to them to speak first, she decided. She knew exactly who would be jealous and who among her fellows would take the news on their chins. The trouble with women was that they usually held an opinion, and they clung to it

49

even when they were wrong. On the occasions when they knew nothing about a subject, they became polarized in spite of or perhaps because of their lack of knowledge.

Belle was an expert in massage; Cynthia would do anything if the price seemed right. Angela used aggressive implements on men of seriously flawed character and Judy knew all there was to know about feet. Babs glanced from one to another, remaining determinedly silent.

Sally Hayes, seventeen and learning the trade, realized that she would probably be expected to take Babs Schofield's place, and she felt uneasy. Still at the age when hope burgeons without nourishment, still waiting to be swept off her feet by a client who loved her enough to ignore her past, she now faced a future filled by men who wanted little girls, and she needed to talk to Babs in private, if that could be arranged. For the first time since coming to the farm, she felt afraid. An escapee from an abusive stepfather, Sally had been happier to get paid for her favours here at the farm, but now, she felt...? Mixed up, that was how she felt, so she kept quiet for the time being and ate as much as she could manage of the meal.

Belle Horrocks, who offered massage with additional privileges, was thirty-five, pretty, and almost past caring. If one of the girls found a cushy number with a stupid old man, all power to her. Like Eve in years past, Belle was saving and saving for a deposit on a place in town, because she had ten years at best to carry on as a night owl, and she wanted what she termed the ordinary life. She had a daughter who lived with

50

grandparents, and Belle wanted to get off the game before Lisa reached her mid-teens. The child understood that her mother worked away, but beyond that nobody was aware of anything approaching the truth.

Cynthia Greenhalgh, at twenty-six, served men who needed extras from a whore with no limits, and since she was capable of managing the bizarre and the twisted she received a higher share of the takings than the other girls and great tips from her clients. Nothing fazed her, as she had become inured to the unusual during her eight years here at the upmarket brothel designed by Eve Mellor. Meadowbank would never be raided – of that Cynthia was reasonably certain.

But Angela Dyson was ambitious. A classically beautiful dominatrix in her early forties, she collared clients, hit them with an assortment of implements, and made them pay in pain as well as in cash for her attentions. She continued to be well groomed and attractive, and was now annoyed. 'We can all wear baby clothes and be pwetty for our pwoud daddies. God, what wouldn't I give to get out of here? Babs, if you don't want to do it, I will.' She looked daggers at Baby Babs; it wasn't fair.

Babs simply smiled. 'I'm still thinking about it.' She hadn't mentioned her hope of featuring in his will, kept to herself the knowledge about his valuable property and his half of a promising racehorse.

'Let us know when you've decided,' Angela snapped.

Mo Thompson felt the same way as Angela. She

51

was twenty-four, a bubbly, shapely, dark-haired woman. Like Babs, she didn't tolerate the un-usual, though she might have been able to act the baby for a man who was almost impotent. 'It'll be a walk in the park, not like here where we have to keep having baths or all-over washes before the next lot arrives. She keeps us at it, doesn't she?'

Babs shrugged. 'Don's two butties short of a pic-nic,' she announced. 'I have to take a nurse's uni-form to Southport and feed him and give him his medicines. So no, it won't be a walk in the park at all. And he wants me, says I'm the love of his life.'

'You're turned thirty, Babs,' was young Sally's belated contribution. 'I'm seventeen, so I should be the baby.'

'You will be,' Babs replied. 'You'll have my pink room.'

'I don't really want it,' Sally whispered mourn-fully, 'but I'd like the chance to get out for a while even though I don't like dirty old men. Mr Craw-ford always smiles at me; he seems kinder than some of the others. Here, I'll have loads of them, but you'll have just him, Babs. I wish I could go to Southport.'

The rest of the girls giggled.

Babs stared at Sally; she pitied the poor young-ster.

Judy Robson, trained in reflexology, put in her tenpence-worth. 'Don smiles at everybody, Sally. Anyway, he's a foot fetishist, and I do feet. I'm ten years younger than Babs, too.'

Babs began to feel like the cat that got the cream. She wouldn't have to stay in Don's house all day every day, would she? And Eve had mentioned negotiations, so the first item on Babs's list was going to be her own bedroom; she didn't fancy spending whole nights with old Denture Breath and Comb-over. Those thin strands on the left side of his skull probably touched his shoulder when not glued to his head with hair cream. Yuk.

'When are you going, love?' Belle asked.

'When I'm ready. Eve's taking me for a few visits first. He's called his place Wordsworth House, because he's mad about poetry, and there's a Dove Cottage in the grounds. I'm going to ask if he'll let me live there, in the cottage. If he says no, I'll still insist on my own bedroom.'

'You're going to call all the shots, then?' Mo Thompson sneered. 'If he's paying you a wage, he'll expect some say in where you'll sleep.'

Babs awarded Mo her coldest stare. 'If you get any greener, Mo, you'll be on the gardener's list for trimming when you go rusty in autumn. Look, I'm not delighted about living with the mad old bugger, but it's a chance, isn't it? I can get to the shops and even to the beach. Southport's not my idea of a lively place, but it has to be better than here. And it'll be for a few months, that's all.'

Angela spoke. 'Oh? Why will it be just for a few months?'

'Because he's dying,' Babs answered without emotion.

Even the sound of cutlery against plates suddenly stopped. Sally's jaw dropped. 'If you're the only person there, Babs, you'll find his body.' She shivered in spite of the heat. 'I've never seen a dead body,' she added lamely.

The girls stared hard at the one who was about

to get away from Ma Eve's. Yes, they were safe here, but it was so isolated, so bleak. Shops selling clothes were things of the past; there was no joy in this area.

Babs exploded, though this time she was laughing. 'Listen, girls, he has a cleaner who comes in every day, even at weekends. And if I have anything to do with it, he'll slip away in hospital after Christmas.' She wouldn't mention the bet. 'I hope he lives till then, because he'll buy me something lovely, and I'll make him a good dinner.' She giggled. 'The condemned man ate a hearty meal.'

The rest of the brunch was eaten in silence except for requests for the cruet or the water jug. Babs began to feel smug, especially when one of the envious ones scowled in her direction. But she pitied sweet little Sally. For the first time in her adult life, Babs wanted to help someone. Yes. She would have a word with the poor kid this afternoon.

The day dragged towards evening. Babs pulled on frilly knickers and the school uniform, painted freckles on her nose, and did her hair in plaits with pipe-cleaners in the braids so that they would bend outwards in a cute, silly way. After tying pale blue ribbons to the plaits, she wandered next door to Sally's room. 'Can I come in?' she called after tapping on the door.

'Yes. I'd like to talk to you if you don't mind.'

Babs entered. 'Aw, Sally, you do look pretty.'

'Thank you. Eve says she thinks I'll have three tonight.' She was dressed in baby doll pyjamas. 'This is me turned into the next Baby Girl, I suppose. She gave me these clothes and said to

54

expect slightly older men tonight. When they're young, they live in hope of getting the real thing, you see.' She stared through the window. 'My stepfather got the real thing – me. I feel sick.'

Babs shook her head in sympathy. 'I know, love. Listen to me, Sal. I'll have to be quick, cos she's already took the van down to town for the straight-after-work lot. I'm not promising, but I might come into some money – don't ask how or when, because I can't say. If I do, I'll get you out of here and we'll have a life. I'm fed up with all this. A working girl got strangled the other night – did you hear about it?'

Sally nodded. It had been the biggest story in the papers and on television.

'We need to find a way of knocking this lark on the head,' Babs muttered. 'Proper jobs and a decent place to live. We can do it, girl.'

'Can we?'

'I'll try my damnedest, Sal. Be sweet and kind to the men who use you, and save as much as you can.' Babs's ambitions had reached new heights. She wanted a good house, a semi-detached with a garden and a decent kitchen. She wanted a proper job in a shop or an office … no, she would have her own business. 'Whatever happens, I'll not forget you, girl. You and I are going places, and one of them places will not be bloody Southport.'

'Thank you, Babs.'

'Don't thank me, Baby Girl. Just hang on in here. I'll try to visit Meadowbank, but first I've got some acting of my own to do. And don't for-get, we've the doc coming in the morning, so try to get rid of your last client as fast as you can, because we'll be woke up early.' She smiled and left Sal's room.

Back in her own domain, Babs embroidered a brand new plan, one that seemed to have developed of its own accord only today. She was going for the bull's eye, and she was good at darts. Her latest brainwave had arrived at its destination during brunch, and it would involve stamina, tenacity and a strong stomach, but it was the only way to be certain of a decent future. Five hundred pounds? No, she was going for the jackpot. She spoke to Baby Babs in the mirror. 'Sally and me deserve a chance, and a chance, no matter how small, is worth fighting for.'

Could she force him to marry her?

Mr Sherwood sent for me after the shift ended yesterday morning. He reckoned that lads on the section were fed up with my mistakes. 'Your concentration's slipping,' he said, 'so keep your mind on the job. You've mixed up Tithebarn Road with Tithebarn Place in Crosby, and two packages for Halewood were on their way to Bootle and Formby. Fortunately, some of the others work with their eyes open and their brains switched on, which is more than can be said for you these days. Are you sickening for something, Neil?'

I told him I was sorry, but he gave me a peculiar look. Am I behaving differently? Am I giving myself away by acting or talking in a new way? I don't think so. Things are still the same as they were – we all go for a pint together unless we're on night shift.

Perhaps it's because I know that in the eyes of

ordinary humans, I'm doing wrong. I was hoping for another visit from Jesus, but I suppose He's testing me. So anyway, I rode my bike home at dawn yesterday morning, and the sky was beautiful. The sun comes up over Yorkshire, but sometimes it seems to throw an echo on all the pretty white clouds over the Mersey. I wish Laura could be with me at times like that. But she has her own schedule, kids' breakfasts, get them off to school, clean the house, washing, ironing, shopping and cooking. I make my own breakfast after a night shift, because my Laura works hard enough as things are. She has to be quiet, too, when I sleep in the day. It's not easy. She can't use the Hoover till I wake up and spend time eating and playing with the kids before getting ready to go on shift.

And there I was at sunrise, just riding home, and I saw the old woman again, that one who stumbles about on her high heels – did I tell you about her? She must have been up to no good all night, but I didn't bother stopping. I see milkmen early in the mornings, and folk like me who work turnabouts, so it's not worth the risk. Two in the afternoon till ten at night's the best shift when it comes to street-cleaning. That will be me come Monday.

I stood for a while and gazed at God's sky. It looked as if He'd been busy with a paintbrush, so stunning was the picture. It's an amazing world. The police aren't here any more; I used a route further inland when the cops were sniffing, went home through Bootle.

I still had the cross and chain at home, but I'd hidden it. I would get rid of it soon enough, I hoped. She's going to be the next one, that stumbling woman old enough to know better; she will wear it, because they all have to be linked so that the message will be clear. That was my thinking yesterday morning, anyway.

But when I got home, Laura wasn't in bed; she usually sleeps till turned seven, which is when the kids wake her. She stood in the hall, arms folded and with a frown on her face. 'I found this in your sock drawer,' she said, and she looked angry. It was the cross and chain I took from Number One. My feet felt stuck to the floor. Number One's mother had identified the body and had said that her girl had always worn her gold cross and chain. Did Laura know that? Had she read it in the paper or seen it on the news? She doesn't often take notice of current affairs.

'Where did you get it?' she asked, and she didn't sound like herself; her voice was cold, and she separated all her words as if talking to a two-year-old.

My brain kicked in – all my extremities had felt frozen stiff until that moment.

'Second-hand shop,' I said. 'I was trying to find a nice box so I could give it to you for your birthday.'

She held it up high and looked at it. 'It isn't a crucifix,' she said. 'It's just a cross with no Christ on it.'

'I know, Laura, but it's real gold and very pretty.'

She didn't seem angry any more. Perhaps she'd been wondering whether I had a girlfriend, and worrying that this thing might have belonged to the other woman. There's never been anyone but Laura for me. I hated seeing that thing in my

58

sweet wife's hardworking hands, because the object is contaminated by a whore.

'It's a lovely thought, Neil. Here, put it away till you find a box, and I'll forget I ever saw it. You'd better get the first owner's initials taken off, though.'

I felt my pores opening. Every hair on my body stood to full attention as if on guard. Initials? Jesus, help me. I never noticed them.

So I took it from Laura. Yes, there the initials were on the plain side where there was no diamond cutting, *JD 21 today.* Number One was Jean Davenport – her name was in the *Echo.*

What must I do now? I wondered. If I took it to a jeweller to have the initials removed, he and others in the trade might have been warned by police to look out for it. Perhaps I could rub the initials off in the shed. Maybe I should pretend to lose this one and buy another. If I kept it, my wife, my lovely wife, would be wearing the embellishment of a street walker.

After breakfast, I went up to bed. My mind was all over the place. I could buy her a gold crucifix with a Christ figure and say I'd sold the 'secondhand' one, but if I put it on the next body, Laura might read the paper for once; she could well find out that Number One's jewellery had been left on Number Two. My plan's going wrong. Jesus gave me a clue by bringing Judas and his joined-up thirty pieces, didn't He? What should I do? Does anyone have the answer? Because my brain seems to be going on strike.

I prayed. I asked for Jesus to intercede and guide me through this ... this mess. And He did!

Well, He tried. From nowhere on the earthly plane, a scene entered my head. The cross was there on a desk or a table, and I saw myself prising Jesus off another cross, maybe one attached to a rosary, and fastening the figure over the initials on Number One's cross. But that isn't the pretty side, is it? The engraving's on the flat side.

And I heard a voice saying a name. It mentioned Jimmy Nuttall. Jimmy has a high-class repository in town, all mother-of-pearl-backed prayer books and New Testaments, leather-bound hymnals and missals, expensive rosaries. He sells First Communion clothes for girls and boys, Extreme Unction sets with everything a priest might need aside from the oils. It's a posh place, and not cheap. Yes, I would go there.

'Thank you, Jesus,' I told Him. If you pray, He never lets you down. Jimmy might have a gold rosary, and all rosaries bear Christ figures... But Laura would still be wearing the whore's cross with the figure from the rosary on the plain side. I was getting confused. If I bought a new chain – no. Jesus, thanks for trying to help, but I'm going to stick with the plan. But no again. If Jean Davenport's cross turns up on the old biddy's corpse, it will all blow up once more, and Laura might notice and remember Jean Davenport's initials. I have to get rid of this one and buy Laura another, a proper crucifix this time.

Right, that's it – it's going in the river and Laura will have a new one, a proper one. I'm walking on sand now towards the pretty echo of a rising sun, and it's almost as magnificent as it was yesterday. I'm throwing the thing in the river wrapped round a big, flat pebble – anyone watching will think I'm stone-skimming. When the water's still and glassy like it is today, I sometimes bring the kids down to play this game. We count the bounces. Everybody says I'm a very good dad.

When the Lord left them, His apostles had to make decisions. I've been co-opted. I'm a new disciple, a secret one, and I have to follow the path prescribed by the Son of God.

Oh, and if your mail's been a bit dodgy lately, I'll do my best to get it right in the future. God bless you. Neil Carson, servant of the Lord.

In Ian Foster's limited experience, things never worked out according to plan. Nobody went in the cellar the night following the attack on Healey. After all the trouble the lads had gone to while in prison, digging at cement and brickwork, loosening bars so that they might escape, nothing happened. No, that wasn't true, because Brothers Healey, Ellis and Moorhead disappeared from the face of the school. At morning assembly the following day, pupils were advised by Brother Bennet that the three had gone on retreat and that new teachers would arrive within days.

On retreat? Ian's fury continued white-hot. Oh yes, they were on retreat, all right, but from their evil doings. They were a cowardly army, and they'd fled to regroup far from the front line of battle, that was all. Ian still needed to get away to tell the Queen and all the rest what had happened here. The flight of the three yellow-bellies served only to verify allegations. 'I'm still going,' he told John-the-Stammer Lucas, who nodded his agreement.

Phil Sharples announced his intention to flee with them, but the rest of the escape committee withdrew. The abusers had gone, and that was case closed as far as they were concerned.

Ian was angry with them, too, though after some thought he began to understand why they weren't coming. It was fear. Like concentration camp prisoners, they were too terrified to take risks, and Ian certainly understood terror.

So just three boys wandered from the route during cross-country running. They picked up envelopes, paper and stamps from behind an empty milk crate, turned right, and legged it to the top field where their stash, including outdoor shoes, was kept. They kept on their running shoes, though flight wouldn't be easy with all the baggage. John knew where they were going, so the other two simply trudged behind him, weighed down by spoils and tired after a shorter than normal supposedly character-building cross-country run.

'What if Brother Jerrold notices we aren't with the rest?' Phil Sharples asked. 'He'll throw a blue fit.'

'Don't waste your worrying on that,' Ian suggested. 'And if he does throw a blue fit, let him do it in Bluebell Wood, cos nobody'll notice with all the flowers being blue.'

'And what if the rest of the escape group tell where we are?' Phil mumbled. 'What if they get questioned and beaten till they talk?'

'They won't, because they don't know where we're going.' Ian adjusted his burden in an attempt to make carrying easier. 'Only Stammer knows that.'

'But–'

'Shut up, Phil. We've miles to walk.'

'But what if–?'

'Shut up. Like I said, we've miles to go.'

He was right, of course. The school was south of Liverpool, and they had to get north of the city via a circuitous route, since they needed to stay away from populated areas to avoid being noticed.

'We're getting nearer,' John told them. 'Another hour or two, and we'll be there.'

The other pair stopped dead in their tracks. 'What happened to the stammer?' Phil asked, wiping sweat from his brow.

'I'm n-nearly OK away from them bastards. As long as you don't talk about it, it'll g-g-go away.'

They stopped for a rest in a little copse outside Netherton. 'We've passed it twice,' John told them, 'but that was so we could avoid houses and th-that. We should be there before dark. There was a p-paraffin stove and mattresses last time m-me and me mates went in. Sacks and blankets and boxes of stuff and tents, too. Unless they've been back and t-took them away, like.'

'Or they might come for them while we're there,' Ian said.

'Chance we'll have to take,' was Phil's expressed opinion. 'We won't be there at night, anyway, cos we'll be out on the rob looking for disguises and stuff. We might have money for paraffin, but we'll need to dress up when we go for it. During the day, we'll take turns to be lookouts.'

'Oh, bugger,' Ian exclaimed. John was snoring.

'We'd best sleep, too. If we move about after dark, there'll be less chance of being noticed.'

They slept, though not deeply. Inside three heads in the small copse, images played in full colour and with sound. Healey, Ellis and Moorhead were up to their tricks in the teachers' rooms near the dorms. The boys saw, felt and heard all they had endured, and, when they woke from time to time, relief was their main emotion. What they failed to realize was that these nightmares could last a lifetime, and they would never be completely free, since a part of each soul had been excised by evil men of God.

When darkness descended and spread its blanket over three damaged boys, they skirted the edge of a housing estate, Phil and Ian leaving John with their bags of loot while they slipped in and out of gates gathering forgotten washing from quiet gardens. When the stealing was over, they re-joined John, renamed Stam since he now had just half a stammer. 'Ian,' Phil asked, 'why did God let all that bad stuff happen to us?'

'He didn't.' Ian was sorting socks in near-darkness. 'Where's this bloody hut, Stam?'

'Other side of them trees. What do you mean, He didn't?'

'We got free will and some of us choose to do bad things.'

'But He could have stopped it,' John said.

Ian threw the socks in a bag – his task was hopeless in the dark. 'Look, everything bad in the world is done by us, by people. He gave us a beautiful planet, a set of rules and free will. Some people are crap. Healey, Ellis and Moorhead are bad, but they could stop being bad if they wanted to. Even diseases are our fault, because we don't live right. Now, pick these bags up – remember, we need some proper sleep.'

Phil shook his head. 'How do you know all this stuff, then?'

'Books. You know, them things in the library with pages of writing in 'em. We don't all stick to the *Beano* and the *Dandy*, you know. Come on, shift your arses.'

They dragged sore feet across the last few hundred yards. The door of the hut wasn't locked, and the three boys literally fell in, hit the floor and slept. This was night one of freedom. There was a great deal to be done before they got caught, and they needed a long rest. Tomorrow, their scribe would begin letting the world know about the Brothers Pastoral.

Helen Carrington pushed her Silver Cross pram into its resting place. She closed the door of the Anderson shelter and applied the padlock before turning towards the house. Ignoring front and rear entrances, she descended cellar steps and reached her own domain. Everything she needed was to hand in her basement flat. When her filthy clothes were locked in a seafarer's trunk, she ran a bath and immersed herself in tepid water; it had been one purgatory of a day.

There was no further news about Jean Davenport, a young mother whose corpse had been found near the river. Quick Mick had died in hospital; even the two young constables had shed tears. Thirty-nine years of age and the product of battling parents who had died when he was in junior school, Mick had managed to murder his own liver. Constables Earnshaw and Barnes, currently on night duty in the Lime Street area, had both expressed the intention to attend Mick's funeral even at the expense of much-needed sleep.

'They'll be on days soon,' Nellie mumbled to herself, 'or they could be sent to patrol the riverside in case Jean is a serial killer's first.' She scrubbed her flesh with a loofah. For how many years had she led this strange life? Five, six? She climbed out, dried herself and donned a clean, white nightdress.

When she returned to the large living, sleeping and kitchen area, one of her sisters was there with food. 'If you don't empty this plate – and I don't mean in the bin – I'll be displeased.'

Helen stuck out her tongue.

'Infantile,' Beatrice said. 'I'm off to bed.'

Alone, Helen ate the ham salad. Eating was hard work on a hot evening.

She thought about Quick Mick, who had gone from quick to slow, from slow to death. 'The quick and the dead,' she muttered through a mouthful of lettuce. 'Am I doing any good at all out there?' She was. She should pull herself together and thank goodness that Mick was no longer in pain. Runaways had been saved and taken home or to places of safety. Three alcoholics had gone for treatment, and one of those had turned his life round. Mick and another were dead, but a third man was very much alive, working and happy.

Oh well. Another day tomorrow, stinking clothes and that silly pram. 'God help me,' she begged.

'I'm not as young as I was.' As soon as her head hit the pillow, she fell asleep.

'Look, it's a goer, I'm telling you. Only do you think you could take your foot away from my face? It stinks like fish gone bad. How many days have you had them bleeding socks on? Go back to sleep, you're getting on my wick.' Roy Foley pushed Billy Tyler's leg away.

'I can't help it,' Billy moaned. 'We're like a full tin of sardines in this bed. How am I supposed to get clean clothes when I can't go home? We've been stuck here for weeks now, babysitting weed. And it's roasting when them bright lights are on.' He sat up. 'And we'll go to prison if we're found out. Or when they start pulling the houses down. We'll have to shift all this stuff somewhere else, and–'

'Shut your face.' Roy rolled off the bed. 'Listen, we'll get thousands off the resin. Like I said, it's a goer, and I know how to make it. We can cut it with anything brown, even dog shit. Holy Mary and Dopey Ginger can arrange to sell it, because nobody'll suspect them two daft buggers. We'll be millionaires.'

Billy sniffed. 'Can't we be millionaires with two beds instead of one?'

'Not yet. If we get found out for using electricity from the street lights, we'll be buggered and we'll have to scarper, and we'll lose every leaf of this crop. So shut up, put up and get your sunglasses on, because I'm doing a burst.' A burst meant light too fierce for human eyes.

Billy was fed up, and he said so.

Roy offered no answer; he was fed up with Billy's fed up-ness.

Every part of the upper floor, including the boys' bedroom, was crammed with plants. Roy, who had suffered all his life from sudden enthusiasms, was building a career in drugs. With all the upper windows blacked out, he was able to give the plants the unbearably fierce light they needed. He fled downstairs with Billy Tyler hot on his heels. Hot was the right word, because the house was stifling. Demolition had begun in streets nearby, though their borrowed premises were reasonably safe for now.

They ate jam butties and drank tepid lemonade.

'Are you sure you know what you're doing?' Billy asked.

Roy nodded. He'd had lessons in Halewood. 'Buds are worth a lot. They can be smoked in a pipe. Leaves can be brewed to make tea, and the resin goes in ciggies. Them who don't smoke can put it in cakes and bake it. I could sell the lot to Halewood and Speke, but we'll get more if Holy Mary and Dopey Ginge find somebody to flog it for us.'

'We could go to jail.' Billy bit into his second butty.

'Don't talk soft.'

Billy was far from comfortable. They were stealing electricity, money and food, and living with a load of smelly weeds in a house due to be flattened at any time. 'I seen that film,' he muttered.

'What film?' Roy glared at his inferior assistant in crime.

'They all went blind except them that were

68

asleep or had bandages on their eyes. Plants done that.'

Roy Foley shook his head. *'Day of the Triffids?* That's science fiction, you clown. No wonder you were in the bottom stream at school. These plants don't walk, and they'll make us a fortune. Sneak out, cross the main road and pinch some milk off doorsteps. You've got to pull yourself together, lad.'

'No. You go for a change.'

The senior executive blinked. He'd picked Billy because he always did as he was told. He suddenly realized that Billy Tyler was intending to run. 'We'll both go for milk,' he said. 'And if you're thinking of backing out or dashing off home, I'll find you, soft girl, so forget it.'

'I'm not running.'

'You'd better not.'

Billy was beyond confused. He'd already stolen dishes, ladies' stockings, small sieves and rubber gloves for the making of super-hash, as Roy termed the best of the crop. They'd eaten no proper food for days, and Billy was becoming light-headed. There was enough foliage in the house to merit the hiring of a workforce, yet he and Roy *were* the workforce, so how would they manage? It would take a month to sift the top of the crop through nylons...

'Billy?'

'What? And I want to be Bill, not Billy.'

'Right, Bill. Where've you gone in your head?'

'It's too much for two people, Roy.'

'Dopey Ginger will help.'

'What about Holy Mary?'

69

'Too busy doing charity work and going to church. It's her cover. She'll be great at the selling side of the job.'

'So who's going to turn that drum all day? And the thing that makes compressed hash?'

'We'll work it out. I always think of something, don't I?'

Bill pondered. Roy hadn't thought of much when they'd nearly been caught shoplifting and when they'd burgled a house on Picton Road; Bill had been dreaming about being locked in a cell, the same dream for three nights, then he'd had a nightmare about magistrates. Roy Foley was good at ideas, but no good at keeping himself and others out of trouble.

'Come on,' Roy ordered again. 'We need milk.'

They went to steal milk.

Belle Horrocks was in a state of excitement that spread the full length of the farmhouse kitchen's table. She was going home for a week. She was going home in a grey suit with a white blouse and black shoes and carrying a smart black handbag. Her mother and father believed that she was part of a peripatetic team used by companies preparing for audit, and Belle had to look the part.

Home was new, as her parents had moved to Wavertree; that was also the place where her three-year-old daughter Lisa lived. Belle's duties at Meadowbank would be undertaken by one of the part-timers who filled in when necessary. 'Lisa's growing so fast,' Belle told the girls. 'She can write her name and count to twenty.'

'You should go home more often,' Babs opined.

'You get a few days off every month like the rest of us.'

But everyone knew that Belle was careful with money. She saved assiduously, keeping a close eye on the balance in her bank book. Eve supplied working clothes, massage oils and food, so Belle was steadily accumulating funds in order to acquire living quarters for herself and her daughter. Nothing on earth meant as much as Lisa did: Lisa would have a decent life and a good education with a career at the end of it; she'd be a teacher or a nurse, something respectable, anyway.

'Where will you take her?' Sally asked.

'Oh, parks, libraries, Crosby beach, maybe Formby.'

'Anywhere and everywhere free,' Angela sneered. 'You won't even find the bus fare to go home more often.'

Babs was a bit fed up with Angela Whiplash Dyson. 'Oh, shut your mouth, or wear one of your gags. Belle's saving for little Lisa. And she's travelling free today, too, because Eve will drop her off before we go to Southport. So try and make something out of that, you bad-minded bitch. Look in a mirror at your mean mouth, Ange. You might have good bones, but you've the gob of a bloody snake, thin and nasty.'

Three women leapt from chairs. Kate jumped up and pressed the panic button, which would sound in Eve's office, while Babs and Angela indulged in hair-pulling, scratching, biting and kicking. Angela was the taller of the two, but Babs was the product of meaner streets, and she knew a few tricks when it came to caring for herself. She

71

threw Angela at a wall and followed through by seizing the woman by the throat. 'You are an evil tart. I hope one day a client will lose it with you and break your effing neck. Get your hands out of my hair, bitch. And Belle would make a dozen of you, you useless article.'

Belle dragged Babs away. 'She's not worth it, babe. Let her take it out on her victims tonight.'

Angela strode purposefully towards Babs. 'I'll kill you next time,' she promised.

'You and whose army, Whiplash? Do you know where I come from?'

'From a bad egg,' was Angela's swift reply.

'From Scotty Road, actually. I don't need whips or canes or handcuffs, because I'm street-smart, see? When you shuffle off the face of the earth, it will look like an accident. I have friends in low places.'

Eve, responding to the panic buzzer, entered the room. 'Babs?'

Everyone froze.

'That fourth attic is sound-proofed now and full of rubbish. Would you like to spend a few hours calming down among boxes of crap? Angela, behave yourself, or you'll go up with her, and you can ruin each other's looks for life. Get out of here, the lot of you. Belle, I'll drop you at home. Babs, you start negotiations with Don Crawford this afternoon. I'll do a bit of shopping on Lord Street.'

Babs stood her ground. 'I want to take Sally with me, give her a few hours off in a place where her stepfather can't find her. She never goes to Liverpool, because she might bump into him, but Southport's safe, so I'm taking her.'

72

'No,' Eve snapped.

'Then I'm going nowhere.' Babs sat down and wrapped her arms round her upper body.

The others left, though Sally lingered where she was.

'OK.' Eve's face wore an angry expression. 'But you'll have to be back in time for work, both of you, so I'll pick you up at about five.' Was she losing her grip? Babs had bested her on at least two occasions lately. 'Go and get ready. We're leaving in ten minutes.' Eve turned and plodded down the corridor. 'Up to your rooms, now,' the two remaining in the kitchen heard. It was clear that the rest had been listening on the stairs.

Sally grabbed Babs's face and deposited a sloppy kiss on her forehead. 'Are you up to something?' she whispered.

'Oh yes. And you'll soon see what, Baby Sal.'

The younger girl swallowed audibly. 'Why are you helping me?'

Babs shrugged. 'You remind me of somebody.'

'Oh? Who?'

'Me. You remind me of me, Sally. I still remember being young and frightened, you see. We might have a couple of wrinkles, but we don't lose our memories at thirty.'

'Are you working on a plan?' Sally asked.

Babs nodded. 'I want you out of here. Say nothing. Just get dressed in something girlish and come with me to Southport. I've no idea what his place is like, but it's in grounds and there's a cottage. Sometimes there's a horse, too. I know he'll take both of us. He'll compensate Eve, and we can have the run of his house. For a kick-off,

73

we might lose his cleaner, because we can do her job. And we'll get time off, so we can go out and meet people. Decent people, not johns. Go on – get ready.'

Sally gulped. 'So Eve will lose two of us.'

'She has a queue of part-timers. Look, stop worrying about other people and think about yourself for a change. When were you raped for the first time?'

Sally blanched. 'I was nine, going on ten.'

'So that's how you think of yourself, as just a toy for men. I am going all out on this one, sweetheart. Don Crawford's not a bad man – he's sick, like your stepfather, but I'm sure he never raped a child. Look at it this way, Sal: there'll be three in the bed. We can keep him happy, and we'll have each other.'

'And if he says no?'

'He won't. I'm the love of his life, and if I want you there, you'll be there. When he dies, I'll get the lot.'

Sally frowned. 'Are you sure?'

'Oh yes, especially if I can manage to marry him. Don't say anything, because he doesn't know yet, and neither does Eve. You can be my bridesmaid.' Babs grinned. 'I think your jaw just hit the floor, Sal. You'd best shut it – there's a bus from town due.'

Sally laughed before pressing her lips together. 'I'd feel safe with you, Babs.'

Babs shook her head sadly. 'Women are never safe, kiddo. Men have the upper hand out there in the real world, which is why we have to make a life without them. You know what your dad is,

74

and mine's no better, always beating my mam, me and anything else that moved. So we have to go all out for a better life for ourselves. I was reading about it.'

They went to get ready, both dressing young, both with pony tails, ribbons, short skirts, white socks and flat shoes. Babs drew the line at freckles, because she was going out today, so this was different. Wotsername Sefton-Hope in the magazine reckoned that there was more to emancipation than a cross on a little piece of paper. It was about raising women to the top of the pile, about decision-making and the enhancement of life. 'Me and Sal are going to be enhanced,' she told her reflection, 'so watch this space.'

Three

'If I'd known you were going to act so daft, I'd have brought buckets and spades and little paper flags for sandcastles,' Eve grumbled. The two girls were counting green doors along the route and getting on her wick. Most exterior woodwork had been painted a dark shade of green in wartime, and Babies Babs and Sal were calculating how many folk hadn't bothered to redecorate since 1945. Eve had dropped Belle at her parents' new address; Belle had been happy to sit in the body of the vehicle, while Eve's two other passengers had travelled from bad through worse and all the way to bloody ridiculous in the best seats at the front with the driver.

The pair of giggling idiots sat beside her cracking stupid jokes. The back, a separate compartment, was where clients were contained while being transferred to and from Meadowbank Farm. It was dark and dingy, and it smelled of men – hair cream, tobacco, sweat and semen. 'You're like a couple of kids,' the driver complained. 'Behave yourselves.'

She should have forced them to sit in the rear of the van with Belle, but Babs remained in an almost unbearably uppity frame of mind. 'It stinks like our bedrooms,' Baby Schofield had pronounced. 'We'll ride in the front with you.' And Eve had felt like kicking herself, because she'd allowed Babs her own way yet again. Who was the real madam here? Who owned the business? Who had sunk every last cent into a safe place where girls didn't need to fret about being worried by pimps, beaten up by punters or arrested by coppers for working the streets?

Babs grinned broadly at her companion, who was clearly enjoying the childhood of which she'd been robbed by her mother's second husband. Sal hadn't been out for months, as she dared not return home, and was too afraid to spend a day in the city centre, where her stepfather pretended to sweep the streets between taking furtive sips from a small bottle kept in a pocket. The younger girl exclaimed over posh houses in Ainsdale, and even got excited by the sight of desert-like sand dunes along the coastal road into Southport. 'We came here years back, before Mam married *him*,' she said. 'We went somewhere called Peter Pan's Play-

76

ground. It was dead boring. Somebody sold tea, and it was always stewed. And there was usually sand in our butties, so we called them sandwiches.'

Eve bit her lip; if she spoke, she might explode. Constant references to St Peter's Waiting Room, Death Valley and Pensioners' Parlour were wearing thin, and the girls were at it again.

'That's Southport all over,' Babs giggled. 'But I've got to get used to it. Sold to the highest bidder, you see. I'm owned by an old man with false teeth, bad breath, greasy hair and a mad horse. I'm a slave, Sally. Do you think I should complain?'

'Oh, shut up,' Eve growled. 'He's a decent enough bloke with a big house and plenty of cash, so be grateful for once in your life. Don's lonely, that's all. There's no harm in him – it's younger men who make most trouble.

'He should have got married,' Babs declared. 'Then he would have had some company.'

'He's scared of women,' was Eve's sharp reply.

'Why?' Sally asked.

Eve had a ready answer. 'His ma was a tartar by all accounts. He looked after her right until the day she died. She left him rich, but isolated. A lot of men who don't marry are reacting to something or other in their pasts. His mother was enough to put anybody off marriage for life.'

Sally's right hand clutched her companion's left. She now understood fully what Babs intended to do. She would insist on marriage, and Sally would become Don's new baby. 'He'll have two of us,' Babs had said, 'and between us we can wear him out faster than I could on my own.'

Would the old man agree to marry Babs? If he was so afraid of women, why should he marry at this late stage?

They travelled up Lord Street. 'See?' Babs laughed. 'They're all old. Look at her with the two walking sticks. She came for a fortnight last week, and she's aged thirty years in a few days. You won't want me back, Eve, cos I'll probably be in a wheelchair by next year. Unless you get a weirdo who wants a girl who can't run away. I'm sure if you look hard enough you'll find somebody who'll play that game.'

Eve shook her head and remained silent. Little Miss Clever Clogs was up to something, and God alone knew what it was. The girl was bright, too bright for her own good in Eve's opinion. What was the besom planning this time? A revolution? Eve would be glad to get shut of her, that much was certain. But oh, she was going to miss her...

She parked the van and studied the map closely. Don Crawford had an estate, a tract of land so valuable that local builders were gearing up for a fight, since the Wordsworth site was probably large enough to contain twenty or thirty high-class detached dwellings with decent gardens. Yes, there was a queue waiting for the poor old bugger to die, and that queue included local government whose compulsory purchasing ability might well raze Don's assets to the level of about seventy corporation houses.

And now Babs was going to join the rest of the retinue, one more greedy gob waiting for Don Crawford to kick the bucket. Where did young Sally fit in? Babs didn't give a damn about anybody else, which was often the case with working girls. They didn't always start off hardened, but the lifestyle made them tough and self-protective, and Babs was as harsh as they came, so why was she helping Sally have a day out? What did she want from Sally?'

'Are we lost?' Babs asked. 'Remember, we have to leave early.'

'Shut up,' Eve advised, 'and behave yourselves while you're there. In fact, Sally should come with me and help with the shopping, because she's not involved, and you need to talk things through in private with Don.'

Babs gave birth to a loud, wet raspberry. 'She's having a day out, Eve. When did she last get away from the farm? Never, is when. Even a dog needs a walk and time outside for a bit of a wander. She's coming with me, and she can sit in another room while I talk to him.'

Eve stared hard at Baby Schofield. 'Are you thinking what I think you're thinking, Babs?'

'I don't know what you think I'm thinking, do I? I'm not a bloody mind-reader. Sally needs a break, and she can come to Southport and visit me any time when she's not working.'

'Have you taken a turn and gone charitable, then?' Eve asked.

Babs was suddenly serious. 'She's like me, like I was. With her, it was her stepfather; with me, it was my uncle. I'm lucky, because he's dead, but Sally's corpse is still leaning on a brush down Lime Street. So don't take it out on me for having a friend. You've got Kate to talk to, and nobody complains about that. What you can't stand is us

79

having minds or mates of our own.'

They'd be forming a union soon, Eve told herself as she drove towards Wordsworth House. Someone like Babs would be shop steward, and they would all pay into a pot and get badges and printed matter telling them how to work to rule. They'd ban pensioners, baldies, sweaty feet, moaners and warts. She pictured them sitting round a bucket of fire in the yard, placards at the ready, a Babs-like figure in the middle screaming about not taking life lying down. Yes, Barbara Schofield would leave a hole in Eve's life, because she was always good for a laugh.

They travelled through a pair of open metal gates with *Wordsworth* and *House* woven into ornate wrought iron. Dove Cottage stood near the gates, and by most people's standards, the grounds were vast. 'Blimey,' Eve muttered, 'so this is how the other half lives.' Even though they were round the back of the building, Wordsworth House was stunning; it looked as if the young troublemaker had fallen on her feet here.

'Stop!' Babs yelled.

The van slewed to a halt. 'What the hell's up with you now?' The driver was fast approaching the outer rim of her patience.

Babs offered no reply. Like one in a daze, she clambered out of the vehicle and stood stock still next to it. Love at first sight? she pondered inwardly. He was tall, well muscled, and even from this distance she could see his eyes shining. Next to him a short man leaned on a fence, his gaze fixed on Babs. Dragged along by a force she didn't understand and didn't want to question,

Barbara Schofield walked towards them across a large expanse of lawn.

It was unreal; it was almost like a dream. Why was she doing this? It was as if some strong and undeniable magnetic force was drawing her across the grass. Eve was right – what was the matter with her now?

Gordy Hourigan stared hard at the approaching young woman. She'd scarcely glanced at him, because she was focused completely on his companion on the other side of the fence, and there was confidence in the way she walked. He looked back at the horse. Mad Murdoch resembled a statue, which fact was nothing short of a miracle, especially in the presence of an alien vehicle on the distant gravel driveway. When the girl reached him, the animal whinnied softly.

'Hello,' Gordy Hourigan said, his accent definitely the property of western Ireland with just an occasional bit of Lancashire thrown in as flavouring.

Babs returned the greeting before climbing partway up the tall paddock fence. 'So you're the mad bugger, eh? Pleased to meet you.'

Gordy doffed a flat cap and scratched his head. He felt like someone eavesdropping during an intimate moment. She was stroking the horse's nose and whispering softly at the lunatic. This had been an insane morning; Mad Murdoch had regressed to foalhood, prancing sideways as if practising for *Swan Lake,* and trying to unseat his rider by stopping suddenly and bending to eat something invisible on the ground.

'Do you work with animals?' the trainer asked.

81

'Human ones, yes,' was her terse reply. 'But this is the most beautiful thing I ever saw. Can I sit on him?'

The man frowned. 'Not dressed like that, you can't – unless you want broken bones. He bolts sometimes, so you'd need a hard hat, at least.'

'He wants me,' she said. 'He wants me as a friend.' With no hesitation, she climbed higher, while Murdoch parked himself parallel to the paddock's wooden boundary.

Gordy had seen this sort of thing before. Some people were made for horses, and some horses were made for some people. And there she was, lying face down across the back of a crazy, temperamental, skittish beast, no tack, no saddle, not so much as a bit of rope to hang on to. With her right hand in Murdoch's mane, Babs clung on and whispered, 'Walk, matey. Let's have a little ta-ta, eh?'

'Well,' the trainer said to himself, 'now I've seen everything.' Murdoch walked carefully right round the paddock, returning Babs to her point of origin and standing motionless while she dismounted untidily.

She patted the horse's neck. 'You are gorgeous, and you know it, don't you?' Babs grinned when the animal shook his head. 'Cheeky.'

She spoke to the trainer. 'The world looks different upside down,' she pronounced. 'I like this horse,' she added when she had clambered back over the high fence. 'He's a bit tall, though. I felt like I was on a bloody skyscraper.'

Gordy closed his gaping mouth. 'Are you Mr Crawford's Baby Babs?' he asked.

'Yes. What about it?'

He shrugged. 'Will you be living here?'

'Maybe, maybe not. Why?'

'Just asking. Because if the horse likes you, you could help me.'

She folded her arms. 'Would I get paid?'

'Yes.'

'I'll think about it.'

Gordon Hourigan took to the little madam immediately. Although blissfully unaware of the truth, she had been blessed with a gift, and that ability should be put to good use. People like her were few and far between, while Mad Murdoch was a one-off, a powerful machine who, like this little lady, was unaware of his talent.

'Where do you live?' she asked.

'In the gatehouse – Dove Cottage,' he replied. 'The boss is poetry mad. Murdy's best friend's a donkey called Nicholas Nye – that name's from a poem, too. Dove Cottage is where Wordsworth lived for a while; it's up in the Lake District, I think. Mr Crawford reads a lot.'

'Does he?' Well, there went her chance of living in Dove Cottage, she supposed. 'How many horses?' she asked, pointing towards the stable block.

'Just this loony gelding and his mother. She was called Dead Loss, but we changed it to Murma because she's Murdoch's mum. The rest are donkeys rescued by Mr Crawford. He's a good man, Miss ... er...'

'Just Babs will do. And you are?'

'Gordy. Gordy Hourigan.'

Babs continued to stare at the horse. 'It's like

he knows me, isn't it?'

'Aye. It happens. I've seen it before. They can seem to recognize people from the future. Have you really never worked with horses?'

'No. I've never even touched one before; look at me, I'm shaking like a leaf in a gale. Where's Murdoch's dad?'

'Ireland.'

'Who owns him?'

Gordy guffawed. 'Who owns him? Whoever can bloody catch him is who. He's a great horse, though – an Arab. Murdy's mother has all the grace of a crippled elephant and the temperament of a saint. His dad's a perfect shape, but the devil's his master. Out of that accidental mating came Mad Murdoch. The boss is an animal lover, so he bought Murdoch's mother at the same time as buying him. He came cheap. They both did.'

'But he has promise, or so I was told,' she said.

'If we can get him to run and jump in a straight line without unseating a jockey or starting a world war, he'll take prizes left right and bloody centre, believe me. I've been in this daft game for years. Watch him now. Look at his eyes, because he listens to every word. Ah. I see he doesn't like your friends.'

Eve and Sally arrived. 'What the bloody hell are you up to now, Babs?' Eve hissed. 'That thing could have put you in the wheelchair you were talking about

Murdoch raised his upper lip, displaying huge, tombstone teeth.

'He doesn't like you,' Babs announced while Sally tried to swallow a giggle. 'See? He's walking away. Good taste in my opinion, Eve,' Babs concluded, giving Eve a cheeky wink.

The horse strolled nonchalantly across the paddock. He travelled again along the perimeter, breaking into a casual trot, a canter and... 'Oh, my God,' Gordy breathed. 'Get behind me,' he ordered. 'Not Babs – he won't hurt her or the other young girl, or me.' He glanced at Eve. 'You're the one he doesn't like. Babs, he's coming over.'

She gasped. 'Has he done it before?'

'No. But a young man in love isn't containable, even if he is a gelding.'

Eve tried to conceal about a quarter of herself behind the trainer. Sally held Babs's hand; if Babs was going to be hurt, Sal intended to be by her side.

The sun disappeared; it was like a slowed-down film that had stuck on its reel, because the animal seemed to be in the air for many seconds, and he cast a large shadow – the event imitated a brief solar eclipse. 'Jesus,' Gordy breathed, 'we've tried for months to get him to ... whoa, boy.'

The boy whoa-ed, leaving marks in the carefully manicured lawn. He tossed his head and looked daggers at the fat woman. Turning his attention to Babs, he seemed to grin. She was clapping and shouting, 'Well done; who's a clever boy, then? Are you going to win the National for Don and Gordy and Babs, eh?'

Clever Boy neighed his agreement. So this was what they wanted from him. It was against his nature, against the nature of any horse, since the skeletal structure is frail, with a huge body balanced on stick-thin legs. But the two-legged thought they were in charge and he needed to please them, especially a pair of these here, the trainer and her. He had to jump over obstacles. Well, he would, as long as she could be there. He stood beside her, his nostrils in her pony tail.

'Riding lessons for you, girl,' Gordy said, a grin splitting his face.

'Are you having a laugh? I even fall off bikes,' Babs told him.

'Ah, but you've an affinity with this insane bugger. He won't throw you.'

She folded her arms. 'Women don't ride in Grand National types of races.'

The trainer nodded. 'Not yet, they don't. But by the time he's ready, it will be a different story. And he likes you, so he won't buck you off.'

Babs grinned. 'I'm glad you said buck instead of ... look, the bike doesn't buck me off, but I still hit the floor.'

The trainer shook his head thoughtfully. 'You're a natural. I'm going to talk to the boss. Open the paddock gate and take Wonder Horse back to his mother. She's up the top end talking to donkeys.' He nodded wisely. 'Welcome to my crazy world, Babs. Before you leave later on, cuddle a donkey. Very comforting things, donkeys. Make sure you pick Nye, Murdoch's favourite. You'll know him, because he wears a bell.'

'Why a bell?' Sally asked.

'Because he's blind,' the trainer replied, employing the tone of one answering a stupid question.

Sally blinked. 'Er...'

Babs rescued her friend. 'Why a bell? He's a

donkey, not a cow. I never heard of a donkey-bell.'

'Two reasons,' Gordy continued. 'One, it tells the rest of the stable he's coming, and two, he has excellent hearing. Something in the bell's noise lets him know how far away from things he is. Murdoch looks after him.'

'Aw, that's sweet,' Sally said.

Eve, sweaty and embarrassed, strode off towards the van. She'd had just about enough of Babs, Sally and that damned horse. As for the trainer – well, he looked as if he'd like to get close to Babs Schofield, too close for Don Crawford's liking. 'I don't know why I bother,' she told the steering wheel. 'Oh well, I've done my bit. Now, what am I looking for? The list. Ah, here it is.' She started the van and prepared to drive off towards Lord Street. Don would just have to do his best, because Eve Mellor was sick unto death of the whole business. Red velvet for curtains, that was what she needed. And a couple of cream cakes would set her right.

Just as she was about to reverse, something caught her eye. From what was presumably the back door of Wordsworth House, four dogs spilled. Behind them padded two cats, a goose, and a clutch of fussy hens with a second goose bringing up the rear. Eve blinked. 'What is this?' she asked herself. 'The RSPC-bloody-A? Jesus, I feel nearly sorry for Babs Schofield. I never thought I'd see the day.' Smiling grimly, she set off in search of red velvet, gold tassel trim, a nice pot of tea and a plate of cream fancies.

There's something wrong with him. He's still kind and affectionate, still good with Matt and Lucy, but he wouldn't join me at Confession on Saturday, said he had a chance of overtime, and he would go to Confession in town. On Sunday, he didn't go up for Holy Communion. I've no one to talk to, because I wouldn't betray him to his parents or to mine, so I may have a word with Father Doherty.

Neil's a good man, very religious. I don't know what to think. Is he having a crisis of some sort, like a breakdown? A man down Musker Street had one of those, and they put him in a mental hospital over towards St Helens; we never saw him for months, then he came back deadly quiet and unfit for work. His wife Annie says it's as if she has four kids now instead of three, and she does several part-time jobs, too. The poor man's on all kinds of drugs, and the children look after him while their mum works.

Our parish priest often says that the holiest people have the most trouble, because they try so hard to get close to their faith that the intensity of it can knock them sideways. They think too much, he says. But if I ever put together a list of the great thinkers I know, my Neil wouldn't be on the list. Not that he's stupid; no, I don't mean that, but he thinks in what you might call straight lines. He decides what he's doing, goes for it, achieves it, then moves on to the next item on his list.

He re-covered our three-piece suite in beige Dralon, a bit like velvet, only easier to keep clean. That nest of tables he bought second-hand looks new now, because he worked so hard to make the set pretty. Then he does sweet things like buying a gold cross and chain for my birthday, skates for Matt, and a talking doll for Lucy.

Is it me? Has something changed inside my head, something that makes me look at him differently? He's preoccupied, a bit distant, worried. It might be a problem at work, of course. For ages, he's been looking for promotion to management level, but he's always talked to me about that. Until now.

A few times in the evenings, I've caught him staring hard at the fireplace. There's nothing remarkable about it; it's a tiled thing with a clock and some candlesticks on the mantel and a mirror on the wall above next to the Papal Blessing of our marriage and a Palm Sunday cross. He used to discuss getting a new fireplace, but he seems so attached to it these days.

The other night, he came home injured. I heard him groaning while he bathed his arm. Says he fell off his bike.

I've asked him what's changed, of course. He looks at me as if I've grown a second head. 'There's nothing wrong with me,' he always says. I know shift work tires him and upsets his digestion and his sleep pattern, but ... but there *is* a marked difference in him. He doesn't touch me any more. We don't want any more children, so we've always used the rhythm method since having Lucy; we keep a calendar with the safe days underlined, but he's not interested in me. How do I say that to a priest?

He told me he fell off his bike and his arm landed on a broken bottle. Three great big scratches, he has, as if some wild cat dragged its claws from elbow to wrist. He's wearing a bandage till it heals. I don't know what to do, where to turn. Perhaps I should take that job in the chip shop. It's for just three hours on weekdays, from eleven till two. At least my mind would be occupied, and I'd be back home when the children come in from school.

Oh, look at the state of me. I'm staring at the fireplace like Neil does, and this duster in my hand's getting nowhere fast. The ironing's done, and that was today's main job. A quick flick round, and I'll be ready for the children. The steak's braising, and I'll leave a plate for Neil. He's two till ten this week. I think he's worse when he's two till ten... Dear Lord, what is going on? Oh, I'd better finish dusting.

Of course, everything happened at once. The whole crop burgeoned beautifully, and the boys weren't ready for it. Roy Foley stood, hands on hips, mouth gaping, his breathing equipment on strike. 'Overnight?' he managed finally.

'What are we supposed to do now?' Bill Tyler asked.

'Erm...' Roy was making progress, managing to scratch his head and taking in some oxygen. 'Get the flowers off. Well, I think so.'

'I thought you'd learned all this?'

'We didn't do exams, you know. I got no certificate for being qualified in grass. We need help.'

Bill shook his head. 'We have to be away out of here, Roy. Them demolition blokes are getting nearer by the day, and the electric will go off soon.

90

Get some help, and I don't mean Ginger and Holy Mary.'

Roy sat down and pondered. From the little he knew, he understood that this was an excellent crop. Somehow, possibly by accident, he had successfully produced a sizeable load of cannabis. The Halewood lads had a new wrinkle, too, because something called LSD was available and, if sprinkled on a joint, it gave a massive high to the smoker. 'We'll sell it to Halewood,' he announced. 'They can buy it off us, harvest it and make it fit for sale. OK, we won't make as much as we'd like, but it's better than ruining it, eh?'

Bill was past caring. He wanted to get home, have a bath, a bowl of scouse and some clean clothes. Drugs were not his scene; he'd be better off being a builder's labourer with the firm his dad worked for. 'Go to Halewood, then,' he suggested. 'I promise I'll stop here and wait for you even though I'm shit scared.'

'Will you be too shit scared to get paid a few quid, then?'

'No. I want compensation. It's been like prison, but with bright lights and sweat and stinky plants. Just sell it – get rid of it, for God's sake. When I see the back of this lot, that'll be an end of it as far as I'm concerned.'

'You won't run and let me down when I go out now?'

'On me mam's life.'

'Fair enough.' Roy went for help.

Bill sat on a chair, on his frayed nerves and on a burgeoning temper. He wasn't as clever as Roy, wasn't as brave as his friend, who had just gone for a three-bus ride into the hands of professional dealers. 'I'm not that stupid, though,' he told a blank wall. He could feel something in his gut, and it was nothing to do with indigestion. He heard an echo of Dad telling him that Roy Foley was trouble. 'Stay away from him,' Dad had said countless times. 'Do you want to serve time in Walton Jail, Billy?'

And here he sat, waiting for the big boys, the sort who had bullied him all the way through school. They probably already had Roy under their thumbs, though Roy would never admit it. Perhaps Roy didn't know it, because although clever enough, he didn't seem capable of fear. How would he survive in the world of drugs if he couldn't feel afraid enough to be careful?

Bill stood up. 'If I run, he'll come after me, and he won't be on his own. Our families won't be safe, either. Why did I listen to him?' He paced about aimlessly. Everybody called Bill Tyler daft, and they were probably right. But was Roy Foley any brighter? He might be able to read, write and count properly, but he was still crackers.

Bill knew that he and Roy were locked into something from which there might be no escape, no emergency exit. 'I don't want to live in a secret,' he whispered, tears pricking his eyes. But he had to. In this matter, he had no choice unless he went to the police and grassed on Roy, too. 'I'm already in prison,' he said.

It was a long wait. The alarm clock that had timed the spillage of light onto plants showed ten o'clock on its luminous dial before the back door opened. In they walked, the cannabis kings of

Liverpool South. Bill did as he was told, carrying plant after plant through the yard and into a parked van. Two men stood guard, one at each end of the narrow alleyway. A third helped Roy and Bill with the carrying of the crop, while a fourth sat smoking a cigar in the kitchen. That was the boss, Bill told himself. Yes, the seated man was the big boy, and this was the beginning of a journey into danger. No, it wasn't prison; it was hell.

Belle Horrocks was in her parents' terraced house in Wavertree. They had moved here recently for the bigger back yard and an extra bedroom, because Lisa was now a lively three-year-old, and Belle came home whenever she could, so she needed a room, too. When Belle wasn't here, her room might be used as a play area for Lisa.

Sam and Frances were proud of their daughter, an auditor with a firm that travelled hither and yon to help companies account for their dealings whenever the taxman growled and showed his teeth. Belle was an expert in tax law, and she was much in demand, because she was the garlic flower and the crucifix that stayed the Civil Service's fangs before they dripped red with company blood. 'Have you been busy, love?' Frances Horrocks (usually Frankie) asked her girl.

'Oh, yes,' was Belle's ready reply. 'We've been cooking books on gas mark nine, though we're breaking no laws, of course.'

'Of course,' Sam grinned. 'Go get 'em, Belle.'

She chuckled. 'Is this place costing more rent because of the third bedroom?'

'Don't worry about that,' Frankie said quickly.

Sam shook his head. 'It needs a fair bit doing to it, plastering, carpentry, new window frames, so I said I'd fix it up if they'd buy the materials and keep the rent low for a couple of years. I'm still working part time, so we should be OK for a while. Lisa needs space to play, Belle.'

Belle had put her daughter to bed, a privilege she enjoyed far too rarely. And for the first time, Lisa had asked for something. She'd always been easy to please, greeting colouring books, a cheap doll, a skipping rope, a box of crayons or paints with equal delight. But the move to Wavertree had brought Lisa face to face with Amelia-across-the-way, and Amelia had a child's version of a Silver Cross coach-built pram with proper blankets and a pillow and a baby doll with nappies and clothes and everything, Mummy.

So Mummy asked about prices, looked in her bank book and wished Mam and Dad had given Wavertree and Amelia's pram a miss. After she'd handed over Lisa's keep and clothes money, the sum saved towards deposit on a flat was almost non-existent and, at the age of thirty-five, she'd be lucky to last on the game for many more years. But her baby wanted a doll's pram, so her baby would have a bloody pram by fair means or foul.

What to do? It would be a couple of days before she could earn money in her usual way, because this was, for her, the wrong time of the month. Mam and Dad had little to spare, and they believed she had a top job with a good firm, so they had to stay off the list.

List? What list? Everyone she knew was in a similar situation – everyone but Eve, that was.

'She wants that pram,' Belle said now.

Sam grunted. 'We told her Christmas. We said we'd all save up and she could have it then. I'm good at making used things look new.'

Belle glanced through the window. Although dusk had arrived, the temperature remained kind. 'This is better pram-pushing weather. I'll see what I can do. There's a pram shop nearer town, so I'll find out if they do second hand in good condition. I think I'll go for a walk before it gets too dark. Sitting in cramped offices for a living makes me glad of fresh air.'

When their daughter had left, Sam and Frankie stared at each other. He broke the silence. 'What's up with her, Frank? She seems a bit down in the mouth.'

Frankie shrugged. 'The job makes her tired, and she's just realized how expensive a child can be. With our Belle, it's all about saving for when we're gone. This Silver Cross pram's just the start, I suppose. Kids cost a bomb.'

'I wish we could help,' he said.

'We do help, Sam. Without us, our Belle couldn't work.'

He nodded. 'True. But I don't like seeing her so worried.'

The following afternoon, their worried girl walked through the streets of Wavertree. It was nice round here, decent houses, almost all of them pretty and cared for with clean paths and tidy little front gardens. A few hundred yards away from her parents' house, she found a phone box.

Kate answered. 'Hiya, Belle. Are you and the family all right?'

'Everybody's fine, love. Is Babs with an un-expected client?'

'No, not now. Eve's on a run in an hour or so. Shall I get Babs?'

'Please, Kate.'

Belle fed the phone's ravenous money box while waiting for Babs. Yes, there was a list, but there were just two names on it – Babs and Eve. The latter would want interest on a loan, but Babs had a soft spot for Belle.

'Hello?' Babs breathed after running downstairs.

'Babs, sorry to ask, but I need a loan and I'm desperate,' Belle said.

'How much?'

Belle breathed deeply. 'A tenner,' she said.

'OK. You can have it, Belle. Looks like I've fallen on my feet, but I'll tell you more when you're here. Can I ask what the money's for?'

'For Lisa.'

'Fair enough. I won't be asking for it back. You keep it.'

Tears spilled down Belle's face. 'How can I thank you enough?'

'Stop crying, you soft cow. You can thank me by buggering off while I have a quick swill. One of the men last night stank like an old dustbin, and I can't get the smell out of my nose. Ta-ra, queen.'

The line went dead. Belle fished a handkerchief out of a sleeve. She'd always admired Babs's honesty, but this was something else. The girl was enjoying good fortune, and she wouldn't keep it all to herself. There was genuine kindness in the world, then. It wasn't just a queue of men want-ing massage plus sex plus someone to moan at about a wife who didn't understand, a terrible job, ungrateful children and bad neighbours.

She dried her eyes and left the phone box.

'Thanks, Babs,' she murmured into the square of cloth. 'I won't forget this.' Tomorrow, she would raid her bank account and buy a pram. Mam would make covers and pillows, and Lisa already had a baby doll. Money from Babs would fill the hole in savings, and all would be well for a while.

Beyond that, Belle knew she had a friend for life, and there was very little she wouldn't do for Babs if called upon. Where there was trust, there was love. And vice versa.

Well, it frightened the living daylights out of me, I can tell you that much. She died quickly, went so fast that when ... when her head nearly came off, there was no blood because her heart must have stopped with the shock. You don't expect to decapitate somebody through strangulation with a bit of wire, but she was small, under five feet tall and thin as a reed.

Waiting for her, I turned my bike lights off and wheeled it along the pavement. And there she came, teetering on high heels, mutton dressed as lamb, skirt too short, frilly blouse probably made for a teenager, red plastic handbag swinging from an arm. When I got close, I could see she was lathered in makeup, and it had set in all the creases on her face. She was ugly. She became a lot uglier, too, with her head hanging to one side and her legs splayed at strange angles. Like a broken marionette puppet, she was.

She had a chiffon scarf hanging out of a pocket, so I took that. It would supposedly do for the next whore I found. There's a herd of them in the city, but that's a bit busy for me. Some use I'd be to Jesus and Judas if I ended up in court for murder, so I have to stick to roads that run parallel to or at an angle from the docks.

On my way home, I tried to calm down, because Laura knows I'm not myself these days. She stares at me as if she's going to ask questions, though she's asked none yet apart from wondering aloud about my health and Confession and Holy Communion.

I've told her I'm thinking about things.

'What things?' she enquired.

So I made the excuse that I was worrying about the Spanish Inquisition and bad Catholics. 'There are bad ones now,' I said. 'The police are looking for three young lads who ran away from some evil monks. Is it the one true faith?'

Laura asked how I knew about the boys, so I told her about the piece in the *Echo* and the men who'd run away from that school. 'The *Echo* has their names, though they can't publish them, but they followed up the story, and the monks have disappeared. The runaway lads have written to the newspapers, the Queen, the government, archbishops, cardinals – even the Pope. No one knows where they are. It's just made me wonder, Laura. Don't get upset about it,' I said, 'it'll work itself out.'

But it isn't working itself out, because I'm a mess. Laura wonders about the physical side, but I can scarcely touch her, because my hands have been on other women. Like that queen in a Shakespeare play, I feel that nothing on earth will clean my fingers. The old one fought, too, so I've had her hands raking down my arm, and I feel like a biblical leper. She had fingernails like razors.

Worse was to come, of course. The old woman was named in the paper as Dolly Pearson, an eccentric who spent most evenings, six nights a week, with her ninety-three-year-old mother. She used to sit with her mum from six until ten, then from ten in the morning until two in the afternoon. Other family members did the rest of the shifts, but she'd been filling in for a sick brother who was in hospital because of a burst appendix. I have killed a decent person.

Dolly Pearson was not a prostitute; she was an oddball on her way home. She was an ordinary, caring being who wore too much makeup and the wrong clothes. Her brothers and sister are heartbroken, and the healthy brother and the sister have to care for their very old mother for twelve hours each. I made a mistake. Christ could have prevented that, as I am supposed to be working under His guidance. So alone, I am. After sharing everything for ten years with my wife, I now am unable to say a single word.

I watch the fireplace, willing them to come back, but I never see anything except her in my sleep, head and legs in impossible positions, my heart beating fast, hers stopped forever. By me...

My screams probably wake the whole street. Laura tries to comfort me, but I push her away. Got rid of the chiffon scarf – it's no use to me, is it? And if this carries on, I'll be getting rid of my marriage, too.

Why me, Jesus? Why did you pick me?

I'm on earlies next week. Maybe I'll settle down then.

Ian, John and Phil were not enjoying the good life in their scout hut. The only thing on the mend was John's stammer, and progress in that small area was sporadic, since they all lived in fear, because Ian's letters to the high and mighty had reaped a media reaction that would result in eventual discovery, and they didn't want to be returned to the Brothers Pastoral. 'We're all over every news-paper,' Phil said after one of his forays into Knowsley.

'They'll be searching everywhere f-for us,' John the Stam moaned. 'I mean, you didn't put any address on them letters, Ian, b-b-but once the cops get on your tail—'

'Shut up,' Ian growled. 'They believe us, and that's the main thing. It said in the *Echo* that three bastard teachers have gone from the school, so everybody's on our side.'

'Except for Catholics,' Phil offered. 'Blind as bats, the one true faith, thou art Peter and upon this rock I will build my church. Bloody churches and temples – give me a football match any day of the week. It's all crap, religion.' He sighed. 'What are we going to do?'

It was hot and stuffy. No one bothered to answer Phil's question. Stealing food, money and clothes was exhausting work. It was a worry, too, since now it was known that even the Queen and the Pope had received letters, the hunt would definitely be on.

They lived for the most part on cold food, as the little paraffin stove sent the temperature in the hut to an unbearable level. The only real fun they had was when they dressed up to sneak out during hours of daylight. Even then, disguised in stolen clothes, they needed eyes in the backs of their heads. Phil had managed to steal a bike, and he'd shoplifted a small tin of black paint and a brush to disguise it. There was little money left because of buying fish and chips on some evenings, and life seemed grim.

'We c-could get paper rounds,' John suggested hesitantly.

Phil laughed, though he didn't sound happy. 'Which bloody fishing boat did you arrive on, soft lad? We can't mix with people. I sometimes wonder whether you're the full shilling. Paper rounds?' He spat the two words. 'Why don't we just go to the cop shop and say we're the missing boys?'

'Sorry,' John muttered.

'Leave him alone,' Ian ordered through gritted teeth. 'John's not had it easy – none of us has. Do you want him going worse with his talking?'

Phil hung his head. 'Sorry,' he said.

'It's all r-right I'm used to it.'

They settled down to sleep on sacks and folded tents.

'Stam?' Phil whispered.

'What?'

'You know I never meant no harm, though, eh?'

'You're OK, Phil. We're all in the sh-shit together.'

Babs and Sally lay together in Babs's double bed. Like a couple of five-year-olds, they giggled and whispered instead of obeying parents' rules and going to sleep. 'I still can't get over it,' Sally mumbled. 'How did you do it?'

'I'm special.'

'I know that.'

Babs chuckled. 'It's the force of my magnetic personality. Don likes you, and he likes the idea of sleeping between two pretty girls. He paid more for you than he did for me.'

'Never.'

'He did. Eve's lost both her Baby Girls and wanted compensation.'

The younger girl giggled. 'My mam used to get that on her glasses when it was hot. She always said they were covered in compensation.' She paused. 'Mam knew it was the wrong word, but she did it deliberately. We used to have fun till she married him.'

Babs stopped laughing and held her companion close. 'Did he hurt you?'

After a short pause, the answer arrived. 'Yes. Said he'd kill me and Mam if I told anybody.'

'I know, Sal. I've been there. Do you ever wonder if that's why we're on the game?'

'I'm sure it is. It's like I'm making him pay.'

'Don't cry, love.' The older girl held the younger in a gentle embrace. 'We've got each other now. And if the RSPCA will take Don's offer and get permission, we'll have a home in an animal sanctuary when Don dies. You didn't see the will, but I did.'

'He's a nice man, Babs. And you don't need to marry him.'

'The property goes to animals, and the bank account comes to me with his half of Mad Murdoch. We're made. We can have rooms in the house for life, and Dove Cottage will be mine outright. No need to marry him, babe. Belle rang, by the way, wanted a tenner to buy something for the kiddy. We can do some good at last. And I will look after you, I promise.'

'And I'll look after you, too.'

They lay for a while thinking about the great luck they appeared to be having, and the loving seemed to begin of its own accord. Neither girl would ever be able to say how it started, though both were grateful for it. After being handled and used by men, they were happy to discover a softer, gentler way, something meaningful, pleasurable and non-invasive. After sweaty feet, sharp elbows and tobacco-tainted breath, this was heaven.

Babs grinned in the half-light from a small lamp on the bedside table. 'Are we terrible?' she asked.

Sally returned the smile. 'I've loved you for a while,' she said shyly. 'All I want is to be wherever you are.'

'Then you shall go to the ball, Cinderella. I'll lend you my glass slippers, but don't break 'em, or I'll wring your neck.' The promise was sealed with a kiss.

It was the middle of the night when the door opened, and all three boys sat up, alarm causing hearts to jump about and sweat to form on foreheads. Light from a torch travelled over John, then Ian, then Phil. 'Who the bloody hell are you?' asked the bearer of the torch.

No one answered.

'You'd better say something.' The tone was threatening.

'Are you the police?' Ian finally managed to say.

The man laughed. 'Not likely.'

'You won't g-grass?' John the Stam asked.

The door closed. 'Your photos have been in the paper, but not your names – not yet, anyway,' the intruder said. 'I know who you are, but I'll say nothing. We thought this shed was empty.'

He sat on a wooden crate. 'If you'll mind some packages for me, I'll pay you.' The new crop grown by Roy Foley and Bill Tyler was now stashed and ready for harvest in Hunt's Cross, but there was too much stuff stored in Liverpool South, so hundreds of pounds' worth of hash and resin needed shifting to a new location. 'I will pay, I promise. Me or one of my lads will bring you food, drink and cash every Thursday. What do you say to that?'

Phil was uneasy. 'Is it drugs?' he asked.

'You don't need to know what it is,' was the ready answer, 'because if you grass us up, we'll get you and anybody close to you. If you're found, you say the stuff was here before you came. OK?'

'Yes,' Ian answered for all three.

The large man stood, lit a cigar, then opened the door. 'Right, lads,' he said.

The boss's minions, including Roy and Bill, filed in carrying sacks.

'Hide them behind the scouts' stuff,' Ian

suggested. 'Let's hope they don't come back for their tents and sleeping bags.'

The leader laughed mirthlessly. 'I'll leave you my phone number. Any worries at all, get to a phone box and call me. Here.' He placed a card and a five pound note in Ian's hand. 'You don't know me, and I don't know you, so learn this number and burn the card. OK?'

'Thanks.'

'And watch out for your neighbours.'

'There isn't none,' John announced.

'Meadowbank Farm, a few hundred yards behind the trees,' the boss told them. 'Mind, they've got plenty to hide as well, but be careful.'

'We will,' Ian promised.

Alone once more, the three boys tried to settle. Phil spoke first. 'I wonder what they've got to hide at the farm?'

'Never mind them,' Ian said. 'We're the ones sitting on drugs.'

'How d-do you know?'

'I just do. Go to sleep.'

No one slept well that night.

Four

Nellie Carrington pushed all her worldly goods along Rice Lane. She'd had a minor surgical adjustment done to her vehicle in the pram shop, and life was suddenly a little smoother on uneven pavements and kerbs. Passers-by greeted her as she sallied forth; even in her smelly clothes, she was appreciated, because she had a heart of gold and was notorious for saving people, with alcoholics as her speciality. She also held secrets, and she guarded them well.

A familiar figure walked towards her. 'Well,' Nellie exclaimed, stopping in her tracks. 'Well, I never did – if it isn't our Belle. Isabella Horrocks. I haven't seen you in years. How are you? Still with Eve Mellor and the rest of her gang miles away from civilization? You're looking very well, I must say.'

Belle forced a smile. The one thing she dreaded was her parents finding out about her true area of work. The idea of auditing had been stolen from a client who had given her the details of his job. 'Hi, Nellie. Keep your voice down, please, because Mam, Dad and Lisa still have no idea about what I get up to.' Nellie's voice, though seldom raised, travelled well. 'How are you doing? And yes, I'm still at the farm.'

'Good, because at least you're safe, pet, and you know me – I say little or nothing about private business. I still keep an eye on the other Lime Street ladies, but it's not easy. Jean Davenport was killed, you know. Terrible business – the work of a madman, or so it would appear. She'll be missed by her family.'

'Yes, we all heard about it. She had children, didn't she?'

'She did, bless them. Her parents have taken them since she died. But now we've lost a woman who dressed like an older working girl but wasn't. There's a very sick person out there looking to

106

clear the streets of prostitutes. Stay safe; stay where you are. Eve's a tough old boot, and she'll look after you. How's young Babs, by the way? I miss that cheeky young madam – she led many people a merry dance. I suppose she's still as cheeky and bossy as ever?'

Belle relaxed. Perhaps the inquisition was almost over. 'She's fine, Nellie. Going to live in Southport quite soon, I think.'

'Why?' Nellie asked.

'Not sure of the details, sorry. But she's turned out decent. Still feisty, but good-hearted.'

'Pleased to hear it. And where are you going on this fine day?'

'Pram shop. Do they sell second-hand doll's prams? It's for Lisa.'

Nellie put the brake on her own vehicle. 'Yes, he does have doll's prams. I've just been in there, and I saw a beauty with a new doll and all the linen and covers for a penny short of twelve pounds, but I reckon he'd bite your hand off for ten. Stay here and look after my old wreck while I go and negotiate for Lisa. Trust me – I have a way with men.' She winked and grinned before retracing her steps. 'I'll think of something,' she mumbled under her breath.

Belle rested against a wall. Encounters with Nellie were often rather harrowing, because she had a tendency to fire questions, as if filling in a form or something official from the government, like a survey or a population census. She was a good woman who tried to save runaways, alcoholics and the homeless, but oh, she did go on. And on, and on. The man in the shop would probably agree to almost anything just to be rid of Smelly Nellie's aroma and her chat. 'There's method in her madness,' Belle muttered under her breath. But she knew, as did most folk, that Nellie Carrington was a saint right through to the marrow.

After about ten minutes, Nellie returned with the doll's pram. 'Here you go, Belle. I told him a tragic story that was almost true, and Lisa got a free pram with doll and covers. I'll need to make an Act of Contrition, but it was all in a good cause, so I'm calling it a venial sin. So here's your problem solved.'

Belle swallowed. 'Free? But it's beautiful, Nellie. It looks brand new, not a mark on it.'

'Lisa deserves the best, as do you.'

Belle gulped again. People were suddenly so kind. 'Babs is giving me ten quid, Nellie.' She opened her bag and recovered her purse. 'Here. I got it out of the bank. Spend it on food for the alkies and runaways. I'll tell Babs when I see her. She won't mind you having the money instead.'

Nellie shook her head. 'It won't always be summer or autumn. Use it for a winter hat, a coat and strong shoes or boots for Lisa. Babs wanted you to have it. Good luck, pet.'

There came the accent again, just a slight echo from the north-east, Belle mused inwardly. 'Were you born up Newcastle way, Nellie?'

'I was.' Nothing further was offered.

'And you went to a good school?'

'Yes, I did.'

'Thought so,' Belle said. Although this little woman knew almost everything about folk she met, she seldom breathed a word concerning herself.

'Quick Mick died,' Nellie said now. 'His liver gave up the ghost and took him with it. He died on Lime Street Station, poor soul.'

'Oh, no. I liked him,' Belle said. 'He had a wicked sense of humour.'

'Not towards the end. He was making very poor sense and shaking like a leaf. Yet I have noticed with most alcoholics that they're interesting people. But we've another mess starting up. Some bad creature is selling cannabis with hallucinatory agents added. There's always something new to worry about.'

Belle nodded, though she failed to understand the terminology. That was another thing about Nellie Carrington; she was knowledgeable. 'What does that mean?' she asked.

'LSD. It's poison. People on that can have weird flashbacks. They see blue snow, or red rain, or ghosts. Some believe they're being followed or picked on, so paranoia's a danger, while others get the idea that they can fly. They can't, of course, so they end up like pancakes all over the place. Alcohol's bad enough, but drugs?' The little woman shivered.

'You can't save everybody, Nellie.'

'No, but I can die trying. Be as good as you can manage. See you soon, I hope. And enjoy your time with Lisa. She's precious.' Nellie turned, had second thoughts, and came back. 'If you ever want a change of career, I'll see what I can do. All the best to you and your family, especially the little one.'

Belle watched the old woman walking away. Where was she from? Why did she live such a strange life when she was so clever and astute? She carried all kinds of stuff in the Silver Cross, a clean plastic box of pasties and sandwiches for the hungry, holy water from Lourdes for the sinners and the sick, biscuits, a New Testament, her own lunch, St Christopher medals for travellers, bandages, foot salve for those who walked miles, and God alone knew what else. Like a missionary, she went forth to help; she was a mystery.

Belle began to examine Lisa's pram. It looked factory new, its body cream, hood and waterproof apron navy blue. The doll was dressed in a christening gown, and the top sheet had broderie anglaise trimming. Over the sheet lay a pink, padded eiderdown, while the pillow matched the sheet. Belle suddenly couldn't wait to see her daughter's reaction to this gift. Thanks to Nellie and Babs, she could now have the pleasure of handing the pram over to her child. Lisa was going to love it, she told herself as she travelled homeward. It was a bit of a walk, especially while pushing a pram that was too low, but she progressed as fast as she could.

She entered her parents' property via the rear gate, parking the pram in a small building that used to house an outside lavatory. As she stepped back into the rear alleyway to walk round to the front, Belle froze. Oh, no. No, no, no! The man was walking away from her, but she recognized him even from the rear as Tom Duffield, a client of hers. With his upper body covered only by a short-sleeved shirt, the abbreviated arm was clearly visible.

He was a good, likeable soul who had lost a hand in a factory accident, yet this was a moment she had dreaded for years. She was fond of him. But her two lives were colliding, and panic took firm root in her chest. Although she'd always known that it was bound to happen one day, she felt weak with shock.

She re-entered the back yard and stood staring at the house with her arms spread across the gate as if trying to block out the person she had just seen. Why had Mam and Dad moved? The other house had been adequate, since Lisa had always been happy to share a room on the few occasions when Belle had spared the cash to go home.

Where did he live? Was he a close neighbour, had he been visiting a friend, had he seen his masseuse and sex partner? After doing her best to reclaim a level of calm, she entered the house by the scullery door. 'That you, Belle?' her mother called.

'Yes, Mam.' After setting the kettle to boil on a gas ring, the terrified woman found her mother in the room commonly known as the kitchen. 'I just saw a man with one hand,' she said as casually as she could.

'Did you?'

'Who is he?'

'Oh, it'll be Duffy,' Frankie said. 'Tom Duffield. Lost a hand, then his wife and children. She couldn't bear the sight of his stump, or so I've been told, so she upped and offed back to her mam, took the little lads with her.'

Belle gripped the door handle. 'Does he live

111

near you?'

'Number forty-two,' Frankie replied, 'just three doors down that way. He's a ... oh, what is it? A voluntary social welfare worker for a few hours once a week, helps people who've had bits amputated.' She stopped dusting and looked at her daughter. 'You look like you've just seen a ghost, babe.'

Belle mouthed her next words quietly. 'I've got a pram for Lisa. I think I've walked too far, Mam.'

Frankie grinned broadly. 'Where is it?'

'In the old lav shed down the yard. Where is she?'

'She's in Amelia's house, so you don't need to whisper. It's opposite us, blue door, blue and white flowers in tubs under the bay window. Go and get her.'

'Will you do it, Mam? I'm exhausted after steering that pram from the bottom end of Rice Lane, and my back aches.'

While Frankie went to fetch her granddaughter, Belle sat and pondered. Was this the time for truth? Should she tell her parents about what she really did for a living? She shook her head. They'd already accepted their daughter's illegitimate child. The rest of the facts might kill them, and even if they survived, the truth would reside thereafter in this house with Lisa, who must never find out. But the situation was already on top of Lisa, because Tom Duffield was living within spitting distance. 'I'll visit him,' she muttered. 'If I plead with him, he'll keep my secret, because he's suffered himself and he's not unkind.'

112

Frankie entered with Lisa. 'Ask your mam,' Frankie said. 'She's the one with the surprise.'

Belle gazed fondly at the love of her life, such a pretty little thing, blonde curls, a sweet face currently wearing a huge smile. 'It's somewhere,' she told the child. 'You'll have to find it.'

Lisa jumped up and down on the spot. 'What is it, what is it?'

'A surprise. If I told you, it wouldn't be a surprise, would it?'

'Is it a book, Mummy? I can read some words, cos I'm nearly four now.'

'No, not a book.'

'A toy?'

'It might be. But you find it. No more questions, Lisa.' For about five minutes, the little girl tore round the house like a whirlwind, finally returning to the kitchen. 'Is it a little surprise?' she asked, 'cos I can't find it anywhere, even in drawers and under beds and behind furniture.'

Frankie grinned. 'It's not little.'

Belle couldn't bear her little girl's tension. 'If it's not inside the house, it must be outside – not at the front, though. If it had been at the front, it might have got stolen.'

Lisa ran to the window. 'There's nothing in the back yard.'

'Go and look where Granddad keeps his brush and shovel and tools.'

The child disappeared at speed, returning without her prize. She stood in the doorway between scullery and kitchen, blue eyes huge and watering. 'Oh, Mummy. It's the bestest present I ever had, betterer than Amelia's.'

Belle blinked hard. No matter what, no matter how, her days as a working girl must end sooner rather than later. She had to get away from Meadowbank Farm. 'I'm glad you like it, love. I'll bring it out of the shed, because we don't want it scratched. Then you can take it across the street and show Amelia. What are you going to call your new dolly?'

'Louise or Lulu.'

'They're both nice names, sweetheart. Wait here.'

Belle went to retrieve the item from her dad's small brick shed. On shelves stood the tools of his trade; there wasn't much Dad couldn't do when it came to improving houses. He'd worked damned hard every year of his life, as had Mam. 'I'm a disgrace,' she told herself.

She wondered what Smelly Nellie meant about finding her a job. What could Nellie know about jobs? If she knew about jobs, why had she never found one for herself? Whatever, Belle needed to find work somewhere not in Liverpool, and start all over again, because her Lisa deserved a decent mother. For the time being, a beautiful Silver Cross pram would have to suffice. And the kettle was whistling.

As is the way with most groups of women, differences were usually forgotten when it came to a true parting of ways. Another common factor was bawdiness, at which skill females are definitely as adept as (if not better than) males.

The party was held at brunch time, since Eve closed her premises only at Christmas, New Year and Easter, so all the girls would be working in the evening. Two very excited part-timers were to take on the duties of Babs and Sal very soon, but they were not invited to the party. Belle, too, was absent, and Babs was sorry about that, because Belle had been her best friend until Sally had arrived.

The love between Babs and Sally was celebrated, as it was not uncommon for girls on the game to turn to each other. All the women present discussed the opinion that some lesbian feelings are formed in childhood. Most agreed that fear or distrust of men could be a factor when a girl clung to someone of her own gender.

When Kate wasn't looking, Angela Whiplash poured vodka into the fruit punch. Kate, the eternal invigilator, worked quietly at her end of the kitchen while the girls occupied the comfortable side. Angela winked at Babs. 'Hey, remember that bloke who made you wear a nappy?'

Babs almost choked on her drink. 'Don't remind me, Ange. I was OK till he told me to pee in it. That was when I ordered him out. It was a brand new towel, too, and one of the nappy pins shot open and went through my hip. I was in a bad mood with the daft bugger, I remember that much.'

Sally stepped in. 'Did any of you get Weigh Anchor?' she asked, her face as innocent as only she, at seventeen years of age, could manage. 'Or was it just me? He usually shouted "Hoist the mainsail" when he was ready for the main event, then "Weigh anchor" when he was finishing. I think he used to be in the merchant navy or something. When he was getting dressed to go home, I thought about thanking him for leaving me lost at sea in the crow's nest. Was it just me, then?'

'Yes,' the company chorused.

'Belle had Mustard Man,' Cynthia told them. 'She has all these lovely perfumed oils, lavender, vanilla, geranium and all that jazz, and he wanted Dijon mustard, the soft sod.'

'On his frankfurter?' Angela asked.

The whole room was filled by howls of raucous laughter.

'Well, she did kind of drop some accidentally on purpose. I got the feeling that she didn't like him. He had to sit in a big bowl of cold water till the pain stopped. She never saw him again.'

'I wonder why?' Kate shouted from the other side of the kitchen.

'What was your daftest one, Angela?' Sally asked.

'Ye gods – that's not an easy question, girl, because I specialize in domination. There was Nick the Vick – he doesn't come any more. Actually, he never came at all, because I had to beat the wickedness out of him every time his body showed a flicker of interest. He was a vicar, read the Bible while I whipped him till I all but drew blood. Mad as a hatter, he was. I mean, he's supposed to lead us all to heaven, but he's too busy fighting his own hell.'

'Any more?' Cynthia asked.

'Erm ... oh yeah, there was U-Bend. He was a very funny shape, and he wanted me to straighten him out. So I tied his hands, strapped him to my bicycle pump, stripped, and let nature take its course. I bet they could hear his screams in Manchester. There was one who wanted me to cut him, but I got rid – no way was I having that. Then Snowflake. He got painted in watered-down glue before having a pillow fight with me. Too time-consuming, that one was, cos he needed a long bath to lose his feathers, and he could have blocked the drains. Oh yes, I get them all, everything from gentle flagellation to brutal punishment. Never mind – the exercise keeps me in shape. Though old age is catching up on me, but we carry on, don't we?'

Mo spoke of a client who was useless unless Beethoven's Sixth was played on the Dansette, and another fascinating chap who ate bananas to keep his strength up. 'We tried without, only he went as limp as washed lettuce. But listening to somebody chewing a banana right down your ear hole isn't my idea of fun, so I told him to bog off. Eve soon replaced him with one who used the rhythm method.'

'Isn't that for Catholics?' Babs asked.

'Not with him, no. He liked traditional jazz, so he was a fast mover, thank goodness. By the time the saints had marched in, he was done and dusted.'

When the laughter died of exhaustion, Judy, who took her job rather seriously, produced a diagram of a foot. 'Every metatarsal takes its own path,' she announced with the air of one delivering a lecture at the university. 'Nine times out of ten, I go for the ball of the foot behind the middle toe.'

Sally gaped. 'What's a meta-thingy?'

'A row of bones,' Judy snapped. 'Small, circular

117

strokes at the ball end of the foot just below the toe should travel the neural path and give the client strength to perform. With some, it's the toe next to the little one.'

Babs nodded sagely. 'So if every doo-dah takes its own path, why does the foot walk in a straight line?'

Judy rolled her eyes heavenward. 'I might as well talk to the wall.'

Cynthia, though pressed by the others, told no tales. As the busiest and best paid, she kept her clients' secrets to herself. Unlike the rest, she accepted the truly unusual, and the men she entertained trusted her to keep their confidences. 'Sorry,' was all she said when urged on by her colleagues. 'Let's just say some of them have a lot to lose, and they trust me.'

'Professionals?' Angela sneered.

'Some are, yes.'

'Don't you mean most?'

Cynthia shrugged. 'Leave it, Ange. Ask Kate or Eve why I keep quiet, because you'll hear the same from them – nothing. I've signed papers. My lot don't arrive in the van – they make their own separate ways here, and sometimes in disguise. And to be honest, I've no idea about what any of them does for a living. I'm not allowed to ask, and they keep the truth to themselves.'

Kate studied the group at the sitting room end of the enormous area. Although Babs had a temper, her amusing side would be missed. Sally was a sweet little thing, so nobody wanted to see the back of her, but this was karma. Things happened, and life had to go on.

Eve came in. 'Kate,' she snapped, 'they're pissed.'

'It's just fruit juice,' Kate replied defensively.

The large woman strode across the floor. 'Vodka,' she announced after dipping in a finger and tasting.

Angela laughed. 'How did Don Crawford take the news about Babs and Sally being in love?'

'None of your business,' Eve hissed. 'Did you put vodka in the juice?'

Angela nodded. As the establishment's sole dominatrix, she felt secure.

'Don't kid yourself about being irreplaceable,' Eve said as if reading Angela's mind. 'I know of at least three who'd be happy to take your place, and there's new stuff out there, stuff they've been bothered to learn about. You're in a rut, Angela, so take this as a warning.' The boss turned. 'Kate, come and pour this rubbish away, please. Drunken clients we have to deal with, but the girls stay sober till business is over.'

Angela's jaw hung slack when Eve had left the scene and the vodka punch was being emptied down the drain. 'Shit,' she cursed after a few seconds. 'You know what, girls? I am not being spoken to like that, not at my age.'

'She'll calm down,' Babs said.

But Angela was boiling mad. 'I am out of here.' She quick-marched her way through the room with Kate hot on her heels.

'Oh, bugger,' Babs exclaimed. 'I'm no fan of Angela's, as we all know, but I don't want to worry about her being out on the streets. Cynthia, go and talk to her. There's a loony wandering

119

about killing working girls.'

Cynthia shrugged. 'It's all right, because she has a plan. Her sister runs a wool shop down Knotty Ash way – it's a lock-up with a flat upstairs. The tenant's gone, and Ange was already thinking of setting up her own business. She's turned forty, love, so she's old enough to know what she's doing.'

'But does her sister know what Angela does for a living?' Sally asked.

Cynthia shrugged; she had no idea.

Upstairs, war had broken out. 'I don't need to work notice,' Angela screamed at Eve. 'I'm going. If you don't leave me alone, I'll blow you sky-high to the cops.'

'In that case, I'll take you down with me,' was Eve's quiet response.

Kate nodded in agreement. 'One down, all down,' she mumbled.

Eve took a step in Angela's direction.

'Stalemate,' Angela snapped in the boss's face. 'It's all falling apart, isn't it, Eve? You've two rookies taking over from Babs and Sal, and you need to persuade an educated dom to come and live happily ever after in the middle of nowhere.'

Eve stood her ground. 'You have to stay till I choose somebody.'

'I was planning on leaving anyway, and I'll be paying rent on a flat, five quid a week. It should be a lot more, but I know the owner.'

'I'll pay that,' Eve said, realizing that this was an admission of defeat. Between Babs and this one, she'd been well and truly cornered.

'Spit on it,' Angela suggested after a pause.

120

Each spat on her right palm before shaking the other's hand.

Back in the office with Kate, Eve said, 'I feel as if everything's coming apart.'

'We've weathered storms worse than this, Eve.'

'Yes, but we're not getting any younger. Sooner or later, we'll have to let the girls go, clear the place of all evidence and sell it, or make it into a B and B.'

'Not yet, Evie.'

'No, Kate. Not just yet. But there's too many changes for my liking.'

'I understand that better than most. We have to keep going because it's what we know. Safety first, Evie. This bit of trouble will pass, and we'll be up and running as per usual.'

When Kate had gone, Eve sat with her elbows on the desk, head in her hands. Where the hell was she going to find another dominatrix? For all her clever talk, she was in a pit dug by Angela Whiplash. 'I'm a fool,' she told herself. 'When will I learn to keep me gob shut? And oh, blood and bullets, when will I learn that nothing lasts for ever?'

That very sentiment was being expressed in an old scout hut beyond Meadowbank's trees and bushes. 'We can't stay here f-for ever,' John said, 'and we're sitting on a pile of d-drugs worth a fortune.'

'We don't know anything about that,' Ian snapped. 'We don't know the drugs are here.'

'And I'm nearly past caring,' Phil added. 'If the coppers find us, we might be put somewhere decent away from the Pastorals. And John – the drugs were here before we came, so they're nothing to do with us. Can we see them? No, we can't, because the dealers hid the lot under the scout stuff.' He sighed heavily. 'It's the boredom that's killing me.'

John nodded his agreement.

Life was easier, but duller. The baron from the southern end of Liverpool kept his word. Every Thursday night, he or one of his cronies arrived with fish and chips, a crate of pop, tinned food, bread, butter, jam, cheese, ciggies and five pounds. The message was always the same once Boss admitted that drugs were in the hut – 'Don't touch them. We don't want you lads smoking filth, because you've been through enough trouble already.' It was almost like having a few uncles, as if somebody cared at last.

'We could ask for some games like Monopoly and cards,' Ian suggested.

'It's fresh air we need,' John answered. 'Going out once every b-blue moon to spend the fiver isn't enough. Anyway, I hate bloody Monopoly. They g-got the name wrong; it should have been Monotonous. I wouldn't mind p-playing dominoes or learning chess.'

They were still discussing their plight when someone knocked at the door. It wasn't the big fellow or any of his attendants, because their knock went bang, bang, bang, pause, bang, bang, bang, pause, then four quick, quiet taps. Anyway, it wasn't a Thursday. The boys were safe in theory, because three huge bolts had been fixed to the inside of the door and, in case they all went out together, there was a massive padlock for use on the outside.

'Sh-shit,' John whispered. 'Th-they'll have heard us.'

Ian crept to the door and placed his ear against it. The other two lay down beneath the window.

'We know you're in there.' The owner of the voice was female. 'We only want to help, that's all.'

Ian turned and shrugged at his mates.

The woman spoke again. 'Look, we won't get you charged with trespass or whatever, because the cops aren't exactly friends of ours, either. Open the bloody door – we mean you no harm.'

Sal and Babs stared at each other. They'd been up in the spare attic looking for bits of Sal's stuff to pack, when they'd seen a boy walking into a hut in the distance. The place had belonged to one scout group that had merged with another, and it was supposed to be empty. 'Open up,' Babs said again. 'You'll be fine, I promise you, cross my heart and hope to die.'

'What do you want?' Ian asked at last.

'To make sure you're all right, that's all. We'll be back with our boss if you don't open this door. Believe me, you don't want to tangle with our boss, because she's built like the *Titanic,* and it'd take a bigger iceberg than you to put a hole in her.'

'How did you find us?' Ian asked.

'We were up in the roof and some of the conifers have been trimmed – they grow fast. You can't be seen from the rest of the house. It's just that one attic, and it doesn't get used except for storage. Open the door.'

Slowly, reluctantly, Ian drew back the bolts and opened the door. 'Come in before you get noticed.'

The two girls entered the shed. 'God, it stinks in here – you've no ventilation. What are those two daft sods doing on the floor?' Babs asked.

Phil was annoyed. He wasn't a daft sod, and he said so. He and John stood up awkwardly.

'Matter of opinion,' Babs snapped. 'Right. What are you hiding from?'

'From nosy parkers like you,' Phil hissed.

'We're serious,' Sally said, her tone gentler than Babs's.

Ian the leader came to the fore. He didn't care any more, wasn't afraid of language, of the words he needed to use, because he was tired, and so were both his companions. 'We ran away from a boarding school because we were all interfered with by monks. I was bleeding from my backside, and it was a mess. Took ages to heal.'

Babs sat down suddenly, depositing her behind on a rough wooden box. 'Bloody hell, lads. You've been in all the papers. The cops are spending a fortune trying to find you. But me and Sal are moving away in a few days–'

'Belle,' Sally said, interrupting her girlfriend. 'Belle will help.'

'We don't need help,' Ian insisted. 'We've got ... mates who look after us. Don't tell anybody else.'

Babs took a pen from her pocket. 'If things get bad, phone this number. It's in Southport.' She wrote the number on the wall, low down near the floor. 'Get to a phone box and ring me. Ask for

Babs or Sally. This is Sally, and I'm Babs. And you could all do with a bath, but I can't do anything about that just now.'

'We could sneak them in during the night,' Sally suggested.

'No thanks,' Ian said.

Babs took the bull by the horns. 'Do you know what a whorehouse is?' she asked, pausing to see the boys' reactions. All three blushed. 'Well, that's where we live until Saturday. Nobody will get the police, because we're all prozzies, and we could end up in big trouble. Understand?'

'Yes,' they chorused.

'Where are the bastards that raped you?' Babs demanded to know.

'Disappeared,' Phil answered. 'On retreat and waving white flags, I reckon. Some bishop will be looking after them.'

'Let me tell you this much, lads. There isn't one woman in that farmhouse who wouldn't kill the buggers for what they did to you. Don't make the mistake of thinking that prostitutes don't care, because that's not true. In our job, we prozzies save young girls from the sort of thing that happened to you, and we all hate rapists. Trust us. Belle will look after you.'

John found his courage. 'C-can you get us some playing cards and d-dominoes?'

'Course we can,' Sal said.

Babs sniffed back some confused emotion. 'Listen, boys. Sally and I were both raped when we were kids, so we know what you've been through. My uncle's dead, but Sally's stepfather is still out there. You're not alone. If the monks get caught,

125

there'd be thousands of us on your side, boys and girls alike. According to the *Echo*, you've sent loads of letters with no return address on them. Now I know why. Sally and I won't betray you.'

Ian shuffled, his cheeks pink. 'So ... er ... you two get paid for doing it now?'

'Yes, we do, mostly because we were so messed up as kids that we didn't do well at school.' She paused. 'How old are you?'

'We're all nearly fifteen.'

'Then you'll soon be old enough to stand on your own two feet. They keep talking about raising the school leaving age to sixteen, but the powers are good at talking and useless at doing.' Babs reached out and took Ian's hand. 'We'll work this out. I'm not sure how, but we will.'

'Thanks,' he managed. 'Erm – what will you be doing in Southport?'

'I'll be learning to ride a horse that's going to win the Grand National.'

'You're kidding,' Phil cried.

'Am I? Well, remember his name – it's Mad Murdoch. He's stubborn, daft, naughty and beautiful. And when he jumps, he flies.'

'P-Pegasus,' John stammered. 'Winged horse. It was in a b-book.'

'He used to read a lot,' Ian explained. 'Spoken words were kicked out of him and he got the stammer, so he liked his words printed. He's clever.'

Sally spoke to the other two boys. 'Babs makes things happen. She'll find a way of helping you – you'll see.'

The girls walked back to the farmhouse, forcing

their way through bushes. 'This is one fucked-up world,' Babs mused in a whisper. 'Them lads have been through hell just like we have. We are getting out of this game sharpish, babe.'

'How?' Sally asked.

'Any bloody way will do. We go and live with that sad, randy old bugger and we take it from there. Just watch me and do as I say. There's always a way, Sally; it's just a matter of biding our time. The horse is the key.'

'How do you know?'

Babs shrugged. 'I don't know how I know. I just know.'

Laughing without quite understanding why, they entered the place they would soon be leaving. As they lay together that night, each held in her mind a picture of three frightened boys in a smelly shed. 'We must find some games for them,' Sally whispered. 'There's a compendium in the kitchen. It won't be missed.'

Babs deposited a chaste kiss on her girl's cheek. 'I love you, Sal. You care in spite of all that's happened to you.'

'Or because of it. You're the same. We'll be OK, won't we?'

'Of course we will.' Oh God, she hoped so. 'Get some sleep, Sally. We're going to need all the rest we can get, cos there's big changes coming.'

'Goodnight, Babs.'

'Goodnight, love.'

I got the first one right except for the cross and chain. The paper said Jean Davenport had children. Well, they may have a chance of a decent upbringing without her in their lives. The second was a disaster; I must learn not to judge a book by its cover, and I think I know how. If I smile or speak, real ones will ask whether I want business. But I wish I could stop thinking and dreaming about Dolly Pearson and her mother, God help the old girl on her deathbed.

Anyway, I overheard a conversation at work. There's a place called Meadowbank Farm that doesn't get mail delivered – it's picked up twice a week by a mountainous woman in a large van. She has a post office box, because the farm is a whorehouse, or so some people think. It's accessible from the East Lancashire Road. I suppose the women think they're safe there, off the beaten track and at least a couple of miles away from their nearest neighbours.

That conversation I listened to should never have happened, because members of the public ought to have their privacy respected, which is why we have post office boxes, but Jesus made sure I heard it. And here I am with aching legs, wheeling my bike with its lights turned off as I stumble along a dirt track that shows signs of use by a heavy vehicle, probably the van that was mentioned. There's a sign on one of the open gates, and it bears the name of the farm.

I'm pondering the subject of beehives. Why? Because one normal female bee is over-nourished, cared for by drones and fed whatever is collected by worker bees. This super-sized grub becomes the queen; the fat woman who drives the van is probably monarch of the farm. This particular home for bees is Sodom and Gomorrah, with

Lime Street and the Dock Road included in the mix. Worker bees will have their own cells where they serve customers, while drones will keep the hive in good order and feed Fat Mamma.

The van's coming – its engine is noisy. I throw down my bike and dive into a bush. The vehicle passes me, and I'm sure I haven't been noticed. It stops outside the house, and its back doors open to spill out half a dozen men. Fat Mamma keeps her girls off the streets, then. She picks up their sex partners and brings them here – well, there's a novelty. Oh, this is a good place for me. With paraffin and a box of matches, I could wipe out all of them, clients as well as those who serve them.

I booked a few days off work, and Laura thinks I'm sea-fishing, but oh no, I'm here watching and waiting. I hide my bike in the bushes, sit and remain as still as possible. The front door closes. There's no hurry, because I'm supposed to be out on a boat over the bar, trying to catch fish in the Irish Sea. Laura will go to bed soon – she's a creature of habit, as am I. We scarcely talk these days. I'm a different person, I suppose, because I am under hallowed orders.

After about an hour, I'm getting cramp, but I have to know the place and what happens here – I'm not risking another Dolly Pearson. The door opens, spilling pink light out onto a gravel path. Men climb into the van while the fat woman wedges herself at the steering wheel. The vehicle turns and travels past me. Queenie has left the building, so I move to the other side of the house away from the driveway.

At least one ground floor room is a bedroom.

129

Through a small gap in the curtains, I see an almost naked woman washing herself at a small sink. There's a mirror on the ceiling above a double bed with a purple quilt and pillowcases in the same shade. The wall facing me is red, with pictures of naked people above the bed's head-board.

The woman's voluptuous. She strips off her transparent black clothing and is changing into something as red as that wall. My body is responding; I suppose this is another test sent to me from above. Oh, how rounded and comfortable the whore is. Laura is thin except when pregnant. She's the only woman I've ever had, and now I understand how men get tempted into fornication with these shameless hussies.

I am confused. I haven't touched Laura since ... since Jean Davenport, but I could touch this one. Anybody can touch this one. How do I get picked up by that van? To discover the layout of this house, I need to be a customer. It will be my duty to copulate with one or more of the whores. Moving my eyes away from the vision is difficult, but I must go, because I have to be alone and hidden while I rid myself of terrible discomfort and indulge the need. I am a bad man.

Back in the hedge, I see the fat woman returning in the van. Again, about six men disembark and enter the building. I lie down for a while. Behind my eyelids, the ground floor prostitute is stripping and washing herself. Oh God, spare me this torture. Still, it's better than the vision of Dolly Pearson, I suppose.

For a while, I doze, but am woken by the sound

of the engine as Fatso drives her customers away, and back I go to the window with the gap in its curtains. She's washing again. Her hair is brown and shiny; it looks like silk against alabaster. Of average height, she has a tiny waist, flaring hips and large breasts. This time, she's dressing in white, which is supposed to be a sign of virginity.

A man enters the room, and I realize that I've been too engrossed to hear the vehicle returning. I must have been standing here for ages. So the creature in white will have had several men tonight. I won't be seen here; the van comes nowhere near this side. There is a strange beauty to what's happening in the room. All my married life, I've been with a good, hardworking wife and mother who just ... just lies there. A few feet away from me at this moment, there's a limited view of joy through a small gap in curtains. She moves. She touches him. She laughs. She holds him. She climbs on top of him. She's beautiful.

Jesus, help me. This wasn't meant to happen, surely? I'm only human. I want what that man is getting from her. She's naked now. So is he. In ten years, I have never seen Laura in the nude. When we do get together, my attitude is almost apologetic, as if my wife's doing me a favour.

Look. Look at her head thrown back and all that shining hair hanging lower down her spine, almost reaching her waist. Listen. She's almost screaming, while he seems to growl like an animal. The deed has been done.

They lie side by side for a while, and they're having a quiet conversation. I've never had that, either. Laura always rolls away from me and falls

131

asleep, sighing as if she's glad the whole business is over. There's seldom anything to say, anyway, because she knows nothing of life beyond the house and the children, doesn't even read the paper or listen to the news. We're a boring pair, I conclude. And now I almost understand why men use other women. Wives cook and clean and raise children, while these female receptacles serve a different purpose.

He's stroking her hair. They talk and laugh while he winds a long strand round his finger. I can almost feel her crowning glory, silky-smooth and long. Laura's is sensible, I suppose. She keeps it short and easy to deal with, because she's busy running the house. A wash-and-go style, she calls it. It's wiry, with no shine and very little colour. I married a blonde, but she's gone mousy as she's got older. There seems to be more to living than waiting for safe days and a quick fumble in the dark. I love Laura, yet there is no pleasure to be had with her, no happiness in mating.

The man's getting dressed. He turns towards the window, startling me for a moment, but he doesn't see me. I'm panicking for two reasons. First, I was afraid of being noticed; second, I know who he is.

I step away and sit down under the window. That man is our butcher, a happy chap with red cheeks, smiling eyes and the best lamb chops for miles. Trevor Burns is his name. His wife works with him in the shop; he calls her Em, so I suppose she's Emily. I'm sitting here on a hard and unforgiving path and I'm shaking my head. He has five children. He goes to our church with his wife and kids. Like most butchers, he's slightly overweight, as is Em. Trevor Burns. Will he burn in hell? Is his name prophetic?

Life is a learning process, and Trevor Burns is my key to this house. I hear the van driving away. When I stand, the woman inside is wearing a shabby old blue robe and clutching a large towel. Business is over for tonight, I guess, and she's going for a bath. Water will not cleanse her soul of sin. And if I do what Butcher Burns just did, there'll be no absolution for me, either. It's all very confusing. It's also exciting. I have never felt as alive as I do tonight.

Jesus, is this part of it? Do I have to know these women in the biblical sense? Must I taste the sin before spitting it out and grinding it to dust?

This is confusing, exciting, bad, good – and perhaps it's connected to my mission. I must bow to the will of my Master.

Roy and Bill were in it up to their necks. 'You owe me,' Boss told them. He focused on Bill. 'I've brought you back here for a reason. I gave you over the odds for your crop, and you can make it up by doing drops or manufacturing for me. You'll get paid. When you've worked off your debt, you'll get paid more.'

Bill was white as a sheet. 'I'm starting work with my dad,' he said. They were on the big man's territory, and both boys were terrified.

The reply arrived through a fog of cigar smoke. 'That's OK. You can do evening and weekend drops.'

'But I live at the other side of Liverpool.'

'That doesn't matter. We'll come to you with the big drop, then you can do the smaller ones when we give you the meeting places. If you're caught, you say nothing. All drops will be in your area.' He turned to Roy. 'You can stay here. You'll be fed and paid to work, and your wages will increase depending on how hard you work.'

Bill cleared his throat of fear. It tasted terrible. 'I can't do drops. We'll be working in Chorley and Preston – he's with a big firm, me dad. But I'll keep my gob shut, like.'

'Make sure you do, or accidents will happen.'

'Er – what will I be doing, Boss?' Roy asked.

'You'll be on ready-made spliffs with an extra ingredient. Don't use any of the LSD yourself, because you might have a bad trip.'

The boys looked at each other. A bad trip? The whole situation was a bad trip. They should have run away and let the plants die, since Roy was now tied into a life under Boss, who never used his real name, while Bill didn't feel exactly safe.

'And don't do anything clever. We know where your families are,' the big man said, his voice low and threatening.

Roy shuffled on the spot. At least Bill would be going home and working with his dad. And yes, he did know what happened to families. A guy who had grassed up some big drugs people got his photo in the congratulations column of a local paper. *Well done with the interview,* the message had read. The interview had been with the cops, and the guy's mother had been tied to a chair at home and beaten halfway to death. There was no hiding place.

Five

Constables Eddie Barnes and Dave Earnshaw were among many who had volunteered for low-paid and sometimes unpaid overtime. While some officers searched for a murderer, others chased about looking for the three supposedly abused boys who had fled and disappeared to God alone knew where. Both cases were of interest to national media, so the whole country was watching the Liverpool police force.

It was a hard job for uniformed men who made their presence felt in the city for at least eight hours a day. After a shift in the Lime Street area, the two constables were fed in the station canteen, after which they enjoyed an hour's rest before returning to duty when dusk began its descent. Somewhere out there, a serial killer was indulging his pastime.

After their too-short break, Eddie and Dave joined colleagues spaced along the riverfront, which stretched for miles. Since the brutal murder of Dolly Pearson, whose broken body had upset even pathologists, nothing further had happened. As August peeped over the horizon, no new evidence had been found, and nobody else had died at the hands of a person nominated by the press as the Mersey Monster.

'Maybe he's moved on,' Dave suggested. 'He might go from one river to another, and he could be in Chester now, looking for women along the Dee. Mind, they won't get many merchant sailors down the Dee, will they? Perhaps he's given up.'

Eddie held strong opinions, because he'd been reading everything he could find on the subject of serial killers. 'They don't give up, Dave, they get stopped by us or by their own death. I just get the feeling – and don't ask me why – that he's trying to clear Liverpool of prostitutes. Of course, he knows now that Mrs Pearson was just an eccentric elderly lady who wore the wrong clothes, so I think he's having a pause. He's a bad bugger on a mission; I feel it in my bones.'

Dave pondered. 'All these coppers and detectives will be putting him off. But this is a bloody long stretch of riverfront, Eddie. He could be anywhere from Otterspool to Waterloo.' He paused. 'It's almost as if we're wanting him to do another one, but we're too visible.'

'Then lives are being saved for now, which can't be a bad thing. Come on, we'll get a cuppa in that late-night cafe. What with murdered women and runaway boys, we're all a bit overstretched and we deserve a short sit.'

They stepped into the decrepit place known as Pat and Paul's Cafe. A smell of rancid fat hung in the air and clung lovingly to curtains and table-cloths. The floor was covered in ancient lino that boasted stains in various colours. Dave went to order tea while Eddie settled in an uncomfortable chair and lit a longed-for Navy Cut.

The dump was quite busy, filled mostly by lorry drivers, but with a few policemen and detectives scattered about. There wasn't a single clean item in the place, and the staff, just the man and wife, looked totally unfit to be in human company. They were sweaty, and their supposedly white overalls bore almost as many shades of colour as the lino.

'What the hell are we doing in here?' Eddie mouthed quietly after blowing a perfect smoke ring.

A man at the next table smiled. 'Not a pleasant place to eat, is it? My wife would be sending for a fumigation unit.'

'We're desperate,' Eddie replied. 'Been on our feet for ten hours.'

The man nodded. 'This is the only cafe open along here at this time of night. A lot of hard work for you just now,' he added. 'The murders, I mean. Any idea who it is yet? He must be very different from ordinary folk, I suppose.'

'It's a psycho,' Eddie said. 'A psycho looks just like everybody else. According to an expert in these things, he's possibly even married with a couple of kids, a wife who has no idea what he's up to, and a very ordinary job. A clever nutcase on a mission can take some catching, but we'll get him.'

'Are you sure?' the stranger asked.

'Even brilliant psychos make mistakes. Dolly Pearson was one of them.'

'Let's hope you put a stop to him, then.' Neil Carson finished his cuppa, said goodnight and walked to the door. He got his bike and wheeled it past the window, waving to the policeman as he raised a leg over the crossbar. 'Good luck,' he mouthed. They would need luck, because Neil Carson's target now sat out in the wilds, a farmhouse shielded by bushes and trees and a fat queen bee. They would catch him? Oh no, he was too clever for that.

Eddie Barnes shivered, though he didn't know why, because the evening was warm. What did Mam always say when she shuddered involuntarily? 'Somebody walked over my grave'? Yes, that was it.

Dave arrived with two mugs of tea and some wrapped biscuits. 'We should get the health inspectors in here. Folk could be poisoned.' He gazed at his partner. 'Are you all right, lad? You look done in.'

'I think I'm OK. I'm a bit tired, that's all.' But he still felt cold.

'Who were you talking to?' Dave asked.

'Just some bloke who agreed with me about this wonderfully clean, high-class restaurant. He said we should try the caviar and the smoked salmon, but what can we do on a cop's pay, eh? Glad you bought wrapped biscuits, Dave. I wouldn't want anything touched by either of them at the counter.'

They sat together eating their biscuits and sipping at strong, stewed tea.

Dave frowned. 'I wonder when this was brewed. Yesterday?'

Eddie looked at the owners. 'It could be him,' he whispered. 'Always open late. Maybe he sends the wife home early while he closes the cafe before going out to do his other job.'

Dave grinned. 'Look at him. About six stone wet through. I reckon he couldn't lift the skin off custard, and he's certainly a stranger to cleaning up.'

'You're right. It's more likely somebody the same as men we see every day. Average height, average weight, average looks, ordinary job, maybe shift work. He'll have read about Dolly Pearson, and I reckon she was a big error, because he's after working girls like poor Jean Davenport. He knows the docks are crawling with cops, so he'll be working on new ideas.'

'Is he crazy?'

Eddie raised his shoulders. 'That's a matter of opinion. Does he know what he's doing? Yes, he does. Does he know why? Maybe he does, and maybe he doesn't. Another thing I heard was that he can't appreciate how other people feel. He could even be an excellent dad, a genuinely good family man till he gets out and about. I bet he's OK at his job, too, although that psych bloke at the station said he's probably working at a level he considers beneath him. But I think he'll steer clear of the docks for a while.'

Dave grinned. 'I bet you've passed your sergeant exams, Ed.'

'I have. And I think I'm trying for CID. I like the whys and the hows and the whos. Listening to that expert in our office, I thought how interesting it was to dig into the human mind and work out the type we're hunting.'

'Are you and me getting a divorce, then?'

'Let's see, shall we? Come on, we should get out of this hole before we come down with cholera or typhoid.'

They stood outside on the pavement. 'It might even be him,' Eddie said quietly.

'Him who?'

'Him who was talking to me, sitting at the next table. Ordinary chap, knows the right thing to say, the right way to behave. They're good actors, these psychopaths. The killer might even be a policeman or a judge or a clergyman.'

'You serious, Ed?'

Eddie nodded. 'Yes. And he hasn't finished his work, Dave. The odd thing is that he should have left a trail earlier in life, because they don't usually kick off with killing people. They might hurt animals and other kids first, but everyone on our books has been checked. He could have moved here from just about anywhere.'

'So he might be on another force's list?'

Again, Eddie nodded. 'Could be Scottish, Irish, Welsh. Or he might be what they call inspirational.'

'What's that when it's at home?'

'Our killer might have been given orders from voices only he can hear. So he could have a completely clean sheet so far. But he still knows what he's doing is wrong.'

'Bloody hell.'

'Yes, that as well. Let's get back to the cop shop. We're on earlies tomorrow.'

A few yards away, a man with a bicycle watched the two policemen as they walked towards town. They would catch him? They probably couldn't catch as much as a cold. He left the recessed doorway and rode homeward back to Laura. Whatever it took, he must make love to her tonight. It was a safe day; it was marked on the calendar.

Belle Horrocks tucked her precious girl into bed.

And the big, bad wolf was never seen again. She kissed her beloved daughter's hair; it smelled of childhood, happiness and Johnson's baby shampoo. Lisa Marie Horrocks was the most beautiful child in the world.

Lisa frowned. 'Did he have to get killed, that wolf?'

'It was either him or Red Riding Hood's grandma, love. Which would you choose to save?'

'My grandma.' The child grinned. 'Well, when she's not trying to make me eat stuff I don't want, like trees.'

'Broccoli's good for you, babe. It'll make you strong and healthy. All veg are good for you.'

'She does spinach, too. It's horri-bubble.'

'Horrible.'

'Do you not like it, too?'

Belle grinned. 'I have a secret, but I'll tell just you, shall I?'

Lisa nodded enthusiastically.

'It was carrots with me, love. I hated carrots. So I cut them small unless they were already mashed, and I put them with something I did enjoy, like gravy or potato or meat. It was easier when they were mashed.'

'Trees don't get mashed, Mam. If they were mashed, would they turn into leaves like lettuce?'

Belle laughed. 'Cut 'em up, stick 'em in gravy and Bob's your uncle.'

'Is he? I thought I hadn't got no uncles.'

'It's just a saying, Lisa. It means everything's all right.' She left the room, making sure that the door was open by two inches and the landing light was on because Lisa didn't like total darkness.

'Night, Mummy.'

'Goodnight, my sweetheart.' Belle stood at the top of the stairs. She'd be back at the farm in a couple of days, and she'd been shut in this house for what felt like a lifetime, too scared to go out because Tom Duffield lived nearby. It was time to face the music, she told herself firmly. She couldn't carry on like this, could she? And Tom was a decent chap...

Downstairs, she informed Frankie and Sam that she was off for a walk.

'It's going dark,' Sam said. 'Somebody out there's killing women.'

'This isn't the docks,' was Belle's answer. 'I won't go far.' That was true, because she was intending to visit a house that was very near. She didn't dress up. Her hair was tidy, her shoes flat slip-ons, and the dress itself was a sensible one from Marks & Spencer: blue and white stripes, a buttoned blouse-type top with a bow at the throat. She pulled on a navy cardigan.

'See you in a bit, then,' Frankie called as her daughter left the room.

Belle walked to the end of the terrace, the side that didn't pass the front of Tom's house. Counting the back alley gates beyond her parents' she tried the one that led into the yard of number 42. It wasn't locked. Sighing her relief, she entered a client's territory for the first time ever, and stopped when she saw him seated in the window. The main light was on, and a brighter lamp shone on the table at which he worked. His missing left hand had been replaced by a hook, putting Belle in mind of pirate stories from her childhood. A parrot might have completed the picture.

She found herself staring at him. With up to three clients a night, few of Eve's girls bothered to assess unimportant details like looks. They were just lonely men who needed a woman, and the quicker they boiled over, the better. Tom was unusual; Tom tried to please her. He wasn't bad looking, not bad at all. He often joked about his missing hand, saying his mam had always told him he was 'armless.

He was fiddling about just now with small items on the table, concentrating too hard to bother looking through the window. Sometimes, he placed an eye against a jeweller's glass on a stand, so the work was detailed. For the first time, Belle realized that he was very pleasing to the eye, and that made her smile, though she couldn't imagine why.

Her palms were damp, so she rubbed them down the sides of her frock. 'You're visiting a neighbour, that's all,' she whispered to herself.

She knocked at the rear door. 'He won't let me down, not Tom,' she mouthed silently to herself. A dog barked, and Belle steeled herself, because she wasn't used to dogs.

The door swung inward. Tom stood with his right hand attached to the dog's collar. The hook had opened the door. His face suddenly wore a wide grin. 'Belle?'

'Yes, it's me. That's a big dog.' She pointed to the black Labrador. 'Is he friendly?'

'You'll be in danger of being licked all the way to death by drowning, but Max doesn't bite. Get

143

yourself inside.'

She entered the house and looked round the small scullery. It was wonderful, clean, tidy and very well decorated with tiles up to the ceiling on every wall. It housed a large porcelain sink, an English Electric automatic washing machine and a pulley clothes line. 'Where do you cook?' she asked. It was clear that he'd turned the minute scullery into a laundry.

'This way.' He led her into the kitchen. It sported not only a bungalow range with an oven, but also a gas cooker with four rings, a grill and another oven, a sink, a fridge, and rows of floor-standing and wall cupboards along two sides of the room. The table at which he'd been working was probably where he ate, and a two-seater sofa faced the range. 'Who did all this?' she asked.

'Amazing what a one-handed man can do with a hook,' he replied, smiling at her, 'and my mates helped with plumbing and electrics. Your dad's going to plaster upstairs for me.'

Belle stood still. 'How do you know he's my dad?'

'He brags about you. So does your mam. It's OK, you're safe as far as I'm concerned, Miss Bookkeeper. We all have our secrets. I'll put the kettle on.'

She placed herself on the small sofa and was joined immediately by the dog. Tom was right – she was getting a thorough wash. 'Give it a rest, Max,' she said.

The animal stopped and leapt off the seat.

'That's why they're used as guide dogs,' Tom said. 'They love people, they're intelligent and obedient. All he wants from me is food, a walk and love.'

'Do you see your sons?' Belle asked apropos of nothing.

He paused, tea scoop frozen over the caddy. 'No. The wife disappeared from her parents' house on Queens Drive after a matter of days.'

'Are her mam and dad still there on Queens Drive?'

'They went with her and the boys, or so I was told by a neighbour.'

'Because of your hand? She left because of your hand?'

'You've talked about me to your parents?'

'Yes. I asked who the one-handed man was. I saw you in the back street walking away from me. You were in a shirt with short sleeves. No hook, though.'

'I use it mostly for work. Yes, my other half couldn't bear to look at my stump, refused to help me dress it, so I had to go every day to the hospital after being discharged. I came back from the dressings clinic one day, and she'd gone. They'd all gone.'

Belle accepted her cup of tea. 'Did you try to get her back?'

'No.'

She didn't ask why he'd made no effort in that direction. 'You must miss the kids.'

'They'll find me when they're old enough. I didn't want them to see me and their mam fighting over them. Anyway, they're why I'm doing the house up. I've a television in the front room, and I'm saving for colour. It's not worth getting yet, because it's mainly just BBC2 that broadcasts in colour, but the others will catch up.' He took a sip of tea. 'You look nice,' he said.

'Different from the way I usually dress at work.'

'I know I'm not your only client, but you're my only girl,' he said. 'And I'm sure this will sound corny, but the massage is as important as the sex. You stop my nonexistent left hand hurting.' He returned to drinking his tea. Belle Horrocks was special, but she wasn't his. Sometimes, when he was with her, he imagined that they were a couple, though he'd never told her that.

'Judy does reflexology,' she told him. 'That can help, too.'

'I know. I don't want Judy. She reminds me of Mrs Duke at school, a pretty face spoiled by disappointment and sulking. You make me laugh; you make me feel good, as if I'm normal.'

Belle frowned. 'You are normal. Just because a bit's been cut off, that doesn't make you abnormal.' She glanced at the table. The bright light remained on, and the area was covered in tiny cogs, springs and other bits of metal.

He followed her gaze. 'I mend clocks and watches. I'm self-taught.'

'With one hand?'

'Yes. The hook's adaptable. Smaller-gauged bits clamp to the end of it, and my right hand's a good labourer. Clocks are easier, because they're bigger, but I manage with watches, too. So I earn a good living.'

Belle relaxed. This was ridiculous, because their relationship was strictly professional, yet she felt as if she'd known the man all her life. He was the

146

sort of bloke who couldn't be pictured in a bad mood. 'My dad will always help you in the house,' she told him. 'You just need to ask

'I know. I'm his landlord, though he doesn't know it, and you mustn't tell him. I got a pay-off from Watkinson's because the machine that took my hand had a failed guard. We never went to court. I bought this house which I'd been renting, and theirs – your parents' – too. I use a letting agent, and he chose your family when the last lot moved out. The name was familiar, so when I found out for certain that they were your mam and dad, I told the agent to charge less rent and Sam would get the place right. I'll provide the materials, of course. Your little girl's there too, isn't she?'

'Yes.' Belle no longer felt relaxed. Tom liked her; she could tell that he liked her. 'It's a lovely house.'

'It will always be their home, Belle. They're smashing people with a great daughter and a lovely grandchild. She looks like you.'

Not for the first time just lately, Belle was in danger of being overcome by gratitude. There was Babs with the ten quid, Nellie with the free pram, now Tom promising to look after Mam, Dad and Lisa. 'You're a good man, Tommy Duffield.'

He smiled. She looked wonderful, so much better as an ordinary, if rather pretty mother. 'When you have an accident like mine, your view of life changes. Once the anger left me, I was grateful that it was just my left hand. I got to thinking about all the lads who never came home after wars, and about those who survived with burnt faces and no legs.'

'I know what you mean, Tom.'

He shook his head. 'I decided to be grateful for many mercies,' he said. 'I'm better off than some.'

Belle remained motionless; he needed to talk. It felt as if she might be the first one he'd opened up to, and he needed to offload the traumas to someone who wasn't a doctor, some lay person who cared enough to listen.

'I went wild again when she took my sons. Hit the bottle, hated the world, didn't even eat properly because I didn't like myself much. Then I got the payout from Watkinson's and I thought right, buy this house and that empty one a few doors down, be positive, work towards a legacy for my kids. They will look for me in time, and I'll still be at the same address.' He glanced at the floor. 'Max likes you. He's gone to sleep on your foot.'

Belle laughed. 'He has a heavy head, so my foot's asleep too.'

Tom leaned back and closed his eyes for a few moments. Working with timepieces was hard on the vision. He liked Belle's company, especially here, in a setting so different from the usual environment. She was radically different from her colleagues at the farm, and he had grown fond of her. 'Do you kiss any of your clients, Belle?'

'No,' she answered quickly.

'Not just me, then. Is there a reason for not kissing?'

'Yes. Kissing is human and personal; the rest is just what any animal does. The only person I've ever kissed was Lisa's dad. He died in a car crash before she was born. Eve warns us against getting fond of a client – she says that's a very bad idea. I imagine that Cynthia kisses, but she's a no holds barred type.'

'Did you marry Lisa's dad?'

'He was already married. I couldn't even go to his funeral.'

'Sad,' Tom said.

'Yes. I've been to the grave. His family keeps it nice and tidy.' She was quiet for a while. 'He said he was going to make sure I stayed off the game, that he would leave his wife and set up home with me and the baby, but I knew he wasn't going to do it. As things turned out, I'll never be completely sure either way, will I?'

He thought about that. 'It's the same with me. I wonder whether she would have separated from me if I'd hung on to both hands. In a way, it was a relief except for losing the kids, because there was nothing much left between the two of us. She might well have stayed after I got paid off by the factory; she was very fond of money. It was probably the love of her life.'

Belle glanced at the mantel clock. Her mother and father would start to worry if she stayed out for much longer.

'There's no point being bitter,' he concluded. 'Bitter people end up on their own, no company, no friends.'

She sighed.

'What's up?' he asked.

She hesitated through a few beats of time before replying, 'I won't be able to see you again

149

at Meadowbank, Tom. We're not allowed to have male friends in our rooms.'

'Am I a friend?'

She blushed for the first time in years. 'Well, I know you away from work now, don't I?' She paused again. 'I suppose I could pretend not to know you, but the boss'd go purple if she found out.'

Tom shrugged. 'Purple might suit her. Well, it might improve her. She carries more ballast than a hot air balloon, and she certainly looks like one.'

Belle chuckled.

'And I could tell you how your mam, dad and Lisa are. Nobody needs to know.' He didn't want her to go; he certainly didn't want her to be with other men. So far, he'd managed – just about – to ignore the fact that he was one among many, but he was hurting now, and not just along the path to his missing hand. Having spent years avoiding love and the pain it could bring, he was now teetering on the brink of loneliness.

'OK,' she said. 'We'll watch how it goes, shall we?'

'Yes. I'll see you out.'

'Front door,' she announced. 'I'll tell Mam and Dad that we got talking and had a cup of tea together. It'll be all right, because they like you.'

He showed her his best room. It was spotless and very beautiful. 'See?' he joked. 'I'd make somebody a good wife, wouldn't I?'

Belle wondered why her heart was racing. Was she afraid that Tom might let something slip, thereby allowing her family to know how she earned her living? Or was he getting fond of her?

'I'll be discreet,' he promised, as if reading her mind. 'Tell them you know me – that's no lie. You could have been doing books for a jeweller and you met me there.'

'Discreet's my middle name.'

'Nice,' he said. 'Isabella Discreet Horrocks. Put a hyphen between the two last names and you'll be double-barrelled.'

'We've enough barrels with Eve,' she replied. 'See you.'

He watched her as she walked the short distance home. She was a whore who served upwards of twenty clients each week. But he knew there was more than that to Belle, and that she shouldn't be defined by the job she did. Behind the masseuse's white coat and under the colourful underwear, there resided a decent woman, a woman who might hurt him if he opened his heart, a woman he almost feared.

Belle entered the Horrocks house and leaned against the front door.

'Belle?' her mother shouted.

'Coming.'

'Where've you been till this time?' Sam asked as soon as his daughter entered the kitchen.

Belle kept her tone casual. 'I met that man with one hand. I met his dog, too. We got talking and had a cup of tea in his kitchen. Max nearly licked me to death.'

Frankie inhaled sharply. 'You went in his house? He's a stranger, and you never can tell. You might have been hurt or raped or anything.'

'Mam, he's decent to the bone. And he's no stranger, because it turns out I met him when we

151

were doing a jeweller's prep for audit. He mends watches and clocks. Don't worry, I'll not be fooled again like I was with Lisa's dad. I'm not as daft as I used to be. Shall I put the kettle on?'

'Yes,' they chorused.

In the scullery, Belle splashed her face with cold water before filling the kettle. There was a degree of turmoil taking place in the area of her stomach, and she breathed deeply through her mouth. What the living hell was up with her? Yes, Tom Duffield was a good man, but ... but what? Everything she knew, everything she understood might be whipped out from beneath her feet like a bath mat on ice. She was thinking differently, hoping for change, yet dreading it at the same time. This, she concluded, was confusion; it was an example that illustrated the concept of being in two minds. Well, in several minds.

'What do I want from life?' she asked the kettle. It was so tempting, but was it love? Might it become love? What sort of man wanted a woman who'd been so well used and paid for her favours? He had a nice house, a good job, and he lived near Lisa, Mam and Dad. Perhaps she'd got him wrong. There was a strong chance that he wanted things to carry on as they were, and yet...

'Belle?'

'What, Mam?'

'Bring the biscuit tin.'

'All right.' She put the tin on the tray, hoping that her mind would slow down a bit. If she carried on like this, there'd be no sleep for her tonight.

Meanwhile, just three houses along the street,

152

Tom Duffield popped a watch back inside its casing. He wound it, listened to the tick, then put it to one side for an hour. If it kept time, it could be returned tomorrow with several other time-pieces to Martindale's, a jewellery shop in town.

He suddenly hated the silence with which he was surrounded, so he turned on the radio. It was the shipping forecast, but there'd be a play in a few minutes. There was a slight dip where she'd sat on his sofa. He picked up her cup and placed his lips where hers had been. 'God, I'm a soft swine,' he said.

Max sat in front of the range, his head tilted to one side.

'Do you miss her too, lad?' Tom asked.

The dog sniffed.

'I remember reading something, Max. It was a saying about things turning out better for people who make the best of things – along those lines, anyway. We have to go with the flow, son.'

'Woof.'

'I'm glad you agree.'

The radio play began. Although he sat through it, Tom would never be able to account for its subject matter. All he could think about was a young woman in a striped dress, sensible shoes and a navy cardigan. The idea of living with her made a kind of sense, anyway, because her parents were here, as was her child. 'But I want to marry her,' he advised his sole companion. 'She needs to feel safe.'

The dog whined.

'All right, Max. Let's go for a walk.'

I can't do it. I just can't do it. I'm useless.

Laura lay there as she usually does, like a half-empty coal sack with some sharp bits sticking through the cloth. She's bony. I tried thinking about that well-upholstered woman at the farm, but it didn't help. It did when I was there, straight after looking through the gap in the curtains, but it was a solo performance in the bushes, and I felt sick afterwards. It made me remember my mother checking my underpants for what she called filth when I was a teenager. Pyjamas got the same treatment, and I can scarcely touch myself to pee without hearing her screaming 'You filthy boy.'

Laura told me to go and see the doctor about what she delicately termed my problem, but there's no point, is there? I mean, would you? 'Hello, doc. I've gone limp with my wife, but I'd be all right with a bit of rough in a whorehouse.' No. I can't do that. Nor can I go to Confession. As for Holy Communion – well, with a soul as stained as mine, I'd be committing sacrilege. Or would I? After all, Jesus told me to clean up, and getting rid of that farm and all its occupants would give me a high score.

So here I sit in a scruffy pub waiting for my butcher to put in an appearance. Some louts are playing darts very noisily, while the brassy tart of a barmaid keeps giving me the eye. I wonder what she does in her spare time? Knitting? Not likely. I wonder whether she's one of *them* when the pub closes for the night.

He's late. I don't do late if I have an appointment. But I mustn't let my anger show when he gets here, because I'm asking for a favour. I have to say there's a lot more to this job than Jesus was willing to let on about. And I'd have thought He might have come back to me just to check on my progress and my plans.

I go to order another half of mild. She asks if I'm all right and I nod. 'I've not seen you in here before,' she remarks, smiling at me. There's lipstick on her teeth, but I say nothing about that.

So I tell her that's probably because I've never been in here before. I feel like saying I haven't missed much by not patronizing this hole in the wall, but there's no point in being provocative. She has a flourishing moustache. Women should look closely at facial hair before piling on the powder, because makeup only makes the fuzz more noticeable.

Oh, my goodness, here he comes, jovial Trevor with his red cheeks and halfway-to-purple nose. The cheeks are probably the result of too much beef, but the nose looks as if it's had a close, long-term relationship with a bottle, and I don't mean milk or Vimto. So cheerful, he grates at times.

'Hi, Neil,' he says. 'What are you drinking?'

'I'm fine,' I tell him.

He comes back with what looks like a triple whisky. He should save his legs and get the whole bottle, or a bucket. I am being rather less than charitable, and I'm trying hard not to lose my temper with this overfed animal.

'Right,' he says.

'Right,' I answer.

'Why this meeting, Neil? What do you need to say that you couldn't say across my counter?'

155

I take a sip of my mild. 'Your wife was there, Trevor!'

'And?' He raises an eyebrow – well, he almost raises both, because they're joined in the middle above that colourful nose.

I lean forward. 'It's about Meadowbank Farm.'

'Say again,' he mumbles.

Is he deaf as well as ugly?

'Meadowbank Farm,' I repeat. 'You know it. Out in the middle of nowhere, nearest shops in Knowsley village.'

Interestingly, his whole face changes colour. The nose is now puce, while the cheeks are scarlet. It's an unbecoming combination, especially on a man whose residual hair is ginger. 'What?' he growls, as if hiding his voice behind fear at the back of his nose and throat.

'I want to ride in the van to Meadowbank Farm.'

He looks round the room as if expecting to see a flock of nuns, some priests and an archbishop or two. 'What?' he asks again. 'How do you know about it?'

I tap the side of my nose.

'It's by recommendation only,' he whispers.

'Then recommend me.'

'You're married,' he blusters, clearly upset.

'So are you. We both have kids, too, and we've a lot to lose. Get me in, and I won't say a word to Mrs Burns. Do you understand me?'

He nods.

I stand and walk out, leaving him to wallow alone in his misery.

She'll be asleep when I get back. Or she may pretend to be asleep. My Laura is a good, caring woman, an excellent housekeeper, a perfect mother, great with money, but ... but she's not desirable. I'm confused. If I try and fail again, she'll start on about the doctor, or she may talk to him herself. Jesus has made a mess of me.

There's one of them hanging about on a corner. Well, she might be one, or she could be a police-woman dressed up to look like a tart. I wheel my bike past, pretending that I haven't noticed her. See, I'm wondering whether I might have finished with the outside jobs in order to concentrate on something more spectacular and efficient – a brothel.

I switch on the bike lights and ride homeward, remembering how I used to look forward to time spent with my family. The bedroom curtains are closed, and no light shines, which is rather symbolic, because my whole life has become dark, no sun, no moon, no stars. I don't pray any more, not since I begged Jesus to come back and talk to me. Even Judas would do, because he'd be familiar with my dilemma.

After putting my bike away, I go inside and look for the meal she always leaves for me. She's been baking. My portion of steak pie in suet pastry is on a plate with vegetables, gravy and baby potatoes. Her cooking is mouth-wateringly good. I set the pan to boil, put the plate covered by the pan lid over the bubbling water, and read the newspaper while my dinner heats up. It smells wrong; perhaps it's my imagination.

It isn't my imagination. Laura loves kidney, as do Matt and Lucy. Me? I can't stand the stuff, and she knows it, which is why she's always made pies containing just steak. Is this her not-so-subtle way of telling me to leave or to make my own dinners? I feel a shift under my feet, as if the planet is re-aligning itself, a bit like an earthquake so tiny that it wouldn't register on any scale. My world is changing, and there's no turning back.

Boss was hopping mad, literally. Normally, he sat in his chair, far too chilled and laid back to stand, but he was upright, furious and shifting his body weight from one foot to the other. 'Who let him near the white room?' he roared. 'After all I've said about keeping to your own side of the business. Well?' He waited.

Nobody offered a reply.

'Who brewed it? Who injected him?'

Silence continued to reign.

'Because he was never a user. Whoever gave him the shot is used to a big dose of heroin, but he wasn't used to any, and he got too much. He grew a crop of decent cannabis, that's all. More by luck than good management, that lad produced top whack stuff, and I want to know which of you bastards killed him and what you intend to do with the body, because I am not taking the rap for this.'

No answer arrived.

'Right,' he said, 'if it wasn't somebody, it was everybody. I'm not talking about people working the grass, but yous lot on the white stuff had better get busy, because you'll be grafting tonight to make up for time lost today while you bury the boy.' Too furious to stay, he stalked out of the office. Roy Foley was dead, and his friend, Bill

158

Tyler, would want to see him in the not too distant future.

Boss walked back to the cottage, his mind working at about ninety miles an hour. The grass people would carry on in the left side of the barn, but the white team had a grisly job to manage. Damn them. He didn't mind them using a bit of 'wastage', but injecting and overdosing a new worker from the cannabis side was ... well, it was murder. 'Bloody months I took finding and developing this place, and what do I get? A dead boy, that's what.' He lit a cigar.

Bill Tyler. What the hell am I supposed to say to him? He's not the sharpest knife in the drawer, but he's not exactly backward, and he was a close pal of the dead boy. 'Shit and derision,' he cursed before pouring himself a double Scotch. 'I'll have to move again, take the whole shebang to another isolated place.' Isolated places took some finding, but there was no alternative. They couldn't stay here. The only one left behind would be poor Roy Foley...

'He won't come out. He won't do anything he's told.'

Eve held the phone away from her ear. For an old man with a bad heart, Don Crawford was a blast when it came to injuring eardrums. She spoke to him quietly. 'I'll be there tomorrow with your girls, Don.'

'Gordy needs Babs now. Murdoch's been sulking ever since she left, and he's stuck in the stable with Nicholas Nye. We can't even muck them out.'

'Who's Nicholas? Bloody room service? Don, I'm up to me eyes here, up past the eyebrows, actually. I've two new girls training, Belle's not back, I'm hanging on to Angela Whiplash by the skin of my teeth, and it's Friday. This is one of our busiest nights, and it's your damned horse, nothing to do with me.'

'He's his best friend,' Don said, sounding rather choked.

Eve, feeling lost, glanced at her watch; she had to do her first run in ten minutes. 'Who's whose best friend?'

Don was clearly losing his temper. 'Nicholas Nye's Murdoch's best friend. He's a blind donkey. They're inseparable.'

Eve tried hard not to seethe; she felt like a pressure cooker about to blow its top in a big way. She still had her curlers in, the books weren't balancing due to an oversight relating to a greengrocery order, the electricity bill had arrived, Babs and Sally, supposed to be helping the new girls, were lolling about in love all over the place... 'Don, I have to go.'

'But—'

'I'm going, Don.'

'And I'm coming to get my girls.'

'You can't. They're educating their replacements.' She slammed down the receiver and began dragging out her curlers. The phone rang again, but she ignored it. Let the old bugger stew – he'd had enough out of her lately. Her two new girls were nowhere near as pretty as Babs and Sally, so she was in danger of losing business.

On the drive to town, Eve thought about Trevor

Burns. He paid well, tipped the girls, was usually cheery and jovial, and he wanted to bring in a new client. A guy called Neil with a stick-thin wife and a boring job needed a bit of pleasure from time to time. She would need to interview him first on neutral ground, because she could usually assess men after just one brief encounter. Like kids, they were fairly transparent. Anyway, a woman with so much to lose had to watch her own back yard, since she didn't want men as guards, because they smacked of pimps. God, life was on the heavyweight side these days.

Still, she did her best. Getting a man into Meadowbank Farm wasn't quite as difficult as making a Freemason of him, but it was no walk in the park. Eve was a woman of well-honed instincts, and she would be meeting Mr Neil Carson in a week or so. Time would tell. All she needed was ten minutes with him, and her radar would have him sorted.

Where was the pick-up tonight? Ah yes, last Friday of the month – the Pier Head. She parked, listened to them grumbling as they climbed into the rear of the van. She was three minutes late. A couple more, and they'd probably have hanged her for treason. Or did treason merit a bullet? And if that greengrocer thought she was going to pay fourpence for a head of lettuce with more slugs than leaves, he had another think coming.

I probably went too far with the kidney in the pie. It's perhaps because I didn't know what to say, who to tell, whether to pack up the children and take them off to my mam and dad's house. I'm helpless, literally, so I'm in a strop like a teenager, even throwing my toys out of the pram like a baby. I can think of not one single person who might be able to guide me over this patch of rough ground. It's all too embarrassing, too personal to describe. Just thinking about what's happening is hard, because the words I have to use, even inside my own head, are difficult to live with.

But why the kidney? That was a very foolish act, because he's always hated it. I'm punishing him. This is my pathetic attempt at scourging, at sackcloth, ashes and no forgiveness, ever. His behaviour – is it behaviour? Can a man be responsible for things he does and says when he's unconscious? How can my husband sin while asleep?

By the way, I don't think I can take the job at the chip shop, since the way things stand just now I've no idea where I'll be in the next few months. There's a spare bed in Lucy's room, and I'm in it, because I can't spend another night in our bedroom, not after what's been happening. And I have to explain myself. Words. Words I must say to him, to my husband, the father of my children.

He's coming up the stairs. He's in the bathroom. The toilet flushes. He's at the washbasin, hands and teeth.

Neil's a very ritualistic person, everything in order, every day the same except for his shifts. That used to please me, but after ten years home no longer feels like a safe place with a predictable man in it.

Something dreadful has happened to Neil. He talks in his dreams and he ... well, he abuses himself while asleep. Words again. Words he says when he's dreaming... I have to change the sheets every day. In the past month, he hasn't made love to me. Does he not feel the wetness on the bedding? Why do his triumphant screams not waken him? I have so many questions, but no answers.

Does he think I don't see the dried stuff in the bed? I don't want this good, honest, trustworthy man near my children or near me. St Jude, hear my prayer. Why is the father of Lucy and Matt having ... those wet dream things that happen to teenage boys when their bodies are ... developing?

I gulp down some iced water from a glass next to my bed, and lie down with my face pointing to the wall. The door opens. Go away, please go away.

'Laura?'

He's whispering. That'll be for Lucy's sake.

'What?' I almost growl.

'Come downstairs,' he says.

I hear him padding down in slippers. Brown slippers. They last two years exactly, almost to the hour. Every alternate Christmas, he asks for the same brown slippers. On the in-between Christmases, it's a scarf or gloves or socks. He winds the grandmother clock fourteen times every evening, careful not to over-tighten the spring. When making cocoa, he pounds away at the original mix in the bottom of the mug, pours on hot milk mixed with boiling water, adds sugar, then does twenty-one stirs with the spoon. Forty-two if there are two mugs, eighty-four if the children want some too.

I'd better go downstairs.

Babs and Sal spent their last night at Meadow-bank Farm in a small ground-floor spare bedroom with their luggage piled all round the walls.

'We'll be OK, won't we?' the anxious Sally asked.

'Course we will. He's fascinated by the idea of watching two girls making love. If he doesn't have a heart attack, he'll be a very happy man.'

'I'm not sure I want anybody watching,' the younger girl moaned. 'And who's going to look after them poor lads in the hut?'

'Sorted. Go to sleep.'

Sally did as she was told, dozing with the top of her head nestling against her beloved's neck. As she drifted towards sleep, she saw a beautiful house with beautiful gardens and lots of happy animals.

Babs had left a letter for Cynthia to give to Belle on her return. Cynthia, in spite of her broad spectrum of sexual adventures, was a thoroughly dependable girl. If she borrowed cash, she returned it; if told a secret, she sat on it. So she held the letter, and Belle would get it as soon as she returned to Meadowbank. Belle would keep an eye on the occupants of the scout hut.

The lads now had a compendium of games, some playing cards, a domino set and a dartboard with darts. Their friends brought food and cash for them, so they were safe for the time being. If anything went wrong, the boys had Don's telephone number.

Sorted.

Six

He was sitting on the sofa, and he tapped the seat cushion next to his, inviting his wife to join him, but Laura chose to place herself in an armchair. She refused to contemplate the thought of physical contact with him, since the very idea of any closeness in the future almost turned her stomach. Even being in the same room wasn't easy.

Once settled, she folded her arms and waited for him to speak, since she was here at his invitation – or had he issued an order? She was the innocent one; she had the axe to grind. As Laura stared at him, something strange happened to her. Although she didn't know how or why, she suddenly found a place inside herself, an area she hadn't visited before. It was a cold island just south of her diaphragm, an isolated region in which this man didn't matter, because she had children, and they came first. Laura Carson had encountered her own strength.

Offended by her stay-away-from-me folded arms, Neil drew back his weak chin until it folded near his throat. His legs were crossed, and he swung the upper limb rhythmically, dangling one brown slipper from the toes. This was a signal that expressed displeasure or impatience. 'What's the matter?' he asked. 'Why the kidney all of a sudden? You know I can't stand any kind of offal.'

She gazed at him, suddenly finding no problem

in meeting his eyes. 'It's a good source of nourishment for the children,' she replied. 'They need variety in their diet. You're looking at the fireplace again.' She congratulated herself for sounding so normal in spite of a quickening heartbeat. Determinedly, she returned to the chilled place below her stomach.

He turned his head so rapidly that a red-hot crick shot up his neck. 'And why were you in Lucy's room? Is she having nightmares again?'

'No, she isn't. I'm in there because I don't want to sleep with you.' Her tone was calm, but brave. 'You can wash that set of sheets; I've had enough of your sick behaviour.' She couldn't believe that she was managing this so well. He seemed smaller, as if he were shrinking into the sofa. 'A man of your age having wet dreams? You really should see the doctor.'

He blinked stupidly, his hands balling themselves into tight fists. He wanted to hit her. She was his wife. He loved her, yet he longed to beat the life out of her.

Laura tutted, her head shaking slowly from side to side. 'And you talk. You talk about body parts, but you use crude words when you do. You wet the bed, not with wee, but with the other stuff, and you shout when that happens. I don't want to spend another night with you. I'm the one having nightmares. First you were screaming, and now you're carrying on like a demented creature. I've had enough of it – more than enough.'

He was still blinking. 'But I've no idea what's going on,' he pleaded. 'I'm asleep.'

'I know you are. You're acting crazy, and I can't

166

cope any longer.'

'What am I supposed to do?' he asked, raising his voice.

'Be quiet; you've made too much noise already, what with your night terrors and now this. You dream of a woman with big ... I'm not going to say the word, but it means breasts. As for her lower regions – well, I'd no idea that such words existed, because most were new to me. But the rest of the phrases left not much room for doubt. My children will hear you; the neighbours might well hear you. It's all too much, Neil. You're shouting the F word.'

He put his head in his hands. 'Jesus, help me,' he mumbled.

She rose to her feet. 'There are two ways of dealing with this.'

He lifted his head hopefully.

Laura continued. 'Neil, either you leave this house or I take the children to my parents' place. The decision is yours. You seem to be having some kind of crisis, but you need to have it in someone else's bed, and far away from your family. Perhaps you have premature senile dementia, but I think you need to turn into a dirty old man well beyond the reach of Matt and Lucy.' She swept out of the room without awarding him a single backward glance.

On the stairs, she found herself shaking, while her knees threatened to buckle. The adrenalin was deserting her, and she felt grateful to return to the spare bed. He hadn't followed her up. She lay, almost as stiff as a board, trying hard to court sleep. It was impossible. What would the neighbours say? What would Mum, Dad and Father Doherty think? The school? She would have to explain the disappearance of her husband there, too. Life so far had been relatively simple, but this was about to be a complicated new beginning.

When she woke from a short doze, it was dawn, and he was clattering about in the bedroom across the landing. She heard the slamming of a drawer and the unmistakable sound of clothes hangers colliding angrily in his wardrobe. He was leaving.

Lucy sat up and rubbed her eyes. 'Mummy? Why are you in here?'

The first lie was born. 'Your daddy's started snoring. He sounds like a train running through the house.'

Laura realized that he was listening, because he'd stopped crashing about. She took advantage of the silence to produce the bigger lie, because she knew he was packing. 'He's going on a course for people who want promotion. Many of the lectures are in the evenings, so they all have to sleep in a big hotel where the course is being held.'

'Oh. All right.' Lucy snuggled herself down under the covers and went back to sleep immediately.

Laura smiled. How precious was the innocence of the young, allowing them to sleep or wake within a split second. She stood up, pulled on her robe and went to check on Matt. He was curled up with his teddy bear and remained secure in the land of dreams.

Steeling herself, she crossed the landing and entered the marital bedroom. 'Thank you,' she told Neil. 'The children can continue at the same school if I don't have to move out.'

'I'll send you housekeeping money,' he said.

'Again, thank you.'

He left the room carrying a large suitcase and a canvas bag. 'Goodbye, Laura,' he said.

She stood at the top of the flight while he descended. Goodbye? That word had never been used in this house, because there was a sense of finality built into it; they always used bye, or see you later, but never the full goodbye. 'Neil?'

'What?' He didn't even bother to look at her.

'Come for a meal when you can.'

At last, he turned and glanced at her for no more than an instant. Without saying a word, he put down the case, swivelled to face the door, opened it, picked up his luggage and set it outside. Taking a Yale key from a pocket, he placed it on the hall table, left the house and closed the door quietly in his wake. Goodbye. He really meant it, then.

Laura sat on the stairs, her mind strangely blank. For several seconds, not a single thought wandered through her frozen brain; perhaps she was in shock. She leaned her head against the wall and wept. Thank goodness the children were not at school, because she hadn't the energy to prepare them. The thinking began, and she wished it would stop.

She'd never paid a bill. The responsibility for a household had not rested on her shoulders, as he had played his part. Children needed two parents, because that was how God had designed

169

humankind. Neil was going to be paying rent somewhere. There was something she needed to do.

Laura dressed herself quickly and started to set the table for breakfast. The job in the Bramwells' chip shop might go some way towards covering the shortfall in household money. Matt and Lucy could play with the Bramwell twins during school holidays, and she'd been promised free wet fish to bring home every Friday to cook for tea. The Bramwells were good, Catholic people, and their children were adorable. She'd promised to let them know by today, and she would. As head of the family, she must learn to make decisions. It wasn't going to be easy, but if she revisited that cold place from time to time, surely she would be able to work things out?

Matt and Lucy clattered down the stairs. The new start had begun.

Mad Murdoch approached the open stable door tentatively. He raised his magnificent head, looked out at his mother, Murma, who was standing still in the paddock and probably considering the wonders of the universe, like apples, carrots, and the misbehaviour of her recalcitrant son. Murdoch nudged Nicholas Nye and emerged into daylight with the blind donkey in his wake.

'About bleeding time,' Gordy Hourigan exclaimed loudly. 'I thought you'd retired without paying any tax or National Insurance. There'll be no pension if you don't buck up, lad.'

The lively gelding sniffed the air, his nostrils flaring and narrowing many times as he analysed the day. With his tail waving almost listlessly at flies that had gathered in his filthy stable, he ambled nonchalantly round the paddock's perimeter. Two stable boys leapt forward with rakes, forks, shovels and wheelbarrows; at last, Murdoch's place of residence could be cleaned. The animal had been in a bad mood for days, and no one but the donkey had wanted to share space with him.

'It bloody stinks in here,' one of the boys yelled. The sitting/standing tenant of the stable and his donkey friend had been given winter feed, as Murdoch had refused to emerge even to graze, and Nicholas Nye had remained by his side. The horse had discovered and perfected a talent for sulking. Gordy Hourigan found himself wondering about the male equivalent of prima donna because the horse had an appalling attitude. It was Babs. Gordy knew this was all about Babs.

Nicholas Nye, guessing his best friend's intentions, clung to Murma, who never suffered from or indulged in flights of fancy. Murdoch had a plan, and the wise donkey knew when to stay away from his protector.

Gordy's gaze was fixed firmly on his naughty pupil. He had never worked with so great a horse; nor had he met a worse one. The powerful yet strangely graceful steed was beginning to prance as if aiming for proficiency in a military two-step with a bit of the St Bernard's waltz thrown in for good measure. If all else failed, he might clatter about in a circus.

Murdoch nodded constantly, urging himself onward, trotting, cantering, picking up speed until at last the nodding slowed and he was streamlined.

'Bugger,' Gordy whispered. 'Here we go again. He knows she's on her way.'

Murdoch cleared the five foot paddock fence as if he owned invisible wings, and after he had landed gracefully he greeted four dogs with a warm whinny as they ran towards him. He stopped, lay on the grass and allowed the smaller creatures to make a fuss of him. They leapt on him, licked him, tugged at his tail, chewed on his mane and barked. He played with them, pushing them gently with a front leg. Murdoch was a star, and this was his curtain call.

'One way or another, that animal will be the death of me,' Gordy mused aloud while watching the tatty mongrels worshipping their master. 'He'll be wanting a bouquet of roses soon.' Geese, cats and chickens remained out of reach, of course. A natural affiliation between equines and canines appeared to exist at Wordsworth House, probably because Mr Crawford had encouraged it, but smaller beasts knew when to keep their distance.

Murdoch raised his beautiful head again just as Eve Mellor's van pulled onto the gravel driveway. The day was living up to his expectations, because he had tasted Babs in the air. He rose to his feet, and the dogs scattered. For Murdoch, nothing else mattered now. She had arrived, and the real fun could begin.

As Babs jumped down from the vehicle, a tall, handsome man of middle age approached her. 'Miss Schofield?' he asked, extending his right hand.

Distracted by the horse, she smiled, nodded and walked past the stranger.

Gordy stopped her in her tracks. 'That's Mr Philip Macey,' he whispered. 'He's a great man, a town councillor, supporter of dozens of charities, and Murdoch's other owner. When he knows you, he asks you to call him Lippy. That's his nickname.'

Babs returned to Mr Philip Macey. 'Sorry,' she said, 'but I love that terrible horse. I've seen you in the papers.'

The visitor shook her hand. 'The nuisance has boundless potential, but he's picky and stubborn. I hear he's taken a liking to you.'

She shrugged. 'No accounting for taste, is there?'

Mr Macey's smile broadened in response to her accent. She was Liverpool to the bone, and Liverpool delivered strong fillies. 'And you don't ride?'

'Not yet.'

He led her into the kitchen. 'Mr Crawford's resting upstairs. I understand that you and your friend are intending to look after him because of his heart problem–' He stopped abruptly; Murdoch was coming through the door.

Babs sat at the kitchen table and waited until the animal placed his nose in her hair. 'He'll be all right now,' she announced, thanking her lucky stars that this man seemed to know nothing about Don Crawford's sexual requirements.

Lippy Macey sat in a chair opposite hers, a frown and a smile fighting for dominance on his face. 'This has been – and continues to be – a difficult young horse to train,' he explained. 'If he has a bond with you, we must take full advantage. He's very intelligent, stubborn and feisty. Where's your friend?'

'Sally? Still in the van, I think. She's not keen on great big animals.'

'And you are?'

She turned and looked at her tormentor. 'It's just this smelly horse. Will you stop spitting in my hair, Murdoch? Go on. I'll play with you later.' She grinned at her human companion. 'I've visited twice so far, and he always goes for my hair. Still, I'll get compensation for shampoo used, I suppose – oh, and I'll have a hard hat with my hair tied up underneath it.'

'He obeys you, Miss Schofield,' Mr Macey said as the horse executed an admirable three-point turn in order to leave the house. 'Have you seen National Hunt racing?'

Babs offered no reply.

'Well, have you?'

She spoke. 'Jumping over fences and stuff? Yeah, I've seen it on the telly. They break their legs and get shot, and I don't mean the jockeys. It wants stopping. Flat racing's all right, but–'

'But Murdoch's a flier.'

'I know.'

'We have our eyes on the Grand National.'

'I know.'

'We want you to ride him.'

'I know.'

'Will you?'

Babs shrugged. 'Look, they don't let women ride, and I've nearly broke me neck falling off a bike, so he'd get to the finish without a rider.'

'If he drops you, he'll stay with you. Can't you feel his love?' He paused. 'The rules are going to be relaxed, and women will ride in the National.

174

Hasn't Gordy told you that?'

She pondered for a moment. 'Yes.'

'He would grind to a halt and stand over you to prevent the rest of the field trampling you. His attitude is that of a warhorse, and if you read about World War One and earlier wars, you'll know how many mounts gave their lives while attempting to shield their riders. You are what we need, and you're all he needs. Gordy Hourigan is a great trainer, and Murdoch occasionally shows him an edge of respect, but that animal runs from the heart. Will you help?'

Again, Babs raised her shoulders. 'You know I'll do my best, but I draw the line at sleeping in the stable with him. And you'll need a man jockey on standby in case I'm not allowed.'

Lippy Macey laughed. 'He has Nicholas Nye to share his stable. And you shall go to the ball, Cinderella.'

Babs failed to hear the last few words. 'And he has his mam close by. Mr Macey, have you seen Murma? I mean, Murdoch looks nothing like his mother, does he?'

'I have seen her, of course. It seems impossible, doesn't it? She looks as if she should be between the shafts of a gypsy caravan. But I understand that his sire's like greased lightning.'

'Nobody can catch him,' Babs said, the words deformed by a giggle.

'Catch him, Miss Schofield? Very few see him. He probably breaks the sound barrier when he's on the run. His real owner lives two counties away from Murma's old stable. He's a bay with a very slender and crooked white flash on his nose, so

175

he's recognizable when fairly still and fairly close, which is seldom. He covered Murdoch's mother, and photographs were taken by the stable manager; that was the sole proof of our foal's rather mixed pedigree. Mr Crawford bought the foal and the dam, because he's soft-hearted. And luckily, we became accidental owners of a very fine animal.'

Sally crept in. 'The horse came in the house,' she gasped.

'We noticed,' Mr Macey said, 'and if he continues to eat Miss Schofield's hair, we may be obliged to provide her with a wig.'

'I'll buy a few,' Babs said, winking cheekily at the seated gentleman. 'I could have a change of colour whenever I fancied.'

Mr Macey laughed.

'Sal?' Babs turned in her seat. 'Just run up and see if Mr Crawford needs anything. The doctor has him on bed rest.'

Sally left the kitchen. She could see that the man at the table was special and that an important meeting was taking place.

Negotiations continued. 'My name's Philip,' he said, 'but friends call me Lippy.'

'Barbara – usually Babs.'

'Right you are, Usually Babs. Don and I will organize lessons. You will go eventually with Murdoch and Hourigan to showjumping arenas just to get used to the rhythm of hurdles. Before that, I have gentler horses for you to ride. Once ready, you will ride Murdoch on my land, which has plenty of fences and hedges.'

'He'll be jealous if I ride other horses,' she

warned him.

'Tough,' was the reply. 'Once you graduate to Murdoch's level, you will learn when to stand in the stirrups with your seat away from the saddle. Don will not allow the whip to be over-used, so you must become accustomed to stroking the horse with it. It will take time, but we have plenty of that, because Murdoch is far too young for the race. The younger mounts have speed, but little stamina. We have five years at least to achieve the right standard. And, of course, you will run in other steeplechases first. Also, remember that Murdoch is a secret; we don't want the racing community to take an interest for a while. The odds for the National will be short enough once he starts winning elsewhere, so we mustn't tempt fate.'

Babs pursed her lips when the soliloquy reached its end. 'So Mr Crawford is an animal-lover?'

'Yes.'

'But he's happy to see Murdoch shot if there's a pile-up at one of those horrible fences? Does he know how many horses die or get injured? Does he know how many get too winded to breathe without help and that the Aintree course is five times more lethal than any other steeplechase?'

Lippy nodded. 'He also knows that Murdoch can make it. Babs, it's about spirit and bravery and love for the rider. Do you have any idea how many jockeys run that race on an animal they scarcely know? Murdoch with you on his back will be carrying a jockey he treasures. He will see you almost every day. Hourigan has always had his mind set on the National, but Don wasn't sure until he learned about you having been chosen by Murdoch. Spirit, love, a good ribcage, great lungs, strong legs, combative attitude – Murdoch has them all. He will win. You will win. We are going to win. You, my dear, will be the first woman to finish first.'

Babs Schofield drummed her fingers on the table. 'I've been reading about it,' she said. 'It's a death trap for the horses, but we'll need to wait for a few more dead or crippled jockeys before the damned race gets stopped. If my horse dies, you will answer for it.'

The corners of his mouth twitched. 'Your horse?'

Babs nodded vigorously. 'Yes, mine. It's nothing to do with money or ownership – you just said so. He chooses me, so he's mine. I belong to him.'

'And he to you?'

'Yes. Anyway, I might be no good at it. No need to jump Becher's till we get there, eh?' She stood up. 'And remember – I'm only a woman. I'll just get our stuff from the van before Eve throws a purple fit with custard.'

'Eve?' he asked.

'She's just our driver.' Smiling to herself, Babs went out to get the luggage. From this day, that's all Eve would be – the woman who ferried passengers and luggage. Babs had met a gentleman, a real gentleman who was going to improve life no end. And she had a horse of her own, a champion in the making who loved her to bits, just the way she loved him.

Murdoch followed Babs to the van. Eve had

deposited the girls' bags on the gravel drive and was safely back behind the steering wheel.

'Thanks, Eve,' Babs said through the open window on the driver's side. 'For everything.' Until this moment, the younger woman hadn't realized that she quite liked Eve.

Eve's jaw dropped. What was little Miss Trouble up to now?

'I mean it.' God, this falling in love with a horse was a strange business. Babs was softening, even towards people she'd never liked. 'Bets are off, Eve. I don't want to gamble with a man's life, so get my five hundred back off Kate, yes?'

Eve managed to speak. 'Right you are.'

'Open me a bank account at the Trustee, will you? Just send me the bank book here. Me and this lunatic breathing down me neck are going to have adventures. Don't say anything, because I'm still shocked about it, too.'

Eve frowned. 'Are you all right, Babs?'

'Never been better.'

'Well, good luck to you and Sally. You'll be missed, especially by Belle.'

'But not by you, eh?'

'That loony horse is eating your hair.'

'Yes, he does that.'

'Ta-ra then, Babs. No hard feelings, eh?'

'None at all. Ta-ra, Eve.'

The younger woman stood with her horse and watched as Eve reversed through the open gates. The new chapter had begun, and a real gent was in charge. Sorted. Again.

BODY OF LIVERPOOL BOY IDENTIFIED

The body found yesterday evening in the Halewood district of Liverpool has been identified as that of Roy Foley, aged 18, from Seaforth. A post mortem examination will be performed today. A local woman whose dog unearthed the body during a walk has been taken to stay with family members in London. She is said to be requiring medical treatment due to shock and anxiety.

Buildings close to the burial site have been cordoned off, though police have given no reason for this action. According to a local businessman, a cottage, a barn and some dilapidated sheds are now under police guard. As far as we know, there has been no arrest and no one is being questioned at this time.

It took a while for Bill Tyler to read the column before he folded the newspaper and left the house. Everybody was out, so he had no explaining to do and no one to help with the reading, though he'd got the gist of the article. He shoved the paper into the saddlebag before mounting his bike; it wasn't strictly his, because it was shared between him and two brothers, but this was an emergency. If somebody else needed it – tough luck. The shock hadn't yet sunk in properly, and he was reacting as sensibly as he could manage.

The other boys. They were in a shed with a load of drugs belonging to a chap called Boss. Roy had been working for him and Roy was dead. Murdered, probably. 'I have to go now,' he mumbled, 'because I'm working tomorrow.' Poor Roy. Poor,

180

clever, stupid Roy was dead. He'd had brains enough for English, maths and science, but not enough sense to keep himself safe. In Roy, there had been scarcely any fear, so he'd copped it in his teens. 'Is it right or left here?' Bill mouthed. Roy would have known... Roy wasn't available; he would never enjoy another day on earth. It was all so bloody wrong, but more lives were at stake, and only Bill Tyler could save them, as long as...

He swallowed, his throat painfully dry. As long as they weren't already dead.

According to the *Echo*, there had been no arrests made, so the buildings mentioned in the article had probably been abandoned in a hurry. If Boss and his gang were in need of money, they'd be going for the stash in the hut.

He swallowed again, wishing he'd brought some water or pop. Any killing was one too many, but this time it was Roy Foley, Bill's best mate, so his fury was strangely hot and cold at the same time. The icy bit sat in his stomach like a lump of lead, but his overtaxed brain burned furiously.

They'd been at nursery together. They'd gone through infants and juniors as an unlikely pair, and had graduated to seniors, shoplifting and burglary in each other's company. 'Stay away from that boy,' Dad had yelled almost daily. 'He's a wrong bugger, just you mark my words.'

Oh well, all the proof Dad needed was now in a saddlebag on the back of a shared bike, and it was on its way to a shed in a field in a deserted part of ... of where? Hadn't Boss mentioned Knowsley? Wherever, Bill had to find the place, because those boys mattered. He pedalled till his feet were sore, his legs ached and his backside was numb. A field and a hut. He had to find the three lads. Roy was dead, and more people might need saving.

Stopping at a newsagent's shop, he spent his last few coppers on a bottle of sarsaparilla. Nothing in his life thus far had tasted better. With his terrible thirst finally slaked, he sat on a wall to have a think. They'd approached the place from Halewood that first night with Boss, but he should remember the route from the hut to Seaforth, because they'd been given a lift home, and he was doing the same in reverse, wasn't he? It had been dark and ... oh, what if he was too late?

Bill and Roy had been to the scout hut only once, on the night when all the cannabis had been sold to Boss. The big man had needed to hide another stash, and it was stored with three teenagers in a smelly, hot building in the back of beyond. Roy and Bill had been commandeered to help transfer their own stuff from the condemned house to Halewood, then to help shift surplus from Halewood or Hunt's Cross to ... to where? They'd gone along in the second of two vans, the first having been used to carry cannabis and so forth. The so forth was the real worry, as it might be worth a bomb, while boys were clearly of little value to Boss, since they were replaceable. 'We know where you are; we'll know where to find your families...'

Again, he stopped pedalling and sat on a grass verge. Where was he? Where were the lads? Bill glanced to his left and saw red. A phone box. 999. He needed Roy, but there was no Roy. He could be ... what was the word? Anonymous? It

182

was something like that. Jesus, his heart was going like a train with no brakes, and his brain was on fire. Think, think. Remember the details. There were tents and stuff belonging to scouts; the drugs were under that lot. The place had just one big window and one door. It was a single door, not a double like garages had.

He opened another single door; it was bright red with rectangles of glass in it. 'I don't need money,' he whispered. Which was just as well, since he had none left. 999. His hand shook as he pulled the dial all the way round three times. 'Police,' he said to the operator, his voice high-pitched and girlish. O God, O God.

It poured out of him as soon as a cop answered. 'Don't ask for me name, cos I can't say it in case they get me mam and dad.'

'Calm down, son.'

'I can't; I'm too scared.'

'All right. Where are you?'

'In a phone box and I don't know where I am. It's about them what killed that lad down Halewood. There's three more in a hut—'

'Three more boys?'

'Yes.'

'Are they dead?'

'No. Er ... I don't know. There's drugs under tents and all that, cos it used to be a scouts' club-house. One window, one door, it has. The lads is them what run away from that school a few weeks back. I think the nearest place is Knowsley, but I'm not sure. There's a bloke called Boss. He's tall and a bit fat and he smokes cigars. He's from Halewood, I think.'

183

There was a slight pause. 'Anything else?'

'They'd kill me if they knew I'd grassed 'em up, like.'

'Can you find your way home?'

'I think so.' Bill slammed down the receiver, left the box and picked up the bike. His legs shook, and his hands didn't seem to be working well either. He couldn't get his knees to support him, so he sat down again next to the bike. At the age of eighteen, after mucking about for years, he was starting proper work with his dad. He had to be grown up now. Yet he sobbed like a baby, tears storming down his face, vision distorted, heart going like the clappers again.

Although he didn't realize at the time, Bill Tyler became a man that night. He would always be slow when it came to reading and remembering, but his long walk on the wild side had finally ended. The law would never again be broken by him. In a sense, Roy Foley's death had been a blessing, since it gave Bill a push in the right direction. He finally found the way homeward, got back and listened to a big row about the bike and a spoilt meal.

Without saying a word, he allowed his brothers to rant on. When he gave them the *Echo* opened at Roy's page, they quietened. He stared at them blankly, turned and went to bed, taking with him the remains of his sarsaparilla. Nothing mattered now except for two things: he hoped the lads in the hut were safe and that he wouldn't let his dad down at work tomorrow.

In the absence of Babs and Sal, Ian, Phil and John

the Stam had accepted Belle Horrocks as their new champion. When she banged and shouted at the door one evening, they didn't hesitate to open it. 'Get out now,' she told them, 'and put as much space as you can between here and yourselves. I have to go back before I'm missed. Now, run as fast as you can.' She shoved a bit of paper into Ian's hand. 'Get gone. There's police everywhere.' She fled into the gathering dusk.

The lads grabbed their running bags; all three had been ready to escape almost since their arrival here. 'S-s-stay together,' John begged as they left their shelter. They could hear the bells on police cars driving through the lanes. As the sounds grew louder, panic beat hard in the breasts of the fugitives.

'Come on,' Ian urged. He had been on a recce one night while his fellow escapees had slept. The scout motto *Be Prepared* seemed to be rubbing off on him – it was the only vaguely decorative item in the shed. 'Coal cellar under the brothel,' he managed on what felt like his last breath. They fought their way through trees and bushes, running down the side of the farmhouse until they reached the rear expanse of garden. 'In here.' He lifted the grating and held it while his two companions jumped into blackness and onto sharp lumps of coal.

'Are you not coming with us?' Phil asked.

'No. Cover yourselves in coal dust and hide. Climb into the coal if you can. I'll be back.'

'Don't l-leave us,' John pleaded. 'I'm s-scared.'

'Hide,' Ian snapped. With no idea of his destination, he ran blindly towards another field. It was

185

almost time to give up; they had made their point, they were nearly fifteen, and they all stank to high heaven for want of a decent bath. Did police stations have baths in them? He doubted that. Where could he get clean enough to give himself up and betray his friends? They stank, too...

Ian ran until he could run no more. When he was beyond exhausted, he stopped and listened; silence, blessed silence. 'I should have brought the bike,' he mumbled while crouching in a ditch. He had to act quickly, as his mates had very little food and water in their packs, since escape equipment needed to be lightweight. It was time to talk. He might go through the *Echo* if the beans needed spilling; the paper would have an exclusive, and deservedly so, because it had been on the side of the runaways since day one. Yes, let the journalists arrange for a meeting with the cops.

He would sleep on it. Where could he sleep? Should he carry on moving in the hope of finding shelter? It wasn't cold, wasn't raining, and he suddenly felt too exhausted to move. There was another point to be considered. If he, Phil and John left it too long before giving themselves up, the public might forget them and the abuse inflicted by the brothers.

The ditch was dry, so he might as well stay where he was. Tomorrow morning, he would reach a decision. He wrapped himself in his coat...

A sound woke him. It was a whistle, a police whistle. God, had they found the other two in the cellar? He peeped over the rim of the ditch and saw that the cops were walking away, flashlights directed westward, so they were going back across

186

the fields in the direction of the scout hut. Reminding himself to breathe, he lowered his head and lay flat. God, he was still holding the piece of paper Belle had given him! He pushed it into a pocket and tried to relax. The police would not come back tonight; some would stay to guard the shed, though.

Meadowbank Farm was in a state bordering on the chaotic. Cynthia had been entertaining a person of importance, so he was collected by Eve and taken out to his car in a state of near-undress. Belle, who had no client, returned from her foray to the scout hut and followed Kate round the house, turning pictures so that erotica became bunches of flowers or scenes of pretty little cottages with smoke emerging from chimneys.

Angela Whiplash shifted anything that was mobile and hung curtains and sheets over fixed items. Nothing much could be done with ceiling mirrors and the like, but in all rooms, purple and red bed linens and covers were hidden under pastel blankets or plain sheets. The girls dressed themselves in 'normal' clothes, scraped off make-up and gathered in the kitchen. Meadowbank was now a hostel for homeless girls and women.

Eve ran round the house as fast as her weight would allow; she was catching men. After bundling them all into the van, she drove like the clappers down the uneven lane until she reached the East Lancashire Road. Once on the main highway, she slowed down to normal speed. She was possibly about to lose her little empire, but she was determined to hang on to her driving licence.

Things were bad enough even without intervention by the law. Angela was threatening to quit, as was Belle Horrocks. Belle had been the most stable and dependable of the girls, but she was now on the brink of leaving Meadowbank. Babs had gone, Sally had gone, and their replacements were still learning the job. Client numbers had dropped. Trevor Burns had stopped visiting. A butcher, he had often brought gifts of joints for weekends, and had always been cheerful. After recommending Neil Carson, he had disappeared. Neil Carson. Eve didn't like him, though she couldn't fathom why. In theory and when interviewed, he came across as an ideal customer, and yet...

Those who wanted Baby companions were fewer these days. Eve had lost at least a third of Babs's clients. Meanwhile, Barbara Schofield was living the life of Riley up in Southport. If that girl fell in shit, she would always emerge smelling of roses. Don Crawford's place was under consideration as an animal shelter, though Babs and Sal were to be housed there in the event of Don's death. Well, perhaps Babs belonged among strays, though young Sal was a lovely girl. 'What the hell am I going to do?' Eve muttered to herself. Should she close down, sell up and hope to live on the equity?

In town, she decanted her passengers and spoke to those who waited for her. 'The cops are a few hundred yards from the farm,' she told them. 'According to Belle, they're looking for drugs stashed in a shed somewhere, so I'm shutting down for tonight.'

'What about tomorrow?' someone asked.

Eve ploughed through her busy brain. 'The farm will be closed until the cops have given up. Look in the *Echo* personals every night. I'll find a way of letting you know when I'm re-opening. After that, you'll have to phone me for details like pick-up locations. That's all I can do; the police are too close for comfort.'

She drove homeward in the empty van. Her life's work was going down the drain, and all because some stupid vagabonds had stored something or other in a hut that stood hundreds of yards from the farmhouse. There was no doubt in her mind – she and the girls would be questioned. It would be enough to make them all quit, she believed. Perhaps it was time to go. She might well have been thinking right after all. 'I'm getting a bit old for this,' she muttered.

Parking outside Meadowbank, she turned off the engine, closed her eyes and wondered who the hell would want to live here on a windy and ex- posed plain in a house that wasn't exactly pretty. There were no amenities to hand, no decent views, and there was no protection from the vagaries of British weather. 'Sod it,' she cursed. Sighing deeply, Eve Mellor climbed down from the driver's seat, locked the van and entered her house. It was all out of her hands, and she must accept what fate dished up for her.

Acting Detective Sergeant Eddie Barnes visited Lime Street Station at the end of his shift. Dave Earnshaw, still in uniform, greeted his erstwhile partner with a broad grin. 'What time do you call

189

this?' he asked. 'Oh, I like the suit, by the way. My new bloke's a rookie, so he's searching the men's lavs. How was your first day?'

'Grim,' was the answer. 'We just missed catching the runaways from that monks' place. We found a massive stash of stuff, and we think it's Albert Shuttleworth again.'

'Bugger.'

'Exactly. It's always him, and he always gets away.'

'Holy Mary,' said a familiar voice.

Both officers turned. 'Hi, Nellie,' Dave said. 'Are you saying your beads again, eh?'

'I am not. There's little time for prayer when I'm doing my life's work.' She drew Eddie to one side and lowered her voice to a whisper. 'Mary's a double agent. All the churchgoing and preaching is supposed to be a front for her drug-dealing, and she does deal up to a point, or she sets up deals. According to Mary, who deliberately keeps poor company, Shuttleworth's in Moss Side, Manchester, but only the good Lord knows where the rest of his team is. Your Chief Constable has been on to Manchester's Chief Constable. The house in Moss Side will be raided at dawn tomorrow. So you'll have your man.'

Eddie relaxed. 'He could go down for murder.'

Nellie shook her head. 'Rumour has it that one of the lads working with heroin overdosed that poor boy, but they were all ordered by Shuttleworth to get rid of the body. Holy Mary told us yesterday. But yes, Boss – as he likes to be addressed – will go down for something, but it might not be murder. More likely accessary after the fact or some such nonsense. And for being a drugs baron, of course.'

Detective Sergeant Eddie Barnes stared hard at the old woman. 'Who's "us", Nellie?'

She tapped the side of her nose. 'Let's just say that Holy Mary and I do a job very similar to yours, though we answer to a higher authority.' She pulled him further away from his ex-partner.

'MI5?' Eddie asked in a soft voice.

'Higher than that,' she replied.

He shrugged. 'That's a matter of opinion.'

A familiar enigmatic smile spread itself across Smelly Nellie's face. It disappeared when she changed the subject briefly. 'The killer of prostitutes seems to be taking a rest, and we have now acquired a murderer whose target may be teenage boys. He'd been filled with drugs – they found an ante-mortem bruise on his arm, just the one puncture wound and no signs of regular use. The lad was killed by an overdose; he probably had no tolerance for the substance. Drugs are being cleared from the site, and Shuttleworth's fingerprints are all over the cottage. His minions slept where they worked and in sheds in the garden.'

Eddie pondered. 'How come you know so much, Nellie?'

'I make it my business to know.'

'Bu–' The plain clothes officer scratched his head. 'What the hell's going on, Nellie?'

She tutted at him.

'Come on, tell me,' Eddie begged.

'Just know I'm on your side, as is Holy Mary. I may look and smell like a vagrant, but I'm doing a job. Trust me – I'm not here just to hang about looking like the wreck of the *Hesperus*. Method in madness, son.' She walked away with the famous battered and bruised Silver Cross pram.

Dave had wandered off to find his rookie partner, who had been in the men's for at least fifteen minutes. Eddie, wearing his wedding suit, which happened to be the only one he owned, stood and watched Nellie. He was off duty, but he intended to carry on working until he got to the bottom of Nellie's secret. She was a police informant; that fact was as clear as a spring morning.

Neil Carson was confused. Having been set on a path dictated by heaven, he seemed to have taken a turning off the main road, and he had enjoyed every moment of his foray into the unknown. The wilderness was a happy place filled with soft-fleshed women, bright colours, sexual fulfilment and, latterly, the punishment he deserved and enjoyed.

Angela gave him exactly what he needed – a good hiding followed by a level of joy he had never experienced until now, until her, until Angela. But his adventures were over for a while, because the house had been closed down due to an invasion of the district by police.

He sat in his cramped attic room. It contained a bed, a small table, a chair, a cooker, a sink, one cupboard and a wardrobe with a filthy curtain instead of a door. Sandwiched between him and another tenant there was a small, shabby bathroom with cracked tiles, a dirty floor and a bath so ancient that its top surface was peeling and showing rust. He replaced washers in the aged brass taps, cleaned the lavatory and included in his rent book a complaint about conditions. A written message was returned to him. It stated that if he wanted the Ritz he'd need to pay a lot more, and he could leave whenever he chose. Neil was angry, because two thirds of his net income went to Laura and the children, so better accommodation was beyond his reach.

He remembered the ordered, comfortable life with the children and Laura in a clean house. She was a good housekeeper, a loving mother, an excellent cook and–

And she was no longer his because he was no longer himself. Who was he? What was he? He stood up and started pacing about the small area. They had been there that night; Judas had even drunk the beer. Mary Magdalene had been mentioned, as had the city's prostitutes, and he had been given clear instructions to rid the streets of sin.

What if he'd imagined all that? Was he mad? Did a mad person know he was mad? Did being sane enough to question his sanity mean that he was not insane? O God, O God. The pacing had to stop before the old biddy below started banging on her ceiling again. He sat and considered his terrible situation. The idea of returning home had to be discounted, since Laura didn't want him, and he had ceased to desire her bony body and her Victorian resignation in his bed. Matt and Lucy he missed terribly, but he couldn't bring them here and ... oh, he was so lonely. He needed something to do, a plan, a project. 'You have something to do,' he said aloud. 'Clean the streets.'

Detective Sergeant (Acting) Eddie Barnes came to a halt at Miller's Bridge. Nellie walked down towards the river, stopping at a large old house set back from the street.

He watched as she disappeared down the side of the building. It was Magdalene House (pronounced Maudlin, he seemed to remember), and it was inhabited by women. When she did not reappear, he guessed that she had entered the place by a rear door. So this was the answer to many questions.

After waiting for about fifteen minutes, he followed in her recent footsteps. She was below ground in a lit cellar. He peered down through grating and watched as she took off her filthy coat and dumped it in a large chest. Everything in the room was clean to the point of spotlessness, and there was no sign of the pram.

Feeling like Peeping Tom, he returned hurriedly to the street and walked to a pub on the corner. As he was no longer in uniform, he entered the premises and ordered a double Irish before parking himself at a corner table.

Nellie was a Veronica. Veronica had created the Veil of Veronica by wiping the face of Jesus on His way to crucifixion; this sisterhood named after her was a working order as opposed to a contemplative commune. The nuns nursed in hospitals, taught in schools, fed the homeless, counselled the young, cared for the aged and sat with the dying.

He swallowed his drink in seconds. Smelly Nellie

and Holy Mary were brides of Christ, so yes, they answered to the highest of all authorities. Nellie lived her days among filth and squalor, while Mary took her life in her hands in order to mislead those who dealt drugs. Eddie remembered Quick Mick lying on the ground in Lime Street Station. Nellie had touched the head of her old friend, probably with holy water or even the oils of Extreme Unction.

Humbled without understanding fully the reason for his mood, the acting detective began the walk home. He would hold the secrets of Nellie and Mary, as they must be kept as safe as possible. There were good people in the world, and he intended to protect two of them.

Seven

Ian Foster woke when the sun bled over the Pennines to spill its pale, autumnal light onto the Mersey plain. He was afraid, disorientated, uncomfortable and shivering in a ditch under a sprinkling of dew. After the passage of several seconds, he pushed cold hands into coat pockets and found the paper given to him by Belle Horrocks yesterday. He blinked back tears of gratitude, because it was a ten bob note wrapped in a page ripped from a notebook. Among other things, that page bore the address and telephone number of Babs Schofield. The number, written by Babs on a wall in the hut, was already etched into his brain, but he appreciated the thoughtfulness of Belle, who scarcely knew him, Phil and John. There was kindness in the world, but would he ever trust males again?

The certainty that it was time to give up remained with him as he rooted in his bag for food. The letters had been effective, but some people had short memories, and the school run by the Brothers Pastoral needed to be closed down within the foreseeable future. Other boys had suffered, and Ian wanted them to be given the chance to talk. So. He decided to collect his thoughts, two lads covered in coal dust, and a way of getting them and himself clean.

There were public baths in town, but the hatchet-faced women who doled out soap and towels would surely refuse to admit three stinking boys and a load of coal dust. And anyway, the facility was too far away from here, wasn't it? 'Strike while the iron is hot,' he mumbled. They didn't have an iron either, so clean clothes would be creased as well as stolen. For a reason Ian couldn't be bothered to question, he wanted to look smart during interviews with reporters and police. Babs might sort out something or other if he phoned her...

His breakfast was a sickly mix of milk chocolate and lemonade. Having read somewhere that mountaineers and the like always carried chocolate, Ian had made sure that all three escape bags contained Cadbury's and a drink. So, what now? Phil and John the Stam were in a coal cellar, and all three boys hadn't washed or bathed in a month. He couldn't go to Southport, since he was unfit

196

for public transport, while his two mates were probably as dirty as the back of a sooty grate by this time. How was he supposed to get them out of the cellar during the hours of daylight? Could Belle provide them with a means to clean up and dress in the decent clothes they'd stolen from washing lines?

He read the page again. Belle was leaving the farm...

A grin appeared of its own accord. Belle knew Babs well, and Babs had a way of making things happen. If Barbara Schofield decided to go to Mars, the race between the USA and the USSR would be over, because Babs would win. So he had to find a phone box.

Yet again, he kicked himself mentally for not bringing the bike. He wished he had binoculars so that he might creep westward and see what was happening several fields away. Still, he had enough change for a phone call to Southport, so that was something. Babs would soon be on board, and rockets would be launched. God help the guilty; even the innocent might expect a grilling from Miss Barbara Schofield. Ian continued to wear the smile while the sun warmed him and hope flickered in his heart.

Eve Mellor was exhausted. She slumped at the desk in her office, plump hands supporting a plump face and a multiplicity of chins. Wearing an ancient housecoat, plastic curlers under a chiffon scarf, slippers, and a face that might have been described by Baby Babs as a near imitation of a bag of spuds, she was waiting for the farm to be

197

invaded. The police had stayed away thus far, but the night-long pregnant pause had been draining. Sleep had eluded her completely; even good old Kate had appeared ruffled after all the reorganization of the house. But Kate had managed to return to her room and was probably sleeping now. 'It's all down to me,' she muttered bitterly. 'I'm the one who'll end up with the shitty end of the stick.'

Someone tapped quietly at the office door.

'Come in,' Eve called with her last few dregs of energy.

Tom Duffield's head insinuated itself into the room. 'Hiya, Eve.'

Her jaw travelled south rather quickly, and her hands found the desk, because she suddenly needed firm support. 'What the blood and liver salts are you doing here? I took everybody back to town in the van last night.'

He entered the office completely and closed the door. 'You were probably in too much of a panic to count properly. I hid in Belle's wardrobe while you collected the rest of them.'

Eve blinked stupidly. 'She had no clients last night.'

He shrugged. 'She had me. She had me with her all night.' A long pause was followed by, 'I'm hoping she'll always have me.'

'You what?'

'You heard me, Eve. We've got plans.'

'Have you, now?'

Without invitation, he sat across from her at the desk. 'We're getting a vehicle, probably a van, and she'll learn to drive. She can pick up and return

198

like you do, Eve, only her passengers will be clocks and watches rather than men. Well, I might go with her, and in that case I suppose she'll ferry one man. Her mother and father live a few doors away from me, and we'll be with her little girl, too. Lisa can have two homes to choose from.' He waited while his message sank in. 'I'm talking possible marriage here, Eve.'

Eve swallowed. It was all falling apart. After Kate, Belle had been the mainstay of Meadowbank Farm. She was intelligent, gentle, kind and careful; Belle Horrocks was a rarity. 'I got compensation for Babs and Sally,' she snapped. 'Now I'm losing another.'

'You'll get nothing for Belle, sorry,' he answered immediately. 'She's a free woman in a free country, and she's walking out of here with me today. We're just waiting for an old friend of mine to come and help us with her things, then we're gone for good. She needs to get away and start a new life. We might have waited, but circumstances forced us to hasten matters.

'The police.' Her tone was flat, almost resigned.

'That's right.'

Eve shook her head. Angela would be moving on in a couple of weeks, so that would leave the place two girls short, while the amateurs who had replaced Babs and Sal were not yet up to scratch. 'She's used goods, Tom,' she said, sarcasm in her tone. 'Why not wait until somebody with a cleaner history comes along?'

'Aren't we all used or damaged goods? Look at me – one hand missing, and I could do with a new pair of eyes with the close work I do. I used other women till I found Belle, so what's the difference? Is it OK because I'm a bloke and she's just a female? Anyway, it's nothing to do with you. She made me come and tell you because she's too polite to just disappear without a word.'

'She already told me she was thinking of going. I didn't know why or when, but she has mentioned it a couple of times just lately.'

Tom nodded. 'Right, well, she's thought, and she'll be out of here this afternoon. Nobody feels safe at the moment – I'm sure you understand why they're all like cats on hot bricks.'

Eve turned her head and stared westward through the window. 'All right, just go, will you?' Her voice was cracking, and she felt dangerously close to tears. When had she last cried? Mam's funeral? She never wept; she always fought her way back, but where was her ammunition now? Admittedly, there were girls working the streets, some of whom might be grateful for the safety she offered, but the cops were just a few hundred yards away.

'You all right, Eve?' Tom asked. 'You look like you've swallowed a whole lemon without sugar.'

'No,' she admitted, 'I'm a long way from all right. We're shut down because of whatever's happening across the fields – probably drugs or stolen goods or some such thing – I've lost two girls to a man in Southport, and now Belle and Angela are quitting. I'm in a mess.'

He nodded thoughtfully. 'Yes, we've talked about that, Belle and I. She knows some girls – or she used to. One of them was that poor Jean Davenport who got murdered. Let her help you

200

to find replacements. She's what you might call astute.' There was pride in the last six words.

'Would she go to all that trouble for me?'

'Yes, she would.'

'Why?'

'Belle cares about people, and she cares a lot about you. She's always believed that places like this should be made legal, because there's danger out there on the streets.' He reached across and patted a well-upholstered hand. 'Take it easy for a couple of weeks, Eve. I have a phone at home, and Belle can let you know how things go. I'll be with her when she meets the candidates, so she'll be in no danger from pimps and the like. The cops won't be here forever, girl. And they might not bother you, though it's best to play safe and stay put just in case. Give yourself a break, will you?'

She managed a nod. 'Thanks, Tom.'

'You're welcome. And I know Belle would say the same – she'll be glad to help you and some of the street girls. They need to get indoors for safety's sake.'

The big woman looked at him. 'Some days it's like living in a bloody hen house, Tom. There's no cockerel to keep order, and I won't get one, because we don't want folk who remind girls of pimps or heavies. Women fight, you see. Babs and Angela were at it like mad bitches – hair and skin ripped at, black eyes, broken fingernails, and the sort of language you might hear down the docks on a wet Monday. Once Babs put all Angela's false eyelashes in an ashtray and set fire to them, so Angela cut holes in Babs's favourite blouse.'

Tom laughed – he couldn't help it. 'You thinking of giving up, then?'

She wasn't sure, and she said so. 'I'm tired,' she told him.

He stood up and paced about. 'You have to be here while the cops are nearby, so why not do it my way? Let Belle bend a few ears while you look after the farm, then decide after things settle and the police have buggered off. If Belle finds you some good people, keep going; if she doesn't, think about closing down. She won't tell any of them where you are, but she'll let them know it's a safe place.'

'Lap of the gods, is it? Because the cops could close us down in quick-sticks, and we'd all be had up in court.'

'I'm afraid it is the lap of the gods, love. I know so. That day when I went to work, lost my hand and nearly bled to death, I wondered what was the point of carrying on. We're still here, both of us, Eve. If I hadn't lost my hand, I'd be stuck doing a monotonous job and living with a wife I didn't like at all. It got so bad that even the arguments stopped. When you get past quarrelling, it's time to throw in the towel. She couldn't live with my one-handedness, so off she buggered. Yes, she took my boys, but I've met Belle and I couldn't be happier. The lads will find me one day. Try to look on the bright side, because things will get better for you, too.'

She studied him. He was a good-looking man with a bit missing, and he was probably decent to the bone. 'Belle's a great girl,' she managed finally. 'Heart of gold, she has, so you'd better look after her.' Smiling weakly, she nodded her agreement to his proposition. 'We'll give it a try if Belle's willing to talk to girls. And she'd better take care of you, too, lad.'

He left her, and she had seldom felt so bereft. Kate would be down soon, she hoped, because the girls' sleep patterns remained the same, and a midday breakfast/dinner needed to be cooked. 'Bloody burglars or drug dealers in that flaming hut,' she muttered, 'they want wiping off the face of the earth.'

Kate appeared. 'Sausage, eggs, beans and chips do you, love?'

'That'll suit nicely, thanks.'

Kate winked and cocked her head towards the open door. 'There's a handsome young man waiting to see you, Eve. I don't think he'll disturb our tenants; he knows they're homeless women.' Her voice was loud; she clearly wanted to be heard in the hallway.

An invisible knife slid its sharp edge over Eve's heart. The police were here. 'Get Belle and Tom,' she whispered. 'Wait in the corridor on dining chairs. The food can get cooked later.'

So this was it.

'Tom?' Kate mouthed. 'Is he here?'

'Just do it.'

Eve was alone again, but for a very short time.

Sally Hayes placed herself on the landing, her back against a wall, arms folded across her chest, a toe tapping on the carpet. She was fed up with almost everything, so she must speak her mind while her dander was up. At almost eighteen, she should be allowed a say in matters that bothered her.

'What?' Babs asked, stopping in her tracks when she saw Sal's frown.

'There's a long list of whats and a couple of whys.'

Babs placed a pile of laundry on a chair. 'A list?'

'A list. For a kick-off, I don't like him lying in our bed and watching us. I don't like him sleeping between us, because he's keeping us apart.'

'Neither do I, but what we must do must be done. And it's his bed, any road. I don't know about you, but I've never had such good grub in my life. Next item on your agenda?'

'I don't like cleaning.'

Babs puffed out her cheeks and blew. 'Well, cleaning's one of our responsibilities, if you remember. We had to get rid of Mrs Wright – she's too nosy, too much of a gossip. Nobody likes cleaning. Anything else?'

'His bed bath. He messes with me and I have to mess with him.' She pulled a face. 'I hate touching him, and I hate him touching me. He messes with my hair, too, and fiddles about with–'

'I know, I know – he's the same with me. Get used to it, Sally. There's no free tickets through anybody's life, so just put up and shut up. Or would you rather go cap in hand to Eve? Because she likes you, and I'm dead sure she'd welcome you back with open arms and a brass band.'

'No, I don't want that.' Sal shivered. One old man was more than enough.

Babs leaned against the wall. 'Sally, you're a big

204

girl now. I can't change any of it here, in this house. You knew he was an odd bugger before we came to Southport, but he'll look after us in his way–'

'And that horse is in the kitchen again. That's on the list, too. What if it shits in the house?'

'He won't.' Babs glanced at her cheap Timex. 'And it's his dinner time.'

Sally's eyes widened. 'It doesn't have dinners; it eats grass, doesn't it? It should stay outside with its mother and the donkeys.'

'I know he eats grass. They all eat grass. He comes in for his pudding. He likes carrots, apples and bread with a scrape of strawberry jam. When he's finished, he takes something for his donkey friend. Murdoch is very clever.'

Sal shook her head. 'The bloody thing acts like it owns the house.'

'The bloody thing is male, so it's he. And he will own the house, just you mark my words. Murdoch's talented and brave and kind, so stop whinging about him. I'm warning you, Sally – Murdoch is not what Mr Macey would call negotiable. That horse will make us rich. He should be called Pegasus – I swear he can fly.'

'You'd rather have him than me, Babs.'

The older woman picked up her bundle of towels and sheets. It was a close call at the moment, but she didn't say anything. If Sally was going to be jealous of a horse, that was up to her, and Murdoch was going nowhere. 'I've things to do, Sally.'

'But–'

'But nothing. Clean the bathroom. Use that old

toothbrush to do round the taps.' She put the washing in the airing cupboard and walked downstairs. It was a bit strange, she supposed. The whole area between sink and table was taken up by a beautiful animal in a context that was totally wrong for him. He looked like one of Don's paintings of horses by Stubbs, but set against a backdrop by some fool called Picasso.

Fascinated by a dripping tap, he was working on catching drops of water; meanwhile, two cats, who usually kept their distance, sat on the table trying to get used to the sight of a large mammal in a medium-sized room. Four mongrels having a mad half hour raced in and out repeatedly, but Murdoch concentrated on the water until he saw Babs. He drew back his upper lip; this was possibly his version of a smile, though she wasn't sure.

'Hello, baby,' she said. 'Have you been a good boy? If you have, you might be coming down with something. Shall I get you an Aspro?'

The horse answered her with a powerful neigh that seemed to rattle round the walls. Two hitherto brave cats shot like streaks of lightning out of the kitchen and into the hall.

'Who's my lovely bundle of trouble, then?' She opened the tap a little further and put the plug in. 'Now, there's your little horse trough. First, take this apple to Nicholas Nye, eh? And don't tell Gordy I put a teaspoon of jam on your bread, else he'll blame me if you get a funny stomach. Horses can die of funny stomachs, you know.' She'd been reading again. Among all Don's poetry books, there were volumes about horses

206

and how to run stables and names for various items of tack.

Murdoch performed his famous three-point turn and took the apple to his friend. His understanding of English was excellent, even when it arrived decorated in Scouse or Irish colours. His favourite person watched through the kitchen window while he passed the gift to his blind friend. He was adorable, and he knew it.

Babs fed the four dogs and blinked moisture from her eyes. She was a tough girl, hardened by life in grim streets, by abuse, by uncaring parents and by her own determination to stay alive and to win. Win what? Was there anything on the planet more precious than Murdoch? Maybe he was her prize. The dogs were lovely, the cats were usually pleasant, the hens laid eggs, while the geese continued protective of their household. And the dirty old man upstairs had saved them all. Everyone had a flaw. Don's was difficult to deal with, but he swore he had never touched a child, and she believed him.

Murdoch came back. Babs turned off the tap, and the horse decided to play bubbles, breathing into the water before raising his head to grin at her. She laughed at him. 'You're man's best friend, aren't you? Dogs are great, but your lot – even the donkeys...' She stroked his nose. 'And you're a big drip, too. Look at me, I'm wet through, you sloppy creature.'

Sally stood in the doorway. 'I need some bleach,' she said, eyes round and staring at the massive beast. 'It's in the cupboard under the sink. Will you get it for me, please?'

'Come here,' Babs ordered. 'I mean it. Come here now.'

Sally approached the table tentatively.

'Stand on this chair, Sally. Just do it.'

'But I–'

'No buts. Chair. Now.'

Sally climbed shakily onto the chair.

'On the table,' was the next command. 'Any buts and you're on the next train to Liverpool.' Babs moved the chair. 'Now, I'll take his head while you climb on his back. You can sit astride or lie across or do the bloody Gay Gordons on him, because he won't throw you. Use his mane – he doesn't mind.'

It took every ounce of her strength, but Sally managed. Unlike Babs, whose first ride had been taken on her stomach across the shining back, Sally managed to sit properly. 'It's high up,' she whispered, her throat dried by fear.

'Relax. If you're scared, he'll feel it and get nervous.' She spoke to Murdoch. 'Outside, boy. Sally, bend down in the doorway.'

With one girl at his head and the other on his back, he manoeuvred his way out of the house.

'You see?' Babs was triumphant. 'That was the worst of it, because you were in a small space. He'll walk forever unless you gee him up. You're the boss. I know he's a naughty devil, but he's different with a rider. He likes you. Slide off and I'll catch you. Stand, Murdoch, stand steady. Good lad.'

Don Crawford, whose health had improved greatly of late, poked his head through an open window on the upper storey. 'Babs? There's a young man on the phone for you.' He closed the window with a loud bang.

Babs caught Sally, ordered the horse to stay outside the house, then dashed inside to pick up the call. 'Hello?'

'It's Ian, Babs, Ian Foster. Phil and John are in the coal cellar at the farm, cos the hut's crawling with cops. We're filthy and tired – can you help?'

Babs's brain shot into overdrive. She pondered for a few seconds. 'I know a couple of men who will help us. Get as near as you dare to the farm-house – into the cellar with Phil and John if you can. I'm going to try to send a horsebox for you tonight, if that's possible. Don't worry about Eve – her hands are as tied as yours. Phone me back in about half an hour. Don, you don't need to listen in – he's just a kid.' She heard a click as the upstairs receiver was replaced.

'Are you still there, Babs?'

'Yes, I am.'

'It's time to give ourselves up, but we need to be clean.'

'Leave it with me, Ian. Phone me back.' She ended the call.

'What are you going to do?' Sally asked after Babs had given her as much of the story as she knew. 'Will you ring the police?'

Babs snorted. 'As if. No, I'm going to phone Mr Macey – he does a lot for the NSPCC as well as the RSPCA. He'll manage things, because he knows important people. I'm going for a quick word with Gordy first. If the phone rings, answer it, then come and get me.'

'Right.' Sally dashed upstairs with the bleach.

209

When Babs was in serious mode, it was necessary to follow instructions to the letter.

Acting DS Eddie Barnes entered Eve's office. He'd been sent by his superior to explain what was going on across the fields to the west of Meadowbank Farm. By rights, he should have had someone with him, but this was a big case, and he'd come alone due to a sudden lack of manpower. Liverpool and Manchester police had joined together to bring about the arrest at sunrise of a dealer in drugs, so several detectives were missing, presumed busy. Shuttleworth, known as Boss, had been apprehended and was being processed, which was great news. The bigger of two mysteries was solved, but three abused boys were still missing. 'Miss Mellor?' he asked.

Eve frowned. 'That's me. And you are?'

He produced his badge of office. 'Eddie Barnes, Detective Sergeant,' he told her, 'though I'm still learning and I sometimes call myself Defective Sergeant. I'm here to reassure you about what's going on yonder.' He waved a hand towards the window. 'We've found some interesting stuff, and that's all you need to know. The subject is not to be discussed – lives may be at stake.'

'Oh yes?' she managed. 'I thought I heard sirens on the main road.'

'We've cordoned off a scout hut that's no longer in use for that purpose. Some runaway boys have been living in it. Have you noticed any boys lurking about, Miss Mellor?'

'No. It's the trees, you see, and we're quite a long way from any other buildings, huts included.'

210

He nodded. 'You're a very great distance from anything and everything, aren't you? No shops, no proper road to the house – how do you manage?'

She stared at the man. He had a glint in his eye that advertised his knowledge of the situation. 'I have a van.'

'Of course you do.' He watched her face as it began to display a degree of fear. Framed by curlers of many colours and a scarf in pink chiffon, it was not a pretty sight. She was a huge woman in a housecoat that had seen better days, and she wasn't young. How could he say something without saying anything? 'Miss Mellor, I–'

'It's Eve. Call me Eve.'

'Who lives here with you, Eve?'

Her cheeks reddened suddenly. 'A few women who've had troubled lives,' she replied truthfully. 'Some have been knocked about – you know the type.'

'And you shelter them?'

She nodded. 'They work – that's what the van's for. Like everybody else, they have to earn their keep. So I drive back and forth dropping them off or picking them up. It's nearly a full-time job.'

'I see.' He knew what the van was for; he hadn't spent all those cold evenings and nights in the centre of Liverpool without knowing what the van was for. This was still difficult territory, because he approved of Eve yet dared not say so. 'They're safer here with you,' he managed. If his bosses found out that he had given his blessing to the owner of a brothel, he'd be in the rubbish bin long before his new status was made permanent.

'Yes. They're happier away from the city and

211

away from folk who mistreated them,' Eve told him.

'So carry on with the good work.'

'I'll do my best.' Just now, she couldn't imagine how the house might carry on at all unless Belle and Tom found some replacements.

'Eve?'

'What?'

'I have to search the house. Really, the team should do it, but I'm sure you wouldn't like a crowd of blokes trampling through in their size tens. These boys could be just about anywhere.'

She turned down the corners of her mouth. 'They're not here,' she said.

Eddie smiled. 'Don't worry. I'll do my best to keep you sheltered from invasion. After all, vulnerable women must be protected.'

Each stared at the other, both of them recognizing and understanding the other's thoughts. Eve spoke up. 'Four attics, we have. Three are used and the fourth is storage. Three bathrooms and six bedrooms on the first floor, two bathrooms and three smaller bedrooms on this floor. Kate and me share a room behind the kitchen; Kate's my housekeeper. The cellar door is to the right of the chimney breast near the range. The kitchen's the main living room.'

'Don't worry; Eve. I'm on your side.'

She believed him. 'There'll be a bacon butty when you've done, officer.'

'Eddie.'

'OK, Eddie. On your way out, ask Kate to get cooking, will you? Or there'll be raw bacon on your bread.'

He left the office and found three people sitting on chairs. 'You look like a doctor's waiting room,' he told them. 'Eve says Kate has to start cooking immediately, if not sooner.'

Eddie left them where they were. After ascending two flights of stairs, he looked at the attics. This place was clearly a brothel, and his betters would want him to report it as such, but he couldn't and wouldn't. His brief was to search for three lads, not to comment on design and decor. After walking down the attic stairs, he poked about on the first floor. He discovered no runaways, but found plenty of hasty concealment of bed covers and other items.

A ground-floor walkabout disclosed nothing until he came across girls at the sitting room end of the kitchen. Kate was cooking. 'I'll do you a butty, lad. Brown sauce or red?'

'Just as it comes, thanks; no sauce,' he replied.

The rest of the level failed to reveal any boys. He returned to the kitchen and rattled the door to the cellar, which was locked. 'Where's the key?' he asked Kate.

'Bloody hell,' she exclaimed. 'You're not going down there in that suit, are you? You'll be as black as a burnt pot, because it's full of coal. We haven't used much with it being summer, and we've got immersion heaters for water.'

He shrugged. 'I suppose you're right. The wife would kill me, because this is my wedding suit.' He stood still for a moment. 'I can't guarantee that I'll be your only visitor, Kate.'

'I know. I'll tell Eve. Thanks for trying, though.'

At the other side of the locked door, two boys

breathed again. Ian would come for them today, wouldn't he? They were covered in coal dust, running out of crisps, chocolate and water, and they ached after sitting and lying on a hard, flagged floor. They crept away and placed themselves behind a mountain of coal. If he didn't arrive soon, they would escape through the grille.

Neil Carson wasn't completely sure what to do with himself, though he was contemplating a solution of sorts. For the first time in his life, he was living in squalor. He hadn't minded so much when Angela had been available, because he'd had a kind of compensation in his visits to the farm, but the farm was closed, and he had few distractions. Was it time to go back? Not back home, but should he start clearing the streets again? Was Jesus on his side, anyway? There'd been no second appearance, no encouragement, no praise, no criticism. He was confused, and confusion was not something he had experienced until lately. Life had been mapped out, predictable, clean and easy.

'I only managed to shift one,' he whispered. 'I have to make sure I don't make a mistake again.' He could seldom get Dolly Pearson out of his thoughts. The woman had dressed crazily, but that had been her only sin. A way to make amends was open to Neil, because Joseph Turton, another postal worker and Neil's closest friend, was looking after his elderly mother and needed assistance. The house was shabby but clean, and Neil could move in at any time and help to take care of the old lady. So far, Joseph was the only person at work allowed to know that Neil had separated from Laura.

He sat down on his one greasy chair and looked round the cramped, smelly room. It was horrible. At Joseph's house, Neil could have a clean bedroom and a shared kitchen. The bathroom was downstairs, since the house had just two bedrooms, and the front parlour had been made over for Mrs Turton, who could no longer manage stairs. There was a kitchen that doubled as the living room, and it adjoined a small scullery, with the bathroom tacked on as an afterthought. No rent would be required. The only payment expected would be sitting with Mrs Turton and buying some food. 'I'll do it,' he said quietly. It would keep him busy and off the streets for a while.

Having returned to the marital home just once in the middle of the night, Neil had taken his bike from the rear yard, but he would need help to move that and all his other belongings. Joseph had a van, so that was going to be useful. 'I'll ride the bike while he carries all my stuff,' he whispered into the oxygen-starved bedsit. With its window nailed shut, the room hadn't had a change of air in God alone knew how long.

He closed his eyes. Perhaps looking after Joseph's mum might go some way to atoning for the murder of Dolly Pearson. The woman had cared for an ancient mother for eight hours every day, so here was a chance of penance. Joseph had promised to keep the secret about the failure of Neil's marriage, and Joseph was a Catholic, so he could be trusted. Yes, the move must be made, because this dump wasn't fit for pigs.

He pulled on a sweater and went for a bike ride.

215

With autumn on its way, the evenings had cooled somewhat...

On that same autumn evening, Barbara Schofield learned several things. First, she knew a man she liked – or liked a man she knew, which fact was something of a revelation. Gordy Hourigan, failed jockey and successful trainer, was showing signs of being very much her cup of tea, and he needed no sugar.

Second, she cared on some deep level about the three poor lads who had run away from school. School was where kids were looked after and educated; it certainly wasn't a place in which children might be used as punch bags or worse. Another surprise was the fact that posh didn't mean snobby, because Mr Lippy Macey had a wicked sense of humour. The nickname Lippy had arrived in infancy; according to his deceased parents, he had begun talking at the age of two and had never stopped since. 'That's why I hover on the brink of politics,' he explained to Babs and Gordy. 'The council chamber's the only place where I don't get ordered to pipe down. Oh, and I learned the hard way that I must always allow my wife to have the last word. That's diplomacy covered. Now, about these boys...'

Babs grinned at Gordy, who grinned back at her. 'One of the lads is called Phil,' she told the two men. 'I wonder if he's lippy, too? Mind, Ian Foster seems to be the boss.' She stared hard at the gentleman known as Lippy. Under the thick mop of white hair, mischief danced in clear blue eyes. 'I don't know much about education,' she said, 'but I do know Ian's clever. He might be what they call university material. And he's the angriest of the three. Poor John has a stammer, so it can be hard to tell, though he manages better when he's not upset or worried. Ian says John reads a lot, so he could be another bright button.' She paused. 'What?'

'Have you ever considered a future in politics?' Lippy asked.

She shrugged. 'I'm Labour.'

'As am I.'

She glared at him. 'You? Lippy Labour? Owner of racehorses and a mansion off Scarisbrick Road?'

Lippy chortled. 'It's pronounced Scares-brick,' he said. 'The i is silent, which is more than you are, madam.'

Babs squared her shoulders. 'We've three young lads shut down a bloody coal hole,' she pronounced, 'while we're stood here like him outside Lewis's–'

'Who is naked,' Lippy interjected.

'Please yourself,' she snapped, 'but I'm keeping my clothes on.'

Gordy shook his head. 'No sense of fun whatsoever,' he grumbled.

She kicked him none too gently.

'She's right.' Lippy had returned to Mr Macey mode. 'Let's hope Ian made it into the cellar to pick up the other two. You say he'll be at the end of a dirt track near the A580?'

Babs shrugged. It was all a bit complicated, and she couldn't guarantee anything. 'They'll all be there,' she said uncertainly. 'Ian will have got them out after the sun went down if he couldn't go to the cellar in daylight. He said on the phone he would fetch John and Phil at some stage, but it might be after dark. I can't say any more than that, because I don't know any more. We'd better go.'

The horsebox idea had been dropped; if the boys stank, they stank. Anyone who worked with horses knew how to cope with malodorous moments, so the boys' temporary divorce from soap and water would probably be no big deal. Instead of a horsebox, Mr Macey had brought a VW camper van with plenty of seating, much of which might soon wear a coating of coal dust, so sheets had been spread over upholstery.

'Right, we'd better go,' Gordy said. Being a short man might be useful if the worst came to the worst and someone had to search a coal cellar. 'Have you got food, Babs?'

She held up her basket. 'Pasties, butties and cakes,' she replied. 'They're going to need strength if they're planning to face the music.'

Lippy winked at her. 'Worry not, because they can stand behind me and my lawyers.'

The details could wait, Babs decided as they drove towards the main route between Southport and Liverpool. Before anything could happen, they needed to find Ian, Phil and John. She crossed her fingers – the boys had better be there.

Sisters Helen and Mary hugged each other in a corridor of Magdalene House. On their way to Benediction, they stole a few moments to celebrate the capture of Albert Shuttleworth, one of the biggest distributors of drugs on both sides of the River Mersey and throughout the north-west. 'You were close to the wind this time,' Helen whispered. 'You've been taking too many risks, Sister Mary Veronica. One of these days, you'll–'

'I know, I know, Sister Helen Veronica. You're beginning to sound like my mother, God rest the poor woman. I've even carried packets of cocaine to those lower down the animal chain. Speaking of which, we both have to continue watching Lime Street for such creatures. London or Manchester dealers might try to cash in now that the boss has gone.'

They entered the chapel. Both found it difficult to concentrate; fortunately, the *Tantum Ergo* and the *O Salutaris Hostia* were deeply ingrained, so their delivery was automatic. At supper, they sat together. 'We'll have to work on the station as completely separate units until we befriend each other gradually,' Helen said. 'I'm Smelly Nellie, and you're Holy Mary.'

'Plus one,' Mary said.

'What?'

'The local police are giving us a dog. He wags his tail and growls when he smells drugs. Dogs have been used to find drugs in France since 1965, so a constable read all about it and trained up his own dog. The poor man died, and his dog needs a kind owner and a job. A bedraggled article, he is, so he will look the part. The good thing is that he doesn't leap on a carrier of drugs, but hackles rise in time with the wagging and the growling. We'll still be working with the police, Helen. Mother Superior has agreed to it.'

'My heart overfloweth with joy.' Sister Helen

clapped a hand to her brow. 'A dog? I know nothing about dogs.'

'Joy indeed, because you'll be adopting him. You found the poor thing wandering the streets – that's the official line. It's a boy, a mongrel, and his name is Nelson.'

'Oh, Lord.'

Mary nodded. 'That's the chap – Admiral Lord Nelson.'

'Who was a tremendously clever seafaring warrior with a questionable personal life.' Helen paused. 'Lady Hamilton. Between them she and the admiral broke his wife's heart.' She stared hard at her companion. 'What?' she asked. 'I can tell you're up to something. You've gone red along the cheekbones.'

Mary almost squirmed under Helen's steady gaze. 'He'll be living with you.'

'What?'

'The dog. He will get to know you, and he'll work for you.'

'I smell like the bottom of a chip shop dustbin.'

'Dogs don't mind smells'

'An answer for everything, Mary, have you not? I don't understand dogs.'

The younger Veronica sister shrugged. 'Holy Mary can't have a dog, because she's always in and out of church. When I'm Holy Mary, I'm a double agent with no dog.'

'Talk to St Francis of Assisi. He took animals everywhere with him.'

'No, I'll have a word with my friend St Jude, ask him to knock some sense into you. You know that station like the back of your own hand. I have to

220

get used to it, so you're the leader when it comes to Lime Street, because I've been a roving reporter or minister without portfolio thus far. If I'm seen on Lime Street regularly, drug dealers will come to me, so I don't need the dog.'

They ate their meal, prayed with the rest of the sisterhood, then went downstairs to Helen's cellar. The resident of this level made cocoa. A dog. Didn't she have trouble enough without a dog? 'Ah well,' she murmured, 'the good Lord sends these things to try us.'

Mary rattled the biscuit barrel. 'Have you no custard creams, Helen?'

The older nun glanced heavenward. The Lord sent things to try her, but Sister Mary Veronica was a trial too far.

By the time they reached the East Lancashire Road, Babs was certain that gentlemen, in the good old Victorian sense, no longer existed. Lippy Macey was discussing with Gordy the possible methods of harnessing the gas that emerged frequently from the back end of a horse. 'One horse could possibly fuel a domestic cooker,' he said.

'And that would smell lovely with sausage and chips,' Babs mused aloud.

'It would be converted,' Lippy said.

'What to?' she asked. 'Catholicism, Buddhism, socialism?'

'She always has either an answer or a difficult question, and she knows a couple of big words, too.' Gordy laughed. 'Are we nearly there?' he asked Babs.

She nodded. 'We'll have to do a you-ee, cos it's

on the other side.'

'A you-ee?' asked the gentleman at the wheel.

'She means a U-turn,' Gordy explained. 'Turn right at the next set of lights—'

'Not the next set; the ones after the next.' She prodded Gordy's neck. 'I'm the navigator, not you.'

He grinned. Little Madam would always be the navigator; in fact, she would probably draw maps to be followed through life by most within her sphere. Sometimes, he thought he liked her because she was one of the few women who were shorter than he was. But lately he had come to realize that there was a lot more to Babs than her small frame. Like Murdoch, she was a clever nuisance. Like Murdoch, she promised to alter the shape of the future. And for an ex-prostitute, she was extraordinarily bright. Gordy kept to himself the secret of her provenance; Mr Macey thought she and Sally were Don Crawford's nurses/housekeepers, and that was fine by Gordy.

Lippy performed the necessary manoeuvres, and they slid gently off the carriageway, coming to rest on the road's shoulder at the end of the rough track that led to Meadowbank Farm.

'I won't be long,' Babs said as she bent to leave the vehicle.

'True,' replied Mr Macey, 'I doubt you're more than five feet tall.'

'Listen, Lippy Longshanks, good things come in small packets and they're easier to wrap.'

'Shouldn't one of us go?' Gordy asked. 'It's getting dark, and the—'

'They know me,' Babs snapped. 'They're frightened, hungry and worn out to the back of next Wednesday. I know what I'm doing.'

'She says she knows what she's doing,' Long-shanks whispered.

'Perhaps she does,' Gordy replied.

Babs left them to chatter among themselves. She crept up the uneven path and called in a stage whisper, 'Ian? Are you there? It's Babs.'

Privets moved, and she turned to her right. 'Ian?' she repeated.

But bushes to her left were suddenly disturbed. 'We're here,' Ian hissed.

'All of you?'

'Yes. Hang on a minute while we get through a hole in the hedge.'

She looked again to her right, but all was still. There was no wind, so who the hell was hiding? Was it police, or some of Boss's people? Boss would be keeping his distance, as would his workers if the cops were at the hut. She stepped closer to the now stilled privets. Whoever it was could sod off, because she had more serious matters to deal with.

They arrived by her side, three young lads with blackened faces, hands and arms. Babs shone a torch over them. 'Buckets of blood,' she exclaimed, 'who got you ready? You look like blooming chimney sweeps from about a hundred years back. And I swear you've all lost weight. Come on. We've got a van waiting for you.'

'We pong a bit.' Ian's tone was apologetic.

'So do horses and donkeys, but I got used to them.' Knowing there was an audience, she whispered. 'Now, let me explain. There are two men

223

in the camper, and they're both OK. There's Mr Philip Macey – he's famous for looking after folk,' she said, winking at Phil, 'and Mr Gordy Hourigan, an Irish trainer of racehorses. They know you had to run away from bad monks. Mr Macey will drop me and Gordy off at Wordsworth House and Dove Cottage, then you might go with Mr Macey to his house. His lawyers will talk to you tomorrow and they'll help you to make a plan about the next move.'

Ian cleared this throat. 'We heard the women talking in the kitchen when I got in the cellar tonight,' he told her, 'and that Boss man's been arrested in Manchester. We were worried in case he came and found us, cos we left his drugs, didn't we? And another lad got killed. It's scary.'

'Shush,' she warned. She felt as if she could put out her hand and touch the heat emanating from this boy, the leader, the one responsible for most decisions – including the original plan to escape the abusers. He was so taut that she could almost feel his aura as it crackled like static electricity, born of fear and hope and hunger. The lad was reaching out, but he was too tired to find the words, so he just stood there burning internally, the whites of his eyes glowing in a dirty face, his worldly possessions in a bag at his feet, two friends behind him waiting, trusting.

Gordy and Mr Macey arrived just as Babs broke down. She never cried. Even when digging a shard of glass out of her leg at the age of seven, she'd managed to contain herself. 'No!' she screamed when Gordy tried to hold her. 'I'm just furious. I'll be all right in a minute. Get this lot in the van. There's wet flannels and dry towels in my green shopping bag and food in the blue one. They need to clean their hands before they eat.'

While the men took the boys away, Babs dried her eyes and turned her torch on the privets opposite those from which the three had emerged. 'I know you're there,' she spat, her voice still fractured by emotion. 'And I do hope you're enjoying yourself, you sneaky twisted bastard. If you need a whore, try Lime Street.' She parted the privets. The creature had gone.

Eight

Neil Carson could scarcely remember his journey into the stark outback of the Mersey plain; it was as if the bike had set its compass to arrive here, while he had been no more than innocent cargo. What was he doing in this place at this time? Angela wasn't available; nobody was available due to circumstances beyond the control of the fat mamma, Eve Mellor. She didn't like Neil, and the antipathy was reciprocated.

He was restless to the point of scarcely being aware of his own actions. Preparations for his proposed move needed to be made, and he needed to reclaim his senses and start to imitate normality, at least. Oh, why had they come that night and why had they chosen him? There were millions of Catholics and millions of fireplaces...

And who was the harridan in the lane, the one

who had berated him so rudely? Where was Jesus when He was needed? Oh, how he wished his mind would stop or slow down a bit, at least. Tired and jumpy, he wondered who was pulling his strings. Perhaps Judas had a grim sense of humour – after all, he had drunk Neil's beer. And if Judas was hanging around with Jesus, did that mean he was now a saint?

Neil sat near bushes a bit further away from that rude woman, listening while the vehicle on the shoulder started up and pulled out onto the road. At last, he breathed. For how long had he held his breath without knowing it? Clearly, he must have taken in oxygen, but not all the way to the bottom of his lungs. That woman had scared the living daylights out of him.

There was no safe place, not for him. Although things had quietened along the Dock Road, the police were doubtless continuing the search for the killer or killers of Jean Davenport and Dolly Pearson. Now it seemed that the mystery of the runaway schoolboys was about to be solved, though that was none of his business and was of no interest to him.

'I have to see her, even if it's only for a minute,' he muttered, wondering whether it was possible for a man to fall in love with a whore. The girls lived in the kitchen at the back of the house – he had learned that much during visits to the farm. Leaving his bike where it was, he crept up the pitted dirt track and round the side of the house, his body in close contact with the building. Autumn was truly on its way, because it was almost dark by eight fifteen.

She was at the sitting room end with some others. Without makeup and the special clothing she used for her role play, Angela looked like an ordinary woman. The whole group chattered and laughed while he, the outsider, eavesdropped through a slightly open window and read lips as best he could when laughter drowned a speaker's words. She was leaving Meadowbank. Why hadn't she told him she was going? But he must not get angry; perhaps she had discovered only recently a new place to live.

The old woman who cooked shouted from the other end of the huge room, 'Where is your sister's wool shop, Ange?'

'East Prescot Road, Knotty Ash,' was the reply. 'I'm having the upstairs flat. It's not big, but it will do, I suppose. Beggars can't be choosers, can they?'

Neil knew Liverpool well, as did most who worked with mail. West Derby, Old Swan, Broadgreen, Knotty Ash – yes, he could find his way to that cluster as long as he had an address. And he had an address. After all, there wouldn't be more than one wool shop along that stretch. So his journey had not been wasted, then.

He stared hard at Angela, who had taught him that pain was the mirror of pleasure, that a collar and lead could make physical freedom so much sweeter, that flesh sensitized by a whip was always alive and eager for more. She reduced him to slavery, chained and cuffed him before allowing him to dominate her only during the final act, during which she appeared to experience such pleasure. Though he could never be sure, since it

227

was part of her job, wasn't it? Laura had never even groaned, had never said a word. His wife had done her duty, no more than that. 'I want you,' he mouthed silently. 'And I'll find you, because I know Knotty Ash like the back of my own hand.'

One stark fact remained: Neil Carson missed his children. Lucy was quite the little lady, always prancing about wearing Laura's jewellery and Cuban-heeled shoes, forever borrowing handbags, lipstick and scarves. She sang and put on plays in which she played all the parts, because her brother wouldn't join in, since mucking about dressed up was only for girls.

Neil allowed himself a tight smile. Matt was a clever boy, doing well at school, but mad as a hatter when it came to football and cricket. They were lovely kids, they were his, and he missed them. He remembered days in the park: the see-saw, the roundabout, a slide, the swings. He'd taught them to throw and catch, to swim at the baths, to ride bikes. But the reality was that he needed Angela more. He dared not tap on the window, could not entertain the idea of ringing the doorbell. And there she sat in jeans and a pale blue blouse, her hair loose and flowing, her attitude relaxed as she chattered to the rest of the ... of the prostitutes. They were pretty; it was clear that Fat Mamma chose *la crème de la crème*.

He backed away slightly into the shadows. The fact remained that he was supposed to be clearing away people like Angela and her colleagues, yet he was operating on the other side of the business altogether. He was a client. Enlivened by close contact with a clever if somewhat brutal woman, Neil was fast becoming addicted. But he wasn't on the streets, was he? Nothing had been said about women who plied their trade indoors; the emphasis had been placed on the cleaning up of pavements where 'ladies of the night' sold their wares.

Wool shop, East Prescot Road, Knotty Ash.

He crept back to the bushes, picked up his bike and wheeled it out towards the main road. Tomorrow, he'd be moving to a decent house with windows that opened and a place to hang clothes well away from cooking smells. Things could only get better. Couldn't they?

He entered the city centre and pushed his bike towards the water. This was a place where people often stood staring out towards the bar as if waiting for a relative to come home after long service at sea. Two painted whores approached him and asked was he looking for business and did he fancy a threesome? He swept an eye over the pair. 'No, thanks.'

They wheedled, spelling out items on their menu and the prices for each function. One offered to remove her dentures to give him the experience of a lifetime, and he smiled kindly upon both of them. 'Ladies, I am spoken for, but thank you.' They were small, they were ugly, and they were on the streets. Furthermore, they were accosting men and offering themselves at very low cost. He wondered whether they might be diseased. But here, in the glare of city lights, he dared not react. Had they been further along the riverfront, he might have been tempted to do the work prescribed by the Lord.

Tomorrow, he was on the two-till-ten shift. In the morning, he would stand at the school gates and look at his children while they played. At noon, Joseph would come for him, and the move away from squalor would be achieved.

Back in that hellish attic room, Neil packed his cases, sat in the greasy chair and drank a small Guinness. A new page was turning; a new chapter was about to begin. Once he got away from this dump, his mind would settle and he would be in decent company and clean surroundings. And best of all, he knew where Angela was going.

'Why are we standing here like two statues waiting to be bombed by pigeons?' Tom asked, a grin decorating his handsome face. 'It has to be done, Belle.'

She swallowed nervously. 'I don't know. Why are we standing here like a pair of statues waiting for—'

'It's not a riddle, babe. You were the one who decided to wait to tell your mum and dad once the deed was done and you were out of Meadowbank. If you remember, I said they should have been told as soon as we'd made our decision.'

'I'm a coward. And there are no pigeons in your house.' She attempted a smile; he looked wonderful in good clothes and with a smart haircut. Max clearly shared their excitement by bringing his toys one by one and laying them at the feet of the radiant couple.

'I'll put the kettle on, Belle.' He went to do just that. 'You did tell them the auditing firm was closing down, so they'll expect you to be out of work,' he called before reappearing in the kitchen doorway. 'Cup of tea and a slice of apple pie, then we go together and do what has to be done. They like me, love. It's not as if they're going to hit the roof with their clogs on, is it?'

'But they don't know how long we've known each other, Tom. As far as Mam and Dad understand, I met you a very short time ago. Well, apart from seeing you in a jeweller's shop. They'll think it's too soon.' She raised her left hand and studied the rings. 'And here I am, not just engaged, but married five hours ago. You told Eve you were talking possible marriage, but you never said we'd be done and dusted by four o'clock, did you?'

Tom shook his head slowly. 'Listen to me. If you think I went to all this trouble getting a wedding cake so that Frankie and Sam can have a taste–'

'I'm sorry.'

He strode across the room and kissed her gently on the mouth. 'We are not a mistake, Belle. I still think we should have done this differently, but we can't change what's happened. We are not a mistake,' he repeated.

'I know.'

'We're made for each other. Let's face it, three hands are better than one, and there's always my hook.'

'Yes.'

'Then sit down, shut up, and I'll get your tea and your pie.'

After a lovely post-wedding meal, Belle wasn't hungry, but she decided to follow her husband's orders just this once. It would give her a little more thinking time... Oh, heck. Little Lisa didn't know anything, either. 'I've done this arse over tip, as usual,' Belle muttered while her man made tea. He did very well with just the one hand, she thought, and she alone had the power to stop via massage the occasional acute pain in fingers that no longer existed.

Three houses along the street, Mam and Dad were probably watching a bit of telly before bedtime. Lisa would be curled up fast asleep and completely oblivious of the fact that she had acquired a stepfather. Might she want to leave her grandparents and move in with Mummy and Tom? And how would Lisa's grandparents feel if that happened? The child could choose. She could eat in one house, sleep in another, bring Amelia to either...

Tom sat after handing her a small tray. 'Stop worrying.'

'I can't.'

'Well, take the rings off and stay with Sam and Frankie for a while.'

Belle didn't stop thinking. Lisa would want to be a bridesmaid, and the child's grandparents would insist on attending a wedding that had already happened. She shook her head. 'I'm telling the truth. Well, I'll give them most of the truth, because I don't want my family ever to know how I've been making my money.' She gazed at him. 'I still can't believe you chose me, Tom.'

He smiled broadly. 'Oh yes, there was a long queue, eh? There were ten of them lining up wanting to marry me. I love you, you daft mare. Even if there had been a queue, I would have asked you and only you.'

Belle fluttered her eyelashes. 'That would be because I'm such a sweet, innocent young thing.'

'You're nearly ten years younger than me, Mrs Duffield. And we have our alibi, because you've done the audit for several jewellers who give me work, so we've seen each other before on several occasions. Ships that passed in the night, yet we recognized each other without realizing at first. We fell in love in my house while drinking tea together; we wanted no fuss, but we'll have a church blessing if that's what they'd like for us. Lisa could have a posh frock, and your mam would have an excuse to buy a new hat. Women like hats, don't they?'

She giggled, but she didn't know why. 'When I was a kid, Mam always used to say I had a giggle button. Trouble was, I couldn't stop once I started laughing, then I'd get hiccups.'

Tom drained his cup. 'Thanks for that information. I shall take it down and use it in evidence against you. Come on. You can finish your pie when we get back.'

Belle stayed where she was, firmly planted in the chair. 'I'll do it tomorrow,' she whispered.

The master of the house paced up and down a few times. He would sort this out. 'Right, Madam Butterfly, you can stop where you are – I'm going to fetch your parents.' When she opened her mouth to reply, he held up a hand in the manner of a traffic policeman. 'You just carry on fluttering about and I'll bring the mountain here. Don't worry, a neighbour will babysit Lisa. Just stay, for God's sake. Married for less than half a day, and there's trouble already.' Giving her no chance to speak, he left the house.

With her jaw dropping, Belle froze for several seconds.

Pulling herself together, she ran to the front door, but she couldn't shout, didn't want to make a show for the neighbours to chatter about over supper or tomorrow's breakfast. Tom was walking up the path to Mam and Dad's front door. He was all dressed up in his wedding suit, a white rose wilting slightly in his buttonhole. Bugger. She closed the door and returned to the living room. 'Come on, Isabella,' she mumbled, staring at her reflection. She looked good in mid-blue taffeta with navy accessories, but she did a quick job in the makeup department.

Silence ruled. Any minute now ... any minute now...

At long last, Bill Tyler had found his way to the scout hut. He could have gone to his local police station first, but he preferred to visit the scene in case the boys were hanging about nearby. If they were, he could have a chat with them.

Oh, hell on a butty, there was a uniform at the door and a couple in plain clothes with him. What should he do? He should ask about the lads he had seen that night, so he steeled himself. He was going to talk to police anyway soon, so why wait? The boys' safety was his first priority, because Roy hadn't been safe.

After taking a deep breath, Bill squared his shoulders, straightened his spine and approached the scene, leaving his bike on the ground.

'Stay where you are for a minute,' Detective Sergeant Eddie Barnes called. 'What do you want?'

'Are they all right?' Bill shouted.

'Are who all right?'

'Them three lads. Has he killed them as well? I know he got arrested the other morning; it was on the wireless.'

After a short conversation, the uniformed man ordered the boy to come closer. 'You're all right, lad. Say what you have to say.'

So he spilled his guts accompanied by a few tears. Annoyed with himself for breaking down like a girl, he told them about the condemned house, the crop, the stolen electricity, and that his best mate, Roy Foley, had been a clever lad totally devoid of common sense. 'We couldn't manage all them plants,' he explained nervously, 'cos there was hundreds of them, so Roy went down Halewood to get Boss and his gang. They said they'd do the harvest, then me and Roy went in one of the vans. They give us twenty quid each. There was two vans – one for people, the other for the grass plants. We helped to load at our end, then to unload at the other end.' He paused. 'Can I have a drink?'

He was given a cup of lemonade. While the boy drank it, Eddie watched him. This was a lad at Confession; he had come here to unburden himself. 'Feeling better? What's your name?'

'I'm Bill Tyler. Roy Foley was me bezzie mate since nursery.'

'Go on.'

He went on as requested. 'There was a great big

235

barn and a house on its own, not stuck to any other houses, like. We put the plants in the barn, then we had to go to a shed near the house and get all these packets and pile them up in the van where our stuff had been. We were driven here, and the packets got hid under tents and stuff. There was three lads. Boss said he'd look after them with food and money if they'd mind his property and promise not to touch it. They was them three what ran away from school.' He paused. 'Are they dead?'

'We think not,' Eddie said, his tone quiet and gentle. 'What happened after the drugs were stashed, Bill?'

Bill told them about having been taken home and ordered to work for Boss. 'He said he'd come back for us the next day. He told me I had to deliver drugs to people, and he was taking Roy on as a member of staff was the way he put it. I told Boss I couldn't do the job for him because I'm working with me dad now. We have to travel to other towns sometimes, cos it's a big building firm. So I got let off and Roy got murdered. It was in the papers.'

'Yes. Boss or one of his gang overdosed him. Boss is too clever for that, which means it was probably one of his sidekicks. So – anything else, Bill?'

The boy stared at his feet. He was grassing, but he had no choice, had he? And with Boss in jail...

Eddie prompted him again. 'Bill?'

This was another frightening bit. 'He said he knew where our families were. The next thing I found out, Roy was dead. Then I started thinking about this lot who were living in the hut with the drugs. Where are they?'

'We don't know. But thank you for coming forward, son. You'll have to make a formal statement, of course.'

Bill felt the blood draining from his face. 'Will I go to jail?'

The uniformed man put a hand on Bill's shoulder. 'Listen, lad – we'll put in a word. It took courage to come here and tell us all this stuff. Now, if you'd like to go with DS Barnes in an unmarked car, he'll take you to the cop shop and you can write your statement.'

'What about me bike? It's not just mine– I have to share it with me brothers and they get mad when I bugger off without telling them.'

'I'll get the keys to the van,' Eddie said before disappearing into the hut.

A sob escaped from the boy's throat. 'I'm no good at writing,' he told the uniform. 'Roy was.'

'But you've got the common sense. You'll be given help with your statement. And don't be feeling guilty because Roy's dead and you're alive. Loads arrived back after the war and made themselves ill over their dead mates. When it comes to crime and battles, it can be the luck of the draw.'

'I miss him. Dad always said he was trouble, but he made me laugh.'

'Well, I'm telling you now, Detective Barnes is hilarious. He might even get you a bottle of pop and a bag of chips. Stop worrying.'

Bill dried his eyes furiously with the cuff of his jumper.

Eddie emerged with the van keys. 'Good job you came tonight, Bill. We've been here upwards of forty-eight hours, and we're packing up now. Let's get your bike, lad.'

Life without Neil was so much easier. Laura Carson did her five lunchtime shifts at the chip shop, plus a couple of evenings when Mum stayed to look after the children. Mum kept telling her, 'You're coming out of your shell, love. It's good to see you happy at last.' But Mum had never liked Neil. She'd always thought there was something dark about him, and had often expressed the opinion that he was a religious fanatic, a man with no sense of humour, and a miserable so-and-so who seemed to think laughter was a crime.

It was true that Laura was blossoming at last, since she was meeting and talking to people across a counter, while her employers held her in high regard. Only now, in her husband's absence, did she realize how oppressive life had become when he'd been there; everything had revolved round his shifts. Now, she could cook when she felt it was time, iron when she had a couple of hours to spare, and the house, which had suddenly become a home, was allowed to be untidy, even boasting a light sprinkling of dust from time to time.

Having read a few magazines, Laura discovered that she was still young enough for longer hair – she had seven years left before reaching the metaphorical and actual cutting off point – so she intended to let it grow a bit. She was also eating better, and the sharp angles on her face were blurring under a healthy deposit of flesh. At thirty-three, she was beginning to look younger.

She had a bust and three new brassieres to celebrate that fact. Feeling very brave and rather naughty, she bought some blue jeans and a couple of tight-fitting sweaters from a catalogue to which she would be paying a small sum for twenty weeks. The Avon lady furnished her with eye shadows, eyeliner, lipsticks, Skin so Soft and a range of perfumed products called To a Wild Rose. Was she going wild? Did she care?

About one subject, she truly cared. Neil's bike had disappeared, so he had probably come to collect it, although he had not bothered to visit his children once since moving out. He sent a cheque every week, but no greetings were enclosed – he didn't ask any questions about the welfare of Matt and Lucy. They were beginning to be curious, especially on Sundays when he must have had time off from his mythical promotion course.

She sat them down after supper and did what needed to be done. 'None of this is connected to either of you,' she began. 'But Daddy and I no longer get on together, so he has left me. He hasn't left you – he wanted you to stay in the same house and at the same school.'

Matt frowned. 'Is he not coming back?'

'No,' was Laura's quiet answer. 'He and I don't want to live together any more.'

Tears pooled in Lucy's eyes. 'Why, Mummy?'

Sometimes, the simplest questions needed complicated answers, and this was one such occasion, though her little audience wasn't ready for complicated. 'Because grown-ups quarrel just like children do.'

Lucy thought about that. 'I quarrelled with Maria Wilkinson, but we're best friends now. You might get back with Daddy and be friends again.'

How could she deal with this without making her son and daughter even more miserable and confused? As ever, she stuck with the truth. 'Daddy and I don't quarrel exactly the way children do, Lucy. This is something altogether different, and it happens sometimes to big people. We are happier apart.'

'So we only have you now,' Matt murmured.

'That's right, son. You both have me. I grew you in my tummy.'

'What if you decide to leave us?' he asked.

Oh dear. This was the crux of the matter. Children were meant to have two parents, and when half the adults in the family did a disappearing act, the young worried about the remaining half. 'I won't leave you,' Laura said.

'We thought Daddy wouldn't leave us.' Matt looked angry. 'How do we know you're telling the truth?'

'You can both trust me. I promise you faithfully that I'll always be here.'

'Till you die?' Lucy asked.

'Till I die.' Laura hugged them both before clearing away the dishes. At the kitchen sink, she thought about the folded sheet of newspaper in her jacket pocket. She'd never been one for keeping up with events, but one of the benefits of working in a chip shop was old newspapers, and a headline had jumped out at her when she'd been preparing a pile of outer wrappings.

'Mummy?'

'Yes?' She looked down at her beautiful daughter.

'Shall I help with the dishes?' Lucy asked.

'If you like. But you don't need to be extra-specially good and helpful to make me stay. Don't be afraid, sweetheart. Mummies don't just go and leave their children, and I love you and Matt very much, so you won't get rid of me too easily.'

She bathed her babies and put them to bed, set the table for breakfast, sewed a button on Matt's coat and laid out their uniforms for tomorrow. When all the jobs were done, she retrieved the page of newsprint from her jacket on the coat stand. A Jean Davenport had been murdered, and a gold cross was missing from her body. The dead woman had always worn the cross, a birthday gift from neighbours for whose children she had babysat during her teenage years.

A photograph of a similar cross sat next to the news item; it was diamond cut on one side, and her initials had been on the plain side. The initials. What had they been? Oh why, why didn't she take better notice of life's details? The cross had disappeared, of course. But surely ... no. Neil couldn't kill or hurt anyone. Perhaps the killer had sold it to a jeweller, and Neil had bought it... He wasn't a murderer. Nevertheless, she shivered as she placed the paper in the bureau's secret drawer. Neil had changed, and she didn't like what he had become. Perhaps he should stay away from the children after all.

By the time they reached Southport, Ian Foster, John Lucas and Phil Sharples were showing symptoms of coma. After stuffing themselves with goodies provided by Babs, they fell asleep, mouths open, noses and throats delivering snores in several styles, none of which bore any relationship to the tonic solfa.

Lippy Macey pulled into a side street. 'What are we going to do with three bags of coal?' He knew his question was rhetorical. He, Gordy and Babs turned and stared at their charges. 'My wife's a small woman,' the driver continued, 'and my sons are in Africa doing something about irrigation, so there'll be no one to help carry these three. Only my wife and daughter are at home, probably with a few very well-dressed visitors. So, what next?'

'We go to mine,' Gordy said. 'I'll take one up for a bath, and you two can sort the others out in Don's house – he won't mind.'

Lippy agreed. 'When they're done and dusted, I'll take them all to my place.' He paused. 'This has to be handled properly.'

Gordy pondered for a few seconds. 'Are they any good with horses?' he asked eventually.

Babs snorted. 'They wouldn't know a horse from an elephant. In fact, unless it has pedals, a chain and a pump, they'll have no idea.'

Lippy Macey laughed. He loved the way Babs expressed herself.

'What?' she snapped, glaring at him.

'Neither did you know a horse from an elephant,' Gordy reminded her. 'Look at you now, Miss Argumentative. You can groom, saddle and ride an impossible beast; you look after cats, dogs,

242

chickens, geese and donkeys—'

'Not geese,' she interposed. 'Geese are not open to reason or suggestion. And they bite. Murdoch isn't impossible; he's just got a mind of his own.' As ever, she defended her mount.

'All right, all right.' He turned to Mr Macey. 'My stable lads are back at school, so I could use some help.'

'Police first,' Lippy insisted. 'And these boys are still under fifteen, I understand, so they've a little while at school yet. Police manpower needed elsewhere is being used up in the hunt for our runaways. As you know, I have some clout with local powers, so let's see what happens now the boys are no longer missing.'

What happened next would be engraved forever on the minds of several people. In the kitchen of Wordsworth House, the three boys acted like drunks; poor coordination, blurred vision and headaches kept them in Don's house for half an hour. After diagnosing dehydration, Lippy fed them sips of water, while Babs and Sal went through the boys' bags in search of clean clothes, which items were then ironed by Sally.

Gordy and Lippy dragged or half-carried Ian along to Dove Cottage and bathed him. The boy objected vociferously to being assaulted and damned near drowned and to being dried with the rough towels preferred by the man of the house. He was dressed in Gordy's old pyjamas and dumped in the spare room bed, where he took up where he had left off, delivering as a solo artist the second movement of the snoring symphony.

Two exhausted men sat on the stairway of Dove

243

Cottage. 'One down, two to go,' Lippy grumbled. 'We need an ambulance.'

'We need a bloody crane,' was Gordy's swift response. 'They might be young and starving, but they're damned solid. Why an ambulance, though?'

Lippy shrugged. 'Dehydration and weeks of poor diet might cause harm to internal organs. They should be looked at by medics.'

'So you're a doc now?'

'No, but my wife is.'

'Ah yes, I remember now. Phone her.'

Lippy shrugged. 'I can't; we're not speaking. Sign language on a phone's not much use. We have visitors and I'm supposed to be there. I've had the lecture about charity beginning at home, and she expected me back by eight o'clock. I might as well hang for the full sheep.'

'Bugger.'

'Yes, that as well. It's fine – she will understand when I've explained it all, and–'

'How can you explain when you're not talking?'

'On paper. Come on, Gordy, let's relieve the ladies.'

They left the cottage.

The younger man smiled to himself, though he said nothing. Babs and Sally were no ladies. The pair walked to the main house, each dreading two more baths. Gordy had needed to mop the floor after Ian's splashing and fighting, and the thought of a further double dose was not pleasant.

But when they entered the kitchen of Wordsworth House, they found three happy people at the table. Don, looking healthier than he had for months, was drinking cocoa with the two girls.

'Cocoa?' Babs asked the new arrivals.

'Please,' they replied in unison.

'Where are the boys?' Gordy wanted to know.

'Asleep,' Sally answered. 'Mr Crawford has two bathrooms, so John had one and Phil had the other. Babs and I bathed them, though we left them to deal with the private details. Don found some old pyjamas in his tallboy, and all's well. Where's Ian?'

'No comment,' was Lippy's answer.

Babs tutted. 'Men? They've no idea. Where is he?'

'In bed snoring,' Gordy said. 'He put up a fight. We were knee deep in water, and we were accused of trying to kill him by drowning, also of flaying him with my rough towels. It was not a pretty sight; nor was the language elegant.'

Sally chuckled. 'I wonder why lads take more notice of little women than they do of great big men?'

'Sheer, naked terror,' Lippy answered. 'My wife is five feet and one half-inch tall. We must never forget the half-inch. She's a practitioner of general medicine, and she strikes fear into the stony hearts of consultants who are, for the most part, untouchable. Nor must we omit the third l in her name – Lillian. Small women come out fighting, because they feel they've a lot to prove.' He looked from Babs to Sally. 'And here we have two more, God help us.' He went to phone the Chief Constable.

Don sipped his cocoa. 'Lillian visits me some-times, and she's a pussy cat.' He turned to Gordy.

245

'Have you accommodation in Dove Cottage for all three boys? I know the third bedroom's a bit small.'

'I could manage as long as you feed and clothe them.'

'We'll see what Lippy thinks.' Don stood. 'I'm off to bed.'

The two girls glanced at each other. Gordy noticed their silent communication and swallowed anger alongside his cocoa. As the sole confidant of Don Crawford, he knew that the two small women were the boss's 'babies', and the thought of them being touched by the dirty old bastard did not sit well with him. But he could do nothing about this area of their lives.

'Are you all right, Gordy?' Babs asked.

He shook his head wearily. 'I'm fine. Boys are more tiring than horses.'

Babs placed a hand on his forearm. 'He doesn't hurt us,' she whispered, 'he's just very annoying. We're tougher than we look.'

'Thank God for that,' he murmured.

Sally smiled to herself. The chemistry between Babs and Gordy was almost palpable, and she didn't need to be a true adult to notice it. She loved Babs, and Babs loved her, but that was different; it was a phase both had needed, a sort of stepping stone between abuse and a better future. For now, it served as cabaret for Daddy Crawford, so it was a job, she supposed. But Babs and Gordy seemed made for each other, and Sally was pleased for both of them. At seventeen, and not far from eighteen, she was almost a woman, and women were clever – even Mr Macey thought so.

Gordy looked towards the hall. 'I wonder what he's saying to the police?'

'He knows what he's doing,' was the reply from Babs.

Lippy re-entered the kitchen. 'Right. The police know we have the boys, as does my solicitor. I'll come for them in the morning and we can start to plot their next move. That school is going to be hit hard.'

'All the monks?' Sally's eyes were wide.

Mr Macey nodded gravely. 'Some of the others must have known what the three main players were up to, so the guilt must be shared by all. My wife would liken it to cancer and its metastases. There's the main growth, the primary, and it can give birth to other malign tumours in different parts of the body. No one spoke up while the abuse was going on; if it hadn't been for Ian Foster and his allies, the disease would have spread. It may start again, so the school goes.'

Babs swallowed. 'How do you get rid of a school?' she asked quietly.

'I own the building,' he answered. 'Their lease runs out at the end of this year. More important, I have friends in the newspaper business, and the printed word is mightier than the sword. The Brothers Pastoral will be damned. Is there any more cocoa?'

While DC Eddie Barnes helped Bill Tyler with his statement, news filtered through the police force at speed. A uniformed officer knocked quietly on the door of the interview room, and Eddie stuck his head into the corridor for a few seconds.

Wisely, he returned to his seat without saying a word about the message he had just been so pleased to hear.

'Let's get this finished, Bill. So you feared for your family?' he asked, taking up where he had left off.

'Yes. We knew a lad whose mam got beat up after he spilled to the cops. She was in the ozzy for three days with conker something ... er...'

'Concussion?'

'That's the one. She had three broke ribs as well, and some bones in her feet was snapped, too. They jumped on her feet. Yes, we got scared.'

'Are you still frightened, Bill?'

The boy shrugged. 'I'm here, aren't I? Boss is locked up, and his gang will have all ran away.' He pondered for a few seconds. 'Yeah, I'm still a bit worried, like.' He stared hard at Eddie. 'Will you come and talk to me mam and dad and me brothers?'

'If that's what you want, of course I will.'

'You can tell 'em what Roy and me done with them plants. It'll come better from you, cos you're on my side. And when I have to give wotsit – evidence in court, it won't come as such a shock to them.'

'OK. I think we're done. Just let me read this out to you. Listen carefully. You can decide if you want to add anything more. Then I'll want your autograph.'

Eddie read while Billy listened. He then signed his statement and sat back, relieved because the ordeal was over.

Eddie grinned. 'We have most of the gang, Bill.

Boss betrayed them. He didn't stick the needle in your friend, but he said one of his men did it. He couldn't give us a name, but he says it's one of four people who worked with heroin. It's manslaughter, so yes, you'll be giving evidence.'

Billy shuddered.

'But there's good news as well,' Eddie told him. 'The three lads from the hut are safe and well in Southport.'

'Are you sure?'

'I'm sure.'

Bill released a long sigh of relief. 'They aren't druggies. They're just runaways.'

'We know.'

'They were in the shed before the drugs got put there.'

'Yes. And for the first time in weeks, they're sleeping in beds tonight. Come on, Bill, let's get you and your shared bike home. We don't want your brothers arguing with you about that old boneshaker.'

'It's not that bad.'

'It's a wreck. Buy yourself a new one out of your earnings.'

Bill grinned. 'I'm just a brick carrier. With a bit of luck, I might be a cement mixer in a few days. They're going to send me to a sort of school to learn plastering and tiling. One of me brothers is doing plumbing, and the other's learning electrics.'

Eddie nodded wisely. If Roy Foley had owned a tenth of this lad's guts and determination, he would have remained alive...

The door knocker clattered. Belle rose shakily to her feet and walked unsteadily into the hall. Her new husband was back, and her parents would be with him. Oh, God. They should have done it Tom's way with a proper wedding and her family involved. What would Mam and Dad have to say about all this? And Lisa, little Lisa...

She opened the door. Just two people stood there, and both jaws travelled south as soon as they saw their daughter. 'Belle?' Frankie put a hand to her open mouth. 'He said he'd married somebody who didn't know the area well, and–'

'And we're the welcoming committee,' Sam finished for his wife. 'What the hell are you playing at, girl?'

Belle blinked several times before answering. 'I didn't want a fuss. Come in,' she said, before leading her parents into the front room. 'So Tom didn't mention me.' This was not a question. 'It's my fault. I didn't fancy banns and a church wedding and all that messing about, because... She couldn't tell them the because, since it involved her fear of people who patronized Meadowbank. 'After I lost my job, I didn't feel fit to organize stuff, so we just went for it.'

'But we would have helped.' Frankie sounded hurt.

'I've been looking for work. As things stand, I'm going to learn to drive and do collections, returns and paperwork for Tom.'

The visitors sat together on the sofa. 'You don't know him,' Sam accused her, glancing sideways at his wife.

Frankie nodded her agreement.

250

'I do. I did. We'd come across each other a few times in the past while I had the job. Then when I stayed at yours, we recognized each other and ... well, we fell in love. And don't tell me off about that, because you two fell for one another as soon as you met outside a butcher's shop when you were teenagers. You got three lamb chops and a husband, Mam, and Dad got six pork sausages and a wife, so don't kick off on me.'

'And we got married in church with our families there,' Frankie snapped.

'Tom's divorced,' was Belle's reply to that.

A short, awkward silence followed. 'What about Lisa?' Sam asked eventually. 'How does she fit into all this?'

Belle shrugged. 'We'll work it out. She'll probably work it out, and we're only three doors away from each other. Lisa doesn't need to lose anybody, and none of us will have to lose her.' She paused. 'Can't you be happy for me, and for Tom? He's a lovely bloke, as you already know. I love him. Like he says, even from a practical point of view, three hands are better than one and a hook.' She watched while her dad squashed a smile.

Frankie was mellowing. 'I suppose we'll just be a bigger family, Sam. And Tom is a smashing fellow. He'll look after our girls, I'm sure.'

'Where is my new husband?'

'He's babysitting Lisa, of course.'

Belle smiled. He'd planned it this way so that nobody would be inhibited by his presence. There was a lot more to Tom Duffield than bright blue eyes, a handsome face, a mop of dark hair and a missing hand; he was clever. Moreover, he cared about people, because he went about in his spare time helping other amputees to come to terms with the loss of body parts. 'We're not a mistake,' she told them, repeating Tom's words. 'And we need each other.'

Sam stood. 'Then we'd better let him come back home if you need each other.' He put his arms round his only child. 'God bless you.' His voice was hoarse. 'He's a good man, but I hope you're sure that what you've done is right.'

'I am sure, Dad.' Belle's words were thickened by unshed tears.

Frankie rose to her feet. 'Come here, Belle.'

Both parents put their arms round the daughter they loved. And in that moment, Belle knew that everything was going to be all right.

So having been blessed by her family, Belle sat down and waited for Tom's return. The wedding cake could keep till tomorrow, and Lisa could help with the first cut. What a day, she thought, before falling asleep in her chair.

If you remember, it's a while since I spoke about this even to you, my conscience, my spirit or whatever you are. It all started off with that greasy chair. This is my last night at Stanley Road's version of the Dorchester in a room with no view due to filthy windows (I cleaned the inside, but no improvement was achieved), and well ... well ... oh, give me a minute.

My heart's all over the place, going like the clappers, then slowing down to a steady thud, thud, thud like one of those things they use to tamp down bits of tarmac on a pathway. I had to get out. I peeled myself off the mucky chair, but the brown paper I was sitting on stayed where it was, as if glued. And I thought look, it's a nice evening, so I'll go for a walk, perhaps have a half in a pub – anything to get out of the dump.

Just like earlier when I went to the farm and saw Angela in the kitchen with the others, her hair loose and flowing, ordinary blue blouse, her mouth open rather than set in a cruel line... Where was I? Oh yes, exactly like then, my feet moved towards the river, and I followed them, which is compulsory, as they're permanently attached to me. Was that a joke? I don't often do joking. What I mean is that I had no more control over my body than I had earlier over my old bicycle.

I don't even remember putting the wire in my pocket before setting off for my walk. I do remember her voice, though. She offered me business, quoted her list of prices for various functions. Her language was a mixture of filth and guttural Scouse, and she had lipstick on her teeth. At first, I thought it might be blood and wondered whether I ought to have brought some garlic flowers and a crucifix...

She smiled, and as I stared at her the flesh appeared to melt from her ugly face until I could see only bleached bone and bad teeth. I seemed to stand back and watch myself ridding the world of the hideous sight. The wire cut my hands. I must wrap some of it round one of my cardboard packing boxes and tell Joseph I hurt myself while doing that.

She wasn't small, but she dropped eventually,

and I looked at her for a while. No longer just a skull, her face and its features were distorted, eyes bulging, the whites discoloured by red threads where blood vessels had begun to burst. Her hands clawed at me, but failed to touch me. An unhealthy, coated tongue protruded as she fought for oxygen, and the noise from her throat sounded like someone trying to vomit. I hated her. She bled slightly where the wire had dug into her throat. Then her pupils glazed over, and the bleeding slowed all the way to a full stop. Her heart was no longer working; she was dead.

So here I am, back in my luxurious apartment with its lard-encrusted cooker, filthy curtains and sticky floor. I just made my second kill. Not my third, because Dolly Pearson was a mistake. After all, I'm only human. I hope Jesus is pleased. Judas is a mischief-maker, I think, so I've nothing to say to him.

Nine

Don, after a great deal of thought, had finally arrived at a decision. 'I've made up my mind, though somewhat reluctantly,' he announced through a mouthful of scrambled egg and toast. After his long rest, he felt better, though not up for much. 'You see, I need to–'

'You need to stop talking with your gob full of food,' Babs chided, glaring hard at him.

He swallowed the last bite of breakfast and

washed it down with tea. 'It's not that I don't love both of you, but you can have your own room from tonight.'

Babs hit him with a clean pillowcase. 'Have you gone mental as well as physical? What are you jangling on about? It's getting so as me and her don't know whether we're coming or going – and no, I'm not being rude. Well?'

He rubbed his arm where the pillowcase had touched him. 'Hey, if you're thinking of going Angela Whiplash on me, you can think again. I've a dicky ticker, you know.'

'Explain yourself,' Babs insisted. He was making no sense.

'Shut up. My health's not too bad at the minute, only I think I need to have a bit less excitement. So you can choose your own room, run the house, cook, medicate me, help me get a bath, and I'll shout if I want any extras. I can't promise to be a good boy forever, can I?' He winked. 'So remain prepared to be pounced on from time to time when I lose self-control.'

Sally sagged with relief, because she hated sleeping with him. Babs, older and wiser, was cynical. 'By the way, I mean it. Don't talk with your mouth full, Don. It's not just about manners; it's in case you breathe food in and get pneumonia. We'll be right next door, and you can have a bell – there's one in the kitchen. Go and get it, Sally – it's a little brass thing with a wooden handle. I think it's on the mantelpiece at the window end.'

Sally left the room.

'What's up with you?' Babs asked as soon as they were alone. She knew the man well; he

255

needed sexual entertainment as badly as a starving person craved food and almost as frequently as a baby wanted milk. Although often impotent, he continued to enjoy the company of petite women in lieu of little girls. In a sense, Babs admired him, because he had resolutely worked to find a way of defying and overcoming his true inclinations.

He gulped down the final dregs of his tea. 'I want to see you win, Miss Barbara Schofield. I want to live long enough to be there when you and Murdoch cross that finish line with a lot of fresh air between you two and the rest of the field. Lippy and I will be waiting in the winner's enclosure with all the digs and the would-be digs–'

'What's the digs?'

'Dignitaries, my love. People with wallets bigger than their brains. Oh, and Lippy and I will give you a one third share in Murdoch.'

'Oh.' Babs took his tray and sat on the edge of the bed. 'Thanks so much for the share, Don, but five years?' Would Don last five years? 'Murdoch's still a baby, still learning and as daft as a brush, playful and naughty. He ate half a loaf yesterday when we forgot to put it away. And he's taken up football – Gordy's thinking of getting him a trial as goalie for Liverpool. Then, when it comes to me, I could do with L-plates front and back, because I know next to nothing and I get sore – my arse needs to toughen up. I may not be suitable for the job.'

The old man had an answer, as usual. 'Use rubbing alcohol like you do on me when I'm bed-bound. He adores you, Babs. That animal hates most people – it must be genetic from his wild Arab sire. Any gentleness he has comes from Murma, God love her. But above everything and everyone, Murdoch chose you. That's why he'll win, why he'll focus. The horse is determined and talented, one hundred per cent instinct and a thousand per cent love. Only you and Gordy have ever ridden him without being thrown. He tolerates Gordy Hourigan; you, he treasures.' He paused before changing the subject. 'By the way, how are those poor boys getting on this morning?'

'They're very quiet,' she replied. 'I did them eggs, bacon, mushrooms and toast, but they're exhausted, so I hope they've eaten it. Mr Macey's coming to see them soon. He's talking to lawyers and welfare people and the cops.'

Don lay back on heaped pillows. 'You see, I've always felt drawn to little girls. I was even told by a head teacher to stay away from parks and playgrounds because mothers reported me for staring, though I never touched a child except for measuring feet and trying on shoes in the shop. I looked at them, but that was all. Those monks want killing. They'll do it again, you see. Once they start, they can't stop. The answer is not to start.'

'Mr Macey will make sure the lads are all right, I'm sure. They're the ones who matter, Don. Let the devil deal with the monks, eh?'

Don grinned. 'Lippy Macey? Oh yes, he'll sort something out. Babs?'

'What?'

'Were the poor souls raped, baby?'

Babs shrugged; was it her business to tell?

'I need to know. They deserve help, so I must have the truth, the details. They might shut down later and refuse to divulge what happened to them.'

She nodded, her expression suddenly sad. 'Ian was raped. He was left bleeding, and he led what he called the revolution. But it's his secret to tell you if he wants to, Don. Don't let him know I told you. He's a bright lad with plenty of pride. I'm not sure about the other two, but I wouldn't be surprised.'

'And Ian's the one in Dove Cottage with Gordy?'

'Yes. He's the leader. We've got John and Phil. John's clever, too, if he can only get past that stammer. By the way, he plays the piano a bit, and sings. When he sings, he never stammers.'

He grasped her hand. 'Look after them, darling. Give them plenty to eat.'

'I will.' She kissed his forehead.

Sally returned with the bell and a face like thunder. 'It was in the hall.'

'The bell?' Babs asked. 'I'd swear it was in the kitchen.'

'No, the bloody horse was in the hall. I know, I know, it's a he. So I told him to bugger off, and he went in the wotsit – drawing room. He was sniffing at the books on the far wall. Some of them books is leather-backed. And he's dribbled on the piano lid.'

'Where is he now?' Don asked.

Sally shook her head. 'He's in the hall again, bottom of the stairs, blowing and snuffling. I think he's trying to work out how to get to Babs.

Just out of interest – can horses do stairs?'

Babs sighed heavily. 'Can they do stairs?' she asked Don.

Don pondered the question. 'Depends on the horse and the slope of the flight. My stairs aren't steep, and the treads are deep enough. You'll have to start shutting the kitchen door to keep him out of the carpeted areas.'

Babs laughed. 'You are joking, aren't you? He can open doors whether they go outward or come inward. If we bolt the back door, he turns round and knocks with a rear hoof; we're losing paint and bits of wood. As for the paddock – well, he clears that gate twice a day, floats over like a big feather. Oh Lord, here he comes now.'

Sally sat down suddenly in the bedside chair. What next? she wondered.

All three remained stock still and listened while the horse made a determined effort to achieve a more elevated position in life. After a few seconds, a beautiful red-bay face insinuated itself into the bedroom. Murdoch whinnied and grinned, obviously pleased with himself.

Babs and Don stared open-mouthed at each other.

'Do you believe your eyes?' she asked.

He shook his head. 'I've never seen his like before. What a pest.'

The animal strolled in as if he owned the whole Fylde coast. Babs bridled, arms folded, head shaking. 'Don't come running to me if you break your leg on the way down, you soft sod. What the hell on a butty are you doing up here anyway? We might need the roof off and the fire brigade to get

259

a crane and winch you out.'

'God, he's naughty,' Sally breathed.

'Or a builder might manage it,' Don speculated. 'They have big machinery. Babs, go down and he'll follow you. I'll stay with his back end.' He leapt out of bed with more agility than some men half his age. 'Take his head, Babs. Keep him steady – we don't want any accidents.'

For a reason she failed to analyse fully, Sally found herself laughing uncontrollably. Don had just told Babs to take Murdoch's head, but Murdoch had buried his nose in Babs's mop of thick, long hair. It was almost like being at a circus in which she, Sally and Don were clowns put there to be taunted by a horse who thought he was ringmaster.

Don glared at Sally. 'Doesn't take much to make you laugh, does it?'

'What's up with you now?' Babs snapped. 'Don't start with the hystericals, Sal, because we've half a ton of horseflesh to shift. You're at the front with me.'

Sally sobered immediately. 'What if he falls?'

'We all die and get used for dog meat,' was the older girl's swift reply.

On the landing, Murdoch studied the situation while the three bipods fussed and pushed and argued among themselves. After deciding that humanity had no idea where to start, he left his rear legs on the landing while the two forelimbs stepped one at a time onto the first, then the second stair. So far, so good. He put forward his right fore, then his left fore onto the third step before jumping with both back legs in order to catch up within two stairs of his frontage. There was nothing to it. Once he had judged the distance between his back and front ends, which became three clear stairs after a while, he was away.

'Bloody hell,' Babs grumbled, 'we can expect a daily visitor upstairs now. He's stubborn; must have learned that from your donkeys. This has to be dealt with.' She was a bit sad, because she loved the horse's arrogance and mischief.

Sally sank to the floor, tears of laughter flowing down her face. 'Talk about hop, skip and jump,' she howled.

'He rules our lives, Don.' Babs watched the equine lunatic as he reached the end of the staircase. 'Isn't he brilliant?'

'He certainly is. I wonder what Wordsworth would have made of him? Or Coleridge?'

Babs tutted. 'Coleridge wrote about an albatross. Yes, I've been looking at your poetry books. Maybe a horse is the cross we have to bear. Still, as long as we keep him alive, we won't have to wear him round our necks like that poor old sailor had to do with the bird. Oh, sweet Jesus, look.'

Murdoch decided to practise and perfect his new skill. After travelling up and down twice more, he lost interest and made for the kitchen, where he found his carrot and two apples, one for himself, the other for Nicholas Nye. He would return later for his bread with the scrape of jam, because the two-legged were still fussing upstairs. Sometimes, his blind donkey friend made more sense than those who were supposedly in charge.

261

The three people on the landing composed themselves. 'See?' Don said. 'There's nothing he wouldn't do to get to you, Babs. But I'm afraid my beautiful house is about to become his second stable.'

'No, it won't,' replied the soon-to-be trainee National Hunt jockey. 'Discipline. He has to learn what Gordy calls his boundaries. Sally's right when she says he's naughty. There's a streak in him and yes, it's all the fault of that dad of his who's streaking about like lightning all over Ireland. It's not going to be easy, because he's so lovable, but me and Gordy are going to have to start talking tough. He can race blinkered, but he can't spend his life in blinkers, can he? He's too easily distracted, Gordy says'

A muffled laugh reached their ears, and they turned to find John and Phil in a bedroom doorway. Don introduced himself and shook their hands. 'That was Mad Murdoch,' he explained, 'and I suppose you can see why the word mad is used to describe him. Did you sleep well?'

'Yes, thanks,' Phil replied. 'John's a bit nervous, so his stammer's worse today. We don't know where we're going to be put, you see, sir.'

'Well, if it's anything to do with me and Gordy, you'll be in Dove Cottage with him or here with me, Babs and Sally. It all depends on welfare and what the police say, though you've committed no crime beyond stealing essentials. There's a decent school within walking distance, and Mr Macey usually gets what he wants. Oh, and you can help with the animals.'

'Th-thanks,' John managed.

'I didn't know a horse could climb upstairs and go down again,' Phil said.

Don chuckled.

'Neither did the bloody horse,' Babs told them, 'but he's a quick learner, especially when he wants to be naughty.'

Don sat on a ladder-backed chair. He had saved geese, starving mongrels, battery hens, ill-treated donkeys and two near-feral cats. He had rescued Murdoch's mother and changed her name to Murma. It was time to help some young humans, preferably of the male variety. He remembered the struggle while the cruelly contained chickens had learned to walk for the first time. They were now a coven of feathered witches with a metaphorical and actual pecking order in place, the biggest being in charge for much of the time – until the smaller ones formed a posse and bit her legs. These lads needed to learn to live, and they would require support. 'I've got some good shoes down in the laundry room,' he told them. 'Babs will find each of you a pair to fit. Go down and wait for Mr Macey.'

The boys and girls left Don to himself while he considered a philanthropic future, though he wasn't alone in his room for long. 'Oh, bugger,' he heard Babs muttering as she ascended the staircase.

She burst into the room, and she was rather breathless. 'He's done another one,' she blurted out. 'It's on the radio. Shirley Evans was her name, a working girl from Liverpool, though they never said which part. Strangled with wire, she was, and left where she dropped. We thought he'd

263

stopped. Well, we hoped. It has to be the same man, because he always uses the same wire.'

'Shit!' Don cursed. 'What's wrong with this world is that some people won't make room for others. What harm are the women doing? It's the world's oldest profession for a reason. I'm sure there is true love and happy-ever-after marriage, but not always, and men need a release valve. Going with a whore's better than knocking the wife about.'

Babs agreed. 'Then there's women who marry for money. The only difference between them and prozzies is that they have only the one client.'

Don chuckled. 'I know – I've seen them. They're in the winner's enclosure with the digs, all fur coats, jewellery and h'aitches where there were none. It's a mad world, baby girl.'

'With a mad horse in it.'

Don laughed again. 'Go and wait for Lippy, my love. I'll come down before he gets here; oh, and send Sally to help me get dressed.'

In the kitchen, Gordy and Ian had joined the party. Ian smiled at Babs. 'Where's Sally?' he asked rather too casually.

'Helping Mr Crawford to get dressed. He's got a bad heart, so me and Sal look after him and the house.'

'Oh, right.' Ian was blushing.

Babs sat down. Ian was nearly fifteen, while Sally would soon be eighteen. It wasn't too much of a gap, she decided. By the time one was twenty and the other twenty-three, nobody would notice the difference. The sweet, gentle love between the two girls was just a stepping stone; after several discussions, they were agreed on that subject. Both wanted the normal life. What was the normal life? Husband, children, bills and worry? And who decided what was normal? The government, the Pope, God? Questions, questions. But the most immediate was what was going to happen to the boys?

Sally entered with her right arm supporting her employer. She sat him in a comfortable chair near the range, then looked straight into Ian's eyes.

Babs smiled. She was right, and she loved being right. She was right about Gordy, too, because he was working at the opposite end of the scale by looking everywhere except in her direction.

According to Don's will, Wordsworth House would belong to the RSPCA after his death, but she and Sally could live out their lives here rent free. There was ample room for two families, and Babs would own outright the gatehouse, Dove Cottage. She smiled at Don. He was an eccentric old man with a bad heart that was really a good heart. She intended to look after him as best she could manage, because he had done more for her and Sally than anyone else in the world had bothered to try. Eve had always seen what she termed 'bad' in him, but Babs knew differently. He was a bit senile sometimes, but he did his best.

'I hope they're on their way,' Sally said almost to herself.

The camper van rolled audibly through shingle and parked outside the kitchen window. 'Right,' Don ordered, 'drawing room, everyone. He seems to have brought half of Southport with him.'

Everyone sighed, and the boys looked fearful.

'It'll be all right, Ian,' Sally promised.

They transferred to the best room, a rather grand place with two walls of crammed bookshelves, a massive fireplace, four sofas, several armchairs and a baby grand piano from whose lid Murdoch's spittle had recently been removed. All new arrivals introduced themselves briefly before disappearing. The three boys were taken upstairs to be examined by a police doctor and interviewed by two plain clothes detectives, one of each gender, and a psychologist.

Mr Macey's remaining retinue comprised three welfare workers and Mr Macey's wife, Lillian. She and the welfare people followed Gordy to his cottage in order to size up the accommodation and to judge his character. As Dr Macey already knew him, Gordy stood a good chance of being found appropriate as temporary guardian.

Only Don, Babs, Sally and Lippy Macey were left in the drawing room.

'We could have stayed in the kitchen,' Babs said.

Don tapped the side of his nose. 'The stammerer plays the piano,' he said. 'And he sings. When he sings, the stammer disappears. I'm within yards of the gatehouse and I have a baby grand. They'll notice that, and it's a point in our favour.'

'Sorted,' Babs finished for him.

Sally grinned; Ian would be living nearby. She returned a cheeky wink from Babs. Life was getting better all the time.

Within the hour, everyone but the boys and the psychologist had returned to the drawing room. It was time for cups of tea all round, and everyone was given one of Sally's butterfly cakes with real cream, light as duck down and very moreish. The cake stand was empty within a few minutes. Silence ruled while the company enjoyed the offerings.

'You can bake for me any time.' Lippy glanced at his wife. 'Lillian's too busy to bake, aren't you, my love? She has to cure the stomach pains of all whose wives can't cook properly.'

Wisely, the good doctor offered no reply.

They talked about the weather, the unbelievable cost of living, the beauty of Wordsworth House and Don Crawford's love of poetry.

The psychologist entered. 'Remarkable boys,' was his first comment before he looked at the denuded cake stand and asked who had eaten his.

'I saved some,' Sally announced. 'I'll just make a fresh pot of tea.'

'Well?' Don asked.

A female welfare officer spoke. 'There'll be a meeting held in camera, just the professionals involved. It's something that has to happen, especially when children or young people have suffered abuse.'

Psychology stepped into the conversation. 'They all expressed fondness for Babs and Sally. Female influence is vital for boys of this age.'

Babs felt heat arriving in her cheeks. 'Yes, we were staying with friends in a house not too far from the hut. 'What would these folk say if they knew the truth about her and Sally?

'Will you please go away?' These shouted words arrived from the kitchen.

Murdoch, who hated to be left out of anything, entered the drawing room, closely followed by Sally. Jaws dropped as if choreographed to perform simultaneously. The horse made a beeline for Babs and shoved his nose in her hair. Sally stood in the doorway, arms akimbo. 'He's ate two cakes,' she pronounced angrily. 'I was making the tea, and he pinched two of me fairy butterflies. Should horses eat double cream?'

Gordy rose to his feet. 'Out, Murdoch,' he said quietly.

The horse moved his head away from Babs and stared at the trainer.

'Out,' Gordy repeated.

After neighing loudly, the animal turned.

Ian stood in the doorway. 'Come here, Mad Murdoch,' he ordered.

Murdoch pondered. There were too many people in this room, and a young one was summoning him. Young ones tended to be interesting. He walked towards Ian, who stroked his nose before taking hold of his mane. 'Let's go outside, shall we?' Ian coaxed.

Horse and boy, pursued by gales of laughter, left the scene.

The psychologist looked at the doctor who had performed the physical examination of the boys. 'Relaxed household, wouldn't you say, Ryan?'

Dr Ryan, chuckling too hard to reply, nodded his agreement.

'That was indeed Mad Murdoch,' Babs announced when laughter approached its natural

268

death. 'He's a bit of a character. We've got cats, dogs, chickens, donkeys, Murdoch's mother, and geese, too. After Murdoch, who's spoilt, the geese are the worst. One of the donkeys is blind, so Murdoch looks after him. Mr Crawford rescued them all. He's working with the RSPCA.'

Dr Macey spoke. 'Lippy and I know you of old, Don. You have your faults like the rest of humanity, but you do no harm and perform many a charitable deed. You already know that Lippy and I would be happy to take these boys, but I think there's more for them here. Looking after animals is good therapy.'

'Mr Hourigan?'

Gordy turned and looked at the welfare woman. 'Yes, that would be me.'

'You're willing to take them?'

He nodded. 'In a heartbeat. I'm of a huge Irish family, so I'm used to youngsters. Mr Crawford's housekeeper and his nurse will cook meals for the boys, so they'd have two homes and several adults plus the menagerie outside. Donkeys are good company and very affectionate.'

'And school, Mr Hourigan?'

'Just a cock-stride away.'

'And Gordy's a linguist,' Don said. 'Four languages – he speaks Irish, English, Animalish and Rubbish.'

Phil and John arrived at the door. 'Can we go outside with Ian and that daft horse?' Phil asked.

'Of course you may,' replied the owner of the estate. 'If you want to earn your keep, shovel some dog shit and bury it deep behind the garage. Thanks.'

269

Both doctors and the psychologist stood up. 'You've probably won yourselves temporary custody of three needful boys,' the psychologist announced. 'It's good to have them pro tem, because it gives you a chance to understand them and decide whether you want them permanently. This way, we all have time to think. The boys' wishes and decisions will be taken under consideration, too, when we have our meeting.'

The crowd left with several cream cakes over which they would doubtless fight, while Don, Gordy and the girls returned to the kitchen. Babs watched through the window as Lippy told the boys how the meeting had gone. 'They're laughing, Sal. God bless them, they're happy.'

Lippy climbed into the van and drove away.

Immediately, the three lads ran into the kitchen. 'Thank you,' Ian said. 'We'll be good.'

'Just be yourselves,' was Gordy's advice. 'When boys start acting good, we send for doctors.'

'Well,' Phil said, scratching his head, 'you'd best get a vet, because that horse is behaving itself. John rode it. He fell off, like, but that was his fault, and Murdoch just stood over him and made sure he was all right.'

'Come with me,' Gordy said. 'I'll show you how to muck out. Working with animals is fifty per cent fun, fifty per cent shit and fifty per cent hard graft. It's time you met some donkeys, too. They're Mr Crawford's pet project.'

'That was one hundred and f-fifty per cent,' John said.

'I know. The extra fifty is Murdoch.'

Don's eyes twinkled as he watched through the

270

window while Gordy took the boys across the lawn towards the paddock. 'I think they'll be all right, baby girls. I'm going back to bed.'

Babs followed him up to make sure he didn't have a fall. The scent of tonight's scouse floated up the stairwell, making the house smell homely. Homely meant safe. She was OK, Sally was OK, and Don was better than he'd been for weeks. As for Gordy – well, he was promising...

Neil Carson stood at the school gates, a flat cap pulled low over his eyes. Just a few hours ago, he had killed a woman, a piece of dross without which the world would supposedly improve. Now, he watched his children, just two among many healthy, happy youngsters celebrating freedom from the confines of classrooms. How would Matt and Lucy turn out? They no longer had a daddy to guide them; Matt, in particular, needed a leader of the same gender. And little girls loved their daddies, didn't they?

'Neil?'

He ignored the voice. He wasn't expecting company, didn't want to talk, yet he knew who it was. Why now? Why did she have to be here right now?

'Neil – it's me.'

He turned. It was Laura. No, it wasn't. She looked like Laura, but with a slightly fuller face and colour in her cheeks. Laura had no sisters. Her hair was shiny; her hair had never been shiny. 'Hello,' he answered uncertainly. He'd been gone for ... for how long? Days, weeks, a month? And she looked so well. She was happier without him,

271

it would appear. 'Hello,' he repeated.

'Watching them play, are you?' she asked.

'Yes.'

'I brought them packed lunches. They both decided that they don't like school dinners, so I thought I'd start today with homemade stuff. They forgot to pick the boxes up on their way out of the house.' She paused. 'Why don't you visit?' she asked eventually. 'Why not come for a meal with us when you're on a suitable shift?'

Neil stared hard at his wife. She was painted. Although she wasn't as heavily coated as street women, she wore powder and lipstick, some colour on her eyelids – and was that mascara? Oh, God. Had she turned, taken a step away from her old life and towards ... towards the murky side? 'I have to go,' he said abruptly, walking to his bike. He threw his leg over the crossbar and pedalled furiously along the pavement until he was far enough away to stop and check traffic.

He pulled into the road and began the journey back to Greasy Chair Hell. Today, he was moving in with Joseph Turton and his mother, so his domestic circumstances would be cleaner and easier from now on. Joseph was coming at twelve, and Neil's shift would begin at two o'clock, so there wasn't much time.

His heart was beating rapidly. Rumours about a body in a side street by the Dock Road were beginning to circulate; as yet, there was nothing in the newspapers. Although anonymous, he was the most hated man in Liverpool. 'Jesus,' he whispered, 'where are you?' It was a grey day. The only bit of brightness had been in the faces of

272

children at play. Oh, and Laura's features had been decorated... What was the woman up to? Another man. There had to be another man.

He was being replaced. She couldn't remarry because of her faith, but if she introduced a substitute father... He couldn't bear the thought. Perhaps he should visit for the occasional meal. First, he had to move house, so he must try to concentrate on getting today right. He no longer thought clearly, and often lay awake in the night persecuting himself about Dolly Pearson and her poor mother. He continued to nurse the suspicion that he was losing his mind.

'I'll take good care of Joseph's mother,' he mouthed to himself. 'After all, everybody made mistakes.'

Laura walked into the playground after the whistle had sounded, and handed lunch boxes to the teacher in charge. She smiled at her son, then at Lucy, both standing still in lines straight enough for the Trooping of the Colour.

'Are you all right, Mrs Carson?' the teacher asked.

Laura blinked as if waking from a dream. 'Oh, yes. Sorry – I was just anxious to get the children's food to them. Their names are on the boxes.' Smiling politely, she left the school grounds and began the walk to work. Neil had disappeared, of course.

She stood and stared blankly at the road. There was something not right with him. There had been something not right for a while, and now he seemed even worse. The way he'd looked at her –

she shivered. She might have been a sample, some kind of experiment on a slide or in a Petri dish. Whispering, she said her favourite prayer. 'Holy Mary, Mother of God, *ora pro nobis*' – oh, she'd lapsed into Latin again – 'now and at the hour of our death. Amen.' Death. Had he? Could he? Was he a ... a murderer?

He'd never been demonstrative, but neither had she except when it came to her children. Neil was a boring man with a boring job, just one friend who still lived at home with an ailing mother, and no hobbies beyond the odd fishing expedition and a pint after work. He was not a warm person, seldom laughing, never getting upset, and he seemed to have no imagination.

But none of the above sufficed to account for him now, because he was very, very different from the quiet, kind man she had married, the good father and excellent provider. There was a darkness about him; his eyes had changed, seeming somewhat flat and lifeless. He hadn't been able to look at her today, was almost incapable of standing still, as if someone had wound a spring in him and it was nowhere near to running down.

As she neared the chip shop, Laura Carson froze in her tracks. The cross. The initials. The diamond cutting on one side. It all crashed into her head for the umpteenth time. The newspaper she'd discovered among the wrappings. Once again, she allowed her mind free rein. Where had he discovered that cross? Initials – what had they been? Had the murderer of the girl dropped it, sold it as second hand, or...? No, no, he could not be the killer. Perhaps Neil had found the jewellery on the

274

pavement near the murder site; or he could have bought it, she tried to reassure herself.

Mind, he'd stopped going to Confession and Holy Communion. Why? He'd been so punctilious, Confession once a fortnight, Communion every Sunday, Benediction, Midnight Mass at Christmas, wearing the mark on his forehead on Ash Wednesday, kneeling in church for the vigil through part of Good Friday and Holy Saturday, serving at the altar if there were too few boys to do the job. Now? Nothing. There was nothing in his head, nothing in his eyes, no vestige of the man he had been.

She waited for her heart to slow, leaning her body against the wall of the ironmonger's shop next door to her place of work. Should she talk to the police? How might Matt and Lucy feel if their father got taken in for questioning? And the cross had disappeared before Neil had left the house, so she couldn't check the initials.

It was a quarter past eleven, time to start chipping the potatoes in readiness for lunchtime. There was batter to mix, bread to butter, there were soaking marrowfats to transfer to the pan. She wasn't responsible for all those tasks, but she had fast become part of the well-oiled machine created by the Bramwells. They liked her. The customers liked her, while her children and the Bramwells got on very well together.

She pulled herself together, fixed a bright smile to her face and went to do the job she loved.

Sister Helen Veronica had not been prepared properly. She had been in training as owner of a

275

working dog; the detective helping her had travelled all the way from Birmingham in order to teach her how the animal would react in the presence of drugs. 'He's one of the first in this country,' he explained, 'and some of us went to Paris to learn the job. A dog's sense of smell is about forty times superior to ours, because they're wolves, carnivores that had to hunt to live. Watch me, watch him, and watch where the drugs are.'

Helen, happy enough to be educated, wondered what St Veronica thought about the presence of heroin, amphetamines, cocaine and cannabis in the convent. But within days, she and the animal known as Nelson were tuned in to each other. Instructed to keep the dog with her at all times, she put his bed next to hers and took him out with her every day, and he even attended services in the chapel and some meals in the refectory.

Sister Helen, otherwise known as Smelly Nellie, was only semi-prepared. Nothing on earth could have fully prepared her for the love. Nelson was of a serious, almost studious turn of mind. His first owner had grown old, and Nelson had experienced little fun for some time. He knew when he was working and when he wasn't. As a scruffy-looking professional, he wore no collar and required no leash, since he needed to be independent and mobile when at work; as a pet, he sported a leather collar and had begun to play a game named by his owner 'pawball'. She kicked a tennis ball, and he pawed it back to her.

The vet had declared the crossbreed to be part bearded collie, part terrier and part human. 'He's a grand dog, in very good health for a five-year-old, but he needs more exercise and some activity to cheer him up a bit.'

Of course, the whole convent tried to ruin him until the sisters were told not to feed him or fuss him, because this was a special dog, one who must have just the one owner who would nourish him, walk him and keep him well. He must cling to her and only to her, since he should not get distracted. 'He wears no restraints outside,' she told her fellows. 'He has to pin himself to me on the streets, or he'll be run over. At the station, he must concentrate on what his nose tells him, and when he signals I shall inform one of the policemen. Nelson will ensure that I stay undercover by keeping his reactions discreet – he will never jump on a carrier of drugs. So please, leave him to me and Mary. She's the other one who may be at Lime Street, and she is the only exception to the rule.'

So Helen and Nelson became roommates. She talked to him, prayed with him and taught him how to play. When not on duty in town, she introduced him to the convent grounds, where he did all the sniffing and digging that comes naturally to dogs. Yet he never approached the small graveyard where several Veronicas rested. He watched other nuns working in vegetable patches, but he didn't interfere with those areas, either.

When on duty, he accepted without reaction the patting and fussing doled out by people passing through. He seemed to keep one eye on Holy Mary, the *agent provocateuse*, and the other on entrances to platforms. Helen often found herself grinning at the dog she had supposedly found and rescued. If the dealers did but know it, they had a genius on their heels.

Within a week, the club known to police as Nellie, Mary and Tatty Arse caused the capture of no fewer than three dealers who had brought their wares via train to Liverpool. Through a complicated set of signals, the culprits were followed and arrested away from the discovery site, often in excess of a mile from the station. And Helen, at long, long last, had someone of her own to love.

Lisa Horrocks, who insisted that she was no longer three years of age but nearly four, stood on Tom's red rug in front of the fireplace in his best room. Belle was in the living room/kitchen, while Tom Duffield sat on the sofa under the gimlet eye of a child whose mentality was probably closer to forty than four. She folded little arms across her chest. 'How old are you?' she asked.

'Forty-eight next birthday.'

'Oh.' Lisa shifted weight from one foot to the other, then back again. 'Isn't that nearly dead?' she demanded to know.

He felt like an interviewee for a monumentally important job like managing director of the Woolworth chain, a butler for Her Majesty, or a Vatican guard. 'No, it isn't nearly dead, Lisa. Your grandparents are older than I am, and I trust they have many years of happy life to look forward to.'

'You're older than my mummy.'

'That's true.'

'And you've only got one hand. Why have you only got one hand?'

He shrugged. 'A machine stole it. Cut it off.'

278

The child's mouth shaped itself into a perfect O. 'Did it hurt?'

'Yes.'

'Was there loads and loads and loads of blood?'

'Some, yes.'

She thought about that for a few seconds. 'I suppose you had to be a brave soldier, like me when I go for inject-shuns. I never cry; so I always get a jelly baby off Nora Nitty from the Bug Committee.'

He tried not to laugh. 'Is she the one who looks in your hair for crawlers?'

'That's right. At nursery, she visits a lot. She says it's a plague area.'

'Oh?'

'What's a plague?'

He considered his reply. 'It's an illness that jumps from one person to the next.'

'Like nits?'

'Like nits.' He wondered how he was doing in this impromptu interview, because he'd had no warning, no time to prepare a curriculum vitae. He could hear Belle chuckling quietly; he would deal with her later. Dealing with her was very enjoyable.

Lisa took a step closer to her victim. 'Are you my dad now?'

Tom cocked his head to one side and grinned at her.

'Well?' She was tapping a foot, something she'd learnt from her grandmother. 'Are you my new dad?'

Oh, he could see Belle in this one. Belle was sweet, kind and motherly, but there was a tiger underneath the fluffy surface. And here stood the tiger kitten, claws not quite sheathed, teeth not quite hidden. 'That's up to you, Lisa. Do you want a dad?'

She glared at him. 'Do dads buy things for kids?'

'Sometimes. I used to buy toys for my sons.'

His reply stopped her dead in her tracks. 'Where are they?'

'With their mother.'

'Why? Why aren't they here in your house?'

'Their mother doesn't like me any more, so she took them with her when she left.'

Lisa looked at the ceiling, then through the window, then at the floor. 'Just a minute,' she said before leaving for the kitchen.

Tom breathed out. He felt like a footballer at half time during a big international match.

Belle was ready, though she played the innocent. 'Hello, love.'

'He had a Mrs Duffield, but she left him cos she didn't like him.'

'And?' Belle dried a saucer.

'Will you stop liking him?'

'No. She didn't want him because he had only one hand. She wouldn't help to do his bandages.'

'Right.' Lisa returned to the interview room.

Tom removed his ear from the wall just in time and sat down quickly. 'Ah, you're back,' he commented. 'Have I passed?'

'Passed what?'

'I'm not sure,' he said solemnly.

'Let me look at it.'

'What?'

She glanced heavenward again; grown-ups were such hard work. 'The hand that isn't there. I want to see it.'

'It isn't there.'

The child's arms were now akimbo; given a bucket, a mop and a hairnet, she would have looked like a miniature cleaning woman. 'Mummy!' she yelled.

Belle appeared. 'What, love?' She was having a hard time, because she wanted to fall about laughing.

'Tell him, will you? Tell him what I mean.'

'I don't know what you're talking about, Lisa'

The child's voice rose in pitch and volume. 'The hand that isn't there,' she screamed angrily.

Belle looked at Tom. Belle shouldn't have looked at Tom, because both were in a state worse than Russia. 'Show her your stump,' she snapped, just to hold back the laughter.

With mock solemnity, he rolled up his sleeve while Lisa closed the small distance between herself and him. 'There you are, Lisa – the hand that isn't there.'

Belle lost the inclination to laugh. There sat her lovely husband displaying his healed wound to a bossy little madam.

Lisa touched her lips, then carried the kiss on her fingers and gave it to his wrist. 'Right, that should make it all better. You can be my dad if you want. I'm going to Amelia's now.'

And that was that.

'I think I've just been adopted,' he told his new wife solemnly.

'Hmm. There's a strong possibility. And all

281

without a general anaesthetic. I wonder if she'll decide to move in with us?'

'Oh, I hope so, Belle. Though I'd hate to deprive Sam and Frankie. Let's just give it time, baby. What are we eating tonight?'

'Finger foods?' She arched an eyebrow.

'You have a sick sense of humour, Isabella Duffield.'

'I know. Don't you just love it?'

He chased her out of the room, along the hall and into the kitchen where he cornered her. 'Good job I'm handsome then, isn't it?'

'And hand-y about the house.'

He looked round the room. 'Do you need a hand?'

'Can you spare one, Mr Duffield?'

The joke would run forever, but he didn't mind. This wonderful woman loved him, and his happiness cup was full to the brim.

Eve threw down her shopping list and turned off the radio. Another girl was dead, garrotted with wire, exactly the same as the earlier victims. An idea was taking shape in her mind like a series of photographs lined up before her inner eye. The man needed taking out of the mix, and the police had got nowhere with the other murders.

She lit a Woodbine and inhaled deeply. There was something about cigarettes that kicked a mind into gear whenever it showed signs of slowing down or pulling into a lay-by. Unlike drink, tobacco dragged a person into the now instead of placing a layer of mist over thoughts and deeds.

All three murders had taken place close to the

Dock Road under the cover of darkness at approximately half past ten at night. All three women had been strangled to death, and there had been no witnesses. Well, perhaps she might try to put that right. Of course, she'd need a touch of luck, but it was worth a try, especially when it involved dealing with a murderer.

Kate entered the office. 'Any luck getting replacements for Belle and Angela, then?'

Eve nodded, though her mind was elsewhere. 'Belle's found a few possibles. I'm meeting them next Monday. Kate?'

'That's me.' She positioned a cup of coffee under Eve's nose.

'I've been thinking. The van.'

'What about the van?'

Eve shrugged. 'There are a lot of vehicles parked or abandoned down there by the river.'

'And?' Kate placed herself in the chair facing Eve's desk.

'Wouldn't it be wonderful if a couple of heavies came with us and maybe one of the girls? Imagine the poetic justice if we put a stop to him.'

The cook/housekeeper's jaw dropped. She snapped her mouth closed. 'You can't go taking the law into your own hands, Eve. We could get done for murder ourselves.'

'Not if he's got a woman and he's trying to kill her.'

'It could be too late for the poor cow.'

Eve nodded thoughtfully. 'Yes, but she'd be the last, wouldn't she? And some heavies know where to buy or borrow a gun with a wotsit on – silencer. We could get him killed without having to touch him.' She thrummed her fingers on the desk. 'There's a pattern to the killings, Kate. He's killed three at the same time, one on a Thursday, two on Fridays. It could be his way of celebrating the weekend – who knows? There's a gap between the murders. This is a shift worker with a job in Liverpool. I bet he goes home the Dock Road way, parks his car, finds a girl on her own, and Bob's his uncle.'

Kate swallowed audibly. 'I hope you know what you're doing, Evie.'

'Don't I always? Get cooking, babe. At least we've fewer mouths to feed while we're shut.'

The older woman left the office. Sometimes, it was impossible to drum sense into Eve Mellor's head. Anyway, there was a meal to cook and be served up. Life went on. Well, it went on till some heavy with a gun put a stop to it.

Ten

Belle, Eve and Tom had a lunchtime meal together in a sit-down chippy in town. They were discussing the future of Meadowbank, and the noise of other people talking and coming in for takeaways was a good screen behind which they could hide. Even so, the two women kept their voices low while imparting and receiving information. Although Tom sat with them, he distanced himself mentally, concentrating instead on the famous Lancashire combination of fish, chips, peas, buttered bread and a huge mug of strong tea.

'You've worked hard, then,' Eve said. 'And I'm grateful, because you're newly-weds and I know you've better things to do with your time. So tell me about these terrible twins. Are they identical?'

Belle grinned. 'Ah yes, the Gilroys. No, they're chalk and cheese, one fair, one dark, both good company. If you ever get bored, they sing and tap dance and perform old music hall acts. Alice does all sorts of play-acting, including a lot of Angela's kind of stuff, and she's damned good at everything. Theresa – she goes by Terry most of the time – is a direct replacement for me. She's massage with extras, so more of your clients will be pleased. And the twins will have threesomes or foursomes, so that might go down well. A bunch of grapes and sheets worn like togas, and you can call it an orgy.'

Tom went to the counter for three more teas. Although he accepted his wife's past and loved her dearly, he felt uncomfortable about listening to explicit details. He wanted to keep Belle away from all this stuff, but he refused to put his foot down. Victoria was long dead, and most women made up their own minds about life these days, which was fair enough after all the time and effort spent gaining the right to vote and running the country during six years of war.

Eve was correct about one thing, because Belle had worked hard to get more girls away from pimps and off the streets. Belle was a good woman, and she wouldn't return to that other life, would she? But Eve didn't look well, he thought.

'Is he all right?' Eve was asking.

285

'It bothers him a bit. He doesn't want to know about their special skills and threesomes – all that leaves him cold. Tom never sat with me while I talked to the girls – he always parked himself apart from us in the pubs and kept an eye on me. He wants to forget that side of life.'

'But that side of life is part of what you are and were. You've moved on, and he loves you – he can't take his eyes off you. Does he trust you, though? Because that's what matters.'

'Yes, and I trust and love him. Let's get through these while he's in the tea queue. No point upsetting him more than absolutely necessary.'

Eve agreed readily. 'Are they good natured, these twins?'

Belle nodded. 'They should have gone on the stage, if I'm honest. It's all banter and laughter with them; they even make their clients laugh. If you need another baby, Betty Halliwell can be anything you want from a baby to an adult. She's in her twenties, barely five foot tall, and the twins are early thirties and normal height. She passed a small book across the table. 'There's a dozen names with specialities and contact details in there, so I've given you plenty of choice. But the Gilroys and Betty would make for a happy house.' She grinned. 'I know it's a good place already, but with Angela and Babs gone it'll be a bit less like an endless boxing match.'

'Thanks, Belle.' Eve managed to sound all right, though she was having trouble digesting her food. She clung to the subject of girls. 'The part-timers who stepped in were useless, always having headaches and what they called ovulation

286

pain, so they wanted time off twice every month. We miss you.' She glanced at Tom. 'How can he carry three teas?'

'One hand can manage a tray with a few mugs on it, Eve. He rests the other end of the tray on his stump. You should see him working with tiny watches. He uses a hook with attachments in place of his left hand. The stuff he can do without it – he never fails to amaze me.'

'You're happy. I can tell you're both happy. You look about twenty-five, tops.'

Belle smiled. 'I never thought it would happen to me.'

'I've seen loads of girls married,' Eve told her. 'Some happily, some not. Your Tom might be short of a hand, but he's a good man. He was very lonely, and I'm glad he found you.'

Belle launched into an account of Tom's interview panel. 'It wasn't so much a panel as the whole Spanish Inquisition housed inside my daughter. Lisa's my mother all over again.' She told Eve about the scullery being a laundry room and the middle room having been turned into a kitchen and living room. 'So I was right next door while she interrogated him in the best room, the one her granny calls a parlour. I don't know how he got through without laughing or busting a gut. I was in pain – honest, Eve.'

Tom placed the tray on the table. 'Your teas, ladies.'

'I'm just telling Eve about Lisa interviewing you in your own house.'

'Nightmare,' he pronounced before sitting down. 'And it's our house now, love. I felt like giving name, rank and number and refusing to make any further disclosures to the Gestapo.' He picked up a mug. 'She asked me did dads buy things for their children. It was as if I'd gone for a job as head of ICI. I had the distinct feeling that she found me wanting. I'm surprised she didn't turn up with a load of broken clocks and a written list of questions.'

Belle giggled. 'She's been raised by my mam and dad, so she talks and acts like an old woman sometimes. And the way she stands, arms folded, chin stuck out a bit, just like my mother when she's having a word with the window cleaner or the milkman. Then she brought me into it.'

It was Tom's turn to laugh. 'She wanted to see the hand that wasn't there, so I told her it wasn't there, and she set her mother on me.'

Eve was doubled over. 'Stop,' she begged. Any laughter had to be undertaken with care because of corsetry and ill-placed deposits of fat. 'God, I'm dying here.' This joke might not be a joke, because she felt terrible.

'That's not the end of it,' Belle said. 'Amelia-across-the-way has a swing fixed in the back doorway, one you can hang there on a nice day and take down when it's cold or raining. So little madam came back the next day and said she wants one in both houses. Tom and my dad are run ragged fulfilling her orders. Her Christmas list is longer than the Bible, and she's done a birthday list on the other side. She might be only three, but she's already polishing her manipulation skills. Tom was over a barrel, weren't you?'

'Blackmail,' Tom said, his face poker-straight.

Eve smiled. 'I think that's what I've missed most – children and grandchildren. Kate's the only family I've got, and we're not even related.'

'You've got us, Eve.' Belle reached out and patted Eve's arm. 'I'd never have met my Tom if you hadn't given me a place.'

'I'd better go.' Yet again, tears threatened, and Eve needed to leave the cafe before she showed herself up. 'Thank you so much, both of you. And it's nice to know I have some friends.' She tried to struggle out of her seat until Tom helped her up.

He sat down again when Eve had left. 'She has regrets, Belle, and she doesn't look too well. I wonder if regrets can make you ill?'

'We all regret some things.' She sipped her tea.

'What do you regret?' he asked.

'Well, I wish I'd been there for my daughter and I wish I'd met you years ago. I wish I were young enough to carry and bear your child, and I'd like to have learned to drive when I was in my teens or twenties. The instructor isn't impressed with me, and I'm not too keen on him. I'm sure he thinks we're both going to end up in the river.'

'Go to a different driving school, then.'

'What? And frighten another man to death?'

'You'll be OK. It takes time. And I know a very good undertaker...'

They left the cafe, both howling with laughter. He dragged her into the Odeon and bought two tickets.

'What's the film?' Belle asked.

'No bloody idea. We're going courting on the back row.'

So while Dustin Hoffman and his Mrs Robinson cavorted and worried their way through *The Graduate,* a pair of naughty and superannuated teenagers made the best of a double seat in the back row. 'I've never done this before,' Belle whispered.

'Never?' he asked.

She shook her head and had a brief view of the graduate's dilemma. 'He was married,' she mouthed. 'And he knew what I'd done for a living before I met him. If he hadn't died, he might have tried to say Lisa was somebody else's.'

'So you went to Eve's to save up for Lisa?'

'Yes.'

A couple in front turned, and the man told them to shush.

So they shushed, and a good time was had by both. When they left the cinema, it occurred to Belle that once again, she was living her life back to front. Most people courted before they got married, but she was different, as usual. She was arse over tip again, and she'd laddered one of her stockings.

They rode home on the bus, sitting hand in hand like a couple of kids. 'Tom?'

'What?'

'I don't think I loved Lisa's dad. This must be the first time I've been in love.'

'And you're how old?'

'Thirty-five.'

He put his mouth close to her ear. 'My mother was over forty when I was born,' he informed her.

'So?'

'So we should try for a baby.'

She looked round the bus. 'All right. But don't you think it'd be a good idea to wait till we get home?'

'Spoilsport,' he chuckled. 'By the way, what was that film about?'

'No bloody idea, love. Dustin Hoffman jumping some old woman, I think.'

'Bugger,' he said. 'I should have watched it; I might have picked up some tips. Still, never mind. I'm sure I'll manage.'

She placed her head on his shoulder. In that moment, she felt completely happy and fulfilled. She was on the right side of the law with the right man, and everything was ... just right. 'I love you,' she whispered.

'I should bloody hope so. These driving lessons are costing me a bomb.'

DC Eddie Barnes, in the company of a female detective, knocked sharply on the front door. Bill Tyler opened it. 'Oh, hello,' he said, his voice rather shaky. What did the cops want? Did they think he might have stolen some of the scout hut stash? Or was this visit about keeping the family safe? God, he hoped so.

'Are your parents in, Bill?' Eddie asked.

'No. They've gone to the pictures. It's just me and our Danny. Come in and sit down.'

Our Danny was mending a puncture on the bike. 'Hiya,' he said before continuing with the job on the hearthrug. 'I never done nothing,' he said, winking cheekily.

The woman detective smiled – she was finally used to the cheek of Liverpool's teenagers. Most of the time they meant no harm, although when they were bad, they were horrid, as the nursery rhyme said.

'There's no easy way to tell you this, Bill,' Eddie began, 'so I'll just spit it out. Boss has scarpered, buggered off, left the stage, broken out of prison.'

Bill's jaw dropped. 'But he was stuck in Walton Jail waiting for the wotsit – the trial, wasn't he? Didn't they say from the start he was dangerous enough to need top security instead of a cell in a cop shop?'

'Definitely,' the young woman answered. 'The number of kids he's given drugs to and ... oh, shut me up, DC Barnes.'

'Shut up, Sandra.' He continued, 'They did indeed say Boss needed locking up. He got out in a delivery van. He has money and friends, he's under arrest for murder or manslaughter and he's charged with drug dealing in Halewood, so he's desperate.' He spoke to the brother. 'Danny?'

'What?'

'You all need to move, and not necessarily together. We have a place for Bill. Now, we're not sure that Boss will send somebody here, but neither are we sure that he won't.' He turned to Bill again. 'Remember the three runaways?'

Bill, white as a sheet, nodded.

'We put in the paper that they are in a hostel in a place well away from Liverpool, but we never said where exactly. You'll be with them.'

'Oh, right.' Bill leaned against the door for support.

Eddie went on, 'Boss might think they stole his drugs and sold the lot. Or maybe he knows the

police are involved and that his stash was con-
fiscated. It's amazing what they can find out in
prison. All we published was the discovery of the
runaways. The gang does know we found the
stuff in Halewood, but the scout hut is officially
just the place where the three boys lived; we
never had an account in print of the police raid-
ing the hut. Actually, when found, the lads had
been in a coal cellar. It's hard to predict what will
happen, but you and the three runaway lads
might be targeted. We never know which way
Shuttleworth will turn, because he's one slimy
creep, and he just lashes out.'

'OK.' Terrified, Bill swallowed, but his throat
was dry.

Eddie spoke to Danny. 'Your mother, your
father, your other brother and yourself must stay
with friends or relatives. Split into at least two
groups. If you can't, ask for me at the station and
we'll find you a safe house.'

Bill fled upstairs to pack. What would happen
to his job at Dad's firm? Would Boss and his men
come here at all? They might. They might come
if they guessed that Bill had made a certain
phone call which had put the cops on the scent
of boys hiding in a scout hut. They might even go
to Roy's house, though that was unlikely, since
Roy had died before getting the chance to grass
on the growers and dealers.

What would Mam and Dad do? 'Detective
Barnes?' he shouted down the stairwell.

'Yes?'

'Doesn't Boss know you found his drugs in the
hut?'

293

'Not sure.' Eddie climbed the stairs and found Bill. 'We've been waiting for the rest of his so-called staff to come looking for them, so the drugs are just a rumour up to now, because we've made no official statement to the press. If the men we haven't caught yet think there's a chance of retrieving the contents of that shed, they'll walk straight into our honey trap. We have to get you away, lad.'

The policewoman was talking to Danny in the sitting room. It was important to emphasize that as many people as possible should try to avoid the subject of drugs in the scout hut. 'Do your best, Danny,' she begged. 'Shuttleworth's gang has a few members still on the loose. He grassed them all, but we've at least six still missing and they might well be recruiting. Now, there'll be a discreet police presence as near as possible to that hut twenty-four hours a day, seven days a week for a while. If the guys get desperate and come for the drugs, we'll have them. But gossip spreads like flu, so keep quiet.'

Danny nodded. 'My dad was as mad as hell with our Bill when he found out what had happened. Mam and Dad told him for years to stay away from Roy Foley.' He shrugged. 'We all went to the funeral, though. Who killed him?'

'We don't know yet. But Bill's been easily led in the past, you see. Yet he's turned out to be a very brave lad. He alerted us with an anonymous phone call, and he went back on his own to see if he could save the boys who'd escaped from that school. After all, Roy had been murdered, and the three others might have met the same fate.

Please don't blame your brother. Be proud of him – he's a brave young man.' She smiled hopefully at Danny.

Danny knelt on the rug and sat back on his heels. 'Do we really have to move out?'

'Yes, I'm sorry. Shuttleworth has power in the criminal world, and his temper's never been under control. It's all about him, you see. He will punish anyone he decides has betrayed him, and he won't necessarily dish out the beatings or killings himself. I'll stay with you till they get back from the cinema and till your other brother comes home. DC Barnes can take Bill away to safety. We'll get Boss. For a start, you could hardly miss him, because he's built like a brick outhouse.'

Eddie entered the room with Bill. 'Right, Sandra – we'll be off. I'll call back if I can after dropping this one off.' He spoke to Danny. 'This is serious, lad. Make sure your family knows how serious. Take good care of one another.' After nodding at Sandra, he led Bill outside to an unmarked car.

Bill stashed his belongings on the rear seat. 'Where are we going?'

'To the three boys from the hut. Southport.'

'OK.' Bill paused. 'But that's only about twelve miles from Liverpool. I've biked it there many a time.'

'Double bluff,' Eddie told him. 'They won't be found. They're on a private estate and now, with Shuttleworth on the loose, they can't even go to school. We'll have to get a tutor in.'

Bill sat back and kept quiet for the rest of the journey. All this had been started by Roy with a few seedlings and a guy with knowledge about stealing electricity. Roy was dead, but the repercussions continued. It was like dominoes, he decided. You stood them up on the table and pushed the first, which hit the second, which hit the third ... and they all came tumbling down.

We were a bit snowed under at work, so I was out driving a van and collecting mail from post boxes. I was feeling pleased, because this could be a step towards promotion – well, you never can tell, since the fact is that I know every angle of this job. So I did the run in quick sticks and was just locking the back doors of the van after my last pick-up when I saw them.

They were sitting and chatting in Jenkinson's. Everybody knows Jenkinson's. It's that chip shop where you can buy your meal to take away, or you can sit at a table and eat in comfort. It's a great place; they have the sense to make sure the fat's boiling before they start chucking things into it, so the food's not soggy and soaked in grease.

And there they were, bold as brass and like a proper family, drinking tea near the window. Fat Mamma needed help to stand up, and she waddled away up the street as if she were made of jelly, great fat legs and a backside as wide as a dual carriageway, she has. She didn't look well. Her face was grey and I could see that walking was hard work for her.

So I pretended to have a bit of trouble with the lock. The other two came out. One was the chap with the missing hand, and I remember travelling with him on one of Fat Mamma's runs. With him was the one called Belle. As far as I know, she does massage up on the second floor of Meadow-bank. Leaving the van (we're not supposed to do that), I followed them. They walked into the Odeon, and I rushed away to complete the job. By half past five, I was back at the depot, and by six I was out, deadline beaten, smiles all round.

Joseph Turton and I have been allowed to swap shifts when we need to because of his mother. Everybody knows now that I've left Laura, and I don't seem to mind them knowing, because that's the least of my problems. Joseph's at home until quarter to ten tonight, so I thought I'd go and watch that film, *The Graduate*. Mrs Turton's usually no bother in the night as long as she doesn't fall when trying to get to her commode.

Well, I didn't bother going into the cinema. The Odeon's a big place, and it's dark, of course, and I might not find them, so I just hung round in the street imitating a spare part until they came out holding hands like a couple of school kids on a first date. I followed them. On the bus, they sat joking and giggling – it's enough to turn a man's stomach. When they got off the bus, I got off. So now I have their address. Nice houses with little front gardens all neat and tidy. A big dog greeted them as soon as they opened the door. Wavertree.

Neat? Tidy? How neat and tidy can the man be if he's living with a whore? She's from Meadow-bank Farm, and she's quite a looker, too. According to Angela, Belle is good for anyone in pain, because she's done a course in massage. Has she left Fat Mamma? They seemed very close on the bus, almost like newly-weds.

I'll have to go home soon and think about this.

297

Joseph will be worried, so I'll give him a quick ring from a call box before he gets that neighbour in, the one who wants paying. I like looking after Joseph's mum. When she's well enough to sit at her table, we play cards and dominoes. I'm making her a big tray with legs so she can sit up in bed and play games or do a jigsaw. I must remember to buy her a couple more pillows.

My hand's healing well. I wound the wire round a couple of boxes, told Joseph I'd cut myself on it. The police are busy round the docks again, but they've no idea how or where to find me. I no longer shout in my sleep. I think that all stopped when I was living in Greasy Chair Hell. But I do miss the kids. Oh, and I must find out what Laura's up to with her powder and lipstick.

After phoning Joseph, I talk to Fat Mamma.

'Is Belle there?' I ask. 'I usually see Angela, but I think I need Belle.'

'We're shut,' she says. She doesn't like me, and the feeling's mutual.

'I was hoping for a back massage,' I moan. 'I hurt myself at work.'

There's a pause. 'She left,' she pronounces. 'I'll get another masseuse in time, but not yet, because we're closed.'

'Right,' I say. 'Why did she leave?'

Another pause. 'She left to get married if you must know.'

'That's nice, Miss Mellor. I hope she's happy.' I replace the receiver. Now, there's an interesting challenge; Belle's away from the docks, married, probably no longer on the game. She'll think she's fallen on her feet. Oh no, Belle. You're going

298

to drop to your knees like a stone when I get round to you. I can guarantee that.

Eve suspected that she was supposed to feel grateful, since Detective Constable Barnes had been kindness itself. He and a friend called Dave had helped in their spare time, removing the massage table, Angela's range of fixed equipment and just about anything else that might have betrayed the secrets of Meadowbank It was now a genuine-looking refuge for ill-treated women. The decor was loud, but Eve told other cops who used the house that it had been like this when she bought it.

Attic Four, generally employed for storage, was now used by police. Plain clothes cops occupied it in shifts, so there was always a presence. Using a ladder, they took turns to look over the trees through a telescope in the hope of catching somebody up to no good. They had also built a garden shed near thick, evergreen bushes which, after small holes had been cut in foliage, gave officers the opportunity to spy through binoculars trained on the scout hut.

Some clever clogs professor from Liverpool University had installed an alarm under the wooden floor of the place in which those three runaway boys had lived, and a loud bell sounded in Attic Four whenever anyone stepped inside the hut. This might prove useful at night when, even with magnification, very little could be seen in darkness.

Eve was being compensated, but the girls weren't working, and restlessness pervaded the farmhouse. Eve remembered feeling like that when she'd had no income due to her sudden weight gain. As for the money she was being paid – well, the police used most of it in food and cups of tea. Still, they were a decent enough lot, she supposed, and she was truly glad of the chance to rest. She wasn't herself.

Kate came in with a mug and a plate of sandwiches. 'Here you are, love.'

'How are the troops?' Eve asked wearily.

'Well, they're getting nearer to revolting. Angela's leaving tomorrow, and Mo's fed up. Judy's talking about setting up her own reflexology clinic in a practice that offers alternative medicine and treatments. I think Cynthia misses the sex more than the money; I've always said she's a nympho. What the hell next, Evie?'

The big woman shrugged. 'I suppose we got that little shed near the bushes out of it.'

'Yes, and it's a few hundred yards from the house. I won't be walking all the way there to fetch a stepladder or a bloody broom. Maybe we should get a guard dog and use the shed as a kennel.' Kate studied Eve. 'Look, Belle's found you loads of girls–'

'Yes, yes, I know.'

'And Eddie said the police will be gone in a few days if nobody turns up. If somebody does turn up, the cops will go immediately.'

Eve stirred her coffee slowly. 'I've left this place to you in my will, Kate.'

'What?' Kate dropped into a chair. 'What's wrong with you? Why are you talking about your will?'

Eve shrugged. 'Everything's wrong. Bad headaches, stomach pains, stupid knees, a bit of dizziness sometimes. She pulled herself together. 'You'll need to get a driver, somebody you can trust. Do a timetable like mine and take no nonsense from any of the girls.'

Kate clamped her hanging jaw into its proper position. 'I'll get the doctor.'

'No, you won't. I'm not dying in hospital.'

'But they might fix you.'

Eve's laughter was hollow. 'I sat in that chip shop with Belle and Tom – they even made me laugh. They're so happy. And he had to help me up out of the chair. I'll never know how I drove home, but I must have, because I'm here. Look, I can't have an anaesthetic. I'm too fat, I smoke, I eat too much of the wrong stuff, and there's no fight left in me, Kate.'

Kate bit her lip. Eve had changed recently. There was little hope in her eyes, and she appeared to care less and less about the house. Occasionally, she even seemed close to tears. How could she, Kate O'Gorman, run this place without the solid presence of her only friend? Eve had attitude. She ran the business like the commander of some military base, no nonsense while on parade, no quarter given to those who fought each other or neglected clients. 'I can't do it without you,' she whispered.

'You need somebody like Belle,' Eve said.

'There isn't anybody like Belle. Can you imagine Cynthia, Mo or Judy being any use? Anyway, the people in charge here need to be older and without clients. What will I do? Advertise in the papers?' Panic rose like bile in her throat. 'Don't leave me, Eve.'

'Me time's running out, babe.' Eve grabbed her friend's hand. 'I'm scared, too. Now, listen to me. When I go, get Belle. She'll find somebody for you, because she's very clever and she knows loads of people from way back. Make sure you meet a few, and choose somebody you like, a woman you won't mind sharing a room with. And straighten your bloody face in case the wind changes'

Kate fled, sobbing into her hands. With no Eve, there would be no Meadowbank Farm. She rushed through the kitchen; if the girls wanted feeding, they'd have to shape up and cook for themselves.

Mo was alone, reading in an armchair. 'Kate?' she called. 'What's the matter? Why are you running? Kate, for the love of God, stand still and talk to me.'

But Kate didn't stop; she ran right through the large area and locked herself in the room where she and Eve had slept for years. It wasn't a big room, and Eve's stuff was everywhere. Her huge dressing gown hung from a hook on the door, and the top of the dressing table was covered in hair rollers and the scarves she wore over them.

An Agatha Christie novel sat on the shared bedside table; Eve loved Miss Marple and Monsieur Poirot. Next to the book stood a jar of the antiseptic cream Eve used under rolls of fat to stop the effects of sweating. The door to a shower room stood open; Eve could no longer fit in a bath. Twin beds were dressed differently: Kate's was covered in blue, Eve's wore a floral pattern on the top quilt. This was Eve's room. No one else should have this room.

Kate sat on her friend's bed. Eve dying? No, it wasn't possible, because she hadn't finished her book, she was listening to a serial on the BBC Home Service, now named Radio Four, and she'd started knitting a new winter cardigan. Eve was tired, yes, but she would pull round, surely? There was only one thing for it: Kate must find a way to fetch Dr Mannix, the one who looked after the health of all the girls. Eve might be annoyed, but better that than dead.

Mo was banging on the door and making quite a racket. Kate opened it.

'What the hell's up?' Mo demanded to know.

It spilled from Kate's lips like the torrent delivered every minute by the River Niagara. 'She says she's dying. I don't know what to do, because she ... she won't listen to sense, says she wants leaving alone, no doctors. I don't know what to do, don't know where to turn, or–'

Mo blinked. 'Who? Who's dying?'

'Eve. She says she wants to die here, not in hospital.'

'Right. Right.' Mo's mind was running like an articulated lorry with no brakes. Any minute now, it would crash, jack-knife and never move again. She had to do something, since poor old Kate was fit for nothing. 'Let me think,' she begged, leading Kate back to the living end of the kitchen and sitting her down. 'Don't move,' she ordered. 'I'm going to find a doctor.'

'Get Mannix.'

'I will. And I'll tell Eve it was my idea, not yours. So don't be worrying, because I'll keep your name out of it.'

Kate sighed deeply. 'Don't act soft, Mo. She'll know I told you.'

'Tough. If the shoe was on her foot, she'd get everybody including the coastguard to help you. I'm going.' Mo left the room.

Against all the odds, Kate drifted into fitful sleep.

'OK, Thompson,' Mo said to herself. 'How do you play this one?'

An idea hit her out of the blue. She smiled to herself. The blue? They were no longer the boys in blue, because they were detectives, but she would go upstairs with tea and chocolate biscuits, and one of them could fetch the doctor.

Before returning to the kitchen, she put an ear against the office door. Eve was moaning softly. Right. It was time to start the ball rolling.

Bill was given a room named the butler's pantry. It was on the ground floor of Wordsworth House, and it held a single bed, a battered wardrobe and a chest of drawers. It had been used in the past by people engaged to do outside work like gardening, fence-mending and jobs in the stables.

When Bill woke on his first morning, a Mr Macey, who was sitting patiently on a ladder-backed chair beside the bed, introduced himself. 'I thought someone should be here on your first morning, since you must feel out of place.'

'I'm William Tyler,' Bill replied, sitting up and rubbing his eyes. 'People call me Bill.'

'I know, Bill. I also know you're eighteen, and no-one can force you to stay here. The runaways are living in the gatehouse with a Mr Hourigan who trains horses, though he has just one at the present time. Murdoch can be harder work than a stable of twenty.'

'Murdoch?'

'Yes. First name is Mad, second Murdoch. He's a law unto himself, but he has promise if we can but turn the naughtiness into something more useful like racing. Now, we've heard that your parents and your brothers have split up and gone to Belle Vale and St Helens. Your job won't suffer, because I've had a word. And I can take you to a builder friend of mine who is happy to continue your training. You are now Bill Morris.'

'Thanks,' Bill said.

Lippy Macey rose to his feet. 'There's a small bathroom next door, and your breakfast will be on the table in the kitchen in about fifteen minutes. I'll leave you to get on.' He placed a hand on the young man's shoulder. 'It will all turn out well. Try not to worry, because the chances of you or your family's being targeted are minimal.'

Alone, Bill wondered briefly about his parents and his brothers before going for a shower. The man had said it would be all right, and the man's photo was always in the newspapers, though Bill had never bothered to read the details. He showered, shaved, cleaned his teeth and pulled on his next-to-best jeans with a Liverpool Football Club T-shirt. After combing his hair, he followed the sound of chatter till he reached the kitchen.

The three lads were there; he'd seen them only

once before, but at least they remembered him. 'Sorry about the drugs,' he mumbled.

Ian laughed. 'What drugs?'

'I know,' Bill replied, 'mum's the word.'

Ian continued, 'Oh, these two ladies looked after us when we were in the hut. This is Sally.' He blushed. 'And this is Babs. They look after Mr Crawford now. This is his house, and he's having his breakfast in bed. Sit down.'

Bill sat. 'Where's Mr Macey?' he asked. 'He talked to me before.'

Phil answered. 'He's at the cottage near the main gate, talking to Gordy Hourigan. We stay with Gordy, but eat here most of the time. John has a bit of a stammer, but it'll stop troubling him when he knows you better. Ouch! No need to kick me under the table, John Lucas.'

John grinned at Bill. 'I r-remember you. You were with B-Boss and his gang.'

'Yes. They killed Roy. I suppose that's why we're all under wotsit – protection.'

Ian shook his head. 'No. We're here because of the monks; Boss and his load of trouble is a new reason, and another problem since he escaped from jail. Has he threatened you?'

The new arrival nodded. 'And my family. They've moved out.'

'They'll get him,' Babs pronounced. 'From what I've heard, he's too big to stay hidden for long. The best place to put him would be six feet under, but he's clever, isn't he? Anyway, eat your breakfast, Bill. Mr Macey's taking you to a place where you can carry on learning about building.'

Bill tucked into his food. As well as bacon and

eggs, he had black pudding, a sausage, beans, mushrooms and hash browns. This was great. He missed home, yet he felt as if he had another family here, in Southport. Things would turn out well, especially with food as good as this.

Daisy and Barry Bramwell, proprietors of Bramwells' Chippy, were delighted with Laura Carson. She was blooming like apple blossom in springtime, even though this was autumn. As the days and weeks passed, she gained a pretty layer of flesh that was ably supported by well-defined cheekbones, her hair grew and hung in shiny locks, and it was clear that she was almost celebrating her new self.

She did five lunchtimes, Monday to Friday, but there was now a new arrangement. As Friday and Saturday tended to be the shop's busiest nights, Lucy and Matt stayed here, in the flat above the shop. Lucy shared young Diane's room, while Matt slept in Kevin's, and all four children were delighted. Laura's wages increased, but there was yet another reason for the twinkle in her eyes.

The reason had a name – Andrew Martindale. Mr Martindale came to the shop every Saturday night after an evening at his bridge club. He ordered cod in bread-crumbs rather than batter, a small portion of chips and a cardboard cup of butter beans. This was his weekly treat for two reasons. First, he tried to eat healthily for the most part, and second, he feasted his eyes on Laura, whose improvement continued to be more noticeable now that her husband was out of the house.

Whenever he turned up just before closing time,

both Bramwells were suddenly busy clearing up, scooping up utensils or dashing through to the back with enamel buckets that had contained raw chipped potatoes earlier in the evening. In short, they left Laura to get on with it – whatever 'it' was.

Mr Martindale's greeting was always polite. 'Good late evening, Mrs Carson. You know my order.'

'By heart, Mr Martindale.'

He watched her every move, and she knew his eyes were on her. It was almost like two minutes of courtship once a week.

'No sign of the husband?' he asked occasionally.

She answered either in the verbal negative or with a shake of her head.

'He's a fool.' Sometimes 'idiot' or 'lunatic' took the place of the word fool.

After not much more than a minute or two, he would be gone.

Daisy knew all about him, of course. He was owner of several small, select jewellery shops, and he chose, cut, polished, prepared and set gems. A widower, he lived alone except for his dogs, which he treated like children. 'He likes you, Laura,' Daisy would say.

'I like him. I'm married, though.'

'Get rid.'

'Daisy! I'm a Catholic just like you.'

'Yep. It's a bugger, isn't it?'

Both women usually finished up in pleats of laughter for which they could find no valid reason, after which piece of utter craziness Laura returned to her empty house. Without the children asleep upstairs, she felt truly isolated. Never a great reader, she usually found something to do, sewing, knitting, a bit of music on the radio, ironing, or darning Matt's socks, which often owned more holes than a colander. On Sunday mornings, she picked up her children, took them to Mass, and normal life was resumed.

Things went out of kilter one Saturday night when Andrew Martindale's car refused to start. 'My late supper will be much later,' he complained to Laura when she left the shop. 'It's going to be cold and dead beyond retrieval – a truly late and dear departed supper.'

So she took him home. Home was just a couple of hundred yards away, and Laura knew he would do her no harm, even when, after eating his supper, he confessed to having deliberately removed a rotor something-or-other from his engine.

And so began the pattern. He was often the last customer, and he invariably took her home in his car. He always ate his supper in her house, always drank the cocoa she made for both of them, was polite, kind and interesting. When leaving, he would kiss her on both cheeks, thank her for everything, get into his car and drive off with a cheery wave.

Laura was confused by the situation. She couldn't tell Andy (as he now chose to be called) to stay away, because she was too polite to do that. Attracted to the older man, she longed for more than a goodnight peck on the cheek, and she didn't understand herself, since 'that side' of marriage had never appealed to her. And what if Neil found out? She never forgot to close the curtains. Even Neil couldn't see through those. He still hadn't spent time with his children, so he was probably avoiding the area. Anyway, she was doing nothing wrong, was she?

Yet she had to confess her sins of thought to Father Doherty, whose views proved broader than she had allowed herself to expect. 'You're lonely, my dear,' he would say, 'and you have committed no sin. Sometimes, the mind wanders into greener grass, and we can't keep it on a lead, can we? Just do your best. You're a godly woman, and He is on your side. So stop confessing sins you haven't yet committed, woman.'

So she carried on doing her best, though it was no easy feat. Doing her best meant not reaching across the table to touch his hand, denying herself the relief she might have felt had she opened up to him about her defunct marriage. Doing her best meant hoping he hadn't felt the tremor in her traitorous body when he kissed her goodnight on her cheeks. Perhaps she should not work on Fridays and Saturdays, but the money was excellent, and the children looked forward to staying with the Bramwell twins.

But she finally opened up to Daisy Bramwell. 'I think I could love him,' she whispered one Friday lunchtime as they prepared to start frying. 'He's kind and patient and funny.'

'Don't forget rich,' Daisy giggled.

'Stop it, please. It's not about money or a nice detached house or a big, shiny car. It's about Matt and Lucy and my immortal soul.'

'Go on. I won't laugh again,' Daisy promised as she coated fish with the batter mix. 'Leave the chips a minute while I fill the aquarium. Mind, it's more like a crematorium, I suppose. Perhaps I should call it the cremaquarium? Sorry, sorry – go on, love.'

'I want to be with him. I've never felt like this before.'

'Oh, grab him with both hands, girl. What good will morals be when you're sitting at one side of the fireplace staring at the other chair, the empty one? Your kids won't stay. They'll be up, off and married in their twenties, and you'll be there with nobody to keep your bed warm or shift the snow or bring you a cuppa in the morning.'

Laura shook her head. 'I don't want my children upset. They'd love their real daddy to come home.'

'But would you?' Daisy checked on her fish. 'Throw the chips in, love, then answer me – do you want Neil back?'

Laura's answer was immediate. 'No.' The fat spat back at her angrily when it made contact with cold potatoes, so she shut the folding lid. 'I don't. But it's not about me; it's about bringing up happy children who will go on to marry and make their own secure families.'

'And your own happiness doesn't count? Wouldn't they be happier if you were too?'

'He's old enough to be their grandfather. And what would everybody say if I divorced Neil? The church, my neighbours, my parents and Neil's family – it would be a wretched situation.'

Daisy shrugged. 'Well, you must make your own mind up, I suppose. Let's open the door and allow the starving of Liverpool in.'

311

Eleven

'You come anywhere near me again with that sodding horse needle, and I'll stick it up your arse with your stethoscope, your thermometer, and the Penny Lane bus, standing room only. You've had enough blood out of me to feed Dracula for a fortnight, so piss off.' Eve intertwined her fingers and placed the resulting knot on the bed covers, where they imitated a confusion of pork sausages. 'No more blood pressure tests, thanks, or that thing will join the rest in a very dark place. Piss off,' she repeated, glaring fiercely at her victim. She was scared, and fear angered her beyond control.

The doctor took Eve's advice and left the scene immediately. That woman in bed three was fierce, and he was a slight man with a life to live and exams to pass. He sent in the troops. While the troops dealt with Eve Mellor, he peered through the venetian blind that gave the ward sister's office some privacy.

Ward Sister was not alone. Her assistants included Matron, a fierce-looking female in a monochrome uniform. She was hefty, but even she looked slender when she stood near Eve. Behind Matron, a consultant lingered with two more blue-clad nursing sisters and a couple of staff nurses. Several young men in training as doctors brought up the rear. The social skills of all in this crew were

312

about to be tested; a particularly difficult patient was an item worth studying. For a few seconds, they did just that – gazed at the woman who was too large for an ordinary hospital bed.

Matron took Eve's chart from the bottom of the bed, looked at it and passed it to the consultant. 'Madam,' she began, 'I think we need to look at several possibilities here, since your symptoms are–'

'It's Miss Mellor,' Eve snapped. 'M-E-L-L-O-R. Got it?'

'Miss Mellor,' Matron said, stressing the double s at the end of the word Miss. 'You have given us nothing but trouble since you arrived on the ward – well, since before you arrived. They had to send a second ambulance just to have enough crew to lift you.'

'You're no effing plucked pullet yourself,' the patient snarled. 'And I did not ask to come here. You will do no more, because I've had enough with that one that couldn't hardly talk English – he's took half the blood out of me. He must have two buckets full of it by now. Is he a vampire? Should we carry garlic flowers and wear a cross?'

Matron employed a different tack. 'You're a very sick woman, Miss Mellor.'

Eve delivered a hollow laugh.

'There's nothing to laugh at, nothing at all.'

'Do I get fined for laughing? Do you have a chuckle box instead of a swear box? I know I'm a sick woman, you soft cow! Get me home and I'll go to bed and bloody die. Send me them women who ride bikes all over the show – district nurses. They can pump me full of drugs when the time

313

comes. Oh, and I might decide when that time comes. It's my life, my death and none of your bloody business, right?'

'Are you contemplating suicide?'

'Are you contemplating leaving me alone? Bugger off, and take your bridesmaids with you.'

The consultant put in his twopenny-worth. 'Er ... we need to get the results of several blood tests and take some X-rays before you go home. It won't take long.'

'No,' she growled. 'Tests? You've enough of my red stuff here to swim in and get a bloody degree in the backstroke with honours, never mind tests. Watch my lips, Mr Doctor. I will not give permission for you to proceed any further with my case. If you touch me, I'll sue for assault. If this gobshite here – Matron Misery Gob – doesn't stop mithering, she'll be done for harassment. And if you don't get me home, I might stick a kidnap hat on one of your monkeys as well.' She waved her arms at the young doctors before folding them as best she could across a vast bosom. 'There are people I need to kill, so let me out. When I say kill, I mean make their lives a misery like what you've done to me.'

Several jaws dropped. Eve winked at one of the young trainees.

Matron shuffled backwards and spoke quietly to the consultant. He tried again. Trained to understand that extreme aggression was often used to mask terror, he approached the bed and took Eve's hand in his. 'Miss Mellor,' he began in a soft, kindly voice. 'We are trying to help you.'

She pulled her hand away. 'Assault,' she warned.

'And don't be nice – I'm not a child. Keep your hands to yourself. See you at my post mortem, eh?'

Undeterred, the man continued. 'This ward is where we put people who need diagnostic procedures to ascertain–'

'Like a pending tray in an office?' the patient asked.

'Exactly like that, yes.'

She nodded thoughtfully. 'There's your solution, then. Shove me in the out tray, stick a couple of stamps on me gob and post me into an ambulance. You can't make me stay unless I'm crackers, and I'm not crackers. Well?'

'You are ill.'

Eve delivered a false smile.

'Miss Mellor, I believe–'

'Cancer,' Eve hissed. 'I didn't land in Fleetwood on Monday with the rest of the fish. I don't need to be mauled by you lot, because I bloody know what this is – it took my mother. You can't cut me – I'm too fat. You'd need a tree saw to get through this lot.' She stared at the young trainees. 'That boy at the back – yes, the one who looks about twelve, stop laughing or I'll send you to the headmaster's office for detention.'

'But you must understand that we need to try to help you,' the consultant insisted.

Eve nodded. 'I know that, lad. They tried to help Mam, and it didn't work. Bring the form and I'll sign myself out of this hell. You won't get into trouble as long as I sign. Do the tests on my blood and send the results to Mannix, my GP. He's another daft bugger, but he's all we've got out there in the wilderness.'

Matron sighed audibly. 'Will you need help to dress yourself?'

'Yes. Don't forget – I'm dying.' She made no attempt to conceal her sarcasm. 'Phone Kate. She'll help me, and it won't be assault.'

They left her. Sister brought the form, and Eve signed it, but she still found herself stranded like a beached whale. She looked round the ward, which was clearly a holding bay, as it contained people of both genders. The man next to her was connected to several drips, with a bag of pee hanging from underneath the bed, poor soul. A woman directly opposite was spark out with her mouth hanging open like the Mersey Tunnel without traffic. What a bloody life. What a bloody death. She couldn't stay here, wouldn't stay here. The pain had stopped and it might not come back again for a while.

Eve didn't need any more of this malarkey. A fat person became used to having little dignity and no physical grace, but this dump was a stride too far. Her soul was the same size as everybody else's and anyway, she refused absolutely to become a row of jars in pathology, a set of samples kept to display an interesting collection that served to illustrate the results of untreated illness. 'Come on, Kate,' she whispered, 'get me the heck out of this ward before I have a breakdown and get certified.'

A terrified Kate arrived eventually, and she was not alone. Behind her trotted Mo, Judy, Cynthia and Angela. Good God, they'd formed a posse, or maybe they were a wagon train, she thought as they surrounded the bed. They looked concerned for her, but nowhere did she find a trace of pity. Her girls were grounded, and they took life with all its vagaries in their stride.

Cynthia donated a smile. 'They don't normally let five people in at once, but you're a difficult patient, so here we are. We've got clean knickers and stuff.'

Eve spoke to Angela. 'I thought you'd be packing your bags.'

Miss Whiplash blinked. 'If you think I'm leaving Kate to cope with you on her own, even with the help of this motley lot, you can think again. And if you don't behave, I'll be there to batter you. OK?'

'You're staying?'

'Yes, for a while. My sister will keep the flat for me. I've told her my friend's very ill.'

They pulled the curtains round and dressed her carefully. Tears threatened, but Eve held back the storm. This was what she wanted – her own kind, her own girls around her. Yes, there would be pain, but these women would fight to keep her free of it. 'Does Mannix know I'm discharging myself?'

'Yes,' Mo replied, 'and he's hopping mad, like a frog with a moustache.'

'So am I, but with a smaller muzzy. I should have refused to get in the ambulance in the first place.'

'You were in too much pain to care,' Cynthia reminded her. 'They've given Kate medication for that. If it gets worse, you'll be on morphine.' As ever, Cynthia didn't bother to dress up the information.

'I know. I've lived this nightmare from your side of the fence, and it's not easy. But bless you all for hanging in with me.'

Angela blinked again. No way was she going to start crying here in front of everybody. 'Where else would we be, Eve?'

Eve closed her eyes. Yes. Where else would they be? Even Angela Whiplash cared. This was an illustration of true female solidarity, a natural unity men often failed to understand. 'Marching as to war,' Eve quoted.

Kate smiled sadly; the hymn was on Eve's list of funeral instructions.

Mo helped Eve with stockings and shoes. 'Right, you'll do,' she said.

'Belle and Tom are waiting for you with that lovely dog called Max,' Kate said. 'And I've got painkillers for you. Sally and Babs are coming for a visit soon. People do care, Evie.'

'I know. I'm grateful. Now, get me out of this morgue.'

They got her out. The farm van was parked at the front of the building, and the girls helped her into the front passenger seat. 'Who's driving?' she asked.

'Angela,' was the chorused answer.

'Can you drive?' Eve wanted to know.

'You'll soon find out. Climb in the back, you lot.'

Alone in the cabin with the boss, the dominatrix spoke to Eve, and this time she didn't try to stop herself sounding emotional. 'It's been hard for you, Eve. Let's see if we can make what's left as easy as humanly possible.'

'It's appreciated, Angela.'

'It's deserved. Right. Which one of these thingies is the clutch?'

Sally Hayes was in a bit of a quandary. She liked Ian, who was only fifteen, but she liked Bill Tyler, too. He was sweet and funny and sometimes quite magical, especially when his face was alight with mischief. 'I must be desperate,' she told herself frequently. 'I fancy anybody young, anybody not old enough to be him.' *Him. Him* was her mother's second husband, and Sally's nemesis. 'Stop thinking about the rat,' she ordered herself in a whisper. She had the kitchen to clean and Mr Crawford's teatime snack to make. But she kept on thinking about Ian and Bill, Bill and Ian – she was a mess.

She knew why, of course. It was because neither of these young men frightened her, and the relationship between her and Babs had taught her that physical love didn't have to involve pain, so she was almost ready to take the next step towards what might be judged a normal, acceptable life. Yet a few shards of fear remained embedded, probably because her mother had not protected her from the monster, and trust did not come easily to Sally.

Don Crawford's needs were easily satisfied because, as Babs often said, he would have trouble penetrating tissue paper, let alone a girl, but Sally still felt sick in his presence. Babs protected her from him some of the time, but Babs wasn't always here these days, and the old man was unpredictable, to say the least. Although the girls now had their own room, he still came in to look

319

at them, to watch while they slept or gossiped or argued. Babs was forever reminding Sally that this man provided for them, fed and clothed them, and had even included them in his will, but Sally continued to have a problem with trust. Oh, and he made her flesh crawl...

One of Sally's jobs was to keep Bill's room clean and tidy while he was off out learning plastering. He liked plastering, said it was an art form and that he intended to be its most devoted student. 'I'm going to sign my work once I can get the bloody stuff to stop falling off the walls,' he had told her. He intended to be known as Master Plaster. He came home each evening covered in the stuff, but he was always wreathed in smiles. Today, he arrived at Wordsworth House early. 'I done a ceiling,' he announced. 'Most of it was all right, but a bit fell off on the boss's head, so he chased me with a shovel.'

'Did he catch you?' Sally asked.

'Yes, but he never hit me cos that's how his last apprentice died.'

'He *is* joking?'

'All the bloody time, Sally. There's no peace. He sent the lad learning carpentry for a box of bent nails. The boy asked why, and the boss said, 'You bend the buggers anyway, so I thought I'd save you the bother.' Then we found him with two tins of paint, one blue, one yellow. He said he was inventing striped gloss.'

'Why?' she asked.

Billy shrugged. 'No flaming idea.'

'He must be mad as a hatter,' Sally concluded.

'That's what we said, but he wanted to know

why the hell he shouldn't have striped paint. Really, he was making an exclusive shade of lime green for his own front door and windowsills. He's mad. I like him.'

When she'd stopped laughing, Sally asked, 'Is he pleased with you overall, though?'

'We have to provide our own overalls.'

'Now you're the one acting soft.'

He winked and shrugged. 'I think I've caught the boss's illness.'

'Glad it's that boss and not Boss boss from Halewood or wherever. I wish they'd catch him, Bill. Somebody must be hiding him, because he's supposed to be six foot four in his socks and as broad as he's tall.'

'The Met's looking for him as well, you know.'

'The which?'

'Scotland Yard. Hiding in London has to be easier. I'm going for a bath.' He picked up a towel and stared hard at her. 'Can you read? I mean read proper – like fast and without pictures?'

'Yes.'

'Will you teach me? I can read some, but not proper like Roy could.'

'I'll help you.'

'Thanks.' Wearing disgraceful overalls and a broad smile, he left his bedroom.

She finished straightening the room, went into the kitchen, washed her hands and made Mr Crawford's sandwich and tea. She would clean this room later. Bill couldn't read? He'd got to eighteen without learning to read properly? A grin spread itself across her face. 'He told me,' she murmured. 'He asked me, so he trusts me.' Perhaps that trust might work both ways? Perhaps she could trust him. She needed someone who would look after her, keep her safe from ... from stuff she didn't want to think about.

Don Crawford was in frisky mode, and Babs wasn't here to take the front line when trouble started, because Babs was out learning about horse riding and something called tack and how to get a horse to prepare for a nearby obstacle. For Sally, that was mostly Greek. She was no longer terrified of Murdoch, but she wasn't a devotee like Babs.

When the old man put his hand up Sally's skirt, she reacted with a fury of which she had never before been aware, slapping his arm quite hard.

He was stroking her bare thigh when she turned on him. 'Listen, you dirty old man – if I leave here, so will Babs, and that bloody horse will get nowhere. You know the score; your heart's not great, and I can make it a damned sight worse.'

'I paid for you,' he said. 'And Babs is too fond of her horse to leave me.'

'I wasn't for sale. Now, Babs is used to you, and I'm not. I've put up with you leering at us when we're in bed, but don't ever touch me when Babs isn't here, or I'll make sure you have the big heart attack a bit earlier than you might have expected. Babs quite likes you; I don't. Get used to it. She's your real baby girl, anyway. I'm just like a spare part.' She flounced towards the landing, catching a last glimpse of him as she turned to close the door. 'I can soon tell Mr Macey about you; he thinks Babs and I are nurses and cleaners, cooks and bottle-washers. He'll get us somewhere decent to live when he finds out what a shit you are.' She smiled. His jaw hung slack and loose; she could do it! She could tell older men to piss off, and it worked.

Although unaware of the details, this was the day on which Sally took hold of her own power. Layer upon layer of resentment and anger had piled high inside her for many years and, on this afternoon, those layers finally melded together and became both armour and weaponry. At last, she was growing up.

Right, what next? Ah yes, she had a kitchen to clean and a meal to make for four hungry lads... Just now, she liked Bill best.

I think I already mentioned Trevor Burns, who was our family butcher when we were still a family. He was the one who got me into Meadowbank where I met Angela, who is going to move soon to East Prescot Road in Knotty Ash. She punishes me, and I know I need her to carry on doing just that, because I'm bad. Going with a whore is wicked... But it's part of the job, or so I keep trying to convince myself.

Well, I've been out on collections a few times lately. I like the autonomy of that; I like being alone but among people who stay away from me. And I was dragging letters out of a pillar box on Bold Street and shoving them in the bag when he tapped me on the shoulder. My heart jumped a bit, because postmen do get robbed, but when I turned, it was Fatso with his purple nose, red cheeks and ginger hair. He looks like something created by one of these modern artists, all clashing colours and odd shapes. 'Oh, hello,' I managed. My God, he is ugly; his wife's no oil painting either, but she has a lovely smile and a kind heart, always gave me an extra couple of pork sausages for the kids when I did the shopping. 'Hello, Trevor,' I said, forcing my mouth to widen into an imitation of a smile. 'Did you want something?'

The butcher got right to the point. 'Eve Mellor's very ill and refusing treatment,' he told me. 'They say it could be cancer, but they're waiting for results.' He stood back a pace, clearly waiting for my reaction.

'And?' I asked, trying to appear composed and unimpressed.

He shrugged. 'I doubt they'll be opening up again in the near future.'

I thought about that. 'Makes no difference to me, Trevor. My girl's moving out anyway, because she's got her own place in Knotty Ash.'

'Angela Dyson?' he asked. 'The one with all the equipment?'

'Yes.'

A wicked gleam appeared in the butcher's eyes. 'Rather you than me, mate, when it comes to getting whipped. Anyway, I phoned and spoke to Kate about what was going on.'

'Oh yes?' By this time, he looked almost gleeful, and I felt angry.

'And they're all staying to help with the nursing of Eve.'

This news rocked me slightly, though I'm sure I didn't let it show. 'I thought you'd stopped going anyway,' I said. 'So what's it to you?'

'I'm just cutting down,' was his reply. 'We're

saving up to go on holiday next year. I thought we might try the Costa Brava.' He paused, staring hard at me. 'Your wife's looking better,' he said, 'like a flower that's just found the sunlight – that's the way my Em puts it. Mrs Carson seems to be feeling and looking a lot better since you buggered off. I wonder why?'

'No idea. Excuse me, but I have to get this mail back for sorting.' I turned my back on him and carried on with the job. No way was I going to let this overweight freak disturb me.

'Rumour has it that she works Saturday nights in the chip shop and your children stay over with the Bramwell twins while Andrew Martindale takes your missus home. He's a jeweller and a widower.'

I won't forget the gleam of triumph in his blood-shot eyes when I turned to look at him. 'Listen, Porky,' I said quietly. 'I've nothing left to lose, but you have. It'll be the Costa Lot, not the Costa Brava, if I talk to Em.'

'You wouldn't do that,' he blustered.

'Wouldn't I?' I stared at him until he walked away.

Goodness, I seem to be making a list. Belle Horrocks, Trevor Burns, my own wife, somebody called Martindale – who'll be next? There was supposed to be no personal involvement beyond ridding the streets of whores. I locked the box, shouldered my burden and returned to the van. He was still standing there on the opposite side of the street as I drove away.

I did Shirley Evans – have I already told you? I used her and garrotted her. She was stronger than she looked. There was a nice, dark and narrow alley behind businesses closed for the night, and I thought I'd have some fun first. Well, I miss Angela. So I had her on the pavement and she asked for money while pulling her drawers up. She smelled like that cheap perfume called Californian Poppy – it was all women could get during the war years. It was that or Midnight in Paris, and picture houses stank of either or both in a constantly failing effort to cover the smell of urine and sweat.

She clawed at my hair and clothes while I separated her from her breath. I went through her purse and found fifteen quid, just pennies short of my weekly wage. This one was a particularly ugly corpse; she died with her eyes slightly open, peering at me through slits. I remember shivering, because I imagined for a moment that she had been entered by one of Lucifer's minions, a junior devil created to jump into a corpse, collect its soul and take it below to the white-hot furnace of inner hell.

I've booked the weekend off, so I might just take this money up to Laura – she can use it for food and other bits. If she ever found out that I'd taken the money from a whore, she'd probably frog-march me all the way to Confession. A jeweller? Perhaps he can give her a solid gold crucifix. Saturday night? I think Joseph has a rest day this weekend – good.

I must get back to Maude; she needs me, because Joseph's on lates. He'll be home about half ten. I'm supposed to be teaching her back-gammon, but if we get nowhere, we've a jigsaw half done. I made her that tray for the bed; it has interchangeable tops for different activities, one for eating, one for jigsaws and one for other games, and she was so thrilled that she cried. We keep the trays we're not using under the bed. Her son's a good lad, but he's not as handy as I am.

Thinking about Maude and backgammon and Joseph and his shifts is my way of blocking out the thought of Laura's being with another man, a rich man from the sound of things. When I saw her outside the school, there was a change in her, a level of improvement I had never expected. Did she need to be rid of me in order to begin a new life?

Maude's been on her own for a couple of hours, which she doesn't mind as long as she doesn't need to leave her bed. Because I pay no rent, I have to fulfil my obligation to her and her son and get home soon. She's a lovely old soul, quite giddy and giggly for a woman in her eighties. Joseph says she still has a full set of chairs round her table, which is his way of insisting that she's not senile. I love her. With Joseph's permission, I've started to call her Mum. My real mother was a tyrant, and I never loved her. Joseph sometimes addresses me as Little Brother or Our Kid. It's nice. I have a new family, and I've escaped from Greasy Chair Hell.

Matt and Lucy are growing up without their dad. Yes, I miss them a lot, but if I start visiting them, it will hurt me even more when I leave. Better to have major surgery all in one go rather than picking and poking at a sore spot time after time. Better for them, too, I hope.

She is punishing me. Laura is leaving my children in a flat above a shop that has a strong chance of consumption by fire due to the business on the ground floor. In order to be with her fancy man, she is exposing Matt and Lucy to danger, and I am angry about that.

If Laura were to disappear, I'd get my kids back and my house, too. Mum Maude could have the front downstairs room, and Joseph could share the double bedroom with me – the two single beds from his house would do. That way, I could help with Mum, and Joseph could help with Matt and Lucy. The children might even play Ludo and snap with Mum – I'm sure they'd love that. How do I eliminate Laura? Am I capable of that?

So Angela is staying with Fat Mamma and the rest. This was a blow, I have to admit. I found the wool shop, but now I've no idea when she will move there. My hunting ground is infested by cops, because three women are now dead. I must concentrate on Mum Maude and doing my share of housework and cooking. If busy, I can manage for a while without ... without all that.

Sisters Helen Veronica and Mary Veronica continued their vigilance at Lime Street Station. Predictably, Nellie's dog was renamed Nellie's Son instead of Nelson, though he appeared not to care, since he also answered to Tatty Arse. A disgraceful-looking article, he worked in pursuit of drugs as hard as any detective, and it was his signal that finally led to the capture of Boss's (Albert Shuttleworth's) last remaining known cohorts when they alighted from the Manchester train and left the platform. The dog signalled, so he had located drugs. The men, who were carrying cocaine, were arrested and questioned; Liverpool police now knew that Boss was definitely in South London. Nellie and Mary, as auxiliary officers, were the only civilians who'd been told about the arrests and details of their confessions.

The force clung hopefully to the knowledge that Shuttleworth might well return to Liverpool before others could take over all his territory. Boss could soon employ a new set of slaves, and the self-made drugs baron loved his mother, who was not in good health. Yes, he would be home. Lime Street became a tense place; even drunks and tramps began to avoid the train station and the nearby London bus terminus.

All trains and coaches were being watched. The stations were frequently saturated with plain clothes officers, though some had been moved to patrol the dock area after the killing of yet another working girl. Dave Earnshaw spent hours in the public part of the station, sometimes wandering onto a platform when a London train touched the buffers, but police vigilance had not paid off thus far.

Just before midnight one Friday, the last London train rolled in. It had been delayed due to storm debris on the line, and passengers were tired, fretful, and anxious to be home. Friends and relatives prepared to greet people who had travelled up-country, and they closed in on the gate when the train stopped.

Dave was the only man in uniform, as his new partner had been summoned home, since his wife was in labour. The rest were detectives who mingled with the crowd as casually as possible and they, too, were tired due to overstaying their shift while waiting for the arrival of this very late train.

As usual, there appeared to be no tall, broad man alighting. Of course, he might return by car, thus costing the ratepayers of Liverpool a small fortune in police wages, but second guessing a criminal as clever as Shuttleworth was never going to be easy.

Smelly Nellie felt the dog tensing by her side. He stepped forward, hackles and tail rising, the latter waving as if greeting a friend. This meant drugs. The hair along Nelson's spine flattened itself as he approached a wheelchair. He turned and glared at Nellie, who nodded towards Dave. PC David Earnshaw walked towards the bearded, disabled person whose chair was being pushed by a man uglier than sin, as his nose had been broken at least once. A shot rang out.

Time froze for a few seconds.

The screaming began, as did the rush towards exits. At exactly midnight, the first bullet entered Dave's chest, and a second hit him during his descent to the ground. Shuttleworth leapt from the wheelchair and fired again, this time without a blanket to conceal the weapon. Chaos ensued. The pusher of the chair was also armed. He sent a bullet flying above the heads of a small gathering. 'Don't move if you know what's good for you.' His accent had been born in London.

Shuttleworth walked towards the main entrance, his gun waving back and forth across terrified faces in the group who had moved in the direction of Lime Street after travelling up on the London train. Children cried, while one young woman collapsed in a dead faint. Behind Shuttleworth, Broken Nose shuffled backwards, his revolver trained on those who remained on the station's forecourt. 'Lie down,' he yelled.

People inside the station's large forecourt dropped to the floor, though Nellie remained upright with the dog by her side. 'Murderer,' she called. 'Shoot me. Go on, show us what you're made of – shoot a woman in her sixties.'

He ignored her and continued in reverse close behind the now self-propelled Shuttleworth, both travelling towards would-be escapees who remained motionless, some guarding the unconscious female on the ground.

Within seconds, the roar of an engine and the screaming of tyres filtered past the throng at the main entrance.

Shuttleworth and Broken Nose were gone. PC Earnshaw, with two bullets in his chest and one in his lower back, lay in a widespread pool of blood. Two detectives ran towards Dave. Nellie and Mary rushed to his side with Nelson, though the dog carried on until he reached the wheelchair. Its inner pockets were stuffed with small, transparent bags containing a white powder, and he sat nearby until a detective joined him and confirmed the dog's discovery.

Nellie murmured a few words from the Latin *Pie Jesu* and stroked blessed water on the fallen man's forehead. Officers who had tried in vain to discover the make and registration number of the getaway car returned to the scene. Over a hand-held radio, a man shouted repeatedly, 'Officer down, Lime Street Station.'

Dave's bleeding slowed, its pace advertising a faltering heart.

Nellie raised her hand in a small gesture of benediction. 'In the name of the Father, the Son and the Holy Spirit, may you rest in peace, my dear, dear friend.' As he left the mortal coil, Sister Helen Veronica held his hands while Mary Veronica knelt by his head. 'He's gone, Nellie,' she whispered.

'Yes. St Peter had better let him in, or I'll be having words with him one of these days.' Still kneeling, she sat back on her ankles. 'Oh, Mary, Dave has a wife and children. Only then did Nellie's tears flow. Nelson, having concluded all business connected to drugs, walked over to his mistress and began to lick the grief from her face. She smiled through her tears. Nelson was a footrest, a draught excluder, a waste bin for unwanted food, a companion and a very close friend. At this moment, he was a rather damp handkerchief. Even now, he made her grin.

Mary used a real hanky to dry her own tears. 'Sometimes,' she whispered, 'I wish I'd joined the Poor Clares instead.'

Helen made no reply. She rather liked being a co-opted, undercover police officer. She turned and saw grown men, plain clothes coppers, mopping at their eyes. 'If his wife is in need of help, let me know so that I can send one of my friends to do whatever's necessary,' she advised them. The seedy side of life was very much the business of Veronicas. Like the saint after whom their order was named, they were there to mop up the blood and tears of mankind, to help with children, the poor, the criminal, the aged and the disabled. It was not the easy life. She spoke to Mary eventually. 'They don't even have shoes.'

'What? Who?'

'The Clares. It's my belief that contemplation should be left to Buddhists. They make such a lovely job of it.'

The two nuns stood with detectives near the cooling body of a good friend. Shuttleworth was now a marked man. 'You'll find him, won't you?' Mary asked.

'We will,' the nearest officer replied.

Police took statements or names and addresses from all who remained, and the ambulance didn't sound its siren as it pulled away, since the passenger was en route for the morgue via the pathology department.

'Eddie,' Smelly Nellie whispered to Holy Mary.

'Oh, my goodness, yes,' was the answer. 'He's CID now, isn't he?'

Nellie nodded. 'They were like brothers. When they were split up, Dave went quiet. Eddie's down by the docks looking for that murderer.' She shook her head sadly. 'There'll be officers doing voluntary unpaid overtime till they find Shuttleworth.' She paused. 'Why did I nod at Dave when Nelson did his Rhodesian Ridgeback imitation? Why didn't I signal a plain clothes man?'

'Stop it, Helen. Thinking like that will do you and the rest of us no good at all. I could have gone to him and held him back, because he stuck out like a sore thumb, him being the only one in uniform. Just pray for him; we can't save the whole world.'

'He was our friend, Mary.'

'So is Jesus, but no one stopped the crucifixion, did they? Come on. Let's make our statements and go home.'

After some rearrangements of beds and rooms, Belle, Tom and Max moved in to Meadowbank. They would stay for just a couple of nights, since Eve, no longer in pain because of her tablets, refused to rest. The place would be up and running within days, so Eve became Führer once more. Wherever she went, Tom's black Labrador followed her.

'He knows,' Tom whispered to his wife.

'That she's dying?' Belle's eyebrows shot heavenwards. 'Don't talk so daft, Thomas Duffield.'

'Watch,' he advised.

She watched. 'It's because she keeps feeding him all kinds of rubbish.'

Tom sighed. 'O ye of little faith.'

'Dogs followed Hitler,' she murmured.

He grinned. 'Eve would have scared the shit out of him.'

Meanwhile, phone calls were made, carefully worded advertisements placed in local papers, and Eve was on a roll. If she was bloody dying, she would leave a decent business for Kate. Rooms were allocated for the Gilroy twins, for a Joan Warburton and for Betty Halliwell, who was to be Baby. Belle helped, as did the other girls, while Tom did a demonstration with commentary on how to paint a wall with one hand and a hook.

Belle took a cup of tea to Eve in the office. 'How are you?' she asked.

'How am I? I'm sick of people asking. How I am is how I am.'

'They care,' Belle told her. 'There's even a crack in Angela's armour.' She paused. 'Where is it?'

'Where's what?'

'Don't act soft, Eve. Where's the bloody cancer?'

The madam folded her arms. 'It's on safari, travelling through the equator towards the Antarctic.'

'Eve!' The syllable was coated in impatience. 'Can you not answer a question properly for once?'

'Spreading,' Eve snapped. 'Mad Mannix keeps trying to get me into hospital – I suppose it's his job. But I'm not spending the last months of my life in that funeral parlour. I've got the pills, and when they stop working, I'll get what Doc Mannix calls more serious palliative treatment. Is that pink room ready for Betty Halliwell?'

'Yes, it is. Eve, I'm sorry, but Tom and I will have to get home. Lisa's taking full advantage of things; she thinks she's in charge of two houses now.' Belle sighed. 'I had this good little girl who was happy with a box of chalks or a picture book, and now she's walking about as if she owns the bloody street.'

Eve grinned. 'You've a good man there, Belle. You lean on him, because he won't fall over, and Lisa will come good. It's a phase, babe, just something she's going through because her life's changed a bit. It's all a matter of showing off – they do that, especially little girls.' How she wished she'd had a child or two, but feeling sorry for herself wasn't going to help, so she tucked away those thoughts and concentrated on now.

Belle sat down. 'I wish I could stay and help you, I really do, but we need to be home.' She felt the heat in her cheeks. 'I love him.'

'Do you? As if we can't tell? And he loves you, girl. Don't worry, I'll ask for help if I need it.'

'We'll visit, I promise.'

The big woman blinked rapidly. 'You've been an asset, love. Go and live your life with your family.'

When Belle had left the room, Eve sat for a few minutes with her head in her hands. She couldn't work out whether she was being sensible or completely stupid. In hospital, she would have been monitored and kept as free as possible from pain; medical staff would have been available at all times, and– 'And I'd be bored out of my skull.' Here was normality. Here was what she understood.

Eve had learnt that nothing in life was ever perfect. It was a matter of choosing from sets of evils, of compromise, of lining up the possibilities and deciding which would create the least hassle. She knew that her best friend's heart was breaking, and that was another reason for being here and staying here. Meadowbank had to be a going concern for Kate's sake. 'I'll get the business up and running if it's the last thing I do.'

She stood up and walked to the window. If she stayed alive and in control till spring, the garden would be landscaped with lots of flowers and shrubs. For Kate, everything needed to be just right. Belle and Tom were leaving. Max, too. Had she not been dying, she might have got herself a dog. 'At least I've had a life worth writing about.' Worth writing about? Did she have the time? Did she dare? No, not about Meadowbank, but about before this place, the pimps, the weird johns, girls fighting among themselves because somebody nicked somebody's bloke, usually a good payer or one with film star looks. Kate and Eve had escaped all that, though they had certainly known a few victims.

Sitting down again, she thought about the girls here. Who could type? Was it Mo or Cynthia? Somebody had to teach this crazy country to accept the world's oldest profession as valid and valuable. She opened a drawer, then another, then one more until she discovered the item she sought, picking out a hard-backed notebook. How to start? A white, empty page stared up at her accusingly. Title? Ah yes, *The Ladies of Liverpool*. 'Take a letter, Miss Mellor, and make it quick.' She began to scribble.

Babs slid down from the saddle to deal with Gordy. He was getting on her bloody nerves again. 'Who's in charge of this animal?' she demanded to know.

'We both are.'

'Right. And who's the one with the sore bum? Who's the one riding him?'

'You are.'

'Then shut that and open these.' She pointed first to his mouth, then to his eyes. 'Murdoch and me, we know what we're doing.' She paused. 'Well, we nearly know what we're doing. I mean, the National's not tomorrow, is it? Have you never heard of walk before you run? I had to crawl before I walked with this fellow.'

'The National's years away for us,' Gordy conceded.

'Then leave us alone while we get on with ... with paces. We've walked, we've trotted a bit and I never fell off. You're always criticizing me.'

Murdoch whinnied his support.

Gordy Hourigan blew out his cheeks and emitted a sound not unlike Murdoch's. 'You're letting him have all his own way. Get a hold on the bugger and stop giving him his head. And your gob's on the go all the time – you can't talk to him in the middle of a race. They thunder along, you know, and you–'

'Shut up.' Babs glared at him. She was a small woman with a great lump of love growing in her chest, love for the daft horse and love for this short-arse of an Irishman. Sometimes, her overflow threatened to leak because she couldn't contain her joy, her anger, Gordy's disappointment and all the niggles connected to the training of herself and this feisty horse. 'Just stop it,' she snapped. 'I might take time to learn, but once I get there I never forget. Like an elephant,' she concluded.

'Is this you telling me off?' he asked, blue eyes twinkling at her.

'Yes, it is.'

'Well, don't bother. You're only upsetting me, and him as well.'

'So? So now you know how it feels.'

'How what feels?'

'Getting upset. This is my real horse. I've ridden all them dozy buttercups over at Mr Macey's place, but this is my proper horse, the real one that I have to live with, but you're at it all the time, gab, gab, gab, moaning and shouting orders and stood there like king of the flaming leprechauns, as if you know everything, and I–'

'Will you go out with me tonight, Miss Schofield?'

Babs snapped closed her hanging jaw. 'Out?'

Gordy nodded. 'Out. As in not in.'

She folded her arms. 'God, you think you're clever, don't you?'

'Yes, I do.'

She fought a smile and won. 'I can't leave Sally on her own with him. He scares her, and she's frightened of hitting him too hard because he makes her mad. See, she's started fighting back, so I'll have to ask her if it's OK for me to leave her with Don.' Babs bowed her head for a moment. 'You're the only one who knows where Sal and I came from.' She looked into Gordy's eyes. 'Don't you mind what I was?'

'No.'

'Why, though?'

'Because I like who you are now. Would you mind what I was? I gave the Garda a run for their money till they caught me and got me locked away for breaking and entering. Will that make you back off?'

She shook her head.

'Then we're equal, so. Take Murdoch and groom him now. This way, we make sure he is one hundred per cent your boy. Ian and John have done the stable.'

Babs asked how the boys were doing.

Gordy shrugged. 'They're scared. You read about Shuttleworth killing the policeman?'

'Yes.'

'Well, so did the lads. Bill's in less bother, of course, because he wasn't left to guard the last of the boss's spoils. Even so, he's better away from Liverpool.'

Babs led her horse away and groomed him. As she did, he made little noises of appreciation. This was his rider, his teacher and his stable girl. There wasn't much he wouldn't do for her. She whispered to him, 'I have a date. Will Sally let me go?'

He nodded. It didn't mean anything, because he nodded frequently, but Babs chose to take it as a good sign. She leaned her head against his. 'You are so beautiful, baby. But you have to make me look good, OK? Less of the sideways shenanigans and more of the elegance. Come on now to the kitchen and we'll get your carrot and your apple, plus one for Nicholas Nye.'

He followed her through the paddock and across the wide lawn. He would have followed her to the ends of the earth, and they both knew it.

Twelve

Neil Carson was in a quandary. Quandaries seemed to have become a part of his life these days, but this one was special, huge, frightening and humiliating. He didn't know where to start, but he opted eventually for the Picton Library and made for the medical section in the reference department.

How was it spelt? And could he have caught it in such a short time with so few encounters? The little creepy crawlies had disappeared after he'd shaved the area carefully, but this... When had he last been with a woman? When had he killed Slitty Eyes? Shirley Evans. Her real name and her nickname owned the same initials. At night, just before falling asleep, he often 'saw' her staring at him through dead, half-closed eyelids.

Apart from reporting at and departing from work, time meant nothing to him. He knew what shifts he was on, of course, because that part of him was automatic – he'd been programmed for years when it came to the job. But remembering days or weeks, where, who, why and when was becoming more than difficult. Perhaps he didn't need to remember, didn't want to. Now this. How was he supposed to cope with it? By keeping a chart on his bedroom wall, he managed to keep up with the looking after of Maude, but just about everything else seemed to be getting harder.

It was October. Yes, he was sure about that, at least. Days were shorter, nights longer, while the air was becoming as chilled as the inside of a butcher's fridge. September, he had killed her. Beginning, middle or end? Oh God. He'd had no protection with him, so he'd buried himself in her filth. And time was no longer calculable... Gonorrhoea? Ah, here it was in the tome he'd chosen.

Symptoms can appear within ten days, or they may not show for months or years, especially in women. If ignored by people of either sex, the disease may attack other parts of the body, and complications could even be life-threatening if neglected. Even if you are unsure and think you may be in the early developmental stages, be on the safe side and seek help immediately.

Why had Jesus abandoned him?

Discharge in men often displays as white fluid which can turn yellow or green. Urination may give pain, and testicles might hurt, though that is rare if the problem is tackled early. The foreskin sometimes swells and becomes inflamed in time – again, this is variable. If you suspect that you have/may have contracted this disease, see your doctor without delay. Gonorrhoea spreads via sexual contact only, and stories about lavatory seats or shared towels are mythical and mistaken.

Depending on areas of penetration, the lower bowel, the mouth or the throat could be diseased. If infected semen reaches the face, conjunctivitis could be a...

Ugh! He closed the heavy book so loudly that people nearby were startled by the crack. 'Sorry,' he whispered before returning the book to its shelf and leaving the area at speed. The clap. People joked about it, saying it was the applause received after a good session with a whore, but this wasn't funny. It was absolutely terrifying. See a doctor? Could he imagine telling an educated man about the clap? Not likely. He could almost hear Mother calling him a nasty, dirty boy, so what would a doctor think of him?

It was all the fault of women. He'd had a nasty mother who'd been able to see only the 'bad' in her son, and he'd married a woman completely devoid of character, a thin, sexless female who'd cared only for her children and the state of the house. Even she had altered her tune now that she was beyond her husband's reach, all powder, lipstick and coloured eyelids. The desire to scream in the street almost overcame him, though he managed to swallow his anger.

He watched passing traffic and pedestrians, saw ordinary people having an ordinary day in an ordinary life. A clock struck the hour. A doctor? Talk to a doctor? Weren't there VD clinics in the city where people sat and tried not to look at each other in the waiting rooms? No thanks. Pacing about didn't help, because folk were starting to stare, so he slowed down a bit, since he needed not to be noticed. The words he had read minutes earlier were imprinted on his brain. *Seek help immediately ... seek help immediately...*

'Jesus, Jesus,' he breathed silently through tightening lips.

Seek help? How on earth might such a statement be framed for a medic's ears, though? How could he tell a doctor the truth about Angela and that... Slitty Eyes? It must have been her, not Angela; Angela was checked regularly, as were all the girls, and men who refused to wear protection had to leave the premises immediately.

He stood outside the Picton and gazed towards the tunnel's entrance. Surely he would be killed fairly quickly if he went in there? No, no, a person could never be sure. It might mean casualty, operations and a diagnosis delivered in a ward filled with people. Suicide was self-murder and unforgivable, certainly, especially for a disciple. He wasn't right; his thinking was less than rational. This lack of clarity had started ... he couldn't remember when.

He walked about the city for a while. In a town centre cafe, he gazed out at Williamson Square. His mind wandered back a few days or weeks. Once again, time proved immeasurable. It had been a Saturday, he remembered that much. Details returned to him as he sipped coffee. The house had looked the same, as had the road. Nothing had changed except... Except everything had changed.

'Thank you,' Laura said as she accepted the dead whore's money. She was blushing. Never before had she appeared so beautiful and desirable. His wife was wholesome, and he wanted to come home. Here, with her and the children, the predictability of life might help him to straighten himself out and deal with everything once more. For a few beats of time, he even managed to be angry with Jesus.

'How are you?' she wanted to know.

344

'May I come in?' he asked. Her blush deepened and served to brighten beautiful eyes he had never noticed until now. He knew why she was embarrassed, because he'd hidden up the side road across the way next to the Wilkinsons' semi, and had seen her being driven home. There was a man in his house – yes, this was *his* house. He was the one who'd worked for it and paid all the bills. Laura still kept it ticking over, but he was the money man. Her hair was longer and shiny.

'This extra cash will help for Christmas,' she commented belatedly.

They stood in the narrow hall. 'How are the children?' Neil asked.

'Both well.' Laura paused. 'They're staying with the Bramwell twins. It's rather late for a visit, and I've only just finished my shift. I'm about to go to bed. And you should be visiting our children during daylight hours rather than coming to see me at night. They think you've deserted them and that they might never see you again. It's cruel, Neil.'

'Going to bed with him?' The question fell out of his mouth without asking permission from his brain, whose powers were waning fast anyway. 'With your new friend and owner of this car?'

He watched as she straightened her spine. 'Don't be ridiculous. He's a gentleman who buys a late supper from the chip shop and eats it here while it's still hot. I have not committed adultery.' Laura looked him up and down. 'What have you been up to?' she asked. 'Because my conscience is completely clear.'

He shivered. It felt as if she could see right through to his marrow. 'I'm staying with Joseph

Turton and helping him care for his mother. She's old and infirm. We take turns and work different shifts for her sake.'

'Ah. Well, as long as you're comfortable.'

Neil shrugged. 'I was more comfortable here at home, before all this started.'

'All what?' she asked.

'Me being disturbed. It's my mother's fault, because she always was a monster, and I began to get dreams.' He was quiet for a moment. 'They've stopped. I don't have them any more.' She wanted him to go away quietly; she stared so hard at him that he felt forced to lower his gaze. Laura had breasts. Her waist was small, her hips slightly flared, and her face had changed completely. The shoes were black patent, and they narrowed to a point at the toe. Did they have stiletto heels?

'Go,' she said.

'Why?'

'Because I'm asking you to.'

'No,' was his swift reply. He could tell she was frightened of him. Why? He'd never been abusive towards her or the children, had seldom raised his voice, let alone a hand. 'I'll sleep in Matt's bed. Joseph's at home tonight.'

Laura rubbed her forehead as if searching for an elusive thought. 'No, you won't. This may be the house you bought, Neil, but it's my home and the children's, too. You left.'

'You ordered me out,' he answered angrily.

'Because you were screaming and moaning in your sleep. Because you weren't a husband or a father any more. You can't come in here.'

'Why not? I pay my way.' He knew why not; she

346

didn't want him near her any more, and she had no shield apart from the older man inside. The children weren't here, so she couldn't plead their need for quiet while sleeping. 'Do you think I'd hurt you?'

'I don't know,' she whispered. 'I don't know you any more.'

'But you know and trust your jeweller? Oh yes, I know who he is – people have told me. You're being talked about, Laura.' What was the man's name? Had he forgotten it, or had he never known it?

She remained outwardly calm. 'He's just a friend. Tonight, he'll sleep on the sofa or in one of the children's rooms, and this will be the first time he's stayed over. He will stay to protect me from you, since I can no longer believe in you. Neil, you're not the man I married.'

'I'm back to normal. I've changed.'

'Have you?'

Neil gritted his teeth; he must not, would not explode. It was a Saturday night, and people were still coming home from pubs and clubs. 'Are you afraid of me, Laura?'

Again, twin spots of colour darkened her cheeks. 'Yes,' she muttered.

'Why?'

They were now eye to eye again. 'Where did you get the gold cross?'

'What?'

'You heard me. It had initials on the other side, didn't it?'

'Did it?'

She nodded just once. 'You know it did. You

347

must have seen them.'

'I told you. I bought it second hand from a junk shop.'

She closed her eyes for a moment. He noticed again how bright they were when she opened them. What was she thinking? What did she suspect? Was she intending to talk to the police about the cross and chain? 'I've no idea where the cross came from before it was sold to the shop.'

'Which shop?'

He stood his ground, though his ground was uncertain, as if there was a sudden shift just below its crust, a realignment of strata. 'Actually, it was a stall on Paddy's,' he mumbled.

'And what were the initials, Neil? The initials on the plain side?'

'Er ... I can't remember.' JD, JD, JD. Jean Davenport, such an untidy corpse, like a broken marionette, legs splayed, mouth open, head lolling to one side, and a partial denture resting on the lower lip... 'I sold it back to him for a much reduced price, because I decided to get you a real crucifix, probably silver.'

'Right.' She took a small step in his direction. 'I shall stay with the Bramwells at weekends from now on, because I'm not putting up with you any more. I want a decent, normal, ordinary life.' She turned her head and shouted, 'Andy? Would you mind coming here, please?'

The stranger arrived and stood by Laura's side. 'You called?' He was grinning like the Cheshire cat. A definite for Neil's list?

'Yes. Will you take me back to the chip shop, please? I'll just grab some things from my room.'

She ran upstairs.

Neil stared at the man, who returned the favour with compound interest, causing the would-be intruder to lower his eyes. The jeweller was handsome, taller than Neil, and very well presented: shiny shoes, a good suit, a trilby in one hand. And he wasn't exactly old, probably early fifties. So Laura dressed up for this man, used makeup for him. What else was she doing for him? Were they lovers? She came downstairs with a small bag. 'I want to leave now, Andy,' she said. After glaring at Neil for a few seconds, she approached him. He caught a whiff of perfume, good perfume; no Californian Poppy for her.

Neil backed away to allow them access to the short path, the gate, the pavement and the car. Her shoes did have small stiletto heels. The couple drove off. He watched as they rang the shop's bell, saw lights being switched on, stood where he was until Laura was inside and Jewellery Andy disappeared in his car. They were punishing him, making a fool of him by acting out this little scenario while he could only stand and watch.

His heart was beating madly, like a kettledrum doing overtime. Sickness threatened his throat, and he gulped back its evil taste. She knew something. But she had a poor memory for detail and seldom read a paper or listened to the news. All the same, he might be in danger.

'She suspects but has no proof,' Neil muttered under his breath. Female intuition? Could he kill her to save himself? Was he capable of wiping out a girl he'd loved since his teenage years? Confusion, confusion.

Neil remembered, just about, how grounded he had been, how determined and hardworking. He'd mended furniture, made second hand look like new, had bought her every labour-saving device known to man. He'd been a good husband, a beloved father...

'Would you like anything else, sir?' the waitress asked, pulling him back into the here and now.

Neil blinked. 'Sorry,' he replied. 'I was lost in thought.'

'Yes, we noticed that. Are you all right?'

He nodded. 'Another coffee and a buttered Eccles cake, please. And, thanks for letting me think. I needed the chance.'

'You're welcome.' She was nice. But there could be no nice women for him, because he'd found another way. Gonorrhoea. It was perhaps as well that Laura had turned him away that night, because he might have infected her. Instead, he could play pass the parcel and spread the disorder like wildfire through the prostitutes of Liverpool and their clients. He had been granted an easier way of killing, and it might live on long after his death.

Henry VIII. He remembered reading somewhere that the evil, self-promoted primate of Christianity had suffered from syphilis, and that his daughter had not dared to wed because she had been born with it. Catholic propaganda? He had no idea. He had no idea about much, really, kept forgetting names of people, of streets, of all kinds of things. Many of the apostles and disciples had suffered. He was one of them, and it was his turn to feel the pain.

When Eccles cake and coffee had been consumed, he wandered off to pick up his bike. Joseph was at home with Maude, so Neil Carson had the privilege of time on his hands. Although he knew he should seek medical help, he opted for a different tack; he would spread the filth he carried, and he knew exactly what to do.

As he cycled along, he went through a list. There was Belle Horrocks. She had corrupted a man with only one hand. She had left Meadow–What? Meadow what? The farm. Yes, she'd run off to grab at a normal life. Normal? What did she know about normal? Fat Mamma was another, though her death was imminent anyway. She had made no effort to conceal her antipathy whenever she saw him. He was pleased that their names were coming back to him.

Who else? The jeweller. Name? Then Trevor Burns, butcher. Laura? Could he, should he? No, no, he needed to take a chance there, had to hope she wouldn't sound off about that wretched cross, because the children must not become orphans. Though they might get adopted by decent people... So it wasn't a long list, but he needed to begin his research. Er ... was Joseph with Maude? Yes, yes, he was. Maude was his adoptive mother, not the real one. He liked Maude, didn't want to kill her.

People had patterns. They worked, slept, ate and played, but they all did it in their own way. So he did remember some things, then. Wavertree. Oh yes, he recalled that one. A female child ran from one house to another, so relatives of Belle ... he would remember her surname again

351

in a minute, must live nearby. They were probably the child's grandparents, while the little girl was likely to be a bastard. Did that disease – what was its name? – did it damage the brain? If it did, such damage must surely take a while to kick in. Syphilis did. Yes, he'd recollected that from God alone knew where or when. Henry ... a king. He'd suffered from that. Hadn't he?

He stopped outside a newsagent's and bought an exercise book and a Biro pen. When he remembered something, he would make a note of it.

'Writing your memoirs?' the shopkeeper asked jovially.

'Just a few notes,' was Neil's reply.

Returning to the bike, he stopped and pondered. Wavertree. Cecil Avenue or Street, Carlisle – was there a Carlisle Street? Albert Road, Cambridge Street? There was an Earle Road. He closed his eyes and was mentally sorting letters at work, but they were all jumbled up. Newcastle Road? Yes, it was there, or near there.

Oh, God, his head was cloudy. A black door, then two houses, then a dark green door. Picton Road. The Picton Library was in town, not in this part of the city, not on Picton Road. Gonorrhoea. He wrote furiously in his new notebook. Plant pots. They might have moved them, because bedding plants would be past their best. Both houses had plant pots, one house had a green door, and the other was black. He was falling apart. Somewhere behind all the nonsense, he knew he was losing his grip. Laura was no longer a good mother, because she had brought another man

352

into the children's lives. But he couldn't, no, he couldn't...

Kill her. Couldn't. He was probably tired because he never stopped thinking. Even asleep, he thought. Jesus came back in dreams and told him everything was going to be fine, but they were just dreams. Meadowbank, that was the name of the farm. He scribbled it quickly.

OK, he would take his time. Deliberately slow, he followed his nose towards the southern end. Ah, yes, he had the right street. Numbers 42 and 48 were here. Plantpots present and correct, contents rather frazzled, and lights were on inside both houses. Count, count, and go round the back. A convenient knot hole in the gate, nobody about, a good chance to—

Oh, look at them. The man was peering through a glass on a stand, and she stood behind him. It was a beautiful picture of something Neil had never known. She was stroking his hair, and he was turning to look at her. Were they redeemed, then? Tears burned his eyes. *I am ill, and they are well. Did I get the message wrong? Perhaps not, because they are inside rather than on the streets. I can't, I can't do any more. There's the little girl climbing onto his lap. Lucy, oh, Lucy. My boy Matt, my lovely boy. The streets. Jesus said the streets. I must write that down later. I must not put these people on my list; I mustn't kill unnecessarily.*

He rode all the way back to Joseph's house and parked the bike round the back. Removing his bicycle clips, he entered the scullery and found Joseph there in tears. For a reason he couldn't identify, Neil felt embarrassed. 'What's the matter?' he asked.

'Mother's gone.'

Neil allowed a few taps of time to pass. 'Gone? Gone where? Into hospital?'

The grieving man shook his head. 'She asked for half a grapefruit, which I spoon-fed her, then she wanted me to wash her hands and face. I was washing her when she thanked me and asked me to thank you, too. Then a weird thing happened; she closed her eyes, opened them wide again, as if she was getting better, and she said, "Neil must stop." After that, she went. Just went.'

Neil swallowed, his throat dry enough to cause pain. 'Is she ... is she still in her room, Joseph?' She was in heaven and, during her passing, she'd picked up a message from Jesus. Neil tried to clear his throat. 'She must have meant she wants me to stay here with you. Well? Is she still in the front room?'

Joseph finished drying his eyes. 'No. Doctor did a death certificate, pneumonia and heart something or other–' He sobbed. 'Congested heart failure, I think. The McManus Funeral Parlour has her. Oh, Neil.'

Neil wrapped his arms round his friend. 'Let it out, Joseph.'

The man was crying like a baby, shaking from head to foot and pouring his grief onto Neil's shoulder.

Neil patted his friend's back. 'You'll be all right,' he said.

'I used to ... when I was younger ... used to resent her. No life of my own, you see.' He pulled away and tried to calm himself, mopping his face with a handkerchief. 'Where've you been?'

'Er ... library, a cafe, a ride round the city.' He remembered all that well enough. 'Joseph, if I'd known–'

'You can call me Joe now. Mother wouldn't let anybody call me Joe. My dad was Joe, so I had to be Joseph.'

'All right, Joe. And I'll live here as long as you want me to.'

'Thanks. I have to get funeral money from her policy. And a black suit.'

'We'll get dark navy,' Neil said. 'They won't be wasted.'

'OK. Will you be a coffin bearer, Neil?'

Neil marked a few seconds before replying. Could he carry a woman who'd told him to stop? She'd gone towards a light, probably, and peeped through into wherever ... and she'd ordered him to stop. Stop killing? Stop here with her son? 'Yes, of course I will, Joseph.'

'It's Joe.'

'All right, Joe.' He sat on a stool.

Joe stared at him. 'Will you do something else for me?'

'You know I will. What?'

'Strip her bed.' These three syllables arrived on a whisper.

'I will.' The lodger stood and walked through the living room and into the empty bedroom/parlour. There remained a dip in the top pillow, a depression where Maude's head had rested. 'Bye, Mother,' he whispered. He could smell her scent, lavender with a hint of lilac. She'd used Johnson's baby powder too, and the whole melange made

355

him feel at home. Wright's Coal Tar soap sat in a dish by her bed next to surgical spirit and the ointment used for her pressure sores when they appeared.

As he bent to pick up the pillow, he felt a slight chill in the air, and his pores opened. 'Stop, lad.'

Neil turned and saw nothing.

'You'll come to a bad end,' the voice whispered. 'Remember – I warned you. Remember. Nothing good can come of it.' The voice faded.

He ran out of the front room, through the living room and the tiny kitchen, past Joe who was sitting on the stool, finally reaching the small, tacked-on bathroom. He retched until his ribs ached, emptying his stomach into the pan before flushing. He sat on its lid. The small bathroom suited him just now, because he was near enough to the sink to splash his face with cold water and wash his hands. He was ill. The voice was in his head, surely?

Joe tapped at the door. 'You all right, Neil?'

He breathed in deeply through his mouth. 'I think I must have had a bad Eccles cake, Joe. And it was a shock hearing about your mother.'

'Sorry, lad.'

'It's all right, Joe. Who else would you turn to?'

There was a pause. 'We'll leave the bed till to-morrow, then, and we'll do it between us,' the dis-embodied voice suggested. 'We'll need spanners or something to pull the frame apart.'

'OK. I'll have a bath.'

'Right-o.'

Neil lay in the water. 'It's all in your head,' he breathed. 'Maude, Jesus, Judas – you imagined them. Get a grip.' He stood up, found his robe and went upstairs to dress. His bedroom door opened. 'Hi, Joe,' he said.

Joe sat on Neil's bed. 'Why did you leave Laura?' he asked.

'We didn't see eye to eye any longer.'

After a short pause, Joe asked, 'But you still like women?'

'Some, not all.' Neil finished dressing. 'Why?'

Joe lowered his head. 'I like men,' he answered quietly. 'I like you.'

'Oh?' Neil stared into the mirror, past his own reflection and studied his landlord. 'I'm your friend.'

The seated man swallowed audibly. 'I couldn't have left my mother, and I couldn't have brought trouble and shame to her door, so I've never told anybody.'

Icy fingers travelled down Neil's spine. It was his turn to gulp. 'But Joe, I'm not that way.'

'Not queer?'

'No. I could never ... have you ever?'

Joe shook his head slowly. 'Not since school. There was a lad there, and we used to mess about, but I've wanted to talk to somebody – anybody who'd listen. And when you left your wife, I wondered–'

'I'm not like that.' What was he going to do now? He couldn't stop here, could he? This man's mother was hardly cold, yet here he sat talking filth in Neil's bedroom; no shame, no control over himself.

Joe continued, 'I thought with you being my best friend, there might be a bit more to you. Sorry.'

357

Neil fastened his shirt and turned to look at the poor creature who had just lost his mother, who was desperate for affection and possibly close to breaking point. *Like I am. I must look after myself.* 'I'll stay till after the funeral, Joe.'

Joe raised his head. 'What?'

'I can't live here with you now. You'll want to bring friends home, friends who want what you want. I'd be a wallflower.'

'No, I–'

'Sorry, Joe.' Neil left the room, ran down the stairs, and went through the ground floor to a small shed in the back yard. He found a drill, screws, and a bolt. If he had to stay for a few days, he would make sure of his own safety. But could he stay? If Maude was still hanging about, and if Joe was going to carry on acting weird, was this the place for Neil?

And the police were searching for his alter ego. There'd been some distraction in the press, he couldn't recall exactly when, articles about a man who'd shot dead a policeman on Lime Street Station, but warnings were still being issued to women about staying in at night. If they had to go out, they were advised not to go alone. *See? I remembered all that.*

There was no sign of Joe, but Neil could hear him sobbing in the front bedroom. He crept upstairs and entered his own room. As quickly and quietly as he could manage, he installed the small bolt and shot it home. Although he had no reason to suspect that Joe might try to force him into his unsavoury world, Neil wanted to make sure.

It was in the Bible somewhere about not having

physical relations with someone of the same sex. It was a sin. Killing people was a bigger sin, so Joe was a better person than Neil. But Jesus and Judas– Oh, why had they come that night on the hearth of the front room fireplace at home? Had they come? They must have, because that event never left his memory. The names of three women stayed with him, too. Jean Davenport, Shirley Evans and, sandwiched between those two, his mistake, Dolly Pearson. But he'd repaid by staying here to look after Maude, who ... who was no longer here.

Thirteen

Given months or at most a year to live, Eve decided to make the best of her time, and she started by buying a car, a three-year-old Bentley with plenty of leg and belly room. Comfort mattered, since there was enough pain without being squashed at a driving seat, and she didn't want to use the van for her personal expeditions.

Her second decision was also a novelty – she closed the business on Thursdays. When questioned by Kate O'Gorman, her second in command, she had the answer ready. 'I want a bit of freedom, love. I've spent too many years behind closed doors, and I want to get out and about a bit while I still can. Anyway, they could all do with a rest once a week.'

Kate knew she wasn't getting the whole story.

'There's something you're not telling me, Evie; I can always see when you're holding back.'

The large woman shrugged. 'Let me have some secrets.'

'No. Not while you're ill.'

Eve sighed resignedly. 'Look, I want to go out with a bang. He's killed three women so far, that Mersey Monster. One was on a Friday, which is pretty much our busiest night, so I'm staying open, but two were Thursdays, and that's when we'll shut, because one of you might like to come with me. I've tracked him by looking at the killing sites, and he does vary among streets around the docks. But they're all within a mile or so of each other.' She stared through the window. 'I'm going to put a stop to him if it's the last decent thing I do.'

'You and whose bloody army? Eve, you can't – it's a job for the cops.'

'I can try. I'm doing no more van runs, so I can carry on as I like, where and when I like. Belle found us that van driver – Cathie Drake, and she's agreed to take over. She's a retired working girl who had a good thing going – she towed a caravan round to holiday resorts and was never short of customers – and she's used to driving. In winter, she rested abroad for three months, if you please, so she must have been minted. Spain, I think it was. She went for New Year and stayed till Easter. Now there's a woman with what I call a head for business.'

Kate nodded. She quite liked Cathie Drake; Cathie was tough but nice.

'I'll stick to Thursdays and the odd Friday, and

360

you can cover here on the few Fridays when I'm out. When I'm gone for good and you're the boss, you could do a lot worse than choosing Cathie as your deputy. She knows a thing or two. Or Angela. There's more to Whiplash than met our eye for years. As for him,' she pointed at the Liverpool newspaper in Kate's hand, 'he'd better watch out, wherever and whoever he is. Is there anything about another killing in that paper?'

Kate swallowed audibly. 'I've not looked. And when you find him, what then? Because he won't stop whatever he's doing just on account of you throwing a maddy.'

'I might accidentally run over him.' She bit her lip. 'And Angela says she can get me a gun. I'll not leave this world till he's dead, only I have to catch him hurting a girl.' She stared through the window. 'Oh no, Kate. He's out there some-where, and if I'm dying, so is he. I'll not leave him behind to carry on killing, damn him.'

'But Eve–'

'But nothing. I've decided. Give me that *Daily Post* and fetch a cup of tea, please. I'm on me last legs, and my final gift to the world will be to try and make it a safer place for working girls.'

When Kate had left the office, Eve scanned the front page of Liverpool's morning paper. It was her turn to swallow hard. 'Blood and bullets – I do not trust that flaming man. Look at him, standing there like butter wouldn't melt.'

It said nothing about suspicious death, but there he was in the doorway of a small Victorian house that was typical of poorer areas of the city. Neil Carson. He'd been living with a Joseph

Turton and his mother, and the old dear had died suddenly. On the morning after his mother's death, Mr Turton had been found by Mr Carson hanging in the hallway. So to all intents and purposes, Joseph Turton had committed suicide by killing himself just a matter of hours after his mother's death. 'And you were there, you slimy bastard.' Had Carson helped the poor bereaved man on his way?

Eve placed the paper on her desk. There was something nasty about Carson, and she had neither liked nor trusted him. Just suppose he needed somewhere to live? The aged lady was dead, so the house should have passed to her son, but Carson might have had other plans for the old place – it would be just a small matter of changing a name on the rent book. What if he'd smothered the bloke before hanging him up like a rabbit in a butcher's window? No. Poor Mr Turton would have been a real dead weight, too much for one person. Oh, this bloke made her flesh crawl, and she had more flesh than most. Was her intuition getting stronger as she neared her end? Perhaps this might be compensation for the fact that she wouldn't reach her mid-fifties.

Kate returned with tea. 'I put a spoon of clear honey in that,' she said.

Eve made no reply as she took the mug. She offered the newspaper in exchange. 'Have a gander at that, Kate. Look and learn, because I told you I never trusted that postman bloke. The devil's in him, and don't look at me like that. Leave the d off devil, and that's what Carson is, bloody evil.'

The older woman sank into the chair opposite Eve's. After reading, she looked across the desk at her best friend. Eve looked so well today, so normal that no one would have guessed how ill she was. 'What are you thinking, Eve?'

'No idea. I'm waiting for the goose bumps to settle down. There's something in his eyes...' She took a sip of tea, grateful for its heat, since she needed to warm up from the inside. 'No, he's like an empty house, nobody in, and there's bugger all in his eyes; he's like something with no soul, no heart, no care for anything but himself. I reckon his eyes leave space for Satan.'

Kate shivered and blessed herself hurriedly. 'Has Angela said anything about him?' she asked. 'Because she's seen him a few times.'

Eve released one of her famous huge sighs. There were clients and there were weird creatures, and this one was as weird as they came. 'He can take a lot more pain than most. I suppose that's because he feels nothing in his body, either. He's just not right, Kate; he begs Ange to draw blood, and you know that's a step too far for her. Well, he may want to bleed, but I reckon that snake could draw some other poor bugger's blood to save himself. Oh, and she said he's angry about her staying here till I die, because the flat would have been more private. I think Angela wants rid of him. Like me, she senses something horrible in the bloke.'

'So?'

'So we get rid. Next time he comes, I'll tell Angela to send him to me for a word or ten. She has a strong stomach, our Miss Whiplash, and if she doesn't want him, he has to be a real shit. So he's out. It wouldn't surprise me if he had something to do with that man's death, the one whose mother passed away the day before.' She pondered. 'He wants watching,' she added, almost to herself. 'There's something... Kate, you know I'm a woman with what they call intuition, and that intuition is on red alert. I'm not sure I know why.'

Kate nodded. There were times when it was best to keep her counsel, and this was one such occasion. She changed the subject. 'Babs and Sally will be here in a while with a surprise for you to look at. She phoned yesterday and said they'd–'

Eve groaned. 'Not that bloody horse. Oh, for God's sake, Kate, tell me it's not Mad Murdoch.'

Kate nodded, then shook her head. 'But I didn't tell you. Just remember that and be overcome with joy, else I'll thump you.'

'Can I not be ill instead, Mother?'

'No. You can be excited and grateful and pleased to see them.'

Eve, muttering and grumbling under her breath, walked out of the office and went to tidy her hair and change into something decent. Horses? What the hell next? With the Gilroy sisters as clowns, Angela with her whip, and now a mad horse, they had the makings of a small circus.

Left to herself, Kate enjoyed a short, rare and welcome rest. Eve had trouble in her liver, pancreas and intestine. The C word was seldom used by Kate, because it frightened her, but her best ever friend had the big C and would take no treatment beyond pain control. As ever, Eve viewed the problem pragmatically. It was there, it was going to kill her, but she would decide when. 'Well, she'd better not ask me to help her come the day, that's all I can say.'

A vehicle pulling a huge horsebox was trundling its way slowly up the uneven path. Kate watched as the driver jumped down, opened the back of the trailer and walked a beautiful animal down from the box. Babs, in full riding gear, climbed out of the passenger seat and helped the short, handsome man saddle the horse, a process that took several minutes. Boy, that was a good-looking horse, and the man, albeit a short-arse, wasn't bad, either.

Kate watched as he threaded his fingers together and bent so that his hands could act as Babs's mounting block. Sally flapped about excitedly when Babs urged Murdoch to walk on. Meanwhile Angela, at the kitchen window, studied her erstwhile rival as she rode up the side of the house – Babs looked as if she'd been born in the saddle.

Kate joined the others in the kitchen. 'She's happy,' she muttered. It was as if rider and horse were one, made for each other. 'I didn't know there were women jockeys,' she said to Eve when the big woman returned from the hair-tidying and clothes-changing session. 'I know they can be showjumpers, but our little madam's training for races, or so I've been told.'

'Who said that?'

'Belle did. They still talk on the phone. Women are allowed to ride in some races, and in a few years they'll be able to ride in the National.'

The whole household, wrapped in coats or cardigans, assembled outside the kitchen to watch as Babs put Murdoch through his paces. She got him to walk, trot, canter and gallop.

'Bloody hell,' Mo said, 'she couldn't even ride a bike. How many times has she come home bruised and bleeding, jeans ripped and hair looking like an abandoned bird's nest?'

Angela laughed. 'I think our little Baby Girl's found her gift. Look at her standing in the stirrups with her arse in the air. Doesn't she make it seem easy?'

Gordy joined the onlookers. 'She's brilliant.' There was pride in his tone. 'First time she saw him, she tumbled head over heels in love, climbed a fence, lay across the back of a horse that could have killed her, and walked him. I knew then. She owns him; they own each other.' He looked at Eve. 'You were there; you saw it.'

'I was there all right,' Eve replied. 'Frightened me to death, she did.'

Angela stared hard at him. 'Are you two going out together?'

'We are.'

'That's nice,' Eve said. 'She needed settling. I'll just warn you now, when she starts throwing stuff, duck. She's a crack shot with pots and pans. And words. She has a very sharp tongue.'

'I'm Irish,' he answered as if this fact served as sufficient explanation.

Judy laughed. 'We can tell.'

'So I'm used to most things. My mother had a deadly aim with rabbits and hares, so we had to be quick getting out of her road. Daddy always said not to worry if we weren't clean at the table,

366

for Mammy couldn't see a thing close to. She could see for miles, but. Because of that, we had to avoid standing mid-distance between near to and far away when she had the gun, as we weren't sure about where one ended and the other began.' He shook his head. 'A mortallious troubled childhood for sure, we had. Her cooking was ... interesting. But she was a lovely woman in her own way. Like Babs. Babs is a one-off, only in a different sense. She cooks well. She knows the difference between salt and sugar, which helps no end.'

'Babs is a gifted girl who avoided school like the plague,' Eve said.

Sal piped up. 'I do better cakes and pies, but she makes good dinners.' She turned to Eve. 'If you want a little break in Southport, Mr Crawford would be delighted to let you stay. We know you've got...' Her voice died.

'Cancer. It's just a word, Sally. It scares the daylights out of Kate, but it's just a word. Yes, I might enjoy Southport, so I'll think about that.'

Murdoch finished his display, nodding when his audience applauded.

Babs slid down the horse's side like a true professional.

'Get him,' Babs told Gordy.

Gordy disappeared.

'Get who?' Mo asked.

Babs patted her horse. 'Nicholas Nye, of course. Just wait a couple of minutes – we've a two-horse box.'

The blind donkey stole the show. Even the life-hardened Eve seemed moved by the relationship

367

between the two beasts.

'Inseparable,' Gordy said. 'Can you imagine when we go to racecourses with this pair? There we'll be in the winner's enclosure with a sweat-lathered horse and a scruffy little Nye. Without his friend, Murdoch might refuse to run. He's temperamental.'

'Like his jockey,' Eve said wryly. 'They should do well together, cos they're a right pair of loonies.'

'You're right enough, Miss Mellor. I took her for a meal she didn't enjoy, so it was the chef they brought to the table while she educated him in the art of cookery. I can't take you anywhere, can I, sweetness?'

Eve chuckled – he knew exactly what the man meant.

'No, you can't.' Babs watched her colleagues making a great fuss of Nicholas Nye. Placid as ever, the patient little beast stood while he was kissed, stroked, patted and told he was an angel. Angela had changed, Babs decided. There was a softer side to her, as if the knife's edge had been blunted. Eve's illness was probably responsible for the shift in Angela's behaviour. On impulse, she hugged her ex-enemy. 'Sorry for all the fights,' she whispered.

A red-faced Angela responded, 'No problem,' before extricating herself from the shorter woman's strangely powerful arms. 'So you two gave up the lesbian bit, I take it?'

Babs nodded. 'We did. But she's greedy – two boyfriends, if you please.'

'Never!'

'One's younger than she is; the other's the same

age. They're both nice in their different ways, and they both love the bones of her. She's a good girl, Angie, but we're expecting a fight between the two lads.'

'We're all good – well, most of us are. People assume that we're bad because of the job we do. Underneath all that, we're as good as anybody else.'

Babs nodded her agreement. 'One day, probably long after we're all dead, the law will change and prostitution will be supervised and legalized. Until then, we can't do anything except keep safe. That killer's still out there, I'm sure.'

Eve listened to their conversation, but said not one word. There were plenty of vehicles parked in the dockside area, and she would be one of them. It would soon be three weeks since the last killing, and the murderer would be hunting again any day now. The pattern belonged to a shift worker, she felt sure. If she knew that, the cops, too, would be aware. But an extra hand at the pump was always useful; for the first time in her life, Eve Mellor was on the side of the law.

Postmen did shift work, didn't they? Central post offices never closed, because mail needed sorting night and day. He fitted the profile, and Eve was on to him.

He picked up the Biro. If he wrote it, he might remember more accurately.

I'm sure I didn't do anything. The bolt was on my bedroom door, and I remember fixing that and making sure the door was shut – I even stuck a chair

369

under the handle like I've seen them doing in films. My clothes were still on me when I woke, so I took them off and hung them up. The house was very quiet, though the outside world was making noise – I could hear vehicles on the move. It was just after one in the morning, I think.

In pyjamas, I went down to the bathroom. Joe was sitting in the middle room drinking. There were six or more Guinness bottles on the table, and a half bottle of Scotch on the floor. He was mixing his drinks, and I've never known him do that except on special occasions like somebody's birthday party or the Christmas do at work. I said nothing and he said nothing It was the same when I'd finished in the bathroom – not a word spoken, so I just went back to my room, shot the bolt home, put the chair under the handle and lay down.

I couldn't catch my sleep. Hearing Maude talking to me when she was dead must have made me jumpy. I caught the sound of him sobbing and clinking bottles down below. He's no friend of mine, I told myself. He's a nancy boy, I kept repeating in my head. He likes me, and always thought I'd felt the same way about him, but where did he get that idea? Just because I left my wife, he thought he was in with a chance. We were just different from the other blokes, odd men out, and we got together for that reason, because neither of us has much to say for himself.

Then I heard him climbing the stairs. He stumbled a lot, and he swore a few times before reaching the landing. Very suddenly, he went still. I got up, crept across the room and put my ear against the door, keeping a careful hand on the chair to stop it shifting. I could hear him breathing. Then he tapped on my door and started going on about how he loved me and how I mustn't leave him. His tongue stumbled over words, and I knew he was very drunk.

I felt sick. I was imagining what they do to one another, and I almost understood my mother and the way she used to carry on. In my book, there's nothing wrong with making love, but two men? Then I knew I had to get out of the house, because I wouldn't be able to look at him, eat with him – could I even work with him? Why wouldn't he give up and go to bed?

He went all legal after a while, telling me in mixed-up words that the new law accepted a relationship between consenting adults over twenty-one unless they were in the armed forces. His speech was slurred, but I got the gist. What was I supposed to do? Let him in and let him get on with whatever he wanted from me?

I waited until he'd gone away before creeping back to my bed where I lay as stiff as a board listening to him crying in the room across the landing. The crying changed to snoring and I fell asleep. In the morning I got up and prepared myself for work. I'd changed shifts for one day and was on earlies. And I found him. He was just hanging there with his tongue sticking out and the rope digging into his neck.

He looked terrible. It hadn't been a quick death, or so I assumed. There'd been no Albert Pierrepoint in attendance to make sure things moved swiftly, correctly and as humanely as possible. This looked like a case of slow strangulation.

It wasn't me, it wasn't. I was asleep, wasn't I? And the bolt was still on, and the chair was stuck under the handle, so I hadn't walked in my sleep. I think I heard a cry at some point, but it probably got buried in my dream. Well, I had to phone the police and the ambulance, then tell work that Joe and I wouldn't be in and

371

why. I left Joe's body where it was, since he was clearly dead.

The police came. An ambulance arrived. Photographers and journalists, tipped off by God alone knew who, turned up and waded in. How long had I lived here, how long had I known Joe, where did I work, had Joe seemed depressed, had the sudden death of his mother affected him? It felt like I was in the dock at the Old Bailey, but I didn't kill him, did I?

They searched the house and found photos of naked men on top of Joe's wardrobe. So I lied. No, I had no idea about his sexual leanings, and I'd been staying here to help with Maude. Yes, I'm a postman, no, I wasn't here when Maude died. Why was there a bolt inside my bedroom door? I lied again. Joe had put it there so that any lodger might have a degree of privacy – another fib that can't be disproved. Yes, I'm married, yes, I have children, no, I'm not divorced because I'm Catholic, blah, blah, blah.

I got a bit scared, worrying whether they would talk to Laura and whether she would mention the cross and chain. Thinking about it, I concluded that she will keep it all to herself for the sake of the children, who don't deserve to be taunted about a criminal father. I was glad when they all left because I prefer to deal with people one or two at a time.

Thinking more clearly today, probably because I'm writing it all in my notebook. I'm remembering more events, though timescales can be confusing. A double funeral is next. Both bodies are now with McManus the undertaker. Well, I think they are, though they might want a post mortem on Joe. And I'm in this sad little house with old wallpaper, chipped paint and furniture fit for Bonfire Night. It's clean, but shabby.

Poor Maude. She had a pervert for a son, and she never knew it. Perhaps she knows now. So, can I stay here with his ghost and hers hanging about like a smell on the landing? I suppose I can. It'll stop once they're buried, and I've heard nothing more since Maude passed over.

I found the rent book, all paid up to date, nothing owed until next month. My own place. It's an end of terrace, too, and the people next door are deaf as posts, bless them both. They're old; I'll do their shopping. My brain's running at top speed. There's nobody to arrange the double funeral, so I'll have to see McManus and get that biscuit tin with all Maude's papers in it. There are policies. Sideboard, left hand cupboard behind the willow pattern plates.

I'll talk to the landlord. I wonder if Angela would come here instead of me going there? I could buy a bit of stuff, I suppose. We could improvise. I'll phone the farm later when I've sorted through Maude's paperwork.

Eve slammed down the receiver. She was displeased, and the fuse leading to her temper had suddenly been shortened by... She shivered. What an arrogant, selfish son of a bitch Carson was. In her large hands, she twisted a handkerchief, wishing it were his bloody neck. He wanted house calls. He wanted Angie to visit him. He needed massage, too. Both his housemates were barely cold, and all he could think about was his own pleasure and relief. Where the hell did people like him come from? A mating between a devil and a witch?

Kate came through the door. 'What's up with

you now, missus?'

'Don't ask.'

Kate sat. 'Too late – I've asked.'

'Give me a minute – I'm boiling over.'

Kate raised an eyebrow. 'Shall I turn you down to slow-cooking?'

'No. Let me sweat this one.' She took a few deep breaths.

While waiting, Kate wrote out the greengrocery order and the butcher's list. The cost of meat was ridiculous, and with Trevor Burns having ceased to be a customer, there was no longer leeway on that side of catering. She crossed out rump and wrote in braising steak. 'Have you calmed down?'

'About gas mark seven, I'd say.'

Kate shook her head. 'Let me know when you're on simmer.'

'I will.'

Kate continued with her shopping lists, wishing Jesus could come along and pass a hand over a few pairs of kippers and some large white sliced. If she mixed a bit of marge in with the butter, would the girls notice? Angela would. Angela could probably smell Stork through the walls of a lead casket, so mixing was out. Bramley apples weren't dear; Kate would make apple pies and a crumble.

Eve spoke. 'He won't be coming here again, love.'

'Oh?'

'I told him to bugger off.'

Kate said nothing.

'I said if he wanted blood drawing, he could do it himself with a razor.'

'You didn't.'

'I did. He told me he'd blow us up to the police, so I said he should feel free, because he's been a client, and I would say so. Then he threatened to do it anonymously, and I said the same – I'd name him as our chief customer. He started screaming at me loud enough to puncture an eardrum. So I slammed the phone down.' She paused. 'There's something about Mr Postman, Kate.'

'I know. You said that before.'

'He's devious,' Eve mused aloud. 'And a deviant.'

'You'll be calling him the Mersey Monster next. Who doesn't like liver?'

'Judy,' Eve replied automatically. 'He could be.'

'Eh? Who? What?'

'Carson could be the killer.'

Kate put down her pen and sat back. 'Him? He's too weedy.'

Eve disagreed. 'The shock element, Kate. I've heard he uses a garrotte made from wire. Detective Constable Eddie said that. Eddie's mate got shot, you know – that PC killed on Lime Street Station on the stroke of midnight. They mustn't have known which date to put on his certificate. Eddie's taken time off, and I'll bet I can guess why – he's looking for Dave's killer.'

Kate nodded sagely. 'Aye, and he's trained for it. You're not.'

'Don't try to stop me, Kate.'

'What? I'd stand a better chance of stopping a Trident that's just taken off from Manchester. But take somebody with you.' Kate left to check her store cupboards. All the way along the hall, she mumbled to herself. 'Murder first, suicide next –

she'll be damned for all eternity.' She entered the kitchen. 'I can't do pastry while I'm in this mood – me hands'll be too sticky.'

Eve remained in the office. She'd better eat well today, because she was going to find and follow Mr Carson. If she didn't catch sight of him today, she'd be on his tail some time soon. For some unknown reason, she felt sure there was more to him than met the eye. And none of the more was good.

Fourteen

For Laura Carson, life had become an odd melange of joy and fear, a cocktail whose components did not mix well, though she occasionally suspected that terror might be adding a certain frisson to her relationship with Andrew Martindale. As a Catholic, she laboured under commandments from both God and Church, yet her Father Confessor remained lenient. 'I don't know what it is about Neil, Laura, but he was clearly an unsuitable marriage partner for you. Is your new man Catholic?'

From the tone of the priest's voice, Laura could tell that he hadn't liked Neil, so she wasn't the only one. 'Yes, he is Catholic, Father. His wife's dead.'

'*Requiescat.* Then bide your time and pray. I shall pray, too. *In nomine Patris...*' He dismissed her from the confessional box with a blessing and

376

penance of one decade of the rosary.

Smiling to herself, she sat on a hard pew while searching for her beads. There was no such luxury as anonymity here, because both priests recognized voices of regular penitents. Laura blessed herself, delivered the decade to Our Lady, then went to pick up her children from Coronation Park.

Standing at the gate, she watched Lucy, Matt and Andy. Andy had drifted into their lives gradually and without fuss. An avuncular figure, he played games with them, took them and Laura to the cinema, and today they were going into another part of Liverpool to look at the smallest of his shops, the original jewellery outlet created by his grandfather, whose affection for valuable metals and stones had now reached a third generation.

As she lingered near the gate, Laura pondered her situation. She loved this man. Yes, he sometimes acted as if old enough to be her father, but he was real. Neil had been almost two-dimensional, a flat person with no fun in him, always correct, predictable and ... and boring. Was she a bad person? No. Andy loved her, but nothing untoward had taken place thus far, though the regret she felt about the lack of physical contact was possibly sinful. But oh, Andy was so very handsome, she thought as she watched him watching her children.

He noticed her and awarded her a smile that was almost dazzling. Two children, each wrapped up against the November chill, raced towards their mother while Andy followed at a more sedate pace. He was such a beautiful man, and he loved her. Laura felt the heat in her cheeks as she returned the smile.

They piled into his car, two giggling children in the back, a pair of would-be lovers in the front. They were going to Smithdown Road, a busy thoroughfare on which Jacob Martindale had planted the first seeds of a now burgeoning empire.

Laura closed her eyes and walked in her mind down a well-worn path that had been visited by many over the centuries. It was a cul-de-sac, and there was no escape from the fact that love hurt. Neil had been a habit, someone she had known for years and, like a pair of gloves, they had simply stayed together. Yet they'd been separate, divided by the lack of love. 'The left hand didn't know what the right was doing,' she whispered.

Andy glanced at her.

'Sorry,' she said, 'that wasn't meant to be spoken aloud.'

'Stop worrying,' he advised gently. 'Take life one day at a time like they do.' He pointed a thumb over his shoulder at Matt and Lucy.

'What if that gold cross was–?' Laura cut herself off.

'Stop it.' Andy had already offered to accompany her to a police station, though she was having trouble plucking up the courage.

'Mummy, Matt's pulling my scarf.'

Laura turned and shook her head. 'Behave yourselves. You're going to meet a nice little girl called Lisa. She's younger and smaller than you, so start practising gentleness from now, this minute.

Matt, I knitted that scarf, and the stitches will break if you pull too hard. Oh, and stop trying to strangle your sister.' Could she put her children through a mess involving their father? Was Neil capable of... She couldn't bear to think about those women.

'I'm only messing,' the child replied.

'Then don't. Strangling your sister is not a good thing.'

Laura faced front again. 'He does that,' she said softly. 'The Mersey Monster strangles. Oh, Andy – what if...'

He nodded. 'Well, we know that the victim was Jean Davenport. You know what I think should be done. If the cross he had bore the initials JD, then yes, he could have bought it from a market trader who, in turn, bought it from the perpetrator. If he's innocent, there's no problem–'

'If who's innocent?' Matt wanted to know.

Laura inhaled deeply. 'Stolen jewellery. Andy gets offered stolen stuff in his shops.' She couldn't remember the inscription on the cross. She shouldn't put her children through all the stress of having a father charged with murder. She mustn't carry on allowing women to be killed just to keep her own little family safe. No matter what she did or didn't do, the results promised to be harmful.

After a journey along Queens Drive and Menlove Avenue, they turned right into Smithdown Road. Laura straightened her spine; just as Andy had advised, she needed to live in the moment, because no one on earth could predict what the next hour or the next day might bring. For Laura, the next thirty minutes would find her talking openly for the first time to a woman with a trustworthy face. But she couldn't know that yet.

After the shooting of PC Dave Earnshaw on Lime Street Station, Smelly Nellie disappeared with her dog Nelson and her friend Holy Mary. The occasional kerfuffle ensued, since many hungry and homeless people missed the food and drink provided at Lime Street Station by Nellie, but remaining police officers did what they could by collecting from the nuns in Magdalene House. At every level from traffic bobbies all the way upward through the ranks, the force now recognized that Nellie, Mary and Nelson were volunteer detectives/police informants.

Eddie Barnes, secretly in cahoots with the two nuns, had taken extended leave though his bosses knew what he was up to and had given their permission. The women, smartly dressed in suits and blouses, travelled with him in several borrowed cars. It wasn't going to be easy, since Albert Shuttleworth, tall and weighty, would be very well hidden because he was so easily recognized.

They carried with them the blanket that had been on Shuttleworth's legs when he'd fired the first two shots at Dave, and Nelson was familiar with the scent. But even Nelson could not identify a person behind closed doors, so three humans and one dog were searching for Boss's emissaries. As most were locked away and maintaining a long silence, it looked like a needle-in-a-haystack job, yet three people and one dog didn't give in; they concentrated on the boss's mother's house. Dave Earnshaw's killer would be brought to justice, and that would be an end to it.

Neil Carson's frame of mind was wildly inconsistent. He was happy when the landlord allowed him to take over the house, scared when he was inside the end of terrace, furious because of the dressing down he'd suffered over the phone when he'd talked to Eve. Having a place all to himself was liberating, but sometimes, just occasionally, he caught peripheral sight of movement, though it always disappeared when he turned his face to look full on. It might be Jesus or Judas, or both. It might be Maude or Joe's tormented spirit...

He clung to his notebook as if it collected the remnants of sanity.

I carried Maude in her coffin at the double funeral. Didn't go to the wake afterwards, couldn't face it. The house is empty, echo-y. Her bed's in the back yard, dismantled. I miss her. I sit on the couch with the tray I made, the one with three different tops, and I eat my meals. I say meals, but I have very little appetite. My stomach's in knots.

The anger. It won't go away. Who does Fat Mamma think she's talking to? She said Angela's had enough of me because I ask for more punishment than she's willing to give. Old Fatso's dying. Putting her out of her misery might be a kindness. I wish I could eat; I wish I could sleep. Something is coursing through my veins and urging me on to... To what? Is it now? Do I go out and do the thing Jesus asked of me? I need to be stronger...

'It's your bloody fault any road.' Babs stood with

381

arms akimbo, her bright eyes flashing with something that was no stranger to white-hot fury. 'You can't be going out with one lad on a Friday and another on the Saturday. Have you lost your mind? Cos if you have, you'd best find it smartish. The way you're carrying on, you'd need one more brain cell to catch up with a daffodil.'

'Well, how am I supposed to work out which one I want?'

'Fast,' Babs snapped, 'you do it fast, because the three scout hut lads aren't supposed to go off this estate, and well you know it. They're younger than Bill, and he gets picked up in a morning by the builder and brought home most afternoons, so he's safer. It's drugs, you idiot.'

'Are you sure?'

'Course I'm sure, you soft bitch. You're sure, too, so stop asking stupid questions. The big boss is on the loose only twenty miles away, so Ian shouldn't be gallivanting down Lord Street just to please you. Sort yourself out pretty damned quick, because if you don't, I'll put a stop to your shenanigans.'

Sally left the kitchen.

'Don't walk away from me while I'm talking to you.'

'You're not me mother,' came the cry from the hall.

'Don?' Babs yelled.

The master of the house appeared on the landing. He was dressed in a silly patterned smoking jacket and striped pyjama pants. 'You called?' he said. 'Or did you scream? What's going on now?'

Babs pointed an accusatory finger at her friend.

'It's her. She's courting two lads, and there's going to be a big fight any day now.'

Don Crawford frowned. 'Hang on a minute, Sally. Who said you could go out with boys?'

Babs stood in the hall, arms folded, a toe tapping the floor to demonstrate the diminishing level of her patience.

Sally, halfway up the stairs, stopped climbing; she had Don in front of her and Babs below on the ground floor. 'Nobody said,' she answered defiantly, 'because nobody owns me.'

'Careful,' Babs warned in a near whisper.

Sally spun round. 'Why? Why have I got to be careful?'

The older girl saw herself in Sally; she remembered being defiant, furious, confused and beyond control. Baby Sally, although just turned eighteen, was acting like a thirteen-year-old, and it wasn't her fault. Her mother's second husband was responsible for this delay in his stepdaughter's development. Babs spoke to Don. 'It's not her fault. I shouldn't have disturbed you, Don, because I can deal with this. Sorry.'

The old man returned to his room, muttering darkly about the stupidity of females, a bad heart and what the world was coming to.

Babs wagged a finger. 'Kitchen. Now,' she spat ominously.

Sally knew she had lost. Breathing slowly and deeply, she descended the flight of stairs. She really needed to learn to control herself. On entering the kitchen, she saw that Babs was seated at the table. Seated meant a meeting, whether the gathering consisted of two or twenty-two people.

'Sit,' Babs snapped.

Sally sat. 'Sorry,' she said.

'I should bloody well think so, too. Supposing that boss man fancied a day in Southport? Supposing he worked out that nineteen or twenty miles was enough distance from the middle of Liverpool? What then? What if he took lodgings here, huh? There you'd be, strolling up the main street with either Ian or Bill.' She lowered her voice. 'Bill refused to deliver or produce drugs for him, said he was going to work with his dad, so now the family is split up and afraid of being found by that bad swine. Bill's best friend was killed. As for Ian – has he not suffered enough at that bloody school? And he was supposed to stay in the scout hut under Boss's orders. Also, do both boys know you've been a working girl? Gordy does, because Don told him he'd bought two Baby Dolls.'

Sally's head drooped. 'I didn't think.'

'No, you didn't. The last of the drugs were in the scout hut, and those three boys were ordered to guard the stash. So you go strolling about with Ian, no sense in your head, no thought for anybody but yourself and what you want. I've a good mind to send you packing. And you have to tell the boy you choose where we've come from, because you'll get found out, mark my words. Mind, Ian knows already, because we looked after him and the other two.'

The younger girl hung her head.

'Right,' Babs said, 'that's better. So tell me.'

'What?'

'About your stepdad.'

'You what?'

'You heard me.'

Sally snorted. 'He's no kind of dad, step or otherwise. He married Mam to get to me.'

Babs waited before speaking again. 'And what hurt most was that your mother let it happen.'

Sally nodded.

'Ditto, Sal. So I fixed Uncle Charlie all by myself. He stuck part of his ugly body in my mouth, and I bit down. Hard. I just had time to throw bleach at it before he ran out screaming. I don't know what he said to the docs in the hospital, but they found out he had TB as well as a withered willy, and he died of the TB about a year later. I had to go for tests.'

Sally snapped her mouth shut. 'Bleach?' she whispered.

'Yes, bleach. I kept a cup of it under my bed. Just had to wait for my chance. See, we're quicker than they are even when we're kids. The way we're made – well, part of it is to manage men. Think about some animals that give birth and spend the first few days or weeks stopping the father animal from killing the young. If you get a rogue male, he needs isolating. I isolated him good and proper, babe.'

'Weren't you scared?'

Babs nodded. 'I was terrified. But not too scared to crack my mother across the head with a mantel clock when she shouted at me for hurting Uncle Charlie. So she got the lot – the clock, a back-hander across her gob and a bowl of cold water with peeled spuds in it. She was arrested for trying to choke me, and he died in the TB place.

I don't know where she is, and I don't care. I spent a few years with Auntie Phyllis, then I went on the game. So what about you?'

'What do you mean?'

Babs reached across the table and held Sally's hands. 'You have to say it. You have to talk about it.' She paused. 'We can still get him, but first, you've got to spell it out, give it up and let it go. It's not too late.'

'You what?' Sally asked again.

'He's a drunk, yes?'

Sally nodded hesitantly.

'And I have a schoolgirl's uniform?'

'Er ... yes.'

'Sorted.'

'But—'

'But nothing. It's just an idea, and I have to think about it. Eve will help me, as will Lippy. He's got people looking for the monks who hurt the boys, and that school will close. The rest of the brothers wanted to stay, but Lippy Macey said no, end of. Well? Are you going to tell me all the details about what happened to you? Because that's the most important part. It's holding you back from growing up, so the words have to be said.'

Sally bit her lower lip. 'I know what I'll do,' she pronounced eventually. 'I'll write it down, because I don't want to hear me saying it, OK?'

'OK.'

'Then you can read it and we'll burn it together. Sorted?'

'Sorted.'

'Babs?'

'Yes?'

'What are you going to do to him? Bleach in his eyes?'

The senior servant of Mr Don Crawford rose to her feet. 'I'm going to ruin his life like he ruined yours. Let me work it out. I want that stuff of yours written, read and burnt before I start thinking about how to deal with him. But take my word for it, sweetheart, that bastard will be crushed.'

Sally gulped. 'How?' she whispered from a dry throat.

'Eve and Angela.'

'But you don't like Angela.'

'That's all in the past, Sal. Angela knows people. Just set your mind on me in the schoolgirl's gymslip and blouse, little plaits with bows at the ends. He'll follow me when I give him the nod.' She pondered for a few seconds. 'I think we'll leave Mr Macey out of this, because he plays too fair. And there you'll be waiting for your stepdad with a couple of big bruisers.' She smiled. 'The happiest day of my life was when they told me Uncle Charlie was dead. I'd relived most of my story through the doctor, so that was out of me system, which is why you need to let your history fly free. Then, when he finishes up dead or in a wheelchair, you'll be yourself, who you were meant to be.'

'Will I?'

Babs nodded. 'See, you can start growing up after that.'

'Oh, I hope so.' Sally allowed a few beats to pass. 'I think I've picked and I think it's Bill.'

'So do I. You'd better put Ian out of his misery, then.'

'Cruel,' Sally mumbled.

'Cruel to be kind, love. He's not old enough, anyway. Stick to Bill–'

'And hope his plaster sticks to the ceiling.'

As victims of a chronic ailment suffered mostly by females of the species, both girls doubled over with laughter. They curled across the table like a couple of drunks, loud chuckles filling the air, tears pouring down their faces. 'And he comes home plastered,' Sally managed after many seconds. 'I ... oh, God... I can't be doing with drunken blokes.'

'Stop it'

'I can't.'

'Oh, Sal, this hurts. I feel as if I've been stabbed in the stomach.'

'I know.' The younger girl managed to stop for breath. 'What are we laughing at, Babs?'

'No bleeding idea.'

Murdoch wandered in, but he didn't bother to put his nose in Babs's hair. He stood there nodding and neighing frantically.

Babs stopped laughing when she looked at him; she knew her horse well enough to understand his 'come here' stance. 'What is it, lad? OK, OK, I'm coming.' The horse left the scene, and Babs prepared to follow him. But she didn't go anywhere, because as soon as Murdoch made room for him, Bill staggered in bruised and bleeding. 'Jesus, Bill,' she breathed.

Sally stood and held out her arms. 'Who did this?' she demanded to know, although she thought she already had the answer.

'Ian,' he said.

Sally frowned. 'Is he all right?' If Bill was hurt, the younger boy might be in a very bad state.

'I never touched him,' Bill told her. 'I just let it happen.'

'Good for you,' was Babs's delivered opinion. 'Clean him up, Sal, while I take Murdoch back to the paddock.'

In spite of a bloodied nose and swollen eyes, the apprentice plasterer grinned at his girl. 'It was worth it,' he said. 'You're worth it. I read the instructions today and mixed me own plaster. It worked. Thanks, Sal.'

'Is that all you want me for – me teaching skills?'

'No. Ouch. That hurt, Sally.'

'I have to clean you up. You'll have two lovely black shiners tomorrow, and you could have stopped him.' She wrapped ice cubes in two tea towels. 'Put them against your eyes.'

'No. He loves you, Sally, and he's only a lad. You've messed us both about, but no way was I going to bash a kid who's been through what he's been through.'

She sat across the table from him. 'I chose you, anyway.' She paused. Should she tell him now that she'd been a prostitute?

'I know.'

'How? How do you know I chose you?'

'I don't know.'

'You just said–'

'Don't start.'

'But–'

'Don't start,' he repeated, removing the cloths from his eyes. 'We've plenty of time, so don't fret.

I want to be Master Plaster before I think about settling down, and you said you wanted night school for baking so you can sell cakes and pies. We slow down a bit, yeah?'

She nodded her agreement. 'You'll get ragged at work over the state of your gob.'

'It's OK. I'll tell 'em you did it.'

'You won't.'

'Oh, I will.' He covered his eyes. 'Bugger off, Sal,' he advised.

She walked away, though she stopped and turned in the doorway. 'You know I worked at the farm? You know what I did for a living?'

'Yep.'

'Will you throw it in me face when you get mad?'

'Nope.'

'OK.' And off she buggered.

Ian, John and Phil were a bit restless. They liked Gordy, and the house was OK, but they began to feel almost as contained here as they had while hiding in the scout hut. Mucking out stables and doing homework set by their tutor kept them busy, but not full time, and they were bored.

'I'm fed up,' John muttered.

Ian sat in the kitchen of Dove Cottage bathing his knuckles in warm water with a drop of Dettol. 'He just stood there and let me hit him,' he complained.

'You were lucky, then,' Phil said. 'He's fitter than you.'

The pugilist halted his ministrations. 'He's won. He's gone in there bruised and bleeding, and girls like that. It brings out the mothering side. Why didn't he hit me back?'

John, no longer the Stam, shrugged. 'You're a clever lad, Ian, so you've already worked it out. You're stood there now looking after your own damage, and he'll have run to Sally. It'll be all love and bandages in the big house.'

The injured man patted his knuckles dry. 'Right, that's it. We're going out. It's a decent enough day, so we can walk to the beach, have a break from here.'

Phil wasn't sure. 'We're not allowed.'

'I've been out,' Ian said.

'And see where it's got you.' John leapt to his feet. 'Look, first we were hiding from the Pastoral bastards, now we're being hidden from a drugs boss as well. They could be anywhere.'

Ian laughed, though there was no joy in the delivered sound. 'You think the brothers might be in Southport where Lippy Macey lives?'

'They might not know where his house is,' John snapped.

'He owns the bloody school, doesn't he?' Ian was determined. 'They'll know where the owner of the building comes from. As for Boss, he'll guess we didn't grass on him. Come on, you yellow-bellies. Let's take a chance while Gordy's out.'

Phil and John stared at each other. They both knew they couldn't allow Ian to go out by himself, as he was in a very dark mood.

Although only one member of the trio wanted to get away, the other two followed. Ian was in charge; Ian made the decisions, so they followed their leader and hoped for the best.

While Babs walked Murdoch towards the paddock, she noticed Gordy kneeling on the floor talking to donkeys while checking their limbs. They were sweet animals, and he adored them. Murdoch whinnied his approval – anyone who looked after Nye and his friends was a good person in the horse's opinion.

Babs left Murdoch to chew thoughtfully on a bit of grass. This was going to be the moment that could cause her dismissal; Sal, too, might be losing her place here. But no. Don Crawford would never allow Murdoch's trainee jockey to leave the stage, while Sal was part of Babs's package. 'Sod it,' she murmured.

Gordy rose to his feet and brushed a hand over his clothing. She looked lovely today. Well, she always looked good, but there was an extra sheen to her, as if someone had gone over her with a tin of Mansion. 'All right, love?' If anyone had given her a coat of beeswax, Gordy would be set to kill the bugger.

'I'm great,' she replied, 'but the rabbit died.'

'What?'

'The rabbit died,' she repeated slowly, as if addressing an infant.

He tipped back the flat cap and scratched his head. 'We don't have rabbits. There's Victoria and Albert,' he waved a hand towards the geese, 'then the dogs with their stupid names, and the chickens–'

'The dogs do not have stupid names. He got them all on the same day, so they're Onesie, Tutu, Three-step and Four-time. Then his cats are Marmalade and Calico, but the rabbit died.'

He remained confused until he noticed the mischief in her eyes.

'Has the penny dropped?' she asked.

He blinked stupidly until a glimmer of light touched his mind's horizon.

'Well?' Babs asked.

Gordy nodded and swallowed hard. 'When's it due?'

Babs giggled. 'That's the right question. If you'd asked was it yours, you'd have had five minutes at most to live. It's due in May. What's up? What's wrong with your gob?'

Gordy emitted a long sigh. 'You can't ride.'

'I know.'

'And the old fellow bought you. Does he still visit in the–'

'No. He's knackered, and the slow-down pills make him sleep a lot.' It was her turn to sigh. 'But you're right, he paid for both of us, Gord. We have to carry on looking after him, me and Sal. And anyway, he's pathetic – I couldn't leave him like I couldn't leave you or Murdoch.'

'We have to get married.'

'I know. So we should go and tell Don together. He can do or say anything he likes, but this kid needs a father.'

'Shall we do it now and get it over with?' Gordy asked.

'No time like the present. But don't forget to take your cap off while we see the lord and master. He's funny about stuff like that.'

Hand in hand, they crossed the paddock and walked over the lawn. 'Just a minute,' he said. 'Do you love me?'

'Course I do, you Irish idiot.'

'That's all right, then. I love you, too.'

They entered Wordsworth House and found Sally weeping in the kitchen.

'Sal?' Gordy touched her arm. 'What's up?'

'They've disappeared. Bill's gone up to tell Mr Crawford.'

'Slow down,' Babs advised. 'And sit down, too.'

Sally sat and caught her breath. 'The tutor came to give them lessons, and they weren't in the cottage, so he called here.' She cleared her throat. 'Bill was on a half day, and he was with me. After Ian beat Bill up, all three of them scarpered.'

Babs's face drained of colour. 'Bloody hell,' she whispered.

Gordy hugged her. 'I'll go and see did they write a note.'

Babs left Sal and went to phone Lippy Macey.

Lippy was, as usual, cool as a cucumber. 'Stay where you are. I'll be with you as soon as possible.'

Eddie, Holy Mary and Nellie (no longer smelly) were tired. Sitting still in a car all day was an exhausting business, and waiting for Boss to turn up at his mother's house made them jumpy. Every time the elderly woman left the house, she was followed. Relief offered by a bit of movement was short-lived, since she never went anywhere interesting, and Eddie was fast running out of patience and vehicles. 'We've had Sandy's van, Eric's Morris, my neighbour's Austin, and my old banger.'

'True,' Nellie sighed. 'Even Nelson's affected by all this.' She turned to Mary. 'You'll have to try to get through via the other side, Sister Mary Veronica.'

Mary pondered. 'Most of his gang are in jail. There are a few lower down the chain, I suppose, people Boss might recruit in times of what he'd call hardship. I could go back to being deliverer of messages, but I wouldn't know where to start.'

Nellie shrugged. 'If we can't find the whale, we need plankton. Fetch, Mary.'

'I need to think overnight,' she answered. 'I mean, there's—'

'What?' Nellie asked.

'She's talking to somebody. There's a man in there with her.'

'Don't panic,' Eddie whispered. They were parked in a street at right angles to the old woman's house. 'Mary, lie down. Nellie, take the dog for a walk.' When Nellie and Nelson had left the car, Eddie drove slowly and turned right into Boss's street. 'Stay down,' he hissed, 'he knows you.'

'I'm down. Be careful, Eddie.'

He slid out of the car. Be careful? The bastard had murdered Eddie's best mate, so carefulness was a long way down on his agenda.

'We'll get m-murdered when Gordy finds out.' John's stammer was rearing its head due to panic. 'Why the bloody hell do we l-listen to him, Phil?'

Phil shrugged; he had no idea. 'We were supposed to have a walk on the beach,' he said.

Ian spoke up. 'Southport's tame. We're going to Liverpool.'

John opened his mouth to speak, thought for a

second, and closed it again; what was the point? He caught Phil's eye, nodded and communicated silently with a nod. The train was slowing, and the two friends of Ian's rose to their feet and moved towards the door.

'What are you doing?' Ian asked.

'Getting off the train,' Phil replied calmly.

'Why?' the leader of the escape committee wanted to know. 'This is Formby.'

'Because we owe Gordy.' John, minus the stammer, drew himself up to full height. 'And we owe Mr Crawford, Mr Macey, Babs and Sal. The girls will have told all three men, and you can bet your bottom dollar there'll be somebody looking for us in Liverpool. Don't worry about Boss, because you're more likely to be snatched by police or Lippy Macey. Good luck – you'll need it.'

'Traitors,' Ian snarled.

'Come with us?' Phil held out an arm.

'No, there's nothing in Southport for me.' He sat back. 'Go on then, yellow-bellies.'

The cowards alighted at Formby Station.

Ian, wearing a deep frown, stayed where he was and folded his arms. Deep down, he knew he was being stupid, but he clung to the idea of freedom. Would he ever be free? When was this court case promised by Macey going to happen? How could anyone fight the Church all the way to the Vatican? He was scared. What should he do?

The train started to move slowly. Before it got the chance to pick up speed, he hurled himself out onto the platform, landing safely on hands and feet. John ran to pick him up. 'You damn fool,' he snapped, stutter-free. 'Trying to get yourself killed,

396

are you?' Phil sped past the pair, caught up with the quickening train and slammed the swinging door shut.

Ian clambered to his feet and pulled himself away from John's hold. 'Leave me alone,' he snapped. He didn't want to admit that panic had overtaken determination, that he was scared of going to Liverpool by himself, that he was upset because of the near-certainty that Sally hadn't picked him. Bill hadn't even bothered to fight back; how humiliating that had been. When was a fight not a fight? When it was a beating – that was the answer.

'We know,' John said softly, 'because we're hemmed in again like we were in that bloody hut. It's just one of them things, eh? Like we won't be on Boss's Christmas list, and some of the brothers could be looking for us to try and shut us up. We've no choice, Ian.'

With no choice, they stood together in a shelter and waited for the Southport bus; with no choice, they were dragged into Lippy Macey's car to be scolded by Gordy. The seller of tickets at Southport Station had recognized their photographs. They were causing a lot of trouble and showing no gratitude whatsoever. Lippy was bending over backwards for them; he had almost reached agreement with the Brothers Pastoral, who were considering replacing the three sinners with lay teachers, preferably female, who would supervise the pupils' welfare. 'If that's what it takes and they're willing to comply, the school will get an extra year's lease,' Gordy concluded.

Lippy chipped in. 'There's another clause, boys.

397

The three predators must be unfrocked, and they have to face a judge and jury, or no agreement and the school closes.'

'Thanks,' the three boys said in unison.

'Sorry,' Ian added.

'We've all been young,' Mr Macey said, 'but you need to find some patience. This type of reckless behaviour isn't acceptable, and it must stop.'

The leader spoke up again. 'It was me,' he admitted quietly. 'We've been locked up a long time, you see. And I was in charge of the breakout from school, so John and Phil think they need to go wherever I go. I've been in a bad mood, see.'

Gordy shook his head. 'Bill said you battered him.'

'I did.'

'Because young Sally chose him.'

Ian nodded. 'Yes, and he never raised a hand to me.'

'He knows you're only fifteen, Ian. Bill's a man, bigger, older and stronger than you. And he knows how you feel. You shouldn't go through life with your fists, but.'

'I know.'

'Then you stay in Dove Cottage and behave yourselves while Mr Macey tries to get the eejit monks brought to justice. All we ask of you is patience.'

'Don't hurt Brother Bennet or Brother Williams,' John begged. 'They're good blokes, Mr Macey. Bennet's the head, and Williams is an amazing teacher, very quiet and well liked. He's never hit a kid as far as I know, and we nearly always remember his lessons. We don't like to

398

disappoint him.'

'I'll bear all that in mind,' Macey said as he pulled into the Crawford estate. 'Now, go and play with donkeys or stay in and do homework.'

Three chastened boys left the car.

'You took on a lot there, Mr Macey.'

'Did I, now? Well I happen to think those boys are worth saving. Bye for now.'

Gordy stood outside Dove Cottage. He and Babs still had to face Don Crawford. 'Bugger,' he muttered. 'I'm putting the kettle on.'

Sitting or lying on a bed in the vast kitchen of Meadowbank Farm, Eve Mellor had plenty of thinking time. Sometimes, she wondered whether she might be obsessed, yet she remained incapable of controlling her instincts. The farm was up and running again with Kate in charge, so Eve was left to her own devices for several hours each day. It was him; she knew it was him.

She had been out several times on Thursday evenings, but she'd never seen him. The devil seemed to be looking after his own.

'I have you worked out, Carson.' Some woman, possibly his wife or his mother, had pissed him off. So from women he expected punishment in order to be angry enough to go and... She swallowed. Angela had served a purpose, or so it would appear. Perhaps being so close to death made Eve more acutely aware, more sensitive. She grinned. Mam had always said that Eve was as sensitive as a docker's hook.

'Docker's hook?' she whispered. 'I could do with one of them to rip his bloody face off.'

399

It was his eyes, she decided. Most of the time, they seemed flat, expressionless and almost dead. Then, all of a sudden, they would flash, as if some hidden thought had dug its way out of his brain all the way to his face. 'It's him,' she repeated. 'I know it's him.' The medicines were helping, but she couldn't do the job alone, so she would get Kate to phone Bert Heslop. A retired policeman, Bert was good at finding folk. 'I'll put a stop to him,' Eve muttered. 'There's a place in hell for him. And I'll phone Heslop myself.'

Fifteen

Eve soldiered on bravely, trying hard not to make the household miserable. Her attitude remained decided, though she was occasionally visited by pain that became almost severe enough to warrant a scream. With her bed under a kitchen window and a telephone extension by her side, she scribbled her stories, stopping from time to time to ponder the case of the Mersey Monster. She had months or perhaps weeks to live, and she wanted him dealt with before she shuffled off. The discomfort would worsen, and she needed to be tougher than tanned leather.

The nearer she came to death, the more certain she was that Neil Carson fitted the bill. He had shifty eyes and a weak chin, never a good combination. He wanted more punishment than Angela was willing to deliver; any bloke who arrived in a

400

flowered shirt with a matching floral tie had to be weird. And he craved to see his own blood, so he was best out of here. The man was crackers. During that very dramatic phone call, he had lost his temper completely. Yes. He was quite possibly the perpetrator. And he worked on turn-about shifts...

Eve had looked for him twice, but had failed to find him. With winter beginning to tighten its grip, sitting in a car looking for a killer was not comfortable, especially for a sick woman. She needed help.

The running of the business was now in Kate's hands, and she was doing an excellent job, thereby allowing Eve time and opportunity to write and to wonder about Mr Postman. Every day, the girls came in to eat and to keep her company, so living in a kitchen was a sight better than mouldering in some hospital ward. The stories would never be finished unless Kate took them up after Eve's death, yet they served a purpose, as if they cleansed the soul.

It was Friday. Belle had phoned before lunch for a chat, and she had informed Eve that although her instructor seemed on the brink of collapse, poor man, she had sailed through her driving test without killing anyone, so that was a bit of good news. She and Tom were off to Jacob Martindale's jewellery shop on Smithdown Road. Jacob, long dead, had been founder of the chain.

Belle and Tom were returning mended time-pieces, while young Lisa was going to meet the children of Andrew Martindale's lady friend, so Belle seemed happy with her lot as Mrs Tom

Duffield. Babs, too, had phoned, and Eve had laughed enough to cause a stitch in her already troubled right side.

Kate arrived at the bedside. 'Cuppa tea, love?' she asked.

'Not yet, pal. I'm still getting over that phone call from Babs. Sal's got a hobby – well, she had. Collecting boyfriends, she was. Oh, and Babs is pregnant, so she has to marry that horse man – the Irish one. The boys who were in the scout hut ran away and were brought back, but oh...' She reached for a handkerchief. 'Hang on.'

Eve dried her eyes. 'It's the way Babs says it all – she should be writing, not me. She paints pictures with words, and she uses loud colours, but you never know what's coming next. I asked her did Don Crawford know about the pregnancy, and she told me he did, so I said, "How did he take it?" Her answer was that he'd taken it badly, gone a funny colour and might have swallowed too many of his pills, so he was down Southport Hospital getting looked at for overdoses and what have you. Laugh? I had to change me knickers.'

The new boss of Meadowbank sank into a chair. 'Who's with him at the ozzy?'

'The lad who was beat up by the other lad. The one whose mate got murdered by the drugs people. Bill, I think he's called. Only he's being checked for concussion, so Don's likely on his own. His head got banged on the floor.'

Kate's eyebrows shot skyward. 'Don's head?'

'No, the lad what got beat up by the other lad. You don't listen.'

'But which lad was it who beat up the other lad

with the dead mate, Evie?'

'I've got no bloody idea, have I? You know stuff happens round Babs – she's like a magnet for trouble. And that horse comes into the kitchen every day, clears a five-foot fence and wanders inside for apples and carrots and anything else that's hanging about – like cakes. Geese flap in with hens and dogs and cats – it's like Noah's ark. Babs can't ride the bleeding horse while she's pregnant – oh, I do miss her.'

Kate smiled. 'I thought you might.'

'Well, I do, so you thought right for once.'

Kate sighed. 'I never thought I'd be saying this, but so do I. The new girls are great, don't get me wrong, but Babs is tough with a heart of gold underneath all the cheek.'

'She thanked me, and she meant it,' Eve whispered.

'No!'

Eve nodded. 'There was a little tear in her eye and a catch in her voice, know what I mean? But she's got used to Southport, and I think she loves her new job now that Don's being sedated. The two girls cook and clean and give him his medicine and a bath when he's able. When he's not, they give him a bed bath. I know they would have gone with him to the hospital, but Babs has got an appointment with her GP, and young Sal's going with her to the doc's while the Irish fellow keeps an eye on the runaways. Babs will be starting on iron and vitamins, I suppose, all that rubbish you have to swallow when you're expecting.'

Kate delivered a sad smile. 'So many changes, eh?'

'Yes.' The woman in the bed paused. 'And more changes to come.'

'I'm scared, Evie.'

'And I'm not? Anyway, I've other things to worry about.'

Kate's gaze drifted towards the window. Her best friend, her dying best friend, was about to embark on yet another lecture relating to Neil Carson and his weak chin, his bad taste in clothing, his wicked temper and the fact that he begged for punishments too brutal even for Angela.

'I'm handing it over,' Eve said.

'Handing which to what?'

The woman in the bed grinned. 'Bert Heslop. Remember him? Dapper little chap with a muzzy and very small feet, drives a Mini now and makes it look like a big car. For a dwarf, he's a very clever man.'

'Private dick?'

'That's the one. I still see him in town sometimes. He followed some of our nastier customers when we first kicked off here at the farm. He can follow *him* now. Straighten your face before the wind changes, Miss O'Gorman. My mind is made up.'

Kate O'Gorman sighed heavily. 'Yes, I remember the little chap from way back. But how many hundreds of thousands of blokes are in Liverpool, Evie? And out of all of them, you've picked this Neil Carson one. What if you're wrong?'

'Then Bert Heslop will tell me I'm wrong, won't he?'

'I wish you'd just let it go, Evie.'

'I'll let go when I'm in me box. Go and peel

your veg, missus. I've better things to do than waste time watching you in a state. He's a shift worker at the post office. He kills when he's on lates. And thicken your custard a bit; the last lot looked as if it had been squeezed out of a teen-ager's acne.'

'Eve!'

'Bog off.'

When Kate was occupied at the business end of the kitchen, Eve reached for the phone, but it rang just before she lifted the receiver. It was Belle again. Eve listened carefully, inserting a prompt here and there, but never embarking on real con-versation. She was right! Her heartbeat quickened; at last, there seemed to be some sort of proof about Neil Carson.

'I'll call you again from home, Eve. I'm using Mr Martindale's phone in the office behind his shop, so I'd better ring off. He thinks I'm phon-ing me mam.' Belle ended the call.

Eve pushed herself into a sitting position. The words she'd heard rattled round in her brain like marbles in a tin. Neil Carson's wife was in the jeweller's shop with the jeweller, her children and Tom, Belle and young Lisa. 'It *is* him,' she mouthed while reaching for the phone once more. This had to be done properly. 'Mr Heslop?'

'Yes. May I help you?'

'I think so. It's Eve Mellor from Meadowbank Farm. Remember?'

'Ah yes. Would you like me to call by?'

'Tonight if possible. I'll be on my own in bed in the kitchen. I'm dying, you see.'

A short pause was followed by, 'I'm sorry to hear

that. I'll come at about eight o'clock. Will that do?'

'Oh yes. That will do very well indeed.'

Another pause. 'Is there anything you need, Miss Mellor?'

She smiled to herself. 'Just you, your notebook and a pen will do nicely, thanks.' Eve ended the call and leaned back on her pillows.

Belle parked the van outside their house. Lisa was lifted out by Tom, who stood to watch while the child dashed off in near-darkness to show her grandparents the silver St Christopher medal and chain given to her by the kindly jeweller. She would stay with Sam and Frankie this weekend, though she was usually a movable feast during daylight hours. 'Bye,' she shouted as she closed her grandparents' gate carefully.

Tom and Belle walked through their own front doorway. 'What happened?' Tom asked as soon as they were out of earshot.

She kissed him. 'Let me make a cuppa first. It'll give me time to sort my head out. I mean, I didn't know her, did I? Why me, Tom?' She walked into the living room/kitchen and set the kettle on the hob. Tom followed her and sat on the sofa. 'It's your face,' he advised her. 'You've got one of those faces that people talk to.'

She huffed at him. 'You're biased.'

Tom chuckled.

'What?' she asked.

'Yes, I suppose I am biased.' He let her get on with brewing tea. She needed time to think, because he realized that something of moment had happened between her and Laura Carson during

406

their expedition to Cooper's Cakes. Belle had been jittery ever since the two women had returned with custard slices, and she had even asked if she might phone her mother from the jewellery shop.

'Here.' She passed him a mug and sat beside him. 'Just give me another minute,' she begged. Max wasn't here, so distractions were minimal. The dog had learnt how to acquire food in two houses and was intelligent enough to get his own way. Sometimes, an animal could be useful when a pause became necessary.

'OK.' Tom sipped at his tea.

Time ticked on. 'I didn't phone my mother,' she said at last, 'it was Eve. I phoned Eve.'

'Oh, yes?'

She nodded. 'Laura is Laura Carson. Her husband is that chap I told you about, the queer bloke who wanted bondage and flaying till he bled. He told Angela he needed to relive the Stations of the Cross, so Ange put him right, saying if he wanted a crown of thorns he could make his own and wear it at home.

Tom waited.

'Anyway, Laura's not one for keeping up with the news – well, she didn't use to be. She works for some mates who have a chippy down her road, and she saw something in a newspaper saved for wrappings. It was about the murder of Jean Davenport, and it said her gold cross and chain had gone missing. Her initials were on the back of the cross.'

Again, Tom allowed her an uninterrupted pause.

'Laura's husband had hidden a gold cross and

chain in his sock drawer, said he'd bought it second hand and was saving it for her birthday. It had initials on it, though she can't remember what they were, and then it disappeared. Why did she tell me, Tom? Why not her friends in the chippy?'

'Too close to home?' he suggested.

'She's frightened of talking to the cops because of her kids. I understand that, but...'

'But she has a lot on her mind.'

'She certainly does. Andrew Martindale knows, and she says he's offered to go with her to the police, but she's still holding back for the sake of her family. I know it must be hard, Tom, but how's she going to feel if it is him and he carries on killing?' Belle sat down next to her husband. 'Did she tell me because she wants me to send the police to her?'

'No, love. She told you because you've got trust-worthy eyes, and she needed to offload to some-body of the same sex. Complicated creatures, women are. Even if they have a decent husband, a good dad or a brother, they'll usually confide more easily in another woman. Anyway, she told Martindale first, didn't she?'

Belle raised her legs and studied her feet for a moment. She had new shoes and they hurt a bit, so she kicked them off. 'She's in love with him, Tom.'

'And he is with her, too.'

She grinned at him. 'You know, for a bloke, you're sometimes nearly human. He's selling up, lock, stock and diamonds. He's planning on mov-ing abroad and taking her and the kids with him if Laura's husband gets done for murder. If he doesn't get charged, they'll stay in England, but in Devon I think she said. It would be a fresh start all round, I suppose.'

'All planned out, then. Is he her father figure, Belle?'

She raised her shoulders in a shrug. 'Nope. I think they're having trouble keeping away from what she calls mortal sin. Her husband was a cold fish at home, but if he's the Mersey Monster, he must have boiled over down near the docks at least three times. It's a bugger, Tom. Oh, by the way, Babs is pregnant. She's marrying that horse trainer.'

'Good for her. From the little I know, she needs grounding with both feet nailed to the floor. I wonder if she'll improve with age?'

Belle laughed.

'What's funny?' Tom asked.

'She's lovely.' Belle always defended her friends. 'And no, I think she'll always be the same – a nuisance.' She chewed her lower lip thoughtfully. 'I wonder if Eve's right about him?'

'Carson? Well, I'd be thinking about the cross.'

'So would I, yes. I'm beginning to wish Laura Carson hadn't told me. It's like being an accessory, isn't it? If it's him, anyway.'

It was Tom's turn to be pensive. 'Well, you know what the police say – anything, however trivial, helps them to pursue or eliminate a line of inquiry. But at the same time, it's up to Laura, I suppose.'

Belle wasn't so sure. And there was something else that needed addressing, an issue that might well keep her out of everyone's business for the foreseeable future. She looked into the eyes of the man she adored. He was a wonderful husband and lover, a great friend to everyone in the family and an excellent stepfather for Lisa. Belle, treated like queen of the establishment, had learnt early on that Tom Duffield did not and would not ever question her past. Feeling shy with no idea why, she blushed while smiling at him. 'Don't get excited.'

'Eh? What's exciting about poor Mrs Carson and the gold cross?'

'It's not that.'

'Not what?'

'A gold cross.'

'I should hope not. Have you been collecting gold crosses?'

'No.'

She was being playful, so he grinned at her. Being playful often led to chasing through rooms and ripping clothes off. Mind, Lisa might come back, because Belle made a great cup of cocoa. 'Well?' he asked.

She giggled like a schoolgirl. 'What do you want more than anything else in the world? Leave me and Lisa out of it.'

His lips parted as he drew in extra oxygen. 'My lads. Have you heard from my lads?'

'No, love.'

'Then what...?'

She placed a hand on her abdomen. 'Not just Babs, Tom, because I've got a little passenger, too. I know you'll love it even if it's a girl. I'm praying for a boy, but we'll just have to wait and see.'

Motionless, he allowed a single tear to obey the law of gravity. 'Thank you,' he breathed a second before the tear became a flood.

'No – thank *you*,' Belle replied, eyelids in top gear. 'I never wanted Lisa to be an only child. I've made love, kissing included, with just two men in my whole life. He might have been a rum bugger, but I loved him, and I love you more. So they're both children of love. I couldn't feel more for anybody than I feel for you, Duffy. You're all my tomorrows.'

'And you know how to turn my tap on, girl.'

She smiled through the wetness in her own eyes. 'That's good, because what use are you with just the one hand?'

'Exactly.' Wrapped together, dying together, they celebrated a little knot of cells that belonged to both of them; it was the perfect end to an imperfect day.

Sisters Helen Veronica and Mary Veronica were slumped in armchairs in Nellie's subterranean living quarters. On a small sofa, Eddie and Nelson fought for space. 'I'm fed up now,' declared Detective Sergeant Barnes, who had served his plain clothes apprenticeship to the satisfaction of his betters. 'We must have missed him by no more than a few seconds.'

Mary sighed. 'Well, we know he's in a green car with no proper lid. It was parked in the back jigger. The neighbour was clear enough about that much.'

'Sports car,' Eddie mumbled. 'This dog is trying to shift me.'

411

'He does that,' Helen answered absentmindedly. 'Take him in the garden, Mary. He may need to relieve himself.'

Mary chuckled. 'Eddie, Nelson, or both?'

Helen glared at her sister in Christ. 'Please yourself.'

Alone, Helen and Eddie sat in silence for a while. Having kicked open Boss's mother's door, Eddie was now recognizable. Bearing a court order at the time of invasion, he expected no trouble in the legal sense, but he had mucked it up. The murderer of his best friend remained at large. 'I have to get him for Dave's sake, Nellie.'

'I know. Just listen to me, all right?'

He combed his hair with restless fingers. 'What?'

'The house next door to Mrs Shuttleworth's is empty. Mary, Nelson and I should take it. I'm sure she wouldn't recognize us. We might befriend her, and we can certainly keep a wary eye on comings and goings. Ask the police to put a phone in for us.'

He stopped scraping at his hair and began to rub his chin. 'That may not be a bad idea.'

She laughed. 'I knew a first from Oxford would be useful at some stage.'

Eddie blinked. 'Educated, then?'

She nodded. 'By nuns, of course, until I was eighteen. Then off I went into the unreal world of academia, worked my socks off and returned to the nuns.'

'Why?' he asked.

'I got the call.'

He grinned. 'So that's why you need a phone.'

She giggled again. 'Of course. God may ring to

412

tell me it's all been a mistake, and I'll be released to function as a lay person in an unsuspecting world.'

Eddie stared at her. 'We always knew you were different. Smelly Nellie is missed down Lime Street, you know.'

'I miss her, too,' Helen replied. 'Perhaps she'll return in time.'

In a comfortable silence, they stared into the log fire.

'Yes,' Eddie said finally. 'We'll do that, then, as long as the powers agree. Make sure you dress like others in the street, flowered pinafores, curlers sometimes, headscarves – you know the score. Go out as if you have jobs.'

'I certainly do know the score. I'll work mornings, and Mary can do afternoons or evenings. That way, we can make sure there's always one of us in residence. You can come and go. Colour your hair and wear paint-spattered overalls. I'll be your mother and Mary can play the part of your aunt.'

Thus the next step was decided upon. Boss's time was almost up.

Neil Carson set about his new campaign with vigour. He found himself enjoying whores, because not only did he have a good time – he was also spreading his disgusting illness far and wide throughout the city. As his nerves settled, he used every woman who offered herself. He carried protection in case victims demanded it, but each item was peppered with small holes, so he was doing his job. This way, men as well as women would be punished for unseemly behaviour.

Neither Jesus nor Judas put in an appearance. The house settled, as if all vestiges of Joseph and his mother had left at last, and Neil no longer feared voices or muffled footsteps. Now on an easier mission, he did his job at the post office, came home to eat, then set out to do the real work. His pattern changed, since he was no longer completely dependent on darkness; the killing had stopped, and he was now imposing a slower death on prostitutes and those who made use of them. Even if they lived, treatment would be needed, so he was on a winning streak.

He polished off fish and chips, reaching for a bottle of beer to complete his meal. But he never got to drink it, because the doorbell sounded. The days had shortened and, on this particularly cold November evening, he had made up his mind to stay here and do a bit of washing. He was running out of socks and–The knocker hammered. Who the hell was it? A visitor he hadn't expected? It was no use pretending not to be in, because darkness had established itself and he was burning electricity.

He opened the door.

'Hello, Neil.'

Stepping back as if avoiding the fangs of a snake, he retreated from his wife and her companion, who was smartly dressed, tall and graceful. 'Er ... you'd better come in, I suppose. I thought you worked Friday nights.'

'I took the evening off,' Laura said.

'I see.' Unsteady on his feet, he led them into the modest but clean home. His heartbeat, too, was erratic, staggering in his chest like a drunk on his way home from a night on the ale.

They followed him. Laura looked round the room as if assessing its contents – including the resident.

'Sit down,' the host said, his tone clipped.

'So this was your friend's house?' she asked.

'Er ... yes. His mother died and he seemed unable to live without her. Please sit down. Would you like some tea?'

The couple sat together on Joseph's old sofa. 'No, thank you,' Laura answered.

A short silence followed. 'What can I do for you?' Neil's voice was suddenly higher than normal, almost as if he were still waiting for it to break. It was the way they were looking at him, as if they could see inside his head, as if they were accusing him of ... of something or other.

Laura, made bold by Andy's presence, spoke up. 'A woman called Jean Davenport was murdered,' she reminded her legal husband. 'The initials on the back of her missing gold cross were JD. You had that gold cross in your sock drawer.' Although she had no memory of the letters engraved on the cross, she took a chance, and she knew from his expression that she had struck gold in more than one way.

'Really?' His voice was still wrong. 'I never noticed initials.'

'Yes, really. JD.' Laura folded her arms and scowled at him.

A few beats of time crawled past. 'I bought it.'

'From?' she asked, an eyebrow raised.

'I told you – a chap on Paddy's Market.'

415

The other eyebrow joined its twin, and he knew she didn't believe him. From somewhere within his tortured insides, a burp escaped. 'Sorry,' he said.

Andrew crossed one long leg over the other. 'Where is it now?' he asked.

'Nothing to do with you,' Neil managed to snap.

'Anything that concerns Laura worries me, too.' He stared hard at Carson, who reminded him of a deer caught in the headlights of a car. 'Are you the Mersey Monster, Mr Carson?'

The fixated man took a stiff pace backwards and fell over the raised kerb at the edge of the hearth.

'Careful.' Andrew Martindale's tone was soft, dangerously so. 'You'll end up in the flames if you don't watch your step.'

Neil inhaled suddenly. There had been an edge to the man's words, as if he had been talking about the devil's furnace rather than a small coal fire. 'Of course I'm not the killer, Mr Martindale. I may have bought the woman's cross from a market trader, but that means nothing. The murderer could have sold it to him. Or perhaps somebody found it.'

'Do you know the person responsible for the deaths of these women?' the older man asked.

Neil shook his head.

'Where is that gold cross now?' Laura asked.

He tried a shrug, but his shoulders were too knotted to look casual. 'I lost it,' he answered. 'Decided to get you a new one, stuck it in my pocket because I might have got a few bob for it, but ... I don't know where it went.

416

She rose to her feet. 'Well, I know where I'm going.'

Andy joined her.

'Where are you going?' Neil managed to ask, panic trimming the words.

'I'm taking Laura home,' Andrew replied. 'She needs to pick up the children from their grandparents' house and get them off to bed He stared hard at the man who seemed so shaken by that stumble onto the hearth. Neil Carson was not trembling because of a small accident; he was terrified by something else altogether. Had the jabbering wreck been waiting for Laura to announce that she was going to the police? Perhaps she should make a telephone call, at least. But the children, of course; she always put Matt and Lucy first.

They left. Neil collapsed on the sofa, whose cushions retained the warmth bequeathed by his wife and her aged fancy man. O God. O God, God, God. She knew. He had seen in her eyes, in her expression, that she had known. Martindale knew, too. 'Are you the Mersey Monster, Mr Carson?' he whispered. 'I'm dying anyway. This disease will get me eventually, but I'd rather die here than in a prison cell.' He jumped up and began to pace back and forth, from wall to window, window to wall, his mind speeding like a bus with no brakes.

She never cared about me. Thin as a rake, sensible hair, no interest in sex. Look at her now – long, shiny ringlets, makeup, a bust. And it's all for a man nearly old enough to be her dad. They might go to the cops. It's Saturday tomorrow, and I'm not working. Satur-

417

days, she works evenings in the chippy, and the kids sleep there while she goes home with Lover Boy. Am I brave enough? Am I? She won't go to the police tonight, because it's a bit late. Saturday, she'll be washing and whatever else she does, seeing to the kids, looking after them till it's time for work.

She'll go Monday. Except she won't because... Oh, I'll get the kids back, won't I? I'll have to see the doctor about ridding myself of this filthy illness. I mustn't get caught. I must not get caught. I wonder if Angela Whiplash has moved to her flat yet? Soon enough, I'll be in dire need of punishment, the sort of beating my mother used to deliver...

Laura and Andy were back at her house; they would collect the children shortly.

'What are you going to do?' he asked tentatively. She was a good mother; she wouldn't want to instigate anything that might damage Matt and Lucy.

'I don't know,' she breathed quietly.

He enfolded her in his arms. 'Sweetheart, you know you can't stand back just waiting for another killing. This isn't the Penny Lane bus running behind schedule; it's murder. And has it not occurred to you that you might be under threat now? In one sense, you played the right card by pretending to remember the initials, and he was literally and metaphorically on the back foot – didn't he nearly get his hindquarters burnt? This has to be done, Laura. And no, I have no intention of going to the police without you. I won't put you in danger of being named accessory after the fact, but he is a threat to you, me and the children.'

418

Inwardly, he thanked God and the Post Office that a telephone had been installed in this house.

Laura nodded. 'I know, darling. But imagine my children at school when their father's being questioned or charged – or both. They'll be talked about, even attacked, or perhaps ignored by those whose parents forbid them to associate with a child of a possible murderer.'

'It won't be easy,' he whispered into her hair. 'But prostitutes have the same right to life as the rest of us do, and their killer needs to be stopped. We'll just have to move and put Matt and Lucy into another school. We can't go far, because your testimony may well be required.'

She pulled herself out of his embrace. 'I'll have to stand up in court and give evidence about the cross and chain, and about the sudden change in his behaviour, won't I?'

Andy nodded seriously. 'Yes,' he murmured. 'I have managers in the shops. We could move to Southport.'

Laura sighed. 'They read the *Echo* up there, Andy.'

'Then we must go further away and find some-one who'll look after the children while we travel back and forth. It takes ages to build a murder case. If they believe he's the killer, he won't get bail.'

'I'm scared.'

He bowed his head. 'So am I. Which is why we must spend the weekend writing down every-thing you remember. I'll stay with you tomorrow night.'

Laura awarded him a tight smile. 'Then you

419

will sleep with me. It's a new mattress, one Neil never used.' She reached out a hand and stroked his face. 'Adultery's a sin, but there are greater offences.'

'You're blushing.'

A small giggle escaped from her throat. 'I need comfort, Andy. I need you. And I'm blushing because I've never ... never solicited before.'

He swallowed. 'I can just hold you; we don't need to do anything.'

'Oh yes, we do. You're my husband now.'

Barbara Schofield sat on an upturned orange crate. She had a torch and two apples. Murdoch looked down his long nose and sniffed at her hair. What did she want? They'd never before gone riding in the dark, and she was carrying no tack. What strange creatures the two-legged were.

'I've brought you both an apple.' She kissed Nicholas Nye's soft nose before handing him his prize. Murdoch took his apple; she was up to something. Babs was the exception when it came to human rules, because she usually did what she wanted rather than what was expected of her.

'You probably don't remember, Murdy, but not very long ago, Murma brought you into the world, all dangly legs and stringy tail, not much sense, just enough to make yourself stand up and stagger on very stupid feet. She looked after you, cleaned you up, fed you and helped you get strong enough to walk proper, like.'

He whinnied softly.

'Yes, I know you love your mam. Well, I'm going to be a mother, too. It doesn't take as many

420

months to build a human as it does to make a horse, but I can't ride until the little one's born and weaned. I'll be there with you for as long as I can, but I can't ride you – can't ride any horse. The big race still doesn't allow female jockeys anyway, so you'll have to get used to a bloke just in case.'

Change was coming; he could tell that much from her tone.

'I will never leave you, Mad Murdoch. See, we're a pair, you and me. We do as we're ordered when we feel like it. So, when you travel in a horsebox to learn how to outrun and out-jump other horses, I'll be there with Gordy. When you go to leap about on Mr Macey's land, I'll be there. Every time you need new shoes or when the vet comes, I'll be wherever you are. It's nothing to do with who owns you, because I love you – and anyway, I'm one of the three with a stake in you, though that doesn't matter any more. And when you float over all them fences, me and Gordy will be watching you, and Nye will be waiting for you in an … enclosure I think they call it. We love you, baby.'

The animal snorted.

'Don't be rude,' she chided. 'You know we love you.'

In the next stable with Murma and two donkeys, Gordy Hourigan wiped his eyes. For a reason he would never work out for the life of him, Babs and the naughtiest horse he had ever trained understood each other.

He shoved the handkerchief into a pocket. Tomorrow would be their wedding day. Don Crawford had squashed his anger and had signed over Dove Cottage to the couple, so all was well. Madam Horse-Lecturer would be wearing white, because her pregnancy was not yet evident, and she had refused a honeymoon in Ireland because she wouldn't leave that blooming horse. Bill was going to be an usher, as were the three runaways, while Lippy Macey had been cajoled into performing as best man. Bill had threatened to dash round the registry telling everybody to 'ush, and Sally was delighted to be the chief and only bridesmaid.

'Everything will be the same apart from your jockey,' Babs was now informing her favourite animal. 'Gordy and I won't ever leave you. He loves you, too, only he hasn't told himself that yet. And when you and me show the rest of the world how to win the Grand National, everybody will know your name.' She crossed her fingers; women would ride in the race soon, or so she hoped.

The horse whinnied again, and Gordy grinned. He pictured her first day here when she'd draped herself across the back of a semi-wild horse; no fear, no hesitation. 'Made for each other,' he mumbled to the nearest donkey. 'Both winners, both difficult when they want to be, sensible when they need to be.'

Babs hugged her horse and his blind friend. 'It's going to be all right,' she said before leaving them in peace. Outside, she shone light on uneven ground and began to walk towards the paddock gate. A second beam of light joined hers, and she knew Gordy had been listening.

'That was a private conversation,' she told him

haughtily. 'Me and him have stuff to talk about.'

'You're fey,' he said, laughter cracking the syllables.

'I'm not. I'm Barbara. Fay Wardle still works Lime Street, I think. Anyway, I have to get away from you. In four hours, it'll be tomorrow, and it's bad luck if you see me before the wedding.'

He grinned broadly. 'I wasn't listening,' he lied, 'I was checking Murma, because she's been favouring her right rear over her left. But she's well. I think she limps when she wants a treat.'

'A joker like her son, then?'

'No, love. He's probably taken his daft ways from his father.'

'Have they still not found him?'

Gordy shook his head. 'We think he may have emigrated to Australia or America, because Ireland's too small for him.'

'Has he got a passport?'

'Probably.'

They shared a kiss, after which Gordy stood and watched her as she disappeared into Wordsworth House. She was his future, they had a brilliant horse, and life from this day on promised to be rosy. He concluded that he was a happy man. 'And a lucky one,' he whispered as he turned and set off towards home, singing tunelessly under his breath, 'I'm going to be a daddy.'

In Wordsworth's kitchen, four boys stood to attention.

Sally's head entered the room. 'Well?' the mouth asked.

Babs blinked. They stood in a row, three who had escaped from the grip of abusive teachers, a

423

fourth who had mourned the murder of a life-long friend. She swallowed. Booted and suited, they were all so handsome. Don had provided the clothes, which would double as garb for court appearances, and the result of his kindness was pride in the faces of four young men who knew they looked great. 'Well,' she said, dropping into a ladder-backed chair. 'Well, I don't know what to say.'

'First time for everything,' Sal laughed as the rest of her entered the room.

Babs stared at her. The younger woman looked stunning. Given her head, Sally had been secretive about the little frock she was having made by a local seamstress. And the courageous (bordering on outrageous) madam had gone for purple satin with a low, scooped neckline. Her shoes were pink, as was a wide sash round her tiny waist. 'Me flowers are going to be pink and purple too,' she announced gleefully. 'What do you think, Babs?'

For answer, the bride burst into tears.

Sally's jaw dropped. 'Hey, don't worry, cos I bought a cheap pink frock in case you thought I looked ready for a funeral. You never cry.' She addressed the boys. 'She never cries.'

The girl who never cried folded her arms on the table and placed her head on them.

'Blood and sand, Babs,' Sally shouted, 'do you want to turn up red-eyed tomorrow?'

Bill walked round the table and placed an arm across the weeping girl's shoulders. 'Hormones,' he pronounced gravely.

'What the effing hell do you know about hormones?' Sally wanted to know.

'Me sister suffered from it,' was his quick reply. 'Before she had our Simon, she was a wet rag for months, and the doctor said she'd caught something called hormones.'

Sally laughed, though no humour was delivered with the sound. 'You don't catch hormones, soft lad,' she told him. 'You have 'em all the time.'

Bill's eyebrows shot skyward. 'Get away with you.'

The bridesmaid gave up. 'I'll tell you when we're on our own,' she threatened past teeth that were almost gritted.

Bab's shoulders continued to shake, though she emitted a different muffled sound.

Bill patted her shoulder. 'Don't cry, love.'

'She's not crying now – she's laughing,' Ian advised the company.

John was quick to agree. 'She's gone what me mam used to call historical.'

'Hysterics,' Phil explained.

The soon-to-be Mrs Hourigan raised her head. 'Listen, you crazy sods,' she managed, dashing tears from her face. 'Just promise me one thing – that you'll always be part of my life, because you're priceless.' Her tone steadied. 'Wear that, Sal. Be different; be yourself.'

Don marched in with an alacrity that defied his doctors' diagnoses. He wore an immaculate suit, a shirt with a couple of discreet frills down its front, a bow tie and shoes that shone like black glass. 'Will I do like this?' he asked. 'I'm the one walking you up the aisle, Babs.'

'You'll do,' was her reply. She surveyed the whole company once more. 'Take them off and hang them up. We don't want creases.'

Alone at last, Babs sat up straight and thanked God for her new life. She had a good man, a baby on its way, a wonderful horse, a house of her own and a very kind boss who had made all her dreams come true. She promised to look after Don, because she wanted him to be there in five years to witness Murdoch romping home with the rest of the field way behind him in the most difficult race known to man and beast. 'We can do it, Murdy,' she whispered. 'Me, you, Gordy, Don and Lippy will make you famous. Right, I'll go and try me frock on.'

Locking her bedroom door, she released the dress from its prison, a large bag with a hole at the top for the hanger's hook. It was a simple affair in a shiny, silky material, high-necked, long-sleeved, with lace down the arms and at the top, where it met a well-defined bodice in the more solid fabric. Turning sideways, she smoothed a tiny bump and ordered it not to grow any more for twenty-four hours. 'Stay as you are for now, baby,' she muttered.

Someone knocked at her door. 'Who is it?' Babs called.

'Only me,' Sally answered.

The bride opened the door and allowed Sally in.

'He's dead,' the younger girl stated baldly, her mouth curving into a smile.

'Who?' Babs's heart missed a beat.

'Me stepdad. Run over by a coal cart yesterday, pissed as a fart, died in the ozzy this afternoon. Eve heard about it and phoned me.'

'So we won't need to–'

'No, we won't.' Sally grinned. 'God, you look gorgeous. Shall we go back to being lezzers?'

Babs pretended to consider the question. 'No, Sal,' she answered finally. 'I love him. Will you put my cap on?'

'Hair down or up?'

'I don't know. The hairdresser's coming tomorrow and I'll let her decide. Gordy likes my hair loose, but I think the Juliet cap needs to be noticeable. Sally?'

'What?'

'That's the best wedding present, him being dead. It means we can shop in Liverpool as well as Southport.'

'I hadn't thought of that.' Sally's words were forced past hairgrips held between her lips. 'I'd have my hair up if I were you. Gordy can take it down when you get home after the do.'

'Yes – give him something to look forward to.'

'I'm not going to me stepdad's funeral.'

'No?'

'No, because I might laugh or do a jig round the coffin.'

Thus Sally's abuser was consigned to the past, just a wrinkle on a page or an insect glued to hanging flypaper. 'I'll be all right now, won't I, Babs?'

'Course you will. We all will. I'd hug you, but I need to look after me frock. Go on – bed. We have to be up early tomorrow.'

Bert Heslop was profusely apologetic about being late. 'I just needed to hang about for the extra half hour, Miss Mellor.'

She grinned. 'Following a husband?'

'A wife. I left her swinging from somebody's neck outside the cinema,' he said, eyes twinkling. 'She's up to no good. Mind, her husband looks like the aftermath of a bad accident, and he's as miserable as sacrilege, so we shouldn't blame her.' He sat on a nearby chair and took her hand. 'Right. What's all this about you dying?'

Eve shrugged. 'Nothing can be done, Mr Heslop; I'm riddled with it – pancreas, liver, kidneys and a few pounds of best steak. When they read me the list, I felt like a mixed grill minus the eggs and fried bread.'

He lifted a pad and a pen from his briefcase. 'And you make light of it.'

'Do I? Well, what's the point? They wanted to keep me in the hospital so they could study me, so I told them to eff off. I'm stopping here with my girls and my best friend Kate. She's taken over, and she's doing all right.'

He smiled. 'OK, Carson, Neil, postman. Tell me what you know.'

She covered the subject completely, all the way from weak chin, flowered shirts and ties, cross and chain – though she stressed that this was only hearsay – to the main post office, his wife, his kids, and the area in which he currently lived. 'You can follow him home from work.'

'Indeed. Anything else?'

'He likes to be whipped, wants to be scourged till he bleeds, the soft bastard.'

'It takes all sorts, Miss Mellor.'

She became serious. 'The Mersey Monster's out there, Mr Heslop, and it could be him. I need to know before I go.'

He scribbled a few more notes. 'You may rely on me.'

'I know that, which is why I sent for you. Get him. Get him for the working girls he's killed and for those he might intend to kill. Just be as fast as you can.'

'Certainly.' He shook her hand and left the room, wiping his eyes when he reached the hall. Eve Mellor was a woman of strong instincts, and she was probably right about this man. He would start tomorrow. It would be Saturday, but this was an emergency, because Eve Mellor was on her deathbed.

Sixteen

As was ever the case when Babs Schofield was involved in any activity, Saturday morning was a litany of errors right from the start. The men's buttonholes arrived with greenery attached. She didn't want that, because her *Book of Wedding Etiquette* stated clearly that a man's lapel flower should be unadorned. Her own bouquet, ordered by Sally, was white with hints of pink and purple here and there, which shades served to echo the bridesmaid's dress, so that was fine.

Right. She glanced round the kitchen to check that everything was in its proper place. The dishes were washed, there was no lunch to think about today, and Babs was able to devote time to men's surplus foliage. Even so, she remained angry, because she'd ordered just the flower, no green fluff. Some people in shops didn't bloody listen. They'd stuck fern on, and it was miserable, all droopy and limp. Oh, and Sally had done a disappearing act.

The phone rang. Would somebody please find four sparkling white handkerchiefs for the ushers. 'Bog off,' she snapped at her beloved Gordy. 'We're not supposed to see each other or talk till we get to the register place.' She slammed down the receiver. Handkerchiefs? Were they planning on crying their eyes out, the soft buggers?

Babs spent the following half hour of her post-breakfast day remaking buttonholes and cursing quietly under her breath. She stuck the results in a bowl of very shallow water and ordered them to behave unless they wanted to be buried with dog muck behind the garage.

Several minutes were wasted when she found her precious horse standing over the three-tier wedding cake in the big living area, usually named the drawing room. 'How the hell did you get past me? Don't even think about it, you little swine. The cake is for humans only.' The 'little' swine towered over her. He knew this was an unusual day, and he'd been looking for clues. Whinnying softly, he pushed his nose into her hair, inhaled deeply and exhaled loudly.

'I don't want horse snot shampoo today, Murdoch. Can't you get yourself outside and be a horse just this once, eh? And no going upstairs.' She led him out, locking the drawing room door in their wake. The rest of the buffet was in the pantry or on its way with caterers, and he couldn't fit through the small pantry door, so that was OK.

After an extra apple plus one for Nicholas Nye, Murdoch left the house slowly. A wildly swishing tail informed her that he was not best pleased.

Babs shook her head. He had a cob on; she could tell he was in one of his big sulks. 'Shit,' she mumbled, looking up at the kitchen clock. Where did the time go? She had so much to do in the next half hour ... and there was still no Sally.

The providers of party foods entered the arena. Another ten minutes floated away into the ether while she explained the locked door. 'He comes in the house,' she told the gang of three. When questioned, she informed the small gathering that Murdoch was an unusual horse who related best to some members of the human race, plus a small, blind donkey called Nye. The dogs were in a stable, she told them, and geese were unpredictable.

Having never heard of a household like this one, they shook their heads and began the business of bringing in fancy foodstuffs from van and from pantry. This was a very strange place, but they were being well paid, so they got on with the job.

Another man turned up in good clothes including a blindingly white shirt, a tailcoat and a bow tie. He owned an expressionless face and long, elegant fingers with beautifully manicured nails.

'Who are you?' Babs was fast reaching the end of her very short rope. He looked bloody daft in

431

that rig-out. Had nobody ever taught him how to smile? Did he ever laugh?

'Sommelier,' was his curt reply.

Some mothers, Babs decided, were no good when it came to choosing names. 'I see,' was all she managed at first. After a few seconds she asked why he was here.

'I do the wines and serve champagne,' he said. 'I shall also supervise the waitresses when they get here.'

He was posh. Don was posh, as was Lippy Macey, but she was used to them. This chap looked down his nose till he was all but cross-eyed, so he wasn't a natural – oh no, this was a self-made posh. 'Right,' she said. 'I've got to...'S her voice limped away as if lacking energy. She had about an hour at best to become a bride. Where the hell was Sally? How was she supposed to manage all by herself on the most important day of her life?

As if in answer to unspoken questions, Babs's bridesmaid fell in at the door. She was as filthy as mortal sin. 'I'll just...' she breathed, saving herself by grabbing the door jamb. 'Er ... yes.' She shot off upstairs.

'Where've you been?' Babs shouted.

'Doing stuff,' was the disembodied reply.

It was clear that the chief and one-and-only bridesmaid was going to be as much use as a chocolate teapot when it came to helping the bride prepare for her big event. 'Beggaring hell,' she cursed softly. 'Why does everything happen to me?'

The next half hour became a tangle of activity for which she was grateful. Barbara Schofield, soon to be Hourigan, was taken upstairs, shampooed, set and stuck under a dryer while the hairdresser painted her nails. Helen (from Hair by Helen of Lord Street) released the dress from prison, dusted the white shoes, examined one Juliet cap and sprayed the bouquet with a fine mist of water. 'Right-o,' said Helen, 'your dress has a long zip, so I can put your hair up now?'

Thirty-five minutes later, Babs stared at the stranger in her mirror. She was beautiful. All brides looked well on the day, but she ... she shone. With her hair swept backward and upward, she had gained an inch or so in height; at last, she had hit her target of five whole feet. When her shoes were on, she was about five feet and three inches. Sorted!

Helen brought a hand mirror to show Babs the back of her head where the cap sat, its rim decorated by deliberately wayward curls. 'You are bloody gorgeous, love,' the hairdresser told her. 'And the mascara, lipstick and blusher are all you need. Wonderful skin – you're a lucky girl.'

'Thank you. The money's on the bedside table.'

'I've been paid–'

'Take it. You dressed me and made me look wonderful. Please pick that money up, love. When Sal marries Bill, I'll book you.' She posed while a photograph was taken for Hair by Helen's brides' book. 'Oh, and have a look in the next bedroom, see whether my bridesmaid's still covered in muck.'

'What?'

'Don't ask, Helen – just do it.'

Alone, Babs spoke to her son or daughter.

'Thanks for staying small, baby. You have a beautiful mam and a handsome dad, and we're both short-arses. Keep that thought in mind, cos this frock fits where it touches.'

Helen put her head round the door. 'She's fine. I'm just doing a bit of a backcomb on her hair. All the best, Babs.' And she was gone.

'This is it, then,' Babs advised her reflection. She was getting married in – oh, about twenty minutes. 'Mrs Hourigan? More like Mrs Hooligan. I must dress up more often and stop legging about like a bloody tomboy.' She couldn't remember when she'd last worn an adult skirt.

Sally arrived. Stopping in the doorway, she eyed the bride. 'You look absolutely great.'

'So do you. Are we ready?'

'Yes. Gordy's gone with the lads, and Don's downstairs waiting for us.'

'Then let's get the show on the road.'

'Are you sure?' Sally grinned broadly.

'I'm sure.'

They descended the stairs.

'Babs?'

'What?' She had noticed the catch in Sally's voice.

'Still bezzie mates, aren't we?'

'Course. Friends forever, Sal. You, me, Gordy and Bill.'

Sally grinned. 'Sorted, then?'

'Abso-bloody-lutely.'

Don looked smart. He had found a purple waistcoat to match Sally's dress and both bouquets. Babs took his arm. 'You look good enough to make me change my mind, Don. Am I marrying the right bloke?'

The elderly man patted the bride's arm. 'I'm too old for wedlock. Come on. Let's go and hand you over to Gordy. He's a good man.'

'So are you, Don.' And she meant what she said.

As they walked out of Wordsworth House, it occurred to Babs that she would never again sleep in this place, because she now had her own property.

'Nervous?' Don asked.

'Me?' Babs grinned broadly. 'Never in this world.'

Neil Carson sat in Joseph Turton's house with a cup of coffee in one hand and a piece of toast in the other. Nothing tasted of anything; perhaps he should have had marmalade instead of plum jam. Still, it was fuel, so he chewed it slowly and swallowed plenty of coffee to help it on its way. When had he last had a real appetite? Ah, yes – last night. The fish and chips had been great, but she had arrived with her chap, and that event had made his stomach churn. The cross. She was ready to blab about that bloody cross and chain.

Joseph's old van was parked up the side of the end-of-terrace house. 'I'll need that tonight,' he said aloud. His thinking was always clearer in the mornings; by night time he was often confused and uncertain, but after a good sleep he was usually back to normal. She mustn't have spoken to the cops yet, because they still hadn't arrived...

Normal? Did he remember normal?

Of course he did. Normal was taking Matt and Lucy to the park while Laura cooked and set the table for the big Sunday meal. It was a day in Blackpool or Southport, a week in Cornwall, the sorting or collecting of mail, an evening at the cinema, Sunday tea with grandparents, a visit to Port Sunlight or Speke Hall, a bit of sea-fishing with Joseph and others from work. 'I've even stopped missing my children and my wife,' he told the floor. 'But I was all right till Jesus and Judas turned up that night. Were they really there, or did I imagine them? I'm sure I never drank that beer...'

Laura had betrayed him with a tall jeweller. She would probably betray him again by going to the police and jangling on about a cross with initials on the back. He needed punishment. He needed Angela to whip him, bring his flesh to life and prepare him for tonight. Tonight. He wanted an alibi, but chance would be a fine thing, since his one and only friend was dead, as was Maude.

The pacing began, wall to window, window to wall. Think, think. There was a can in the back of Joseph's van, and it was full of petrol. He stopped and swallowed. It was the only way to be rid of both his enemies in one fell swoop; the children would be in the flat above the chip shop ... 'while Laura and Martindale will be in *my* house.' It was his house. He'd worked hard all his married life, had provided for his family while she had probably hated him all along. Now, she was beautiful, good enough for a wealthy old man. She wore makeup and high-heeled shoes, pretty blouses, and soft, silk scarves. Her hair shone, while her head was held high as if she'd won a medal or a damehood, and she had some new jewellery, too.

Hatred flourished in his chest. He had loved her, had been a faithful husband until ... until Jesus and Judas.

He carried on walking. Petrol, rags and matches. Alibi? The Hen and Chickens was busy on Saturday nights; he could go to the men's room, nip out, do what had to be done, then get back to his drink. Before going in the pub, he would make sure that the children were with the Bramwells. Was the Hen and Chickens too close to his target? Think, think, think. No, the pub wouldn't do, since it would close too early...

The solution arrived on a plate, both literally and metaphorically. The very deaf Mrs Wray from next door shouted through the letter box. 'Are you there, Mr Carson?' Oh dear, what did the old girl want?

Neil opened the door and she pushed an apple pie into his hands. 'I have to go to me sister's, love, because she's been took badly with the sciatica, and can't walk. I'll be back some time tomorrow, but will you sit with Norman tonight? You don't need to be upstairs with him; just listen in case he falls again. I'll put him to bed early before I go, like. A neighbour's with our Brenda till eight-ish.'

For answer, he nodded, since shouting at the Wrays was a tiring business. He carried his pie into the kitchen and decided that Jesus had arranged all this. Norman was deafer than his wife, so he wouldn't know that Neil had nipped out to deal with Laura and her aged lover. Ten minutes there, ten back, half an hour to work out how he would set the fire and to do the deed.

First, he would need to go earlier to make sure

that Matt and Lucy would be sleeping elsewhere, because children were not on his hit list. They could live here with him, and the clap would be dealt with, to hell with embarrassment. He'd be a good dad, but he'd need to work days only, since someone must be here for the children.

Notebook. He dug it out of a drawer and plotted his day. At six o'clock, he would watch Laura taking the children to her place of work. By seven thirty, he would be next door with Norman Wray, who should be upstairs and asleep in bed by that time. He stopped writing. 'Am I sure about Laura and her bloke sleeping together?' he asked the empty room. 'If Mr Jewellery's downstairs on the sofa, he might hear me messing about near the door. Front door, back door – which is best? And what if Martindale doesn't sleep there tonight?' He sighed deeply. They both knew about the gold cross, and both needed to be out of the picture.

It was never going to be easy. A man chosen as a disciple by Jesus could not expect life to be a walk in the park. A small smile visited his lips. With Laura gone, the children would go to a park again on Sundays, and they would be accompanied by their father.

Babs carried her disquiet into the chauffeur-driven Rolls-Royce. 'Where were you?' Babs, who clung to the opinion that she had done well this morning, was looking for answers. She eyed her purple-clad friend. 'It was no fun, Sal, because the men's buttonholes were wrong and all kinds of mad people kept turning up.' She eyed Don. 'You've rented a man just to pull corks out of bottles? I don't know about a corkscrew, but he'd a few other screws missing, the jumped-up fool.'

Don eyed his best Baby Girl. 'I want everything to be right,' he replied.

Babs glared at Sally. 'Well?'

'I told you – I was doing stuff,' Sally replied, her cheeks glowing.

'In a coal mine? Or have you worked a quick shift down the docks?'

Don spoke up. 'Leave her alone, Babs. She was helping outside.'

'Leave her alone? Leave her a-bloody-lone? That's what she did to me. Her job was to get me ready, but she came in as black as a stew-pot and the hairdresser had to do it all.'

Sally giggled.

'What's funny?' the bride asked.

'Nothing.'

'Nothing?'

'It's me nerves,' Sally said. 'I start giggling when I get nervous. I used to laugh when we had tests at school – I can't help it.'

Babs blew a loud raspberry. 'In my book about etiketty, it says the chief bridesmaid's main concern is preparing the bride, though that job is sometimes taken over by a relative. I've no rellies here, so it was up to you, you soft mare.'

Don interceded again. 'You'll see the results of Sally's labours soon enough. Behave yourself for once, please.'

'I always behave myself.'

Don nodded. 'When you're asleep, yes. It's just when you're awake we have problems. Calm down, because you'll be married in about ten minutes unless Gordy changes his mind.'

'I'd kill him.'

The giver-away of the bride smiled. 'Exactly. That would be extremely bad behaviour even for you. Calm down and pretend you're a lady.'

'I'm not a lady. I never wanted to be all frills and h'aitches h'in h'all the right places. I'm a woman. Small, like, but still a woman.'

Don resigned from the argument, sitting back in his seat to demonstrate his decision to withdraw from the field of battle. Where Babs was concerned, the least-said-and-soonest-mended school of thought was sometimes appropriate, especially for someone whose survival depended on tablets.

The car glided to a graceful, soundless halt.

Babs swallowed. This was it; Custer's last stand, the final few moments of being single. Still, she wouldn't get a chest full of arrows like poor Custer... There was just one dart in her chest, and that was her love for Gordy.

'We're here,' Don announced unnecessarily. He stepped out of the car, offering his arm first to the bride, then to her attendant. In a small lobby, Sally straightened Babs's dress and her own. 'Aren't you cold?' she asked.

Babs wasn't feeling anything. 'I don't know,' she answered truthfully. She was getting married. Little Barbara Schofield from Sefton Park, Dingle, Bootle, Seaforth and any other place to which her family had fled due to unwillingness to pay rent, was going up in the world. She had a good man, a house with proper furniture and the greatest horse in England. It was like a dream, a good dream.

'It's November,' the younger girl announced. 'Come on, let's get in there, because I'm freezing.'

The inner doors were opened by two smiling ushers, and the strains of a quiet piece of Bach greeted the new arrivals. 'We can't have hymns,' Babs whispered, 'because it's a civil ceremony.'

'Then *be* civil.' These words were delivered from a corner of Don's mouth.

'I'll try.'

The music stopped and was replaced by *Barbara Ann,* one of Gordy's favourites. This livelier music was also played quietly and was turned up just a fraction when Gordy's Barbara stepped onto the scarlet runner that stretched between two blocks of seating. She stopped. Belle and Tom were here, as were Angela and the rest – even the new girls.

Eve, near the double doors and in a wheelchair, smiled at the naughty young minx she missed so badly. 'Just your friends, Babs. Worry not.'

The girl who never cried looked ahead to where Gordy stood with Lippy Macey. Both wore purple waistcoats and purple ties. The girl who never cried blinked rapidly because she never cried. Eve was frail. Skin stretched by too much flesh now hung in loose folds over her collar. The girls looked good, and they knew how to behave in company, so there was no danger of the bride's being categorized as a whore. But Eve, poor Eve...

It was time to concentrate on her future, which would begin at the side of a short but good-looking man who had wanted to be a jockey. His best man, Lippy Macey, towered above the groom, while four ushers stood against walls as if expecting a riot. She heard a little girl laughing and shouting 'Pretty,' the voice rising above the quietened *Barbara Ann*. That would be Belle's Lisa, Babs decided. Belle was pregnant again, though very few people knew about that.

By the time she reached Gordy's side, her throat felt full, as if a bit of food had been lodged in it; she was happy and sad, and she didn't know why. She looked at the registrar, a man of medium height with a pot belly and a smiley face. Bride and groom were allowed to make their own vows as long as the official performed the legal side of the ceremony.

She was going to cry. She would not cry, because she had never cried as a child, even after failing off swings, walls or bicycles.

Gordy spoke about the obstacles they would need to clear, about soft ground, hard ground, easy going and muddy tracks. His soft accent delivered the promise to love and cherish her evermore, to care and provide for any children and to walk by her side always.

It was her turn, but her mind was a blank page. A poem; she had chosen a poem. Not Wordsworth, not Coleridge, not Don's usual lakeside fare. She swallowed. Pushkin, Alexander, died 1837. She knew when he'd died, but the poem eluded her.

'Barbara?' The kindly registrar was prompting her.

Right. It flooded back like a tidal wave, the first and last verses of 'Wondrous Moment.' She would try to talk proper, like.

'The wondrous moment of our meeting,
I well remember you appear
Before me like a vision fleeting,
A beauty's angel, pure and clear.

In ecstasy the heart is beating,
Old joys for it anew revive,
Inspired and God-filled, it is greeting
The fire, and tears, and love alive.'

The registrar was mopping his eyes, while members of the congregation were sniffing and clearing throats. Babs turned on them. 'It's not a funeral,' she announced loudly. Then she looked at Eve and knew that there would be a funeral quite soon. Eve had scolded her back at the farm just like a mam should; she'd recognized fire in Babs, had even allowed her to win from time to time. There had been war; there had been mutual respect – even affection of a kind. Babs blew a kiss at her old friend and enemy. Eve returned the gesture.

Within a couple of minutes, Gordy and Babs were man and wife. And that was when the dam burst.

Gordy dragged a strange item from his top pocket. It was a bit of white handkerchief fastened to a piece of card. 'I had to cut mine up,' he told her, 'because my bride was in a mood when I phoned and asked for help. The ushers have the same.'

Laughter joined tears, and Babs fought to pull herself together before hysteria claimed her. 'Is

443

this how our life's going to be?' she asked, the words fractured by emotions she scarcely understood.

'Probably. Come on now, we must sign the book to get our certificate. And stop the tears before your mascara runs. I don't want a black-eyed wife on the wedding photos. People will think I beat you up, so.'

They signed their names, and a ripple of applause travelled from the back of the room to the front. From the walls stared civic dignitaries captured in the past and trapped behind glass, mustachioed Victorians, Edwardians in sombre hats and dark clothes, a few who looked as if they might have lived more recently, in the 1940s and 50s. Sunlight pierced windows of stained glass, spreading colours over the volume in which the couple wrote their names. It was done, and Barbara was no longer weeping.

Lippy whispered a few words to Sally, who came forward and repaired minor damage to the bride's makeup. They walked down the red carpet while Glenn Miller's music played in the background. Photographs of the main players in the wedding party were taken. Later, when the whole gathering had been captured on film, a black carriage arrived, a splendid affair pulled by two greys with white plumes on their heads.

Gordy and Babs sat in this chariot. A white velvet cloak with a white fur collar was placed by her husband around Babs's shoulders. 'There you are now, pet. That's imitation ermine; you could join the House of Lords, so you could.'

A coach held most of the party, while Eve and

Kate were helped into Lippy Macey's van, which also held the wheelchair.

'Why aren't we moving?' Babs asked.

'Wait. Try a little patience for once.'

From a nearby side street, Murdoch appeared. He shone like polished copper, his tail plaited, his mane combed straight. The horse wore rosettes he'd never won because he was meant to be a secret, while bright horse brasses gleamed on his tack. Lippy Macey's men guided the horse and blind Nye to the carriage, and Murdoch led the procession homeward.

Nye's bell sounded with every step he took. Shoppers stopped in their tracks and stared at the procession – one red-bay horse, one donkey, a carriage pulled by paler steeds and a slow-moving Rolls-Royce, with a single-decker bus and a van bringing up the rear. But this was Southport, so there was no applause, and no children ran by the side of the wedding party.

The bride and groom held hands. 'That's why Sally was missing,' Gordy explained, 'because she was looking for Murdoch and brushing Nye.'

Babs squeezed his fingers. 'She brushed Nye?'

He nodded. 'And we all know what happens to brushers of Nye. Was she muddy?'

'She was.'

'She did it for Murdoch, babe. You know he doesn't like to leave his best friend behind.'

After biting her lip, the bride said, 'I was horrible to her.'

'That's normal, wife. And we are all used to it.'

'Am I horrible?'

'Yes, but lovely with it.'

445

'They're all staring at us.'

'That's because you're lovely, and they haven't seen you horrible.'

She slapped his hand. 'Just wait till I get you home.'

The groom chuckled. 'Promises. Empty promises.'

There had been a delivery of snow for just a few minutes, and the children were outside trying to scrape together enough to make a miniature snowman. Laura watched them for a while, smiling anew at the innocence of the young. She wanted them to stay like that, at a safe distance from life's harsher truths, but she now knew that would be impossible.

Removing her notes from the bureau, she whispered them into the room. 'Started having nightmares towards the end of summer when the killings began. He screamed in his sleep. After a week or two of that, he began to use foul language referring to female body parts. I asked him to leave for the sake of my children, Matt and Lucy.'

She glanced at the window, checking the precious ones again. They were laughing. Would their natural happiness be spoilt by what was about to happen?

'I found a cross and chain in his chest of drawers. It was hidden under socks. There were initials on the back of the cross. The front was ornate and very like the one in the newspaper photograph, diamond cut, and without a Christ figure. At my place of work, I saw an article in an old newspaper. It stated that Jean Davenport's initialled cross had been missing from her body. I could not remember the initials I'd seen on the cross in his drawer, but I confronted him and lied, asking what he'd been doing with a piece of jewellery that bore the initials J and D, and he shook like a leaf in a gale.'

Matt had taken a tumble, but he stood up and rubbed his knees like a brave little soldier. He would need to remain brave, as would his sister.

'He says he bought the jewellery from a street trader on Paddy's Market, but I don't believe him. For years, he was as steady as a rock, then he suddenly became jumpy and strange. He may not be the Mersey Monster, but I thought I should talk to you just in case. I have my two children, and I fear for them if their father gets arrested. On the other hand, I am finding it very difficult to sit here with my suspicions without doing anything.'

Laura tapped her teeth with a pen. The day was growing cold, and darkness threatened, so she stashed away the notes and put sausages under the grill. The vegetables were already in the steamer, so there remained only the tasks of browning Wall's Pork Sausages and creaming the potatoes.

Andy let himself in; he had his own key now.

Laura raised her head from the tasks in hand and smiled at him. 'Did you close early?' she asked.

'No. Mrs Mather's in charge with her son, and the day was quiet, so I stashed the good stuff in the safe and left her totting up the takings. She'll lock up and go home when she's finished. The Christmas trade won't start for a couple of weeks yet.' He looked through the window. 'I see they've made a midget snowman.'

She sighed. 'They may as well have fun while they still can.'

'Laura, I–'

'I've done the notes. When I take the children to the Bramwells look in the top drawer of the bureau and see if I've forgotten anything. We'll talk about it later before we go to ... before we go upstairs.'

Andy smiled; she was blushing like a teenager. Sometimes, she seemed so young, so naive. 'Hey, if it bothers you, I'll sleep down here.'

'No, you won't. I told you before, I've made up my mind. You're my man now.'

He nodded thoughtfully. 'Another thing your children will have to deal with, another change of circumstances.'

'Yes.' There was some power in her voice at last. 'Never forget that my children may be Carsons by surname, but they also have McMahon blood in their veins. I am so much stronger these days, and they will grow into their strength, too. They're fond of you.'

'And their father?'

'Never visits them. It would upset him too much.'

'It's all about him, isn't it?'

Laura paused, potato masher held aloft. 'I think it always was, Andy. His mother was very unkind to him, kept calling him a sinner, especially when he started growing up. She's all right with him now – or she was till we separated, but he was an unhappy teenager.' She pulled herself together.

'Get them in, Andy, then I can feed them. We've a lot to do tonight.'

He raised an eyebrow. 'I'm not as young as I was, Laura.'

'Andrew Martindale, I was referring to the notes. Bring the children in and let's be a family.' While creaming the mash, she stood at the sink and watched as Andy talked to Matt and Lucy. He was a good man. Hopefully, he might become the father figure her children needed.

Bert Heslop, private detective, found Brandwood Street. Carson's house stood on the end of a row; a dark blue van was parked at the side of the building. Neil Carson had taken in his pint of milk very late in the day, and Eve Mellor's description had been good. It was half past four; Bert was scribbling notes on his pad. Miss Mellor was dying, so speed and accuracy must be employed.

The day had been cold with flurries of snow, and evening had begun its descent. He turned on the engine and drove round the streets for a while so that he might heat the chilled air in his car. For a reason he failed to define, he knew there was something very wrong with the man who had lifted the milk from his step. Perhaps it was the eyes? They had shifted from side to side as if expecting to see something or someone he feared.

Returning to a different part of Brandwood Street, he watched as Carson moved past him in the blue van. Careful not to seem over-keen, he followed the vehicle at a slower pace. On a main road, Carson stopped. This section of the long stretch was named College Row and, after parking, Neil wrote down the number of a house at which Carson was staring. 'He's up to no good,' the detective mumbled to himself.

Glancing round, he caught sight of the chip shop mentioned by Miss Mellor. In there, Mrs Carson had found among wrappings evidence of her husband's possible involvement with the murders. Why was the man watching the house? Chills played up and down Bert's spine.

Neil Carson drove a few yards closer to the road, but Bert stayed where he was. Why? he wondered. 'Why am I choosing to keep watch here?' he whispered. Because the killings on the Dock Road had stopped? Because he suspected that Carson's next target might be his own wife? Curtains were pulled into the closed position by a tall man. After half an hour or so, Mrs Carson emerged from the house with her children. She disappeared into the chip shop, which was not yet open to the public. Bert decided to buy his supper there as soon as possible, because a hungry man felt the cold more acutely.

Using a torch, he re-read notes made yesterday after his meeting with Eve Mellor. Mrs Carson had spoken unexpectedly to a new acquaintance about the cross found in a drawer, and that lady had told Meadowbank's madam. Had Mrs Carson confronted her husband? Was she now in danger? When he looked up from his scribbles, he saw that Carson's van had gone.

He switched off the torch. The man in Mrs Carson's house had to be Martindale, a well-known and respected jeweller. The call to Miss Mellor had come from one of his shops, so... So he would knock on the door. 'Should I?' he asked the dashboard. Shivering again, he gave birth to the next couple of thoughts. Was Carson's missus insured? Had he been making sure that the kids were not in the house? He leapt out of his car and ran across the road.

Andrew Martindale opened the door. He held a tea towel in one hand and a plate in the other. 'Yes? May I help you?'

'Let me in, please. He may be planning his next move as we speak.' Bert had to put his head back to see the face of this very tall man. 'I'm a private detective and I'm following Neil Carson. He was watching this house, and he drove away just minutes ago.'

Andy widened the gap and allowed the short man to enter the hall. 'Living room on your right,' he said, placing plate and towel on the hall table.

Grateful for the fire's warmth, Bert perched on the edge of an armchair. 'Hubert Heslop,' he announced.

'Andrew Martindale.'

The visitor held out his hands to the fire. 'Cold night,' he commented.

'Yes, the weather's serving up a taste of winter,' Andy replied. Surely this man was here to discuss something more dangerous than snow?

'I suspect Carson's ready to strike.' The small detective paused and fuelled his lungs with a large intake of oxygen. 'Well, a Mrs ... er ... Belle Duffield was spoken to by Mrs Carson during a visit to one of your shops.'

Andy nodded. 'Yes. It was rather rash, but she seemed to trust the lady.'

'She is trustworthy. Mrs Duffield spoke on the telephone to a very discreet client of mine, someone who has used my company in the past. I am employed by a Miss Eve Mellor to follow Neil Carson, since she believes him to be the Mersey Monster.'

The taller man placed himself in a chair opposite his visitor. 'I see.' He didn't quite see, but he felt he ought to make some comment.

'I know about the gold cross and the behaviour of Mr Carson. He was outside just now, watching while Mrs Carson took the children to the chip shop. Will they be home later?'

'No. Saturday nights are busy, and Laura works late, so Matt and Lucy stay with the Bramwell twins in the flat on the floor above the shop. She will come back, but they'll return tomorrow in time to get ready for church.' He paused. 'What's going through your mind, Mr Heslop?'

'Bert.'

'Right, Bert – I'm Andy. I'll make some tea while you get your thoughts in order.'

But Bert followed Andy into the kitchen. 'When does Mrs Carson come back to the house?'

'About half past eleven, usually. Occasionally, she works till midnight.'

The small man nodded thoughtfully. 'Does he know she suspects him?'

'Yes.'

'And does he know that you share her opinion?'
Andy nodded.

'Then he'll probably be here later tonight. I'm assuming that you haven't yet spoken to the police?'

'That's right – we haven't.'

'Well, I suggest that now would be a good time.'

Andy stared down at his companion. 'We're going to do it together.'

'When?'

'Monday.'

Bert inhaled deeply once more. 'You could both be dead by then. I think it will be arson – that's usually the choice of a cowardly man. With women, it's poison, but men use fire if they want the hands-off approach.'

With his hand shaking, Andy brewed the tea. 'She's frightened enough already, and the children are up and down the stairs at the Bramwells' until bedtime, so she has her hands full. On Saturdays, their curfew runs later.' He followed Bert back into the living room and placed the tea tray on a low table. 'You watch and I'll watch. Let's get the police when he tries to set the house on fire.'

Bert's lips settled into a grim line. 'I'm not sure it will be arson. He could have a gun or...' He ran his fingers through his hair. 'If he is the monster, he's downright dangerous.'

Andy leaned forward, elbows on knees, clenched hands supporting his chin. 'I'll walk her back here in a few hours and I'll tell her then what might be happening. You watch from the side street across the road – you can see this house clearly from there. Laura and I will walk through the house and, after switching on lights, we'll go through into the rear alley. He won't do anything until he thinks I'm asleep, because I could bring him down as easily as swatting a fly.

I may be older, but I'm fit. I'll take her along the back all the way to the Bramwells' place, then I'll return here, put the downstairs lights out, switch on the bedroom lamp, leave again via the rear door and cut through a few streets to join you in your car. She'll be with her children, and I'll be out of his line of fire – no pun intended.'

Bert smiled grimly. 'And you'll leave your car parked outside the house so that Carson can assume that you're inside with his wife.' He looked Andy up and down. 'Will you fit in a Mini?'

'I'm reasonably collapsible. Listen, Bert, if he can be caught red-handed, he'll be put away tonight. Once he's locked up, it will be easier for Laura and me to heap the other pieces of evidence on his head. The story will come out, of course, but if we do it my way, he'll go down for attempted arson, and he'll crumble under questioning about the dead women. I think this will be the quickest way to be rid of the man.'

Bert remained unsure. 'Perhaps we could get the cops out tonight and have them watch what's going on and–'

'No.'

Bert's jaw dropped.

'No,' Andy repeated. 'What if you're wrong? What if he makes no attempt to harm me and Laura tonight? The boys in blue may decide to take none of it seriously – we might even be accused of wasting police time.' He poured the tea. 'Now, I'll make us something to eat. We may be in for a very long night. Do you like eggs?'

'I do.'

'Good, because I'm great with eggs. I'll bring

you some bread – use the toasting fork. Bread singed by fire is always tastier. I'll go and start scrambling.'

By the time they'd eaten together, both were easier. Whatever happened, each felt he'd found in the other a friend for life.

Eve sat near the huge fireplace in her chariot. Chariot was a word so much more acceptable than wheelchair. She watched Baby Babs dancing with her new husband, saw her girls chatting away to others in the party, and felt content, because she'd done a good enough job of raising these surrogate daughters.

Babs and Gordy had their own place at Dove Cottage, and the three abused boys would be staying here in Wordsworth for a few nights, as would Eve, Kate and the girls. Meadowbank was closed for the week, so all its residents were in holiday mood. She shifted in the chariot; the pain was beginning to get to her.

The best man arrived by her side. 'Miss Mellor? I'm Macey, commonly known as Lippy.'

She held out a hand. 'Eve Mellor. I've a small-holding outside Knowsley. Babs and Sal stayed with me for a while.'

Lippy pulled up a chair. 'So the three boys who ran away from school hid in a hut near you?'

'They did, yes.'

'Ushers today,' he told her. 'And I have news for them. The offending brothers have been thrown out of the order and are on bail awaiting trial.'

'Should be bloody shot,' she snapped. 'I've no time for bastards who prey on kids. Still, let's not

455

think about them, eh? I'm staying here for a few days with my old friend Kate. I know it's late in the year, but a change of air might suit.'

There was sadness in the smile he delivered. 'If you need a doctor while you're in Southport, use Don's. As a temporary resident, you retain the right to be treated.'

'Thanks.'

He patted her hand. 'The tiny bundle of fire dressed suitably in red is my wife. She's a doctor, too. You won't be alone, dear lady.'

When he had walked away, Eve fixed her eyes on bride and groom. They were clearly happy. Tomorrow, one of the lads might take Eve and Kate to meet the famous horse, the very one who had hated Eve on sight. She groaned under her breath. Soon, it would be morphine, and morphine would render her less than sensible.

'Eve?'

She turned to find Babs squatting beside her. 'You look lovely,' Eve said. 'I was that proud when you came into the register office – well, I could have cried.'

'We never cry, you and me.'

'It's not every day a daughter gets wed, love. I felt as if you were my girl. If I could choose a child of my own, you'd be high on the list, babe.'

'Oh, Eve.'

'I know, I know. I don't want to go, but this bugger's got a grip of me, and it's going to win. I'd love to be a granny by proxy, only it's not going to happen.'

Babs blinked rapidly. 'I'll see you tomorrow.'

'Yes, love.'

The bride stood up and brought a chair to Eve's side.

When seated, she took Eve's hand. 'I've been watching you. You're in pain.'

'Yes. But make sure I don't die in hospital, will you? Kate's promised, but she might panic when the time comes. She's not as strong as we are. Angela said she'll phone you when ... when or if any decisions are made.'

'OK.'

Gordy joined them. 'Come on now, Mrs Woman. We're going home.' He nodded at Eve. 'Full house here tonight. You, Miss O'Gorman, four lads and all your girls. Still, three of the boys will be back with us in a day or so.'

'Are they safe?' Eve asked.

'I doubt the monks will break bail conditions, but we'll remain on red alert. Goodnight.'

Without announcing their intention to leave, the couple disappeared while the party was in full swing. Don had been in bed for a couple of hours, but others looked set to have fun until to-morrow. It had been the greatest of days.

Babs and Gordy made their way to Dove Cottage and towards their own private celebration. They were a family, and families needed alone time.

Seventeen

There was an odour attached to the Wrays' house, a smell that clung determinedly to everything, proclaiming loudly that the people living here were elderly. The place wasn't dirty; it was just decadent. Maude Turton, who had lived next door, had always given off the scent of lavender or violet, but poor Mrs Wray spent most hours in the day – and possibly the night – caring for a sick cripple of a husband who scarcely knew her. She fed him, gave him bed baths, cleaned up his messes, helped him up and down the stairs, and still found time to make an extra pie for a neighbour.

Neil Carson lowered himself into a chair. 'I won't eat the pie,' he mumbled. He couldn't eat anything that came out of a house as neglected as this one. Surfaces were dusty, while curtains and cushion covers screamed for a damned good wash. Poor woman. She was probably too old and worn out to deal properly with household tasks.

Dolly Pearson crept into his head. Mistaking her for a whore, he had killed her, thereby leaving Mrs Pearson's mother without one of her carers. Shivering, he sat back and tried to eliminate the thought. 'I looked after Maude,' he whispered. 'I looked after her well, even loved her.' Surely that went some way towards compensating for his mistake? He'd tried so hard. Liking women older

458

than himself was never easy. Mother. Oh yes, Mother had a great deal to answer for.

A picture of Joseph's hanging body suddenly occupied his mind. 'Stop, stop.' He picked up a newspaper and tried to read, but nothing sank in. Tonight, he was going to kill his wife and an upstanding citizen of Liverpool. 'Don't think about it, Neil,' he muttered, 'and just concentrate on the newspaper. It wasn't his fault that Joseph Turton had been homosexual... Words on the page meant nothing, and were beginning to melt together like blobs of tar on a hot day.

Nine o'clock. Laura would be in the chip shop for at least a couple more hours; really, it needed to happen after about one or two o'clock in the morning while people were sleeping deeply. If Martindale's car was outside... 'Patience, patience,' he mouthed. There really was no valid reason for leaving Norman Wray twice. As long as he was back by the early hours, Neil would be safe and neither of the Wrays would know anything about his temporary escape. He'd even parked Joseph's van in a different street.

Traffic was still on the move outside. It was Saturday night, it was too early, and he needed to be safe.

'Safe?' he asked aloud. 'Who can be safe after killing the mother of his children?' Yet everything had arisen after Jesus had delivered the message, the request about ridding the streets of prostitutes. Life was a maze... He seemed to be meeting dead end after dead end. Dead. Oh yes, he had brought death to Liverpool, but tonight's would be his biggest crime.

He stood up and began his usual walk, but in a different house. Wall to window, window to wall, dead end to dead end. Hell beckoned. The need to murder his wife and her lover had arisen from tasks undertaken in the name of Jesus. Could a latter-day disciple go into the inferno? Now, that *was* a real and eternal punishment, a fire to end all fires.

He paused. The children would be heartbroken, since Laura had been a good mother. But he would be a good dad; he'd always been an excellent father. He would need to seek treatment, of course.

Fire. With fire, most people were killed by smoke, so Laura wouldn't burn to death, would she? And to think he'd been worrying about Matt and Lucy being unsafe if the chip shop went up in flames. Life was strange, a circle with events, worries and ideas moving and reappearing like the moon and the sun, forever there, yet not always visible.

He placed himself in the hands of the Lord and tried once more to read the newspaper. Five long hours, and he must stay calm.

'Where on God's good earth are you taking me now?' She was a besom, as his old mammy might have said.

'Somewhere sensible,' was the new bride's swift reply.

'Stables?' Gordy asked. 'Will we spend the wedding night with a couple of horses and some donkeys? The dogs are in there too, you know. They seemed not to like the music, so they'll be asking

Murdoch to protect them.'

Babs ground to a halt, as did her husband. 'A stable was good enough for Jesus's birthday, wasn't it? Anyway, we had our wedding night months ago, soft lad. I have to tell Murdoch we're really married now. He already knows I can't ride him because of the baby.'

Gordy tutted.

'What?' Babs snapped.

The besom's partner shook his head slowly. 'And you call me soft when you're the one who thinks a horse understands English?'

'He understands *me*,' Babs insisted, 'because he's mine. He chose me.'

'Hmmph,' Gordy grunted.

She folded her arms and faced him. 'Listen, Hooligan. He knows when I mean there's change coming. I'm not saying he gets everything I tell him, but he senses when I mean change. And he's my horse in his heart, so he listens to me. I do nothing behind his back. Like a kid, he wants to learn.'

Gordy grinned. 'He'll be asleep.'

She laughed. 'He never lies down till about ten o'clock; he does the sleeping-stood-up bit till Nye settles. They're both prey animals, both made to sleep standing up and ready to run. And before you ask, yes, I've been reading again. A horse does flight or fight. There's a locking mechanism at the tops of their legs to stop them falling over in their sleep. A mare would fight if she had a foal to protect, but they mostly bugger off when they see predators. Like we would. They're us, but with four legs and more sense.'

461

She was right, of course. Gordy watched as she picked up a torch and switched it on. Murdoch was on his feet, eyes closed, ears in the I-am-resting or I-am-bored position. One ear moved. 'He knows we're here,' Babs whispered. 'Murdoch? Hello, baby.'

Both ears suddenly pricked up into the ready position. He whickered softly.

'We're married,' Babs announced, 'so we'll both sleep in Dove Cottage from now on, but I'll still be in the big house every day, so you'll get your carrot and your apple. Nothing's different really. I can't ride you, but I can be with you. They're getting a nice young man to ride you, which is just as well, because they might carry on allowing only men jockeys in the big race.'

Gordy leaned against a wall and watched as Murdoch placed his head on Babs's shoulder and the whispering began. Although newly married to his beloved girl, he felt as if he were intruding on a pair of lovers. Babs had proved herself to be a godsend in more than one way; she was clever, funny, loving and would become a great jockey after the child was born. 'What are you telling him, Babs?'

'That we love him.'

Gordy sniffed. Babs had a habit of pulling at his heartstrings.

'Lie down, baby,' she said.

The horse settled down next to his donkey friend. From the shadows, four scruffy mongrels appeared and stretched out, cuddling up to their equine friends. They didn't like parties, so their usual beds at the foot of Wordsworth House's stairs would be empty tonight, and they would borrow warmth from the stable dwellers.

'Come away with you now, Mrs Hourigan.'

'I'm coming, I'm coming.' She put away the torch and took her husband's hand. Never before in her life had she felt as happy as she did in this moment. A good man, a precious horse and a house with three bedrooms and a plumbed-in bath – what more could a woman ask for?

Belle did the driving. For the first few miles, the couple sat in silence, tired after the long but happy day. 'Tom,' she asked eventually while travelling through Ainsdale, 'did you take a close look at Eve?'

He sighed. 'I didn't need to, love. She was nearly as yellow as a new duster.'

Belle agreed; even the whites of Eve's eyes had been stained. 'She can't have long left. I hope they keep her as pain-free as possible. Will it bother you if I go up there occasionally – to the farm, I mean? Just to help Kate look after her? I'll go only when you don't need me to run you round with clocks.'

Tom shook his head. 'I won't mind at all, love. But remember our baby and don't go lifting and carrying anything heavy.'

She continued through Formby towards the main route to Liverpool. 'That private detective is on Neil Carson's tail, Tom. He's going to follow him over this weekend, or so Eve says. There has to be a reason why he had that cross and why he got rid of it. I shiver when I think of him. Even Angela said he was twisted.'

'I'll warm you up when we get home, my love. Until then, don't think about him.'

Belle swallowed. 'I'm scared,' she whispered.

'I'll protect you. I may have just the one hand, but I can swing a poker well enough, and my hook could rip his ugly face off. Anyway, he doesn't have any reason to hurt you.'

'He's killed working girls. I've been a working girl.'

Tom considered her words. 'If Laura Carson told you her suspicions, she'll go to the police soon. He'll be locked up before you know it.'

But she still felt chilled to the bone. Eve was dying, and there was a lunatic about with a private detective on his tail. After such a lovely wedding, Belle should have been happy, but her intuition was on red alert. Something bad was going to happen very soon. 'I love you, Tom.'

He heard the catch in her throat. 'I love you, too. What's the matter?'

'I don't know.'

'Well, when you do know, be sure to tell me.'

Belle tried to concentrate on her driving. Being female was not always a good thing. Women knew stuff that wasn't knowable, and men seldom understood the vagaries of a woman's mind. Was it a sixth sense? Was it imagination? Perhaps hormones were the culprit.

'There's nothing you can do, anyway,' he said.

Ah yes, here came the pragmatism of the male. She smiled. Tom would take care of her, wouldn't he?

Detective Sergeant Eddie Barnes had earned his

invisible stripes. Not that he'd ever lost them, since he had passed his sergeant's exam while still in uniform, but he knew that his boss rated him highly as a plain clothes officer.

At a quarter to eleven p.m. on this November Saturday, he sat in an emergency meeting called by DCI Fox, a man who minced few words. 'So there's a shitty drugs war on,' the man in charge pronounced. 'Boss Albert Shuttleworth is being challenged by the new big boy, and they're meeting tonight.' He stared at Eddie. 'Lime Street.'

Eddie clicked his jaw into the closed position. 'No,' he breathed.

The DCI smiled. 'I think the new drugs baron dictated the terms and the location. This tip-off is from a reliable source, so go to it. Take unmarked cars, suitcases or whatever else you think will make you blend with the scenery.' Again, he addressed Eddie. 'So if all goes well, we won't need to rent the house next door to Mrs Shuttleworth.' He talked to the full meeting. 'Remember, all of you, that Albert Shuttleworth is an escapee. We want him on trial for the murder of the drugged boy and the killing of PC David Earnshaw.'

Eddie asked a question. 'Are they meeting in the station or on the street?'

'The source wasn't sure. So spread yourselves out a bit. You, DS Barnes, will be in charge. I'll be on the station in my best suit. The meeting between our two heroes is scheduled for eleven thirty, hence this rushed gathering. Remember, the man's a bulldozer without wheels. Go. Get the bastard. He'll be lucky if I don't rip his effing head off. Dave Earnshaw was a damned good copper.'

Eddie Barnes swallowed and hoped his eyes weren't red. He took over the job of his superior, allocating officers to certain sites along Lime Street. 'Ideally, we want both of them, but Shuttleworth is the priority.' He allocated three cars to six officers. 'The rest of you are foot soldiers. Pick up bags and cases from the dressing-up box. We don't want to waste overtime money, so make tonight count.' He blinked. 'For Dave. Make it count for Dave.'

While Bert Heslop sat in his Mini in a side street facing College Row, Andrew Martindale left the house and walked down to the chip shop on the next block. Fortunately, Laura was not in the serving area. He spoke to Barry Bramwell. 'Where is she?' The words emerged in a whisper.

'Upstairs checking on the kids,' was the reply.

'I'll be bringing her back here,' Andy said. 'No time for details, but we'll come down to the rear of the shop. Is that all right?'

'Er ... yes. What's happening?'

'Too complicated, Barry. I'll tell you another time.'

Laura appeared in the doorway. 'What's going on?' she asked.

'Nothing,' the men said simultaneously.

She eyed them with suspicion. There was an atmosphere, and they were lying. 'I know you're up to something,' she stated evenly. Her gaze travelled over both guilty faces.

Barry laughed. 'Typical woman, eh? As soon as a man opens his gob, he's telling lies. We'd be better off dumb.'

466

Laura smiled and picked up a knife. 'Line up,' she ordered. 'I'll cut your tongues out.'

Andy smiled in spite of everything. He remembered the quiet little woman he had met. How she had changed. Here she stood brandishing a sharp knife, yet she wouldn't have said boo to a goose a couple of months ago. 'Come with me,' he told her. 'I'll sort her out,' he promised Barry.

'Will you, now?' Laura tapped a toe on the tiled floor. 'I'm the one with the knife, Andy.'

Barry shook his head in mock sadness. 'She used to be such a lovely lady. Put the knife down before you do yourself a mischief.'

Once outside, Andy decided to wait until they were home before telling her the tale. After all, he didn't want her breaking down out here in the glare of street lighting. Although she asked repeatedly, he refused to discuss Neil Carson and Bert Heslop until they were indoors.

'Well?' she asked as soon as they entered the living room.

'Sit down,' he suggested.

She sat.

'Neil has been watching the house – this house. And a private detective has been watching Neil watching the house. In the professional opinion of the detective, your husband has waited for the children to be out of the way before...' He sighed heavily. 'Laura, Neil may be trying to kill us. There's the gold cross, and–'

'He wouldn't kill me,' she insisted.

'If he believes you're about to inform on him, he very well might try to eliminate the pair of us. And here we sit, neatly packaged in one building,

467

no children, just the two people who could have him locked up.'

'Move your car.'

'No.'

'No? Why not? Let's drive off somewhere and–'

'No,' Andy repeated. 'You will walk back with me down the rear alley to the Bramwells' place. I shall take a circuitous route to Mr Heslop's car. He and I will watch and wait. There's a telephone box near where he's parked, so we can get the police and the fire service as and when necessary.'

Laura blinked. 'The fire brigade?'

He nodded. 'Mr Heslop says cowardly men resort to fire. If he broke in and killed us with a knife or a gun, he might leave evidence and he would risk resistance from us. Fire eliminates everything. Now, we are safe for the moment, as people are still walking and driving past, but I shall go upstairs in a few minutes, close the curtains and switch on the bedroom lamp. Later, we can put out the downstairs lights and leave by the back door.'

'But I–'

'But you will stay with the Bramwells – it's all arranged.'

She leaned forward, elbows on knees, head in her hands. So this was what the two men had been plotting in the chip shop. A picture of Neil's angry face entered her head; he had left this house in a cold fury and had possibly remained in a similar frame of mind. She should have gone to the police, but the children might have been hurt. Nevertheless, it was her fault that things had gone so far.

'Laura?'

She raised her head. 'All right. Do what needs to be done, while I must do as I'm told, I suppose.'

'I'm sorry, my dear.'

She managed a tight smile. 'None of this is your fault. I should have gone to the police station.'

'Let them catch him red-handed after a 999 call.'

She rose to her feet. 'We'll be apart on our first night together.'

Andy laughed. 'Do you have Irish ancestors?'

'I do.'

'Ah, well that explains everything. Come along, let's get you away from here. With people still walking and driving out there, he'll try nothing this side of midnight.' He looked at her with love in his eyes. 'As long as you're safe, I'm happy.' And he meant it.

The pills were in the kitchen.

It was clear that Thelma Wray must have decanted them into larger jars, containers big enough to take labels onto which she could write in huge script the purpose of each collection. There were several types, including *Sleeping, Calming Down Mild, Calming Down Strong, Stomach, Fits* and *Painkillers*.

He chose the mild calming down jar, tipping out just one harmless-looking article that imitated common aspirin. Should he? Shouldn't he? It wasn't yet midnight, and he was still tense and worried. This was just a gentle sedative, something to take the edge off. He needed to stop thinking about Dolly Pearson and Joseph Turton, wanted to calmn down, relax, even to doze for an hour or so.

After swallowing the pill, he fed the coal fire and waited for the medication to work. Warmth spread throughout his body, and he felt as if he were drifting on a cloud, carefree, almost happy. He raised a hand and almost chuckled when it dropped back onto the arm of the chair. Never in his life had he felt so calm. No, that wasn't true. He remembered the pre-med before his tonsillectomy.

Drifting towards sleep, he smiled. After a few hours of good rest, he would go and do ... he would go ... do ... what needed to be done.

Just before setting off for Lime Street, Eddie phoned Sister Helen Veronica. 'Sorry to wake you, Nellie, but stop collecting furniture for the house – we may not need it, so leave everything alone tomorrow unless I say different.'

'Why?' she asked sleepily.

'Because with any luck, you two will be Smelly Nellie and Holy Mary again by Monday. Pray. Pray like billy-o.'

'I will. God bless, Eddie.'

'Thank you, Sister.'

He joined his men and set forth to do his duty. No, it was more than his duty; this was for Dave.

Belle suddenly sat up in bed.

Her husband stirred and opened his eyes. 'Belle? What's the matter?'

'I don't know,' she breathed, the words almost

sticking in her throat.

He switched on a lamp. 'Is it the baby?'

She shook her head slowly. 'No. It's nothing to do with you and me – it's something out there.' She waved a hand towards the window. 'I don't even know what I mean. Just a bad feeling; I have this bad feeling.'

'Where?'

'Everywhere. It's in my head, my chest, my throat. I keep imagining I want to vomit, but it passes. And it's not a headache or bellyache or toothache.' She turned and looked at the man she loved. 'It's probably to do with Eve and this bloke she's got searching for the postman. Or it may be that I'm disturbed by how ill she looked.' She plucked at the sheet. 'The thing that woke me was a smell of burning. Black smoke everywhere, there was. I couldn't see his face, but the fire was his fault.'

'You couldn't see his face?'

'No. But I know who he was ... who he is.'

'Carson?'

'Yes.'

Tom slid out of the bed. 'Cup of Horlicks?' he asked.

'Yes, please.'

He left the bedroom.

Belle sat and hugged her knees. She hadn't told him everything, hadn't mentioned Eve's voice in the dream. It was just a dream, after all. 'It's all over,' Eve had said. 'He's done for, finished, on his way to hell.'

The woman in the bed shivered. Perhaps she should not have accepted that second piece of wedding cake. Ah well, the Horlicks might settle her down.

Neil Carson's legs were like lead. He dragged himself up, looked at the clock and made a note of the time. It was only ten minutes to twelve; but it was almost Sunday, the Lord's day, a time for worship and prayer. He stilled. When had he last been to church? Psalm 118 invaded his head for a few seconds, and he whispered the words, his voice almost as unsteady as his legs. 'This is the day that the Lord hath made; let us rejoice and be glad in it.'

Be glad? That pill hadn't lasted long, had it? Should he take another one? No, no – he needed to stay awake. Perhaps he should go now, wind the window down on the driver's side, let the cold air give him a boost. He would park in the side street across the way from College Row, watch the house, look out for their comings and goings. Meanwhile, this drug could leach its way out of his system.

He stood, patted a pocket and smiled when he heard the reassuring rattle of matches in their box. Stumbling slightly on the stairs, he went to take a peep at the old man. Norman Wray was spark out, mouth wide open, teeth in a jar by the bed. It was a good job that Thelma was deaf, because the old man's snores imitated the London express pulling into Lime Street.

Right. Downstairs once more, he picked up the Wrays' keys, his own house keys and those for the van. It was too early, but he needed to get out.

The fresh air hit him hard, making him sway

like a man with eight pints in his belly. 'It'll be that damned pill,' he muttered. The street was deserted. Good. Last orders would have been served, since suburban public houses tended to stick to the old opening hours. He shivered, realizing how hot and stuffy the Wray house had been.

The van was two streets away, and Neil still felt rather shaky when he finally climbed into the driver's seat. 'Glad I didn't take one of the strong tablets,' he said under his breath. Driving slowly, he made his way out of a maze of streets and onto the main road from Liverpool to its northern villages. 'Plenty of time,' he told himself as he neared College Row. 'I can rest down the side street and see what Laura's up to with her old bloke.' He had the petrol, the rags and a box of matches; he also had a slight headache which was probably a side effect of that damned pill.

Lights flashed in his mirrors. Something was travelling close to him, much too close. He picked up speed, but he was too late, because the other vehicle seemed out of control.

And it just happened. One minute, he was hurrying along at about forty miles per hour, and the next he was shunted right across the road. Whatever had hit him was powerful enough to push him and his van through a plate glass window. He hadn't been looking often enough in the rear-view mirror – it was that medicine of Mr Wray's, it had to be. He was a good driver, an excellent driver, but his brain was out of order tonight.

Just before Neil lost consciousness, he caught a

glimpse of the front end of a single-decker coach reflected in his twisted wing mirror. Then something sparked in the rear of the van, and the can of petrol exploded. He was in the chip shop! Matt and Lucy were in the chip shop and... And he passed out.

A few pedestrians stopped walking, knowing full well that they couldn't help. Flames entered the shop and burned furiously, possibly fed by cooking fat. Faces appeared at first floor windows, but nothing could be done. Bramwell's Chippy was on fire, and there were people trapped in the flat.

Bert Heslop and Andrew Martindale heard the explosion, but they were concentrating on Laura's house and were allowing for no distractions. Andy, curled in an imitation of the foetal position, stared stoically ahead. 'It's still a little early for fire-setting,' he remarked. The tiny car was uncomfortable for a man of Andy's height. He shifted, but no position suited him.

'Crazy men do crazy things,' was Bert's response. 'I've been in this business over twenty years, so not much surprises me now.' He glanced at his companion. 'You're the cuckoo in my nest, aren't you? But we couldn't use your car, because it's needed as bait. Sorry you're tied in knots, Andy.'

'Shut up, Bert.' There was no malice in the message.

The detective grinned. The scene reminded him of Laurel and Hardy in one of their many silly predicaments.

They sat through several silent minutes. 'Something's burning,' Bert announced eventually. This statement was underlined by the sound of ambulance, police and fire vehicles. The emergency services passed Laura's house. 'Hell,' Andy mumbled. 'I'll just...' he opened his door and struggled out of the minuscule vehicle. 'You stay here,' he ordered before marching quickly to the top of the street.

'Oh my God!' It was the Bramwells' place, their home, their business, their twins... And Laura was there. He had forced her to go back to her place of work where she was now in danger, and possibly... 'No!' he screamed, running towards the fire. 'Matt? Lucy?'

A fireman caught him. 'Sir?'

'My family – my little family–'

'All out, sir. Some smoke inhalation, but all safe.'

Andy sagged against the young man's sturdy body. 'How many?' he managed.

'Four children, three adults. Sir?' He had seldom seen a man sobbing as hard as this one.

'The coach?' Andy managed.

'Driver dead, van driver in a bad way. Some minor injuries to coach passengers, but–'

Andy blew his nose. 'Sorry about that,' he said. 'Do you know who was driving the van?'

'Carson. Couldn't read the first name, but his address is here on College Row. His licence was damaged.'

'Will he ... will he live?' was Andy's next question.

'Not my place to say, sir. He's in a bad way, like I told you before. They've all been taken to the workhouse,' he added, using as reference the

475

name of the institution whose purpose was now medical.

'Walton,' Andy said quietly. 'Thank you.' For the first time in his adult life, he felt like kissing a grown man. 'Thank you for everything.'

'You're welcome. It's our job.'

Andy continued grateful. 'And it's a mess,' he said.

'Police will be authorizing a check of the coach's brakes for possible failure. A man in one of the flats across the way said the driver was flashing his headlights at the van, but the van driver made no attempt to move out of the way. It's grim, but it could have been a hell of a lot worse.'

The older man walked away. First, he had to tell Hubert Heslop what had happened; second, he must get to Walton Hospital to see how his precious Laura, the Bramwells and four delightful children were faring. There was, of course, a third subject, one Neil Carson who had taken yet another wrong turning in life. Rather belatedly, he gave thought to the people on the coach. Thank God they seemed not to have suffered too badly, though he was sorry for their driver.

He pulled himself together, straightened his shoulders and walked towards the place where he and Heslop had been keeping vigil. They needed to get to the hospital.

Neil Carson lay face down on a bed. They were cutting away his clothes, and the pain was beyond anything he could have imagined. Although he felt as if he were still on fire, his teeth chattered loudly.

'Another quarter grain,' a male voice snapped. A needle was stuck in Neil's arm, though he scarcely felt it. The nurse who had administered the drug squatted down. 'It's your back,' she explained. 'Your front's hardly touched, but there's a terrible smell of petrol on your clothes.'

'Spare can,' he managed finally. 'In the back. A gallon.'

She didn't tell him about the flesh melted away so badly that a part of his spinal column and some ribs were visible; nor did she inform him about the lack of hair on the back of his head. Instead, she held his hand and stayed where she was. Miracles aside, the patient was going to die. 'Can I get anyone for you? Your wife, perhaps?'

'Priest,' he garbled.

'Just a priest?'

'Yes.'

'No family?'

'No.'

The young nurse rose to her feet. 'He wants a priest,' she whispered to the attending doctor.

'Be quick, nurse,' Neil begged. 'I want you to be here. The priest can't talk, but you must.' He knew he was dying.

She ran off to ask the senior doctor's permission. The accident victim's vital signs were not good; he was in shock, and major organs were threatening to shut down. When the priest was on his way, the nurse retraced her steps back to Neil Carson's bedside. The staff had done their best to remove his clothing, and the hole in his back was packed with sterile gauze. 'He won't make it, will he?' she mouthed.

A consultant shook his head gravely. 'Fourth degree,' he said softly. 'Right through every layer of tissue to the bone – the spine. His kidneys are giving up, his BP is off the bottom of the scale, and his heart's like a ferret up a drainpipe.' He raised a hand. 'Sorry, sorry, I don't mean to be flippant.'

The nurse lowered her head. 'It's all right, sir. Cases like this one bring out the best and the worst in all of us. I'll sit with him till the priest comes.'

'Thank you.'

So while Neil Carson made his quiet way towards the end, just one young woman sat with him.

But when the cleric arrived, the patient rallied. He spoke softly, so quietly that the priest had to kneel and lower his head in order to catch what was being said. Ordered by the man in the bed to remain as witness, the nurse joined the priest and knelt beside him on the floor.

Neil gabbled, tripping over words that spilled in a disorderly fashion from a mouth that was twisted in reaction to pain. 'Jesus forgave Judas. On fireplace. Magda ... Magdalene repented. Notebook. Sideboard. It was me. Jesus said that ... told me ... get rid. I killed them. Gave some the clap. Mrs Pears – Mrs Pearson was mistake. Monster is me. Bless me, Father, for I have si ... nned.' A rattle on his breath advertised the proximity of death.

The nurse wept and said nothing.

But the cleric did not hesitate for a single beat of time. He anointed the patient and, on behalf of the Almighty, forgave him his sins. There would

478

be no court case, no prison, so Neil Carson had used a lay person as herald, because a priest could disclose nothing. The nurse would be the harbinger of this man's tale, while the notebook, should it be found, would probably be the real witness.

Neil died on the second rattle, and both people at the bedside sagged with relief.

'Thanks be to God in His mercy,' the priest said.

'Is he forgiven?' Staff Nurse Chalmers dried her eyes.

'God forgives the sick, my child. And I don't mean his burns, because this man was ill in his head. Go now and ask your superior might you be allowed to phone the police. The patient had you here as witness for a reason. You must tell them that the Mersey Monster is probably here, and that a notebook is likely to disclose his truth. I can share this only with you, and the rest goes with me to my grave.' He left to tend other tormented souls.

Avril Chalmers put away her handkerchief. Leaving curtains drawn around the deathbed, she walked to the ward office. A fireplace, Jesus, Judas? Perhaps Neil Carson had been mentally ill, in which case he would surely find a place with God. Now, she had to carry the weight of it, as did the priest. But at least she could talk. And she would.

Police on Lime Street were stood down at half past midnight. The informant had phoned the station to say that the meeting had been postponed for twenty-four hours, since the new drugs baron had business tonight. Members of the force, all plain clothed, were advised to return to base.

Eddie felt glad; with another day to prepare, he could sit and think for a while, organize things better, get more officers on the job. After instructing the rest to move in fits and starts, he made his way back to his place of work. Nellie. He decided that he wanted Nellie's dog, so she would need to be here tomorrow. 'I'll get him, Dave,' he whispered. 'He's finished.'

Eighteen

It was a very full house.

As soon as everyone had been given the all-clear, three adults and four children left the hospital with Andy. Outside, he summoned a taxi to carry the Bramwells to Laura's house. Since the shop and living accommodation had been assessed as probably unsafe, the Bramwells had to stay at the Carsons' home. Matt's bedroom now contained two boys head-to-tail in his bed, and two girls were head-to-tail in Lucy's. Laura had a camp bed in Lucy's room, which was the smallest, while Andy settled on the living room sofa. Daisy and Barry Bramwell took the master, and Andy was plotting downstairs for hours.

By morning, he had sorted everything out in his head and on paper. The owners of the chip shop could remain here, while he, Laura and her children should get away as soon as possible. He glanced at the clock; it was half past seven, and the police had failed to wake the sleepers upstairs. Only Andy knew that Neil was dead. Sighing, he went into the kitchen to make a pot of tea for Laura. This was day one. By tonight, the Carson family and he would be many miles away, or so he hoped.

'Andy?'

He turned and looked at her. Sleep-tousled and in a plain cotton nightdress under an unfastened towelling robe, she looked almost childlike. 'Sit down,' he said softly.

Taking the chair opposite hers, he held both her hands. 'The police came earlier. Neil died.' He paused. 'Laura? Look at me, darling. They wanted to talk to you about the fire and about Neil, but I explained that you'd been suffering the effects of smoke inhalation, so they left.'

'Oh,' was all she managed.

'So we need to get away before the story hits the press. The Bramwells can stay here and keep an eye on their premises. Neil wasn't insured to drive the van – it belonged to his dead friend. So we have to hope the coach company's insurance will cover the rebuild. I'll help if necessary. Laura?'

She stared at him as if they were yards apart. 'What?'

He decided that she hadn't heard everything.

'Did he suffer?' she asked.

'I have no idea, sweetheart.'

'Was he the monster?'

'I don't know.'

Laura nodded absently. 'I'll get dressed. Take me to the presbytery. I want a priest with me at the police station.' She stood up.

'But you haven't drunk your...' She had gone. 'Your tea,' he finished lamely. She was in shock. Did she believe that Neil had tried to kill her *and* the children? The coach brakes had failed, and the whole thing had been an unspeakable accident.

He went back to the kitchen, intending to prepare eggs for scrambling. After breaking eight, he mixed them in the jug so that he might cook breakfast in stages when people came downstairs, but the doorbell interrupted him. Opening the front door with his eyes fixed at adult height, he was forced to lower his gaze for the small man on the front doorstep. 'Bert,' Andy exclaimed.

'May I come in?'

'Of course.'

Bert crept inside. 'You know he died?'

Andy nodded.

'Does she know?'

Again, the older man inclined his head before leading Bert Heslop into the living room. 'Everyone's fine,' Andy said, 'though they did breathe in a bit of smoke.'

The private detective closed the door. 'He confessed to a priest and to a nurse, so–'

'So he was the killer?'

'Yes. There's no doubt. The police are searching his house now. It seems there's a notebook and the wire he used round their necks.'

Andy swallowed audibly. 'Dear God.'

'The police want to talk to Laura.'

'Yes, I know. She's taking me and a priest with her.'

'Very well. I'm off to Southport to speak to Miss Mellor. She hired me, so I should have gone to her first.' He stood up, held out his right hand and shook Andy's. 'At least he can do no more harm,' he said quietly.

When the detective had left, Andy stood and stared through the window, though he noticed little. Neil Carson could cause no more trouble? Oh yes, he could. The man was dead, but the results of his evil might very well hurt one lovely woman and two innocent children. They needed to emigrate.

Eve opened her eyes. The refreshing Southport air had made her sleep well, and she decided to stay where she was and return to the land of dreams ... oh, God, she wasn't alone. Where was Kate? The other single bed was empty. In order to make room for wedding guests, the two women had stayed in a small office on the ground floor, and there was scarcely room for two beds what with the desk, some chairs, several filing cabinets and bookshelves.

He was staring at her. There was no space at all now, because a bloody great horse took up the small gap between the beds. To get out, he would need to reverse. Did horses come with reverse gear? He was whickering at her, the gentle sound emerging from a mouth that seemed not to threaten. This was one beautiful creature. For the first time in her life, she failed to be afraid of a very large animal. Carefully, she sat up. She did this slowly not because of Murdoch, but in order to minimize pain.

'What do you want?' she asked, noticing how his ears pricked up when she spoke.

For answer, he placed his nose against her head. 'You know, don't you, Murdoch?'

He blew a fair imitation of a raspberry against her scalp.

'That's my attitude,' she told him. 'To hell with cancer and therapy. They could burn holes in me, but I ordered them to bugger off.'

The horse sighed and pulled back his head.

She stared hard at him for several seconds, noting the well-defined musculature in the neck and on his shoulders. Were they shoulders? They probably had some posh name given only to horses. 'You're beautiful,' she whispered.

'Thank you,' offered a disembodied male voice.

Eve watched in fascination as a short man jumped on to Kate's bed, walked up it and descended into the small space in front of Murdoch.

'Mr Heslop,' she cried.

He stroked the animal's nose. 'Fine fellow,' he said before seating himself on Kate's pillow. 'A little girl in the kitchen told me where to find you, Miss Mellor. I didn't want to disturb you, though I see you already have a visitor.' He seemed neither surprised nor deterred by the unusual house pet.

'Oh. Right.'

It was like a tennis match. The horse's head changed direction in reaction to each speaker.

'You were right,' Bert Heslop said.

'Was I?'

He nodded. Murdoch nodded. Eve nodded. 'So where is he?'

'In a morgue, I expect.'

Murdoch whinnied.

'Dead?' Eve felt her jaw slackening.

'Dead.'

'Bloody hell. How?'

Murdoch stamped a foot.

'He expects to be included in the conversation,' said the detective. 'Yes,' he advised the largest item in the room. 'A coach hit him and its driver died at the scene while crashing into Carson's van. At first, it was put down to failure of brakes, but the coach driver may have suffered a heart attack. I'm here to tell Miss Mellor that Neil Carson died of burns, one of them fourth degree.'

'What does that mean?' Eve wanted to know.

'Right through to the bones of his spine.'

Beyond exhaustion, Eve lay back on her pillows. 'So how do you know he's the Mersey Monster?'

'He confessed to a nurse and a priest. There's a notebook.'

'What about a notebook?'

Bert tapped his nose with a forefinger. 'He kept a diary, and I have friends in high places.'

'Police?'

He nodded. Murdoch nodded. Eve nodded. Apart from the fact that two humans, one of them at death's door, were discussing a monster, this was fit for a Three Stooges farce. 'He told the nurse about the notebook; all the details were in it.'

'Thank God,' Eve whispered.

'Amen to that, Miss Mellor.'

'Eve.'

'All right, Eve. I'm Bert.' He placed an envelope on the windowsill. 'Deal with that when you're ready, then. I'd better go.'

Hearing this, the horse backed out of the room.

'They do reverse,' she exclaimed.

'They do indeed.' He shook her hand. 'Goodbye, Eve. I wish you all the best with as little pain as humanly possible.'

Alone, she felt tears gathering, but she hung on. This was it; this was the day she had long awaited, and her job was done. But she didn't want to die here. The idea of seeing herself off in somebody else's house seemed impolite.

Kate entered with a tray. 'I've got your soft boiled egg with soldiers – best butter and all.'

Eve smiled at her Lancastrian friend. 'Your accent's gone worse, Kate. Sit down.' She delivered the tale. 'And he's been in our house,' she added at the end. 'We've had a bloody killer at the farm.'

Kate shivered. 'Jesus,' she mumbled, her eyes closed as if for prayers.

Eve nodded sagely. 'Two kids, he had. Imagine the state of them when this hits the headlines. His poor wife, too. What on earth has she done to deserve a thing like that as a husband? She talked to Belle, you know.'

'Yes, you said.'

'Laura, she's called. Nice name.'

'You already told me.' Kate unfolded the legs of the breakfast trolley and propped it on Eve's bed. 'Eat what you can, love. Our girls are all in the kitchen having breakfast served up with laughs by

486

young Sally. She's got a boyfriend – the lad whose mate got killed by them drugs people. He's learning to be a plasterer. Them other boys are here, too – they hid in the scout hut, remember?'

Eve nodded.

'They slept here too, last night. There's all kinds of camp beds and whatnot up the stairs here. Mr Macey's got the date for Crown Court – March, he said. The monks are civilians now, and they have to report to a cop shop every day. I thought Babs and Gordy might have Dove Cottage to themselves, so there'll be four lads and Sally stopping here. Oh, well; it never rains but it pours, eh? I'll go and have my brekky.'

Alone, Eve struggled to eat bits of boiled egg, though she didn't attempt to tackle her toast.

When the tray had been removed, she turned, wriggled to the edge of the mattress and placed her feet on the floor. The windowsill was close by, and she reached for Bert Heslop's bill, which seemed rather bulky for a single sheet bearing lists of expenses. It wasn't a bill. It was a card with a bunch of flowers on its front. Inside, there was no printed message. Instead, a hundred pounds in new notes nestled with a handwritten line. *For a cancer research charity of your choice. God bless you, Hubert Heslop.*

And that was when she began to cry.

Sisters Mary Veronica and Helen Veronica were in a public house enjoying a lunchtime shandy with DS Eddie Barnes. Nelson sat under their table waiting for gifts of potato crisps and pork scratchings.

'I hope you're right this time, Eddie,' Helen said. 'And no more beer for Nelson, thank you. He's daft enough when not on duty.' She looked at her watch. 'So we have just about eleven hours.'

'Yes. Corner of Crosshall Street and Victoria Street.'

'At a quarter to midnight?'

Eddie shrugged. 'That's what we were told.' He spoke to Mary. 'So this new drug boss trusts you? Are you absolutely sure? After all, Holy Mary did run errands for Shuttleworth.'

Mary grinned and winked in a very unholy manner. 'I'm in it for the money. They all know I won't carry drugs, but I'll deliver messages. But isn't that meeting place a bit busy?'

Eddie shrugged again. 'Maybe they want to look normal, just two blokes on a night out.'

Helen gave her opinion that it felt wrong. 'They always stay hidden,' she said. 'They're the most invisible of all this city's invisibles.' She patted Nelson almost automatically; with his head on her lap, he was clearly begging for treats, but no one was forthcoming with titbits. He withdrew, curled up under the table and fell asleep.

'I've changed my mind; I want you and Nelson to stay at home tonight,' Eddie advised Helen. 'We don't want him doing a turn because he can smell drugs.' He focused on Mary. 'Dress in your Holy Mary clothes, but I'm hoping we won't need you either.'

'Right,' she replied. 'One more shandy, then we'll return to being brides of Christ.'

Eddie grinned as he went for three more drinks. These two nuns were excellent police officers, better than many who'd been trained for the job. They were prepared to break smaller rules for the greater good, and therein lay their strength. There was a God, and He was benign.

When they returned to Meadowbank Farm, Eve, Kate and the girls were greeted by Belle, Tom and Max. Liverpool was buzzing with news of the crash, though nothing had been heard so far about Neil Carson's having been the serial killer of working girls.

Belle threw her arms round Eve's neck. 'Was it him? Was Laura right? Were you right?'

Eve delivered a weak smile. 'We were right, babe. I'll just go and get clean, put me nightie on and throw meself in bed. We're closed tonight; business as usual soon enough.'

'Shall I help you?'

'No, you're all right – Kate does it. She's used to me, love. Getting me changed can be complicated.'

Belle lingered with Tom and her ex-colleagues, watching as Eve and Kate went slowly into the bedroom they had shared. While the girls fussed over Max, Belle stared blankly into the near distance. The light in Eve Mellor's eyes had died; it was almost as if she had stayed alive until Carson had been caught. 'She's going, Tom,' Belle whispered to her beloved husband.

'Yes, love,' he mumbled, 'but wear a brave face for her sake. She won't take treatment apart from painkillers, and that's her prerogative. Act normal.'

'I don't do normal, and neither do you.'

He raised his shoulders for a split second.

'Then just be yourself.'

'OK.'

Belle gave herself a silent lecture. For the sake of Eve and the girls, she needed to stay strong. Kate brought Eve to her bed in the kitchen and pulled the covers over her before going to the other side of the huge room to make cocoa. Belle followed her and helped with the task. Looking over her shoulder, Belle noticed that Eve was writing in a notebook. 'What's she writing, Kate?'

'Her memoirs. She's been at it a while now.'

'Yet she seems sleepy, closes her eyes a lot.'

'Yes, she does that, too.'

'She's lost a lot of weight, hasn't she?'

Kate sighed. 'You should see her naked – just loose flesh hanging from her bones. I'm scared, Belle.'

'So am I, love. So am I.'

The girls drifted off to bed, leaving just Tom, Belle, Kate and Max in the kitchen with Eve, who was already asleep. Belle glanced across at Eve. 'Go and get in your own bed, Kate,' she said. 'She's settling nicely, so I'll stay with her tonight.'

'What about Tom?' Kate asked. 'He can't drive home.'

'I'll stay,' he said. 'You're weary, Kate.'

She had to agree. 'Sleep in the spare next to the office,' she advised him before going to look at Eve, who was snoring.

Tom left the room, blowing kisses at his wife as he went.

Kate grinned and took herself off to the bedroom.

Alone with Max, Belle stretched out on a long

sofa. The dog, sensible as ever, lay flat out in front of the fire. It was a quarter past eleven, and Belle drifted off almost immediately – even Eve's snoring failed to keep her awake.

But a wet, doggy tongue woke her. She patted Max, sat up and looked to her right. Eve's bed was near the window. 'What is it, boy?' she asked.

He whined quietly and walked to the bed.

Belle followed after glancing at the clock; it was just ten minutes to midnight – she had slept for no more than half an hour.

Eve was warm, but she wasn't breathing. Had the snoring been the rattle of death? 'Find Tom,' Belle told Max. He ran.

When the covers were pulled back, she noticed the open notebook, a ballpoint pen and an empty pill jar. Eve had done as she had promised from the day of her diagnosis: she had seen herself off. Switching on the bedside lamp, Belle read the final words.

I have had a lovely couple of days and am happy watching you all playing with Tom's daft dog. While you're distracted, I'm swallowing saved pills. Please, no ambulance. Don't try to revive me, because I have a few crabs inside me, and they're taking lumps out of my guts. It's hurting now, especially as I saved many painkillers for this purpose.
I thank and love you all. Please, just let me go.
Eve Mellor.

Belle gulped hard. The woman in the bed had probably been swallowing pills a few at a time all evening. It was possible that Eve might be brought back through medical intervention, but she hadn't wanted that. 'Sleep well, my friend. I always knew there was a good woman behind all the bluster.'

Tom arrived.

'I think she's dead,' Belle murmured.

'Shall I get an ambulance?' he asked.

For answer, his wife pushed the notebook into his hands.

'Ten minutes won't make any difference,' Tom whispered. 'Let's make sure she's gone before waking Kate or sending for an ambulance.'

At midnight Tom would use the telephone while Belle roused Kate.

For Meadowbank Farm, this Sunday night marked the end of an era.

In town, a different tune was nearing its climax. Shops and offices were packed with police in plain clothes. DS Eddie Barnes, in charge of the operation, was dressed in tattered garments and clinging for support to a lamp post. Delivering a mangled version of *Danny Boy*, he kept his eyes open beneath the neb of a flat cap. Tonight, Old Drug Boss would meet his successor with a view to joining forces.

It was cold. Air expressed by passers-by hung in the air like small clouds. A pale silver moon sat against a huge map of faraway stars; there was frost tonight. Late revellers left clubs and wandered about in search of night buses. A loud woman berated her partner for looking at other women at a dance. 'You made a show of me,' she screamed, clattering his ear with her handbag. 'I

492

was ashamed.' The man shielded his face; he was clearly used to such performances.

Another couple joined them, and the fighting ceased immediately.

Eddie, whose pipes were still calling from glen to glen and down the mountainside, tried not to be distracted. He sang on determinedly and tunelessly about sunshine on meadows, valleys under snow and Danny coming home.

Shuttleworth slipped out of a recessed doorway. With his head down, he approached the chosen meeting place, but there was no sign thus far of the new drugs baron. He stilled and lit a cigarette. He was taking a huge chance by being here, and he knew it.

Before Eddie reached the end of sunshine and shadow, chaos invented itself. While members of the force watched from first floor windows, civilians arrived from every conceivable direction, running at Shuttleworth. Whistles blew. Police decanted themselves from shops and offices. They arrested at least a dozen of New Drug Boss's minions, but Shuttleworth was not among the detainees. Eddie barked orders. 'Put this lot in the wagon. After that, you four go left, the rest turn right at the corner. I'm going up Lime Street.' He stood for a few seconds and watched while offenders were stored in a large van.

'Right – go!' he shouted before making for the station. Why was he going to the station? He had no bloody idea. Bloody. Dave's blood. Eddie shivered. Running fast, he crossed the main road and reached his destination. People were screaming; a porter came out and grabbed Eddie's arm.

'He's been stabbed,' the employee of British Railways said. 'You used to work here in uniform, didn't you?'

They entered the station together. Eddie retrieved his arm and walked slowly across the area. This was karma; it was perfect. He bent down. 'Hurts, does it?' he asked.

Shuttleworth clutched at the handle of a knife whose blade was buried in his abdomen. 'Fuck off,' he snapped.

'Oh no. I've waited months for this.' While the felled man removed the weapon from his body, Eddie made no comment. The removal of the knife would mean a complete bleed-out; had it remained buried, there might have been a small chance of survival.

'Pig,' the dying drugs boss spat.

'Goodbye,' Eddie whispered.

As Shuttleworth breathed his last, an ambulance arrived. Eddie allowed himself a tight, grim smile. While blood bubbled in Shuttleworth's final exchange of gases, a clock chimed. It was midnight on Lime Street, and the world was now a better place.

Post Scriptum
1974

Well, the big day's finally arrived and I'm stood at our bedroom window looking out at Wordsworth House where I work part time, like. I'm a lot of things part time, I suppose. Wife, mum, jockey, RSPCA receptionist/animal feeder/guilty party when things go wrong in this house or Don's; he left it to the animal protection as long as Sally and Bill can live in.

Yes, Don died, and I miss him something awful. I knew he was a dirty old man, but he used short women instead of kids, so he done the right thing. There was that time he wanted to watch us with other men, but I soon put the stoppers on that idea – it was a couple of miles too far. God bless, he was no trouble when he died, but Sally was. Oh my God, she was in a state worse than Blackpool beach on a hot Sunday.

She come fleeing down here in her nightie screaming her head off cos Bill had already gone to work, and she set Gordy off crying like a bloody kid, then I joined in too, just to keep them company. I got a passing RSPCA girl to come and sit with our Ellie. Then we went back with Sal to Wordsworth, the big house called after Don's favourite poet (he was a soft arse when it come to poetry) and there he was, all white and still and cold, gone in his sleep, no trouble to

495

nobody. That was when my husband started keening like one of them banshees what they talk about in Ireland. So I thumped him. Not hard, like, but enough to make him breathe in proper.

Don't get me wrong, I adore my Gordy – best man in the world, but he's one of them emotional types, can't keep nothing inside. Reminds me sometimes of Murdoch – mad, but in a good way. It's a bit like living with somebody what's on cloud nine one minute and knocking on hell's door the next. I think it's called being Irish, so there's bugger all I can do about that, right?

It's been a sad and happy few years. In 1968, Eve never even seen Christmas, cos she done herself in one night in November while all the girls was sat there with Belle and Tom and their dog. We thought poor Kate wouldn't be able to forgive herself, but she soldiers on looking after the girls and cooking dinners just like she always did, says Eve's spirit's with her. Angela never left, so she's in charge, too, cos she's getting a bit old for collaring folk and kicking the shite out of them.

Belle and Tom have a little lad called Thomas, and they're really happy even though Max passed away. Straight off, they got another baby dog the same as Max, and they called him Max till he ate the stair carpet, so he answers to Trouble as well. Speaking of dogs, we have a load of them here now, plus cats and even parrots what people have got fed up with. I don't know why some folk bother with pets, cos they don't deserve them, do they? Bloody morons.

We also have a string of bays, some red like

Murdy, some brown. We take them down the beach and walk a long way to the sea some days – you know what Southport's like, all sand and no wet, but salt water's good for horses' leg bones and ankles, so we walk till we find the Irish Sea, usually just a stripe across the horizon.

When I give him his head, Murdoch runs like a gale force wind, took me breath away till I got used to it. I lie low to keep him streamlined. We leave miles between us and the rest of the stable. Well, not real miles, but you know what I mean. He's fast – that's the long and short of it. Haha – he's long and I'm the short arse.

Oh, I do miss Eve, you know. In her own way, she was like a mam to me. I knew underneath all the orders and the bad-mouthing she was a good-hearted soul. Like me, I suppose she was, all gob and always right. The girls will be there this afternoon, but I'll miss Eve and Don. Don wanted more than anything to watch Murdy in the National.

Here comes my Trouble, am I all right and the odds have shortened again what with me and Murdy winning a few other races. I tell him to go and look after our Ellie and to calm down, cos it's just another steeplechase. Well, I realize that's not true, because it's an overcrowded field with jumps like bleeding Everest, but I know it will be what they call a breeze for my horse. He is mine now. Lippy Macey owns a back leg or something, but the rest of Murdy is mine. 'Go on, Gordy,' I say, 'and play with Ellie.' He goes. He knows I need some me-all-by-myself time – not as daft as he looks. There again, nobody could look as daft as he does when he's chasing horses – runs like a ruptured duck, and his hair favours a burst pillow.

That school's still open – Woodside, it's called. They have a few women teachers and a nurse and some good monks. Two of the baddies are still in jail, and one got murdered in there. My Gordy calls that karma, whatever karma means. Fatso Drug Boss copped it on Lime Street near the spot where he killed the copper – I suppose that's another piece of karma.

I'm looking at me silks, purple and silver; they remind me a bit of my lovely wedding day. Not long after we got wed, Belle told me that the serial killer of working girls was done for – done to a turn in a fire by all accounts, with his gob inside a chippy and his backside on fire. Belle's friends with his wife. She's called Laura, I'm told, and she emigrated to Canada with her kids and a new husband what used to be a jeweller.

See? My mind's all over the place today, because I don't want to think about this afternoon – yeah, that's probably the reason. Purple and silver. Don wore a purple waistcoat when he gave me away. He gave me this new life, too, and I'm dead grateful.

I'll be one of the first women to ride the National. It's a terrible race, very hazardous, my Gordy says. He worries about me and I worry about the poor bloody horses. Ooh, look, there's our Sally waddling off to stroke Murdy and Nye. She'll be staying here, because she's eight months gone and anyway, she can mind our Eloise. Sally's expecting to deliver twins, and she says they don't like one another, cos they fight like buggery.

We've got just Ellie, and she's enough, thanks. Reading at three, she was, and now that she's coming up five she has a little Shetland called Periwinkle, and she wants a taller pony as well because Peri's getting a bit small for her. Oh yes, we have a crazy life here, and she's in charge, little madam. I think she takes after me.

Our three lads what were stuck in that stuffy scout hut are off out in the world, every one of them with a good job. It's turned out well for all of us what had a bad start in life. Makes you think, eh? So many damaged people mending theirselves and one another just through talking and listening and laughing and crying. It's all you need, see. Communication.

John lost his stammer and gained a wife, a lovely widow a bit older than him with two kids. He mends cars and sells them. Phil's nearly a doctor serving his time down Walton, and Ian's an accountant. I wouldn't have given sixpence for their chances when me and Sal first met them, but it just goes to show, you never can tell – know what I mean? Look at my mad horse down there, stood with Nye and staring up at me. I know he knows that today's the day.

It'll soon be time. A string of bays has just left for the sands, but Murdoch's made no effort to go with them. His lip's curling; he's talking to me. Murma's further away with a few donkeys holding some kind of committee meeting, I'd guess. Her son never takes his eyes off me except to glance at his companion, Blind Nye.

Now he's chopping the ground with a hoof. He's telling me to come down. It's time.

What a bloody life. I've been weighed, stared at, questioned and I got that mad I told the swines I'd had cornflakes for me breakfast and evackerated me bowel. Well, they were getting on me bleeding nerves. Laughing at me, they were. I don't know what they were doing with me horse, only he's been showing the whites of his eyes. Never seen a fuss like it, I swear. When he shows his whites, folk need to stand clear if he doesn't know them.

He's got to carry some weights, and all the animals are under guard in case some flea-brained scally shoves a bloody needle in their arses so they can't run proper and something else will win the trophy. It's weird. People are weird. This is supposed to be sport, but there must be criminals about.

I grab hold of Gordy. 'Where's Nye?' I ask.

'In the horsebox.'

Me dander's up now. Me dander's up as high as any of them cruel jumps. 'Bring him in here,' I order.

'I can't. They won't have a tatty old donkey near high-bred horses.'

Well, I hit him. I must stop this sort of behaviour, else he'll start thinking I mean it. Tell you what, though, I am pissed off with this lark; more fuss here than at a grandmothers' picnic down Otterspool Prom with gulls swooping down and pinching the butties. I've never been put through this load of crap before. But them other races weren't like this, were they? I'm with the cream of the cream here, dead posh folk and high-bred horses.

Anyway, one minute I'm trying not to laugh at all these dignitaries what Don and Lippy used to call digs, and I'm looking at some terrible hats and wondering who got these people ready for coming to Aintree. Lippy waves at me – he's here with his little doctor wife.

Then all of a sudden, I'm in the saddle and in the line, and Murdy's snorting and tapping a hoof. What happened in between hats and starting line – don't ask, cos I've got a hole in me memory. This is fear – adrenalin, I think it's called. Some of the other horses are snorting, too. Some of them might be dead in about ten minutes. Focus, you soft cow!

And we're off. Oh, God, the thunder. There's one hundred and sixty-ish hooves beating the ground, forty horses going for gold. He takes his time, does my Murdoch, saves himself for a bit later on, like. Now I've gone deaf, deaf as a post. No thunder, no crowd, nothing at all, because I'm not me no more. I'm him and he's me and there's just one of us what have been glued together for six years come July. I do remember that none of these jockeys knows his mount like I know mine, scrape of strawberry jam, an apple for Nye, spit on the books and on the piano, climb the stairs, threaten to eat me wedding cake... Oh, now – this is it, this is how it feels when our invisible wings open.

I daren't look. There's a few horses down, but I don't want to know. We're being passed by riderless ones who carry on because that's what they've been taught, and I ignore them because this day is ours. Floating like a feather over and across Becher's and the Chair, no end to him, no beginning to me, cos we are a thingy – a centaur. Second time. Second time round and we don't flag, no pause, no fear now, just the flying.

We don't get to the finish first, cos half a dozen without riders are there before us. Sound crashes in like a bomb hitting Liverpool. They're screaming our name as we cross the line. Only now do I look back – the second horse is coming in half a furlong at least behind us. I lean forward as he slows down. 'You done it, baby, we won it and I don't half love you.' I'm proud, cos I never needed the whip except to stroke him gently as a sign that I was pleased with him.

He's breathing hard. I pat him and he's wet through. There's telly cameras all over the shop and a helicopter in the sky. Here comes the bit we're going to hate. Still, what can't be cured must be endured – and we did win.

In this world, there are many horses, then there's Murdoch. No, there's Murdoch and me, and we are joined by a thread no one can see, a thread that was made on that first day when I lay across his back and he walked me round the big field – the paddock. Oh, bloody hell, there's Gordy and he's crying again, bless him. I think I'm in shock, because I've lost all sense of time. This is a long race, but I feel as if it lasted about three minutes.

Now, the shit stuff starts. We've a mounted cop on both sides of us. Murdy's not pleased and I have to tell him, 'Easy, boy.' Oh Jaysus, as Gordy would say. The winner's enclosure is packed with hysterical people, and the mounted police try to push them back. Mad Murdoch, winner of the

Grand National, has stiffened all his muscles, but his breathing's calmer. And then he does it so suddenly I nearly lose me hold on the reins. Yes, he's up, front legs thrashing about, people scarpering like shoplifters dashing out of Woolworth's.

And all I can do is bloody laugh, because his legs crash down on one of them ugly hats I told you about before. Dignitaries? Look at that one running away in her slingbacks, no stockings and enough hard skin on her heels to cover an elephant. Her hat's buggered too, cos Murdoch saw to that.

Trophy. Photos. Me talking to a telly camera. There's a long pole with a fluffy end nearly up me nose – it's a microphone. My baby's still wet with sweat. So I do me whistle, that one with a finger at one side of me gob and me thumb at the other side. He stills. The digs and press folk go quiet as well. One of the police says I've cleared the wax out of his ears. Maybe I should charge for me services – wouldn't be the first time, would it?

Gordy arrives at our side.

I smile down at him before speaking me mind into the fluffy bit. 'Thanks and all that,' I say, 'but this animal's me best friend and he's wetter than a ton of cod on a Fleetwood fishing boat. I'm not being funny or nothing, but he needs a rub down and his donkey what's waiting for him. You can have more photos when I've dried him off and made sure his breathing's right. Now, let me through.' Nobody moves. So I carry on. 'This animal is worth more than all the rest of us put together. He matters.' The police clear a way and we get past. And they're all here, Lippy and Lillian (don't forget the third letter l in her name), Angela, Mo, Belle, Tom, Katie and the new girls. Every one of them steps up with blankets and rags to rub my darling horse dry.

We're still being filmed, only I don't care no more. Somebody from a newspaper asks if I'm happy and I tell him I am, because me horse is still alive and not needing his throat opening so he can breathe. And yes, it is great to be the first woman to get the trophy, but will they bugger off, cos I want Murdoch back with Nicholas Nye.

That's when they grab hold of my Gordy to get the tale about the donkeys and Murma and the geese and cats and dogs and chickens and the RSPCA. I hear somebody saying they want to do a shoot at Wordsworth House, and I think to meself – well, as long as they don't mean with a gun. I hear Nye's bell, and here he comes to have his photo took next to Longshanks Mad Murdoch and this dwarf of a female jockey.

I'm sitting proud as a peacock (peahen?) on my bare-back horse while cameras flash. 'It's all right, Murdy,' I whisper, 'it's just the price of fame. Never mind, we'll soon be home.

'I promise,' I tell him as I slide off, and he does that horrible grin, all tombstone teeth and quiet whickering. Honest, he's a right case, this chap.

There's a bit more pissing about with photos, leave me hat on, take me hat off, stand at his head, make him do that grin again. It's boring. And I've a daughter waiting for me at home...

We're back at Dove Cottage. I give Gordy a goodnight kiss, and that's that, cos I feel as if I've been dragged through me granny's mangle. I should be used to it by now, but the National's a bloody killer, isn't it? If I feel hammered, what's my poor horse going through? I'll massage him in the morning; he likes being massaged.

Me eyes start drooping into the closed position. In that stupid world that lives at the edge of being awake and at the start of sleep, I see her standing there, a battleship in a frock, scarf trying to cover them big plastic curlers she always used, pink ones, blue ones, yellow ones. And she's grinning at me.

'Hello,' I say in my head.

'I'm that proud of you, Babs,' she says. 'My girl, my daughter.'

'Thanks, Mam.' And I drift away from here, past her and into a world where there's just me, Gordy, Ellie, Murdoch, his mother and our donkeys. This is my heaven, and here I'll stay until ... until...

I sit up, muscles aching and complaining as I thump my beloved husband. 'You're snoring again,' I tell him before settling back on the pillows. I must stop hitting him, or he might begin to think I mean it.

SOFT ECHOING HOOVES

Ankles strapped. Tightly wrapped
Against disease. Ran with ease
Across the sand, his own land.

Fences cleared, never feared,
Did not go under. Heard the thunder
Forty more with him before
Seldom behind. One of a kind.

Thrum, thrum, the beat of drum?
No. It's the field; to him they yield
Hard and fast, riders cast
To lie on ground while wild hooves pound.
Yet still he rushes, still he pushes
For the line. 'The prize is mine!'

And leaving space, he owned the race,
Took the crown. Then looking down
On mortals less, he nodded. 'Yes,
I didn't fall. I'll never crawl.'

Within this book, you had a look
At Murdoch (Mad), who's quite the lad.
An imitation, my own creation.
A paler horse who runs the course.

But Red Rum was the one I met
On Southport sands. I can't forget
The scent of him, his gentle touch.
I fell in love and cared so much
I never watched the National,
Since love is rarely rational.

I should have known. No rider thrown
No fence refused, no skill unused.
A noble mount whose wins we count.
We had the best. He's now at rest.

Though still I hear on Southport's beach
Soft echoing hooves beyond my reach.

Reader, I hope you love my Mad Murdoch
as much as I do.

RUTH HAMILTON

The publishers hope that this book has given you enjoyable reading. Large Print Books are especially designed to be as easy to see and hold as possible. If you wish a complete list of our books please ask at your local library or write directly to:

Magna Large Print Books
Magna House, Long Preston,
Skipton, North Yorkshire.
BD23 4ND

This Large Print Book for the partially sighted, who cannot read normal print, is published under the auspices of

THE ULVERSCROFT FOUNDATION